ONLY BAD OPTIONS

◄ A GALACTIC BONDS BOOK ►

JENNIFER ESTEP

ONLY BAD OPTIONS

Copyright © 2022 by Jennifer Estep

ISBN: 978-1-950076-15-4

Cover Art © 2022 by Tony Mauro

Published in the United States of America

To my mom—for everything.

To my grandma—who inspired the title of this book.

*To myself—for trying something different
and writing a book of my heart.*

A truebond is like a stormsword. Everybody wants one, but few people know how to properly wield them—or realize that they can cut you to shreds.

—AUTHOR UNKNOWN

PART ONE

EYES AND ARROWS

ONE

VESPER

Sometimes in life, you have only bad options.

Like planning to commit corporate espionage in the morning, becoming a whistleblower by noon, and trying not to be murdered by midnight.

Those thoughts—and a dozen disturbing visions of my own potential murder—zipped through my mind as I perched on the sofa and stared out over the low table in front of me.

Screwdrivers, laser cutters, and other handheld tools covered the scarred faux wood surface, along with colorful gelpens and clear plastipapers boasting sketches and schematics of everything from household appliances to shock batons to a pair of gloves designed to mimic the look and feel of human skin. Squiggles and doodles of blue eyes and black arrows adorned the edges of the thin, reusable plastipapers, since those odd symbols had haunted my dreams for as long as I could remember. Wires snaked out from underneath the papers, while a cup squatting on the corner of the table held the remains of a raspberry protein shake that had stained the clear plastic a dull, sickly pink.

I leaned forward, picked up the miniature spaceship in the middle of the mess, and turned it around in my hands. The cheap plastic model was a little larger than my palm and had been spewed out by one of the multidimensional printers at Kent Corp, where I worked in the research and development lab. Yep, I was a lab rat, responsible for fixing flaws in Kent Corp designs, as well as dreaming up new products for the Regal-family-owned company to sell to further increase House Kent's already hefty coffers.

Velorum was grooved into the side of the model, in the same place it had been on the actual ship, and I traced my fingers over the letters, my skin sinking into the tiny dips and empty curls. Kent Corp products always had boastful, grandiose names, whether it was a new space cruiser, a solar-powered blaster, or a can opener.

I snorted. *Hubris* would have been a much more appropriate moniker, especially given the small but deadly flaw in the cruiser's design.

Footsteps clacked along the floor, and a woman shuffled into the room where I was sitting and clutching the model ship like a recalcitrant child who refused to give up her favorite toy.

The thirty-something woman was dressed in a light beige pantsuit that outlined her trim body, while black stilettos added a couple of inches to her already-tall frame. Gold shadow and liner brought out her dark brown eyes, while plum lipstick did the same for her ebony skin. Her dark brown hair was slicked back into a low bun, and a gold chain made of square links hung from her neck.

Her sleek, tailored look was a direct contrast to the shape-less white lab coat I wore over a long-sleeved light gray shirt, matching cargo pants, and work boots.

The woman yawned, her eyes still a bit bleary with sleep. "Why are you messing with that model? I thought you finished your report on the *Velorum* crash last week."

"Good morning to you too, Tivona," I drawled, ignoring her question.

She shuddered and stepped into the tiny kitchen. "There is no such thing as a *good* morning, especially not a good *Monday* morning."

Tivona Winslow might be a brilliant negotiator, but she was most definitely not a morning person. Still, her love of late nights meshed well with my get-up-and-get-things-done mentality. The two of us were rarely home at the same time, which made sharing our small two-bedroom apartment—and especially the single bathroom—much more manageable.

A grin split Tivona's face, and she gave me a saucy wink. "Although the weekend was *very* enjoyable, especially Saturday night."

I laughed, despite the tension simmering in my body. "Let me guess. True love lost and found on the dance floor thanks to a chembond cocktail."

"Something like that." Tivona scrunched up her nose. "Although she wasn't *nearly* as cute and charming the next morning."

"They never are when chembonds are involved—"

Tivona waved her hand, cutting off my lecture. "I know, I know. A chembond isn't *real*." She sighed with longing. "But it was fun while it lasted. You should try it sometime, Vesper."

I rolled my eyes. "No, thanks. I've sworn off relationships, remember? Especially chemically induced ones. They burn out even faster than regular ones do."

Tivona arched an eyebrow at the bitterness in my voice. "What was it you said after your breakup with Conrad? Oh, yes. That attraction, desire, and love are nothing more than chemicals in the brain. Dopamine and pleasure centers and all that other technical stuff you spout all the time."

I lifted my chin. "And I stand behind every single word."

This time, I sighed, the sound full of the melancholy that

haunted me like a bad dream. "Maybe you're right. Maybe I should go clubbing with you, down a cocktail with someone, and see what happens. At least you know what you're getting into with a chembond—and that it will wear off in a few hours."

Unlike my current heartache, which had been dragging on for months.

Sympathy filled Tivona's face. "This thing with Conrad will wear off too. Especially when you get out there and meet someone new. You'll see, Vesper. Soon you won't be thinking about Conrad at all."

Her cheerful words were completely innocent, but they blared in my mind like an alarm warning that something bad was about to happen. I held back a shudder, trying to ignore the magic suddenly pricking my skin like needles on a medtable.

Tivona hit a button on the brewmaker on the kitchen counter, which let out a series of high-pitched *beep-beep-beeps*, almost as if it was talking to her. Liquid streamed down into the chrome pot, and the rich, dark scent of chocolate espresso filled the air. It looked and smelled far more appetizing than my chalky raspberry shake.

Brewmaker was a misnomer, since the appliance was actually a food fabricator that could produce everything from scrambled eggs to almond oatmeal to a serviceable steak, depending on which protein pods were loaded into it. But people called them brewmakers because most folks used them to whip up drinks— coffees, teas, protein shakes. No matter how advanced technology got, folks still loved to gulp down caffeine, ginseng, and other stimulants, along with massive amounts of processed sugar.

Tivona drew in a deep breath. "Ahh. I'll never admit it, since I am legally obligated to claim that Kent products are perfect as is and defend them vigorously against all lawsuits, but those tweaks you made to this brewmaker last week really worked. Espresso in less than ten seconds that is the perfect temperature and won't scald your mouth? That's genius, Vesper."

"You know I like tinkering with things."

Tivona's dark gaze darted over to the mess of tools, plastipapers, and wires on the table in front of me, and her lips turned down into a disapproving frown. "That's one way of putting it."

When we'd first moved in together about three years ago, Tivona and I had divided the common room into two sections. Her side, which included the kitchen, was spotless, and everything was either neatly stowed away, like her plethora of mugs in the cabinets, or stacked in precise piles, like the latest contracts she was working on that covered the dining table.

My side of the room, which included the sofa and the low table, was far less organized. Like Tivona, I preferred the pile method of storage, but mine were haphazard mountains that contained everything from old technical manuals to appliance parts. I found the clutter cozy and comforting, but it supremely annoyed Tivona. More than once, she had challenged me to find a particular plastipaper or tool to get me to clean up the mess, but I always located the requested item within a matter of seconds, like an old-timey magician pulling a rabbit out of her proverbial hat. Always knowing where things were was one of the few advantages to having seer magic.

Despite Tivona's neat-freak tendencies, she was a genuine friend and by far the best roommate I'd ever had, mainly because we didn't see each other all that often, not even at Kent Corp, where we both worked. Having an in-person conversation with her was a rare treat, rather than an everyday chore.

Tivona poured the chocolate espresso into an oversize mug, then plopped down on the other end of the sofa. She plucked the remote from the end table on her side of the room and hit a button, causing the holoscreen embedded in the opposite wall to flare to life. She yawned and took a sip of her espresso, while her favorite gossipcast played on the screen.

"And now we bring you the latest in the ongoing conflict

between the Imperium and the Techwave . . ." The gossipcaster's voice droned on and on, delivering yet another variation of a story I'd heard a hundred times before.

The Imperium, led by Lord Callus Holloway, who was supported by the other noble families, collectively called the Regals, was one of the major ruling forces in the Archipelago Galaxy, along with the slightly less powerful Techwave and the Erzton. Each group controlled and focused on a different area. The Imperium dealt in magic, genetics, and bloodlines, while the Techwave eschewed such arcane things in favor of cutting-edge technology, experiments, and weapons. The Erzton maintained a neutral stance, selling minerals, wood, and other raw materials to both the Imperium and the Techwave, as well as to other wealthy organizations and individuals. Basically, the three groups boiled down to magic, tech, and minerals, although they would all happily use whatever they could get their hands on to acquire more wealth, weapons, power, and resources.

The Imperium and the Techwave had been at odds for years, but lately, hostilities had increased to unprecedented levels, with the Techwavers attacking several Regal-owned corporations and stealing everything they could. Supposedly, the Techwavers—or Techies, as they were sometimes called—wanted to make personal enhancements, military-grade weapons, and other advanced technology available to everyone and thus level the playing field between the magic-wielding Regals and the common folks. But really, the Techwave just wanted to rule the galaxy the way Callus Holloway had for the last thirty years.

I had little love for the Imperium and even less for the Regals with their self-important Houses, esoteric societal rules, and unrelenting determination to value magic, alliances, and bloodlines above all else, but at least they maintained some semblance of law, order, and freedom. Unlike the Techwavers, who were little more than terrorists who just took what they wanted and left death and destruction behind in their wake.

Like on Temperate 33.

Two months ago, the *Velorum* space cruiser had crashed shortly after takeoff on its maiden flight, killing everyone on board, as well as hundreds of additional people on the ground in the spaceport below. I'd been one of dozens of lab rats sent to investigate the ship's smoldering remains. A group of Techwavers had used the chaos of the crash and its aftermath to break into Kent Corp offices on Temperate 33, steal info on the company's new line of weapons, and blow several buildings to smithereens.

For a group that supposedly wanted to make things better for everyone, the Techwavers hadn't cared whom they hurt as long as they got what they wanted. Greedy bastards. Then again, someone was always rebelling against someone else in the galaxy.

"The fighting is getting extremely intense on Magma 7, where the Techwave commandeered a large metal refinery three days ago," the gossipcaster droned on. "The Imperium has taken heavy casualties trying to regain control of the facility. Another attack is expected to begin later today, with Imperium soldiers hoping to finally root out the Techwavers from their fortified position inside the refinery . . ."

In other words, both sides were going to lay waste to the refinery, then retreat to lick their wounds. Something else that was not surprising.

"And now, on to more pleasant matters: the spring ball being held later this week on Corios."

Tivona squealed with delight. "Finally!"

Like many folks, Tivona followed the Regals' exploits with great interest, especially when it came to their lavish parties on Corios, their home planet. Whereas I did my best to tune out the incessant gossipcasts, which always reminded me of how

I had been tossed aside and twinged my childhood heartache like a finger poking into a deep bruise.

The gossipcaster grinned at the camera, showing off her blindingly white teeth. "The spring ball is one of the most anticipated events of the social season, with several engagements expected to be announced during the event. Some anonymous sources claim one of those announcements will involve Kyrion Caldaren, the current leader of the Arrows, the Imperium's elite fighting force."

The feed cut away from the gossipcaster to show a shadowy figure dressed in dark clothes stalking through a smoke-filled hallway on some spaceship. A dark helmet covered his head, so I couldn't see his face, but I didn't need to. Just the man's tall, imposing silhouette, as well as the glowing stormsword in his hand, was enough to strike fear into the heart of anyone with even a modicum of common sense.

Tivona let out another fangirl squeal of delight, completely enraptured by the image on the screen. Well, at least this gossipcast was about someone I had never met, making it far less annoying than most.

"Kyrion Caldaren is the son of the late Lord Chauncey Caldaren and his wife, Lady Desdemona," the gossipcaster continued, as if everyone didn't already know exactly who he was. "He is also the current head of House Caldaren and thus in control of the substantial Caldaren fortune. More than one Regal lord and lady has tried to catch Kyrion's eye over the years, although, so far, he has resisted all attempts to be caught. Perhaps someone will be lucky enough to finally snare him at the ball."

The gossipcaster chuckled and winked at the camera, as though Kyrion Caldaren was a fat trout just waiting to be plucked out of an aquafarm pool.

I rolled my eyes. "As if anyone in their right mind would want to be engaged, much less wed, to the most notorious killer in the galaxy. C'mon. The man supposedly murdered his own father when he was a teenager just so he could take control of their House."

Tivona flapped her hand at me, never taking her eyes off the screen. "Shush!"

The gossipcaster kept extolling the many supposed virtues of Kyrion Caldaren, while glossing over the fact that the Arrows were among the deadliest warriors in the galaxy and that their main objective was to systematically eliminate Callus Holloway's many enemies. Something Kyrion Caldaren had done more than once if the rumors were true.

But among the Regals, Kyrion Caldaren was *quite* the catch, and this wasn't the first program speculating about whom he might eventually wed, even if he wasn't bonded to the person. Then again, he was rich enough to induce any kind of chembond he wanted for as long as he desired. Such things were common among the Regals, especially since truebonds were so rare, even among the nobility's psions, seers, spelltechs, siphons, and other wielders of magic.

My mother's voice snaked through my mind. *I should be back on Corios. I should be part of the Regals, not rotting away on a useless planet trapped in a useless life with an utterly useless child.*

Pain spiked through my heart like a drill punching through a sheet of steel. I grimaced, wishing I could forget that conversation, which was among the last things my mother, Nerezza, had said to her cousin Liesl, whom we'd been staying with at the time. But perfect recall was part of my seer magic, at least when it came to all the horrible things that had happened in my life—especially my mother's abandonment. Nerezza had left when I was seven, and even now, thirty years later, I could still hear her harsh tone as clearly and vividly as though she had uttered the words a moment ago.

"Vesper? Are you okay?" Tivona asked. "You look like you're about to snap that model in two."

My fingertips had dug into the *Velorum* miniature, and the dull white plastic was creaking in protest. I loosened my grip and tossed the ship down onto the table. "I'm fine. I should get to the lab."

"What are you working on now?" Tivona asked. "A dozen ways to improve your latest brewmaker design? Even though it's already perfectly perfect?"

I forced myself to smile at her teasing. "That is tomorrow's project. Today I have a few final things to wrap up with the *Velorum* crash report."

Tivona toasted me with her mug. She took another sip of her espresso, then focused on the gossipcaster again.

I gathered up the loose plastipapers from the table and stuffed them into the crook of my arm. I hesitated, then grabbed the *Velorum* model. As soon as my fingers closed around it, magic pricked my skin again. A faint silver glow shimmered around the tiny cruiser, even as a cold finger of dread tickled my spine.

Normally, I would have dropped everything, sat back down, and studied the model from all angles. My seer magic often highlighted things, but it was always up to me to puzzle out exactly what my power was trying to tell me. My mother's harsh voice was still ringing in my ears, though, and the ache of her abandonment was still spiking through my heart, so I glared at the light gilding the miniature spaceship.

Go away! I hissed in my mind.

The silver glow snuffed out, although that cold finger of dread kept tickling my spine. Somehow, even without my seer magic, I knew that my plans for the model ship were going to cause me a whole lot of trouble—and maybe even get me killed.

TWO

VESPER

I went into my bedroom and dumped the plastipapers onto my desk. I considered leaving the *Velorum* model behind too, but that would be akin to chickening out of my corporate espionage scheme, yet again, so I stuffed it into my gray backpack, along with the rest of my supplies. Then I said good-bye to Tivona and left the apartment.

By this point, it was creeping up on eight o'clock galactic time. The twin suns were shining brightly, the warm rays soaking into the solar panels that adorned the walls and roofs of the low, squat concrete buildings like the green scales of the enormous dragons that lived on Tropics 5. People were pouring outside to head to work or school, and I fell in with the flow of human traffic.

Three blocks later, I reached the transport station and squeezed into the last car. I gripped a strap dangling from the ceiling and tried not to bump into the other people swaying around me. Just about everyone in this part of Stahl City worked for Kent Corp, so most folks were wearing some combination of the House Kent colors of light gray, dull beige, and dark brown.

Some people were bopping their heads, listening to the music blasting out of their earbuds or implants, but the lucky few who'd managed to snag a seat had their heads down and their eyes fixed on their handheld tablets. Some were reading books, but many were tuned to the same channel Tivona had been watching, and faces and fashions flickered across the small screens as the gossipcaster continued talking about the Regals' upcoming ball. More disgust rolled through me, and I stared out the grimy windows and watched the solar-panel-crusted buildings zip by for the rest of the high-speed ride.

Fifteen minutes later, the transport zoomed into the main station at the edge of the Kent Corp campus. I followed the crowd of people streaming toward the security checkpoints manned by guards wearing dark brown uniforms. The guards sported matching polyplastic helmets with clear face visors that constantly fed them information, as well as letting them communicate with their comrades. All of them had a blaster and a shock baton dangling from their belts, but the guards didn't really need the weapons. Their bodies bulged with muscle, and many of them continually shifted on their feet, ready to dart forward and tackle someone in an instant.

Everyone who worked for Kent Corp received some sort of physical or technological enhancement. Supposedly, the enhancements were a bonus, a perk, a reward for loyal service, but really, they were designed to help us lowly worker bees perform better and faster—and to keep us from being killed so easily while on the job. The guards were given enhanced strength and speed, while the negotiators like Tivona were fitted with watches, contact lenses, and other devices that let them access thousands of corporate documents just by saying certain keywords or blinking their eyes in particular patterns.

Me? Like most of the other lab rats, I had been given an

oxygen optimization—or O2—enhancement. A special liquid had been injected into my lungs that greatly increased their capacity and functionality. Basically, I didn't need as much clean air to breathe as other people, and the oxygen that was already in my lungs and blood would continue to circulate—and thus keep me alive—for far longer than normal.

Most folks snickered when I told them about my O2 enhancement. Admittedly, it wasn't as visually impressive as bench-pressing another person with your index finger or running a mile in less than two minutes, but it came in handy more often than you might think. Accidents happened all the time in the research and development lab, and you never knew what toxic chemicals might be released. The O2 enhancement gave me a fighting chance of not having my lungs melt inside my chest before I was able to escape a contaminated area. Statistically speaking, it was also one of the best enhancements to have outside the R&D lab, since forty-two percent of all deaths in and around spaceships and ports were due to a lack of oxygen.

I advanced through the checkpoint line, ran my ID card through the reader, and let the biometric scanner sweep over my body. Then I placed my left hand on the metal turnstile and waited for it to check my fingerprints as a final confirmation of my identity. The light turned green, and I pushed through the turnstile. None of the guards so much as batted an eye at me, but that cold finger of dread tickled my spine again.

So far, no one had any reason to suspect that I wasn't toeing the Kent Corp line along with everyone else, especially when it came to the *Velorum* crash. That might change in a heartbeat, but for now, I was free and clear, so I tucked my ID card into my lab coat pocket and strode forward.

With more than ten million people, Stahl City was one of the most populous cities on Temperate 42, although you wouldn't know it from walking through the Kent Corp campus, which had been carved out of the manufacturing district. Lush lawns covered with real grass and dotted with equally real hedges and trees rolled out in all directions, along with red-clay tile paths lined with rust-colored polyplastic benches that clustered around matching fountains. The only things that ruined the view and the illusion that this was an actual park were the chrome-and-glass skyscrapers that loomed over the campus like giants about to lift their legs, stomp their feet down, and crush all the workers scurrying around like ants below.

Scores of people dressed in business suits, lab coats, and maintenance coveralls were hurrying along the paths, most with their heads down, eyes focused on their tablets, and earbuds blaring music, but I tilted my face up toward the suns, enjoying the growing warmth of the day. I drew in a deep breath and was pleasantly surprised when the earthy scent of grass briefly overpowered the stench of exhaust that always polluted the air.

Temperate 42 had gotten its name because it was, well, *temperate*, with brief winters, rainy springs, bearable summers, and cool falls. The Kents and other Regal families almost always had their corporate headquarters on such planets in the Archipelago Galaxy, although the locations were more for the higher-ups' benefit rather than any true benevolence toward their workers. None of the Regals wanted their production plants to be shut down due to adverse weather conditions.

As I walked along, more and more guards appeared like patches of dead brown leaves ruining the rest of the vibrant green landscape. Another finger of dread joined those that were already tickling my spine. I shivered and walked faster.

Ten minutes later, I reached the main building, a hundred towering stories of chrome and glass studded with the ubiquitous green solar panels. The energy the panels generated helped ease the burden on the city's electrical grid, which included the nearby Kent Corp production plants that constantly churned out everything from brewmakers to blasters to spaceships.

I waited in another security line, confirmed my biometrics, fingerprints, and identity again, and stepped into the building. Just like the outside, the inside was all sleek chrome and gleaming permaglass, albeit with a greenish tinge, thanks to the exterior solar panels. Not a single smudge, fingerprint, or speck of dust could be found on anything, not even the large, square chrome recyclers in the corners, and the cool, sixty-two-degree air smelled of stale nothingness.

Several security desks were spaced throughout the lobby, and even more guards were stationed in here than were roaming the campus outside. None of the guards paid any attention to me, but even more worry welled up inside my chest. Not for the first time, I wondered if I should go through with my plan, but it was too late to back out now. I'd already delayed getting the files twice last week, and my buyer would walk—and take their money with them—if I failed to deliver a third time as promised.

Besides, the longer I waited, the more people could potentially die.

I squared my shoulders and marched over to the elevators. They too were permaglass, and I squeezed inside one with more than three dozen other people, as though we were pickles packed into a jar. Instead of going up to the negotiator, sales, and other corporate offices, this elevator went down, down, down, to the research and development lab, three stories underground. All the better to contain the hazardous chemicals, stray blaster fire, and other nasty things we lab rats cooked up and occasionally, accidentally let loose.

I popped myself free from the elevator, the first pickle out of the jar, and scanned my ID card for a third time. I also stepped on a mat that sanitized my boots with ultraviolet light. A soft beep sounded, and I moved forward, yanked on a door, and walked through to the other side.

The R&D lab took up most of this subterranean level.

Despite the fact that it was buried half a mile underground, the ceiling soared more than a hundred feet overhead, and enormous models of Kent Corp spaceships dangled from thick steel cables like moon mobiles hanging over a child's crib. Everything was clean and sterile, from the white tile floor, walls, and ceiling to the long, clear polyplastic workstations.

Some of the other lab rats were already hard at work, peering at their latest projects through thick safety goggles and stabbing screwdrivers, pliers, and utility knives into half-assembled vacuum cleaners, recyclers, and other appliances. I called out greetings to several folks, most of whom murmured absently in response, completely absorbed in their tasks.

My steps slowed, and I drifted over to the right, where the ceiling dropped down and the white tile gave way to thick gray concrete walls that formed a bunker housing the weapons lab. On the other side of the permaglass doors, folks tinkered with blasters, handheld cannons, and other devices. My gaze zipped over to a table near the center of the lab, where a long blade perched in a plastic holder—a stormsword.

Unlike the cheap, disposable appliances that Kent Corp produced, stormswords were artifacts made from pure, genuine metals and minerals, often passed down from one family member to another. This sword had a silver hilt studded with three smooth, roundish stones—sapphsidian, a jewel that was such a dark blue it was often mistaken for being black.

Several smaller pieces of sapphsidian adorned the crossguard, which curved out in two opposing directions before ending in sharp points that were perfectly aligned with each other, reminding me of a yin-yang symbol. Matching twin curls of silver snaked up out of the crossguard and touched the blade, which had a faint opalescent sheen, indicating that it was made of lunarium, a rare, expensive mineral often used in psionic and other weapons.

Supposedly, sigils often covered a stormsword's hilt, although no symbols adorned this one. I'd heard one of the weapons techs say the sword had been blasted with electromagnets and wiped clean of all traces of magic and any psionic echoes from its previous owner, whoever that might have been.

Another silver sword also sat on the table, although this one looked like a cheap toy and had several red buttons on the hilt, instead of glittering jewels. The Kents were trying to come up with a stormsword—or something similar—that they could mass-produce and sell to the highest bidder.

A weapons tech was tinkering with the Kent Corp sword. Nothing happened with the first two buttons he pressed, but as soon as he hit the third button, red sparks erupted, and electricity sizzled along the blade before abruptly winking out. Smoke billowed up out of the hilt, a clear sign of fried circuitry. The tech waved the smoke away and used a gelpen to scribble some notes on his tablet.

The longer I stared at the faux weapon, the more my magic flared to life. Suddenly, I could see all the parts and pieces of the Kent Corp sword in my mind, along with all the flaws in the design—and how to fix them. I might not care for the memories my seer magic wouldn't let me forget, but it was quite useful in figuring out how things worked and especially how to make them *better*. I could easily fix the sword's circuitry, although it would never have the psionic power of a real stormsword.

My gaze slid back over to the first weapon. I didn't know if it was a genuine stormsword, like the techs claimed, or just an excellent imitation, but something about it made my magic surge with anticipation, and my fingers itched to grab the weapon and see how it worked—

"Ahem." Someone cleared his throat behind me.

I jerked away from the clear doors, leaving a couple of handprints behind, along with a smudge where my nose had been pressed up against the glass.

A weapons tech rolled his eyes and scanned his ID card.

The doors whooshed shut behind him, and I peered through the glass, staring at the stormsword again.

"She's a beauty, ain't she?" a low voice drawled.

A big, burly guy with a shaved head, bronze skin, and bulging biceps stepped up beside me. Unlike the other security guards in their dark brown uniforms, this man was wearing black from head to toe, indicating his senior, superior status. A blaster dangled from his belt, along with a shock baton, although from the rumors I'd heard, Hal Allaston preferred to use his fists to get the desired results. Hal was the head of Kent Corp security, which was just a polite way of saying he was an upper-echelon mercenary who carried out all sorts of unsavory orders.

Hal squinted at me as though the suns were in his face, despite the fact that we were inside. His eyes were the same flat black as his uniform and utterly devoid of warmth, and I didn't need my seer magic to realize he was very, very dangerous.

"Maybe someday you'll get to play with that stormsword, if you ever get promoted to the weapons lab," Hal said.

I ground my teeth. No one wanted to fix toasters for a living, and everyone longed to get promoted to the weapons lab, including me, *especially* me. Over the past several months, I had submitted designs for blasters, cannons, and other items, hoping to get moved or at least promoted to a supervisory position in the appliances lab. But all my ideas had been rejected as being either too expensive or too impractical, along with all the other polite corporate ways you could be told your work simply wasn't good enough.

Hal stepped even closer to me. "I could arrange for you to be transferred into the weapons lab, although I would require a personal favor in return."

His gaze trailed down my body as though he could see right through my lab coat and the clothes underneath. Maybe he could. Like most corporate mercenaries, Hal had been pumped full of chemicals and enhanced multiple times.

I repressed a shudder. "I should get to work."

Hal grinned, his white teeth flashing like tiny daggers in his face. "See you soon, Vesper."

I walked away at a slow, steady place. I didn't look back, but I could tell that Hal was staring at my ass. I could *feel* it with my seer magic. Ugh.

My workstation was in the back of the home appliances lab and consisted of two long tables that formed a large L, giving me the illusion of a corner office, if not the view and privacy. I slung my backpack down onto one of the tables.

While I waited for my terminal to boot up, I glanced over at the projects littering the other table. A serrated kitchen knife that sharpened and sanitized itself every time you tucked it back into its block. A whisk that moved of its own accord in a magnetized mixing bowl. A pair of thin flesh-colored gloves that were designed to look and feel like human skin. I'd been assigned the kitchen knife and the whisk, but the gloves were my own design. The idea had popped into my mind a couple of months ago, although I didn't know what, if anything, the gloves would ever be useful for.

" . . . Kyrion Caldaren . . ."

A few feet away, Bodie, another lab rat, was staring at his own terminal, viewing the same program that Tivona had been watching earlier this morning. How long was that overly perky gossipcaster going to talk about Kyrion Caldaren and the Regals and their stupid ball—

A chrome brewmaker landed on my desk like an anvil, accompanied by a smooth, silky voice. "Hey, Vesper."

Anger exploded in my heart, and I stared at the shadowy image of Kyrion Caldaren stalking through that never-ending corridor on Bodie's terminal. Perhaps there were some advantages to being the most notorious killer in the galaxy. I bet an Arrow like Kyrion Caldaren never had to deal with the indignity of working for his incessantly smug and infinitely less talented ex.

I plastered a neutral expression on my face and looked at the man standing on the opposite side of the table. "Conrad."

Conrad Fawley smiled at me, oblivious to the fact that I could have cheerfully yanked the kitchen knife out of its self-sharpening block and stabbed him through the heart with it.

Roughly a year ago, Conrad had been transferred from an office on a neighboring planet to the main R&D lab here on Temperate 42. I hadn't paid him any mind until he'd asked me a question about the brewmaker he was working on, the same model I'd tweaked for Tivona last week. Conrad was quite handsome, with shaggy blond hair, ruddy skin, and dark brown eyes, and I'd said yes when he'd asked me out to dinner as a thank-you for helping him.

To my surprise, he'd been attentive and charming and deeply interested in my work, especially my ideas for improving various Kent Corp products. One dinner had led to another one and another one . . . until we'd ended up at his apartment. The sex had been nice enough, and Conrad claimed he was falling hopelessly in love.

Me? Well, I was never one to crack my heart open after a few dates, and I certainly hadn't expected to have some fairy-tale truebond with Conrad, but I'd cautiously started to hope we might have something *real*, something that would *last*.

Then, three months ago, while we were eating lunch on a bench outside, Conrad had said he wanted to talk. Like a fool, I assumed he meant about work, not our relationship. Conrad had smiled, looked me straight in the eyes, and dumped me.

Oh, it had been a little more involved than that. He'd clutched my hand and tearfully spouted all the usual clichés about how much he cared about me, how he needed to figure out what he really wanted in life, and how we were better off just being friends.

Despite how good I was at seeing how things worked, I hadn't seen the breakup coming. Or maybe I hadn't *wanted* to see it. Looking back, there had been plenty of warning signs that Conrad wasn't happy—or at least, that he wasn't happy with *me*. He had started obsessively watching the Regal gossipcasts, going off-planet with his friends to party, and ignoring my calls even when we'd scheduled a video chat.

In some ways, my seer magic had made the breakup even worse. Usually, my power warned me when bad things were going to happen, but it hadn't given me any clue about Conrad. For the first time in a long time, I'd been caught completely off guard, and I was just . . . *stunned*. So stunned that words had deserted me, and I had just sat on the bench and blinked at him, like a warning light on one of those brewmakers I was always fixing.

"You'll be so busy with work you won't even miss me," Conrad had chirped, as if my being good at my job made it perfectly acceptable for him to throw me away like a piece of trash.

Conrad had taken my stunned silence for agreement. Thanks to my magic, every time I saw him now, memories of that moment flooded my mind—the relieved smile on his face, the unexpected jolt of him giving me a friendly slap on the shoulder, and especially his quick, light, buoyant steps as he hurried away from me and toward his wonderful new future.

I'd sat there, as limp and wilted as the hydroponic spinach salad I'd bought from a campus food cart, for five minutes before the shock had finally worn off. Then I'd thrown my uneaten salad away, trudged back to the lab, and returned to work as though nothing had happened. A few tears had stung my eyes, but I'd hidden them behind my safety goggles. Conrad Fawley might have scraped me off the bottom of his shoe like a wad of chewed gum, but I didn't cry over him.

Not then, anyway. I made it through the rest of the workday and then had a proper breakdown in my apartment that night. Tivona even used our new brewmaker and the one small pint of genuine ice cream we had to make me a strawberry cheesecake milkshake to try to cheer me up, although the gesture just reminded me of how I had helped Conrad tweak the brewmaker's design.

But the worst part was that Conrad had come to work bright and early the next morning with the new love of his life hanging on his arm—Sabine Kent, the daughter of Rowena Kent and the heir to House Kent.

Tivona got the story from a friend of a friend of Sabine's who also worked in the litigation and negotiation department. A few weeks before, Conrad had met Sabine in a club on Corios. The two of them had downed a chembond cocktail and had a grand time together. After that, one thing had just naturally led to another . . . ending with me getting dumped and Conrad scaling the Regal ladder like so many others before him. Oh, yes. Conrad Fawley was nothing but a *climber*, a derogatory term for people who ingratiated themselves with Regal lords and ladies in hopes of eventually becoming one themselves.

"You need to look at this latest brewmaker, Vesper," Conrad said now, still smiling at me. "Your design is still a little glitchy, and we can't put it into production until all the kinks are worked out."

I arched an eyebrow. "Funny how it's only *my* design when something's wrong with it. Why, I thought it was *your* design when you pitched it to Sabine Kent a few weeks ago."

As if dumping me for a Regal wasn't bad enough, Conrad had also stolen my ideas for improving the brewmaker and other products and passed them off as his own. Duplicitous bastard.

His smile faltered, then vanished completely under my hot glower. "In case you've forgotten, *I* am the lab supervisor now," he snapped. "So do us both a favor, and just do what you're told."

I raised my hand and snapped off a mocking salute. "Yes, sir."

Anger sparked in his gaze, but it was nothing compared to the fury pulsing through my heart. Once again, I itched to grab the kitchen knife and stab him with it, if only to see how well the self-sharpening and -cleaning block worked. For science, of course.

Conrad sucked in a breath, but a light feminine voice cut off whatever order or insult he'd been about to hurl at me.

"Conrad! Darling! There you are!"

Sabine Kent sashayed over to us. She was about five years younger than me, in her early thirties, and absolutely gorgeous, with green eyes, pale skin, and coal-black hair that tumbled down her back in fat, glossy curls. Her light gray pantsuit and matching stilettos probably cost more than everything I owned, and the diamond studs in her ears twinkled like stars sneering about how much brighter she shone than I ever could.

I had always believed in karma, destiny, magic, fate, whatever you wanted to call the gods or forces or higher powers or whatever steered everything that happened in the galaxy. I just never expected it to be such a heartless bitch to me. *I* was the one who had been unceremoniously dumped, whose heart had been trampled and whose work had been stolen, so *I* should have been the one getting a hot new fling and a promotion and every other good thing that had appeared in Conrad's life the instant he had gotten rid of me.

I might not be a Regal, might not belong to any House, but I had an excessive amount of pride, and I couldn't decide which was worse—getting dumped, being duped out of my designs, or getting traded in for a younger, shinier, and much, much richer model. Any one of those would have been humiliating enough, but add in the fact that I still had to see Conrad every single day . . . Well, it was like constantly grinding salt into a fresh wound.

Sabine's gaze landed on me. Her brow furrowed, and her lips puckered, as though she was trying to recall my name, even though we had been introduced more than a dozen times at Kent Corp events, and we had both dated the same man.

She must have dismissed me as unimportant, because her expression smoothed out and she focused on Conrad again.

"Come, darling," Sabine cooed. "I have a new suit waiting for you in my office. I want you to look absolutely perfect for your meeting with my mother."

My ears perked up. So Rowena Kent was on the premises. Well, that explained the guards I'd seen outside earlier, as well as the extra ones in the lobby. Once again, I wondered if anyone had any inkling of what I was planning to do, but I dismissed the thought.

I wasn't important enough for anyone at Kent Corp to pay attention to—not Conrad, not Sabine, and certainly not Rowena Kent.

"Let's go," Sabine said, tugging on Conrad's arm. "I can't wait to see you in the new suit."

He nodded at her, then snapped his fingers at me. "Get to work on that brewmaker. It keeps shooting off sparks."

Conrad hit the button on the back. Several seconds later, a shower of hot blue electric sparks erupted all around the brewmaker, making me jerk back in surprise. A cruel smile twisted Conrad's face, and he strode away with Sabine.

I sighed and reached for the off switch, but the brewmaker burped out another shower of sparks. One of the sparks landed on my right hand, making me hiss with pain. Still, that was a small sting compared to the anger, humiliation, and loneliness scorching through my heart.

For the second time in my life, I had been betrayed by someone I thought had cared about me. Some seer I was. Because try as I might, I could never quite see the pain zooming toward me before it shattered my heart yet again.

THREE

VESPER

Hal ambled through the lab, making sure all us rats were actually working. Bodie finally switched off the gossipcast about Kyrion Caldaren and the rest of the Regals, put his head down, and concentrated on the new blender he was designing.

I pulled my stool up to my workstation and examined the faulty brewmaker. It took me less than a minute to discover the solar wiring was frayed, hence the sparks. So the fault was not with my design but rather with the cheap, shoddy materials Kent Corp used in all their products. I huffed and shoved the brewmaker off to the side.

I'd fix it later—if I had a later.

I tinkered with a few more projects. When I was sure everyone was absorbed in their work, I fished an ID card out of the thigh pocket of my cargo pants and inserted it into my terminal. When the login screen popped up, I entered a fake name, along with the matching password.

Three months ago, right after he'd dumped me, Conrad had

tasked me with designing some new ID cards for everyone in the R&D lab. Not only did the ID cards grant people access to campus, but they also monitored the workers' movements through the various buildings and made a record of every file, document, and schematic they accessed. The cards were a good way to track theft and sabotage, and they were an even better way to hide what you were doing.

I'd swiped a dozen blank ID cards, then attached fake names and photos to them all. It had been a slow, painstaking process, but no one had noticed there were suddenly a dozen new employees in the system who very rarely logged in and never did any actual work. Then again, thousands of people worked for Kent Corp, and it was easy for folks to fall through the cracks, even if they were imaginary. I had intended to use the cards to surreptitiously access Conrad's files and figure out just how many of my designs he had stolen and passed off as his own, but now, I had another plan for them.

I yawned and stretched, raising my arms high and wide. On their way back down, I accidentally-on-purpose banged my right hand against the terminal, knocking the monitor down and away from the cameras in the ceiling. The higher-ups were always worried about corporate espionage, especially given House Kent's rivalries with the other Regal families, so someone was always monitoring the security feed, much the same way that Hal constantly ambled through the R&D lab like a shark in search of blood in the water.

When I was certain the cameras couldn't see my monitor, I used the fake ID card to pull up all the files related to the *Velorum*, including my own report explaining why the ship had crashed, which I had submitted a few weeks ago and which had been summarily dismissed.

The information was the same as the last time I had checked it three days ago, except for one notable difference: Rowena

Kent had spent more than an hour sifting through the files this morning, according to the time stamps.

Hmm. An unexpected and troubling development. I hesitated, wondering if I should go through with my plan. So far, the gossipcasts were buying the story that the *Velorum* crash had been caused by pilot error, but that wasn't the truth. Then again, most people cared far more about credits and power than they did about the truth.

And I was one of them.

Oh, sure, I could pretend I was being all noble and righteous and other useless shit. And maybe a teeny, tiny part of me was being all those things. Like so many other people, I had lost someone in the *Velorum* crash, although mine was a tiny pang of hurt compared to others' wrenching grief. But I still wanted to avenge the person I had lost, even though I hadn't seen her in years. Plus, memories of visiting the crash site haunted me. Choked sobs and anguished screams rang in my ears, and the acrid stench of burned metal and fried flesh filled my nose at all hours of the day and night.

But mostly, I was angry, frustrated, and disgusted by the crash cover-up and how no one wanted to fix a small problem and save lives. I was also more than a little pissed about how all the higher-ups, especially Conrad, had dismissed my work and said my conclusions weren't accurate, when I knew damn well they were. When every single bit of my intelligence and experience and small scraps of magic were screaming that I was right and everyone else was wrong.

As the weeks had passed, and it had become clear that the pilot—who had died in the crash—was going to be the scapegoat, my anger had turned to resolve and then from resolve to action. Through a series of burner email accounts, I had discreetly contacted *Celestial Stars*, one of the most popular gossipcasts in the galaxy—the same one Tivona and I had watched this morning—and said that I had major dirt on a prominent Regal House. For the right price, of course.

After some haggling, Artemis Swallow, the gossipcast's head producer, and I had settled on a hefty finder's fee, half of which was already waiting in an anonymous, untraceable account. I would get the other half as soon as I delivered the information.

That was the theory, anyway. Time to put my plan into action and see if I could get away with it.

I let out a breath, then pulled a microdot drive out of my pocket. Even though it was only about half the size of my thumbnail, the round drive could hold an incredible amount of data. I placed the drive on the terminal keyboard. Then, before I could change my mind, I hit a button and downloaded all the *Velorum* files.

It only took a few minutes, although it felt like forever to my paranoid brain. After the download was complete, I swapped the first microdot drive out for a second one and downloaded all the files again.

It was shockingly easy and extremely anticlimactic. No alarms blared, no guards sprinted over to my workstation, and none of my coworkers so much as glanced in my direction. A relieved breath escaped my lips. Now on to the slightly harder part: where to hide the drives so that I could get out of the building with at least one of them.

Given the proprietary designs we worked on, all the lab rats were screened from head to toe before being allowed to leave the building. I had been pondering this problem for weeks, coming up with one potential hiding spot after another. A hidden pocket sewn into the lining of my lab coat, a secret compartment hollowed out of a zippered fob dangling from my backpack, an empty locket hanging around my neck. No, no, and no. Clothes, bags, and jewelry were far too obvious hiding places, and I had dismissed all those ideas and a dozen more.

Eventually, I had settled on the old hide-it-in-plain-sight

trick. I glanced around to make sure no one was watching me, then took the model of the *Velorum* cruiser out of my back-pack. I cracked it open, nestled the first microdot drive inside the hollow space, and snapped the whole thing shut again. Then I tossed the miniature aside, letting it land among the plastipapers, tools, and other models that littered one corner of my workstation.

The miniature ship was also a rather obvious hiding place, which was why I'd picked it for the first drive. Another feint on my part, although if someone did think to look inside the model, then I was already neck-deep in trouble and well on my way to being dead.

Everyone was still focused on their own work, so I palmed the second microdot drive, got my backpack, and headed into the nearest bathroom. None of the bathrooms was equipped with cameras. Not even the security guards, who were being paid for their vigilance, wanted to see people use the facilities, and it was one small weakness in Kent Corp's excellent security protocols.

The bathroom was empty, so I went into one of the stalls and shut the door. Then I put the toilet lid down, set my backpack on it, and pulled out a vial of clear liquid glue. Next, I grabbed a bottle of silver nail polish, along with two blue plastic jewels shaped like eyes.

A couple of weeks ago, Tivona had put jeweled stickers on her nails before going out clubbing, and in that *aha!* moment, I'd realized I could do the same thing with the microdot drive. And thus, my problem of how to smuggle the *Velorum* files out of the Kent Corp building had seemingly been solved.

Early this morning, I'd painted all my nails with the silver polish except for my left thumb. Now I crouched down, laid my hand flat on the toilet lid, and placed the microdot drive in the center of my left thumbnail. Then I stuck one of the plastic eye-shaped jewels on top of it, hiding and encasing the drive. The glue went on next to shellac the whole thing to my thumbnail and then finally a smear of the silver polish.

I also stuck the other eye jewel onto my right thumbnail so that it matched the left one. Then I examined both thumbs, along with the rest of my fingers. Mine was not the best or most professional manicure, but it should work well enough for my nefarious purposes. All I had to do was get out of the building with my left thumb still attached to the rest of my body.

A simple enough task . . . I hoped.

I blew on my thumb to dry the glue and the polish, then stuffed my supplies into my backpack, opened the stall door, and headed over to a counter. I set my bag down, then leaned forward and stared at my reflection in the mirror.

My wavy dark brown hair just brushed the tops of my shoulders, a bit frizzier than usual, due to the recent spring rains and humidity. My dark blue eyes seemed bigger and brighter than normal in my pale face, but I didn't bother powdering my nose or swiping on some lipstick. Today was the one day when I wanted—*needed*—to blend in with the rest of the lab rats.

But I couldn't stay in here forever, so I grabbed my backpack and left the bathroom. As the door swung shut behind me, I thought about the other thing I'd seen in the mirror—a faint silver glow around my body, almost as if my magic was trying to warn me how much danger I was in.

As if I didn't already know.

I returned to my workstation and set my backpack down. I was just reaching for my stool when Hal walked up to me.

"Let's go." He jerked his head. "You're wanted upstairs. The meeting about the final *Velorum* crash report."

The meeting had been scheduled for more than a week, but I still eyed the mercenary, wariness surging through me.

Hal looked right back at me, and his gaze didn't flick over to the *Velorum* model on my workstation or fixate on my left thumb. Since my secrets seemed to be safe, I followed him out of the lab.

A couple of other lab rats were waiting in the corridor, and we all stepped into an elevator. No one said a word as the elevator whooshed up like a rocket and floated to a stop at the hundredth—and top—floor.

Hal grinned, then swept his hand out to the side. "After you, Vesper."

Even though I knew he was going to leer at my ass again, I had no choice but to step out of the elevator and follow the other lab rats into an enormous conference room. One entire wall was made of glass, revealing an impressive view of the green campus below, along with the neighboring skyscrapers.

Hal gestured for the other lab rats to stop, then took up a position right beside me. I silently cursed my bad luck, but I couldn't move, given the crowd of people inside the conference room. Corporate types, mostly. Members of the board of directors and other important, wealthy shareholders who wanted Kent Corp to keep making them as much money as possible. Those folks were seated at a long table made of real wood in the center of the room, while the lab rats, salespeople, and other workers were forced to stand along the walls.

Tivona was with the other negotiators in one of the corners. She waved at me, and I waved back. While I had been part of the team investigating the *Velorum* crash, she had been among the negotiators tasked with handing out payments to the victims' families in hopes of staving off lawsuits. According to Tivona, most of the families had taken the payments, although a few folks were threatening to sue, wanting more credits than the meager crumbs Kent Corp was willing to dole out.

If money had a smell, it would be the sour eagerness that permeated the conference room at the thought of the new cruiser launch and the trillions of credits it would bring into Kent Corp. No matter how rich they were, the Regals were always striving for more—more wealth, more power, more workers and resources and production plants.

Sabine Kent swept into the room, followed by Conrad, who had shed his white lab coat for a slick, shiny dark brown suit that made him blend right in with the other higher-ups. Conrad pulled out a chair for Sabine near the head of the table before dropping into the seat beside her. He beamed at her, and she gave him an adoring smile in return.

Not for the first time, several fingers of jealousy pinched my heart tight. Not because I still cared about Conrad. That ship had crashed, burned, and disintegrated into ash the instant I realized he'd been cheating on me with Sabine. No, I was jealous of the power Sabine Kent so easily wielded, the way she could walk into a room and have people sit up and take notice and think about all the many, many ways she could help someone—or destroy them.

Another woman followed Sabine into the conference room. All the conversations abruptly ceased, and not so much as a piece of plastipaper rustled to break the sudden, tense silence. Sabine might have power, but this woman was the true force behind Kent Corp.

Rowena Kent was roughly thirty years older than her daughter, in her mid-sixties, although she had the wrinkle-free face of a much younger woman, thanks to skinbonds, serums, and other enhancements. She had the same green eyes that Sabine did, although her face was even paler, as though she never dared to let any sun on any planet touch her alabaster skin. Not a single strand of silver glinted in her short, tousled black hair, and her dark gray pantsuit looked even sleeker and more expensive than the lighter one Sabine wore.

Rowena took the seat at the head of the table. Just like so many Kents before her, Rowena was a spelltech, someone capable of infusing psionic power into weapons and other objects. Sabine was also a spelltech, although I didn't sense any magic rippling off either woman. Curious.

A man scurried forward and poured Rowena a glass of sparkling water, which she ignored. Instead, her gaze swept over everyone in the room. She studied me for a moment before moving on to the next person.

Cold dread washed over me yet again, but I forced myself to ignore my feelings and think logically. If security had discovered my illegal downloads, I would have already been in a holding cell being beaten, shocked, and otherwise tortured by Hal until I coughed up the two microdot drives. I might be safe on that front, but my magic kept pricking my skin, a clear warning that something was wrong. I just couldn't puzzle out what it was.

Rowena snapped her fingers three times, and everyone leaned forward, their gazes locked on her. "Where are we at with the investigation?" she demanded. "Are you ready to present your final findings?"

Sabine gestured at Conrad, who stood up and waved his hand, activating the holoscreen embedded in the table. A light flared, and reports and schematics hovered in the air like a cluster of colorful clouds.

"We've spent the last two months investigating the crash." Conrad launched into his spiel. "After eliminating sabotage, we studied the design specs, along with other factors, including pilot error . . ."

He recapped all the simulations and experiments that I and the other lab rats had conducted over the past several weeks and all the ways we had tested an identical space cruiser, trying to replicate the *Velorum* crash. After about ten minutes, everyone's eyes glazed over, and Sabine pointedly cleared her throat.

". . . and so we've concluded pilot error is to blame for the crash," Conrad finished, and sat back down.

Even though I'd known what he was going to say, disgust still surged through me. Why had I ever cared about Conrad? Or believed he cared about me? He was just like the rest of the higher-ups, more concerned with what would benefit him the most rather than the actual truth.

But I kept my mouth shut, as did all the other lab rats, although a few of them gave me curious looks, clearly wondering if I was going to speak up. In the beginning, I'd been quite vocal about pilot error *not* causing the crash, but as it had become clear that no one cared about what had really happened and that my reports weren't going to change anything, I had stopped protesting. I might not have a lot of magic, but I had a healthy sense of self-preservation, and I wasn't stupid enough to keep drawing unwanted attention to myself.

"Very well," Rowena said. "I want the press release sent out today, revealing the final, official cause of the crash. I also want the new space cruisers delivered to Corios as planned for the showcase during the spring ball."

Everyone nodded, including me.

Rowena waved her hand, making a diamond ring flash on her finger. "Everyone is dismissed, except for my special guest."

Special guest? Who was that?

Hal clamped his hand around my upper arm. "Stand still, and keep your mouth shut, Vesper," he hissed in my ear. "Or I'll rip your arm off the rest of your body."

His fingers dug painfully into my skin, a clear reminder of his enhanced strength. I couldn't have broken away from him even if I'd tried. Worry churned inside me like a blender had been shoved into my stomach. What did Rowena Kent want with me? Had security discovered my downloads after all?

Everyone else filed out of the room. Tivona shot me a worried look, but some people came up behind her, and she had no choice but to leave. Relief washed through me. At least I hadn't dragged my friend down with me.

Hal maintained his viselike grip on my arm, while another guard took up a position on my other side, his hand curling around the shock baton on his belt.

Rowena smiled at me, but it was the sharp, toothy grin of a shark about to swallow up the guppy in its path. She gestured at a chair on the opposite side of the table from Sabine and Conrad. "Please. Sit."

It wasn't a request, but I wasn't about to let them see my worry, so I wrenched my arm out of Hal's grasp, stalked forward, and dropped down into the chair. Sabine ignored me in favor of swiping through screens on her tablet, while Conrad tapped his fingers on the tabletop, something he did whenever he was anxious or nervous. Despite his cool façade, he was far more concerned than he let on.

Me too.

Rowena rocked back in her chair and steepled her hands over her stomach, making the diamond chips on her polished white fingernails glitter. Unlike the plastic blue eyes adorning my thumbs, her jewels were very, very real and another indication of just how much wealth and power she had.

"Earlier this morning, I finished reviewing all the files related to the *Velorum* crash," Rowena said. "I found your initial conclusions to be most interesting, Ms. Quill."

Another chill swept through me. She'd read my reports, and she knew my name. Oh, no.

"Why is that?" I asked in a calm, careful voice.

Rowena shrugged. "Because you were the only lab rat who didn't follow Conrad's lead and conclude that the *Velorum* crashed due to pilot error. What did you say caused the crash? What did you call it, exactly?" She snapped her fingers, and the sharp sound made me flinch. "Ah, yes, a *safety hazard*."

I knew I should keep quiet, but the smart show-off and smug know-it-all inside me just couldn't stop the words from pouring out of my mouth. "Actually, the ship crashed because of an error in the navigation system. One of the sensors below the observation deck windows is unusually sensitive to laser scans, blaster and cannon fire, and other similar bright pulses of light, heat, and power."

Rowena gave me an encouraging nod. "And?"

Once again, I couldn't stop talking. "And whenever light, heat, or power hits this particular sensor, the navigation system wrongly interprets it as a solar flare and reacts accordingly."

By this point, everyone was staring at me—Rowena, Conrad, Hal, the other guards, and even Sabine set her tablet down to focus on me.

"Reacts how?" Rowena asked, that deceptively pleasant smile still fixed on her face.

I swallowed the hard knot of worry in my throat. "The ship's autopilot kicks in, and it activates an emergency dive protocol. In other words, the ship immediately takes evasive action to avoid flying straight into the sun, star, or other danger it thinks is directly in front of it. Of course, that doesn't matter in space, where there is usually nothing to slam into, but it *does* matter when a ship is in a planetary, gravitational atmosphere and near land, water, or some other geographic mass. That's why the *Velorum* crashed. Because it had just taken off from a spaceport, and the sensor essentially drove it right back down into the ground. Not because of pilot error."

"But pilot error *was* a factor," Conrad cut in smoothly. "You just said the ship went into a deep dive. A skilled pilot should have been able to recover from that."

I should have agreed with him. Should have gone along with everything he said and every wrong conclusion he spouted. But the longer I looked at him, the more I wanted to wipe that patronizing smirk off his face and the more I wanted to get some—well, *any*—sort of revenge for how he'd stolen my ideas and used them to advance his own floundering career.

I shook my head. "Not even the most skilled pilot could pull out of a dive that steep, no matter what magic, enhancements, or tech they had."

Sabine gestured at her tablet. "I've reviewed your reports about this so-called *flaw*, this supposed *safety hazard*. But really, it's a nonfactor. The chances of the navigation sensor interpreting blaster or cannon fire or anything else as a solar flare are very, very small."

"Less than one percent," Conrad piped up, trying to bolster her argument.

"Which will still amount to dozens of crashes a year given how many ships Kent Corp plans to produce," I countered. "And since most of the new cruisers are destined for Imperium duty, then that percentage greatly increases, especially given the recent hostilities with the Techwave."

"Yes, such crashes would be of great concern to the Imperium," Rowena murmured.

I couldn't tell if she was mocking me or not, but I turned my attention to her. "Luckily, the safety hazard is an easy fix and can be done without attracting any unwanted attention. You could do it here, in the production plants, as you build the new ships. And send maintenance teams to quietly replace the faulty sensors on the cruisers that have already been delivered to their buyers."

A ghost of a smile flickered across Rowena's face, as though she found my suggestions quaint and amusing. "I appreciate your attempts at discretion, Ms. Quill, but it's far too late for that. Several new military cruisers have already been delivered to Imperium forces and will go into service right after the spring ball. I can't send maintenance crews to fix things on brand-new ships. Why, the merest *hint* that something might be wrong with the new ships would cost Kent Corp trillions in lost revenue, not to mention reigniting interest in the *Velorum* crash. I've invested far too many of House Kent's resources to have this endeavor fail now, at the last minute."

Even though she was talking about a massive conspiracy that could potentially cost millions of people their lives, her arguments were just as valid as mine were, so for once, I did the smart thing and kept my mouth shut.

Rowena rocked forward in her chair. "But you're right. There *is* a safety hazard in the new cruiser design."

"Mother—" Sabine started to protest, but Rowena silenced her daughter with an angry glower.

"The new cruiser line was your idea, your design, and you were so bloody *pleased* with your own brilliance you didn't even consider that someone else might notice the modifications," Rowena growled. "Arrogant fool. Your carelessness could have set our plans back years, if not scuttled them altogether."

Sabine gasped and jerked back as though her mother had slapped her.

"As I've told you countless times before, all it takes is one person, one tiny mistake, to bring down an entire Regal family. I've seen it happen before, and I will *not* let it happen to House Kent."

I rewound her angry words in my mind. Plans? What plans? And what modifications had Sabine made to the new space cruisers? The two of them seemed to be having a conversation about something else entirely, something far more sinister than letting unsuspecting passengers fly around on ships equipped with faulty sensors.

Rowena kept glowering at her daughter, even as she stabbed her finger at me. "How is it that some bloody lab rat knows more about how our spaceships work than you do?"

I stiffened. I'd heard the term *lab rat* thousands of times, and I often used it myself, but Rowena Kent spat it out as though it was the vilest sort of curse. Even worse, her tone reminded me of that long-ago insult from my own mother: *useless child.*

Rowena's words also struck a nerve with Sabine, whose

cheeks flamed with anger. The younger woman shot me a venomous look, and her fingers curled around her tablet as though she wanted to hurl it at me. Conrad glanced back and forth between Sabine and Rowena, while Hal grinned, clearly enjoying the drama. The other guards shifted on their feet, more wary than amused.

Cold dread washed over me yet again, even stronger than before, but I didn't need my magic to tell me that I needed to do everything in my power to save myself.

I cleared my throat again, drawing everyone's attention. "You don't even have to replace the sensor. All you have to do is tweak the settings, and then the light, heat, and power variances won't matter and won't overload the navigation system."

Rowena gave me a look that was filled with even more venom and disgust than the one Sabine had just shot my way. "And that will still cost me money, not to mention delaying production, both of which are unacceptable. I will *not* give Callus Holloway a chance to sink his claws into my corporation. Not now, when so much is at stake. We will proceed with the new cruiser launch as planned."

Again, instead of doing the smart thing and keeping my mouth shut, I kept right on talking. "But if the sensors aren't fixed, then every single ship is in danger of crashing. And if even just one cruiser goes down, especially one of those in Imperium service, then you're looking at thousands of casualties. And that's just on the ship itself. There will likely be many more casualties on the ground, just as there was with the *Velorum* crash."

"That's the idea," Rowena muttered.

Confusion filled me. "Wait. You actually . . . *want* people to die on your spaceships? But that will ruin everything—your corporation, your House, and especially your standing among the other Regals."

Rowena lifted her chin. "My corporation, House, and standing among the Regals are none of your concern . . ." Her voice trailed off, and she snapped her fingers at Conrad. "What's her full name again?"

"Vesper Quill," he replied in a smooth voice.

I looked at Conrad, and he stared right back at me. Despite his calm features, I thought a bit of regret flickered in his eyes, but most likely, I only imagined it, the same way I had imagined he had ever cared about me. I might have been planning to sell the stolen files about the *Velorum* crash, but Conrad was actively participating in the Kents' cover-up. And for what? So Sabine would buy him another fancy suit? So he could keep being Rowena's corporate lackey? So he could keep enjoying the crumbs of wealth and power the Kents occasionally tossed his way? What a greedy climber. What had I ever seen in him?

Rowena turned to Conrad. "Scrub her terminal and all her work related to the *Velorum* crash. And make sure she didn't download any of the files onto another drive. This information will *not* leak. I don't want to spend the next six months denying rumors that there's something wrong with the new cruisers—or worse, having to repair them on the sly. And you don't want me doing that either, as I would be most unhappy with *you*, Mr. Fawley, despite the fact you are currently fucking my daughter. Do you understand me?"

A sheen of sweat popped out on Conrad's forehead, and he bobbed his head in quick, nervous agreement.

"Get rid of her," Rowena ordered, staring at me again, her face as cold and blank as the beige walls. "The usual method is fine. Let Holloway think we are still loyal and beholden to his precious Imperium."

Hal and the three guards stepped away from the wall and headed toward me. Even though I knew it was pointless, I shot to my feet, grabbed Rowena's untouched water glass, and slammed it against the table. She yelped in surprise and shoved her chair back, as did Sabine and Conrad.

Several pieces of glass dropped to the tabletop. I snatched up the biggest shard and whirled around, ready to stab the first guard who came at me.

But the guards were enhanced with strength and speed, and I was not, and Hal was already standing in front of me.

"Bet you wish you'd been nicer to me now," he said.

I raised the shard, but he lunged forward and punched me. Pain exploded in my jaw, my legs buckled, and I hit the floor. I blinked and blinked, trying to banish the stars swimming in my eyes.

"Finish her," Rowena ordered.

Hal grinned and leaned down. I looked past him at Rowena, then at Sabine, and finally at Conrad. All three of them stared back at me with a mixture of annoyance and disgust—

Hal's fist plowed into my face again, and everything went black.

FOUR

VESPER

I was having the dream again.

I was strolling through the corridors of a . . . Well, I didn't know exactly *what* it was. Not a simple home and not a mere mansion either. It looked more like . . . a castle.

An old, run-down, dilapidated castle that had fallen into ruin.

Most of the furniture was covered with gray sheets, which in turn were covered with dust. Thick wads of silken cobwebs clustered in the corners of the high ceilings, while others hung off the grimy stained-glass chandeliers, slowly listing to and fro like ghosts that couldn't decide if they were going to stir themselves enough to haunt the structure. Still, despite the dust and cobwebs, everything in the castle was *real*—real stone, wood, and glass—instead of the plastic versions in my apartment.

Years ago, when I'd first started having this dream, everything in the castle had been shined to a high, sparkling gloss. But as time had gone by, the structure had fallen into disrepair. Now, an . . . *emptiness* permeated the air, as if all the people, life, love, and laughter that had once filled the castle had fled, and all that remained were the faint, hollow echoes of those lovely things.

Really, though, it wasn't a dream—it was my mindscape.

That was the term the Imperium academy instructors had used, which was just a fancy way of saying this was the place inside my mind, heart, and body where my magic resided. Like all children living on Imperium-controlled planets, I had been tested for psionic abilities when I was five years old, although by the time I was seven, the academy instructors had deemed my magic too weak to waste time training me in how to use it. They had labeled me a failure in that regard, a sentiment my mother had repeated after she had gotten the news.

Useless child. Her words echoed in my ears again, but here, in my mindscape, I was able to shrug them off a little more easily than before.

I ambled through the corridors, but everything was the same as the last time I'd had this dream, a few weeks ago, right before I had decided to blow the whistle on the *Velorum* crash.

Eventually, I ended up in my favorite room, the library. It was among the castle's smallest areas, a cozy space lined with real wooden bookcases filled with real paper books. Sometimes, if I stood in the center of the library and drew in a deep breath, I could actually *smell* all that dry, slightly musty paper. Ahh.

I sucked in a couple of breaths, but the papery scent eluded me, so I walked over to the fireplace in the back wall. No flames crackled behind the grate, and my breath frosted in the chilly air. A silver-framed portrait hung above the fireplace, but I could never quite make out the people's faces, the same way I could never quite read any of the book titles.

Once again, I tried—and failed—to see the people's faces, so I looked to my right. A door appeared next to the fireplace, beckoning me to venture even deeper into this dream. I walked through the opening, stepped onto a tight spiral staircase, and trudged downward.

The gloom that cloaked the rest of the castle quickly receded, and light bloomed, along with pale blue flowers that twined through the dark stone banister and gave the air a sharp but slightly sweet scent, like the sticks of spearmint candy I had loved as a child.

Sigils were also carved into the banister, although I had never been able to decipher them. Still, as I trailed my fingers along the stone, the sigils glowed with various colors and sensations. Some were as hot as fire, while others were as cold as ice. A few even made sounds, as though the markings were people whispering their deepest, darkest secrets to me.

I reached the bottom of the stairs, which opened into a round room. More pale blue flowers bloomed down here, clinging to the walls like oversize spiders. I had never seen a different kind of flower anywhere in the castle, which struck me as odd. After all, since this was my mindscape, I would think my imagination would occasionally conjure up roses, orchids, or some other expensive blossom I had seen on a gossipcast.

And then there were the eyes.

All around the room, eyes glittered like faceted jewels embedded in the walls, and a few even adorned the ceiling, peering down at me from on high. Most of the eyes were closed, as though they were sleeping, but a few were open.

When I was a child, I'd thought the eyes were black, but they were actually a deep, dark blue with flecks of black sparkling in them, like the night sky the instant before it gave way to full, unrelenting dark. In fact, the eyes looked just like the sapphsidian jewels embedded in the stormsword in the Kent Corp weapons lab. Weird.

The unblinking sapphsidian eyes seemed to track my every movement, although I had never been able to tell if they were pleased by my presence or silently cursing the fact that I didn't have enough magic to figure out what, if any, purpose or meaning they had.

In addition to the jeweled eyes, arched doors were also set into the curved wall. The closed doors were varying shapes and sizes—large, small, wide, narrow—and different sigils were carved into the dark stone. I studied the sigils, just like I always did, but I couldn't make sense of them. Still, I knew what lay behind some of the doors.

Memories—my memories.

I stopped in front of the smallest door, which was just tall enough for a seven-year-old child to walk through. Unlike most of the others, which were closed, this door was wide open, with light, sound, and images flickering on the other side, as though I was watching a gossipcast on a holoscreen. But it wasn't a gossipcast—it was one of the most miserable moments of my life.

I should be back on Corios. I should be part of the Regals, not rotting away on a useless planet trapped in a useless life with an utterly useless child.

My mother's voice drifted out from the doorway, and I could see her through the opening, her back to me, her body tense, her fists planted on her hips. Beyond my mother, Liesl threw up her hands in frustration. They kept arguing, and the scene played out just as it had in real life the day the Imperium academy instructors had decided to stop training me.

I'd been hiding on the stairs above and peering down at my mother and Liesl through the railing slats, but the image flickering in the archway was different, as though I had been down in the same room with them. A quirk of my magic I could have done without. Having a crystal-clear view of my mother's disgust only made it more painful to relive.

Especially since sometime that night, after I had cried myself to sleep for disappointing her yet again, my mother had left.

Liesl had claimed my mother would return soon, but I knew it was a lie, that my mother wasn't happy with her life, and especially with me, and that she was never, ever coming back.

And it was all because of magic we didn't have—anymore.

Supposedly, several generations ago, our ancestors had been powerful psions, a catchall term for anyone with extraordinary mental abilities like telepathy or telekinesis. From the stories Liesl had told me, our ancestors had been renowned spelltechs who had been dubbed *Quills* because they had painstakingly written down many of their formulas and inventions with real ink and feather quills on actual paper. Of course, the whole thing was probably a fairy tale, but I'd liked the stories so much that I'd taken Quill as my surname.

Those Quills had supposedly had a house on Corios where they had hobnobbed with the other Regal families. Sometimes I wondered if that was what I was seeing in my mindscape, the dilapidated castle that had once belonged to my ancestors, although I had no way to tell for sure.

But as time marched on, fewer and fewer Quills had been born with magic, and eventually, their power had seemed to vanish altogether—until my mother had been born.

As a teenager, Nerezza had demonstrated enough psionic potential for the Imperium instructors to offer her a position at a prestigious boarding school on Corios where highborn Regals trained to use their abilities to further their families' fortunes. But my mother's magic had seemingly petered out too, and she had been shipped back home—with a baby in her belly, courtesy of an ill-advised affair with some Regal boy.

And so the desperately unhappy portion of my mother's life had begun in earnest. At least, these were the stories Liesl had told when she visited me at the Imperium academy on Temperate 7 where she'd placed me after my mother's desertion. Given what I remembered of their arguments, I had no reason to doubt her. Besides, at least Liesl sent me candy and emails and even visited me a few times a year, unlike my mother, who I doubted ever gave me a second thought.

But perhaps the most ironic thing was that I was just like

my mother—someone with just enough magic to be considered a psion, a seer in my case, but not enough power to be useful. At least, not in the traditional seer way of having grand visions of the future that would steer a House toward greater prosperity. But seeing how things worked and using that power to fix and make them better had gotten me a scholarship to an Imperium university, and then various lab-rat jobs until I'd started working at Kent Corp.

When I was younger, I'd tried to increase my power, tried to unlock whatever potential I might have, but nothing had ever worked. I'd read dozens of books on psionic theory, in hopes of figuring out what the eyes, flowers, and sigils in my mindscape really meant. But the problem with psionic abilities was just how little was truly known about them and how no one had ever been able to replicate them with science and technology.

To this day, psions remained anomalies, with powers that came from someplace or something deep inside them that no amount of gene editing, manipulation, or therapy could mimic. Which was why so many people, myself included, referred to those abilities as magic.

With their emphasis on marriages, alliances, and bloodlines, the Regals had managed to produce generation after generation of psions, but even some Regals were born without powers or found their abilities fading over time. To supplement that loss, Imperium academies were always searching for psionic children, outliers, to bring into the Regal fold. The Erztonians had a similar system in place. Despite their fanatical devotion to technology, even the Techwavers sought out psions.

A couple of years ago, I had finally given up trying to figure out my own limited magic. Being in my mindscape didn't hurt me, and most of the time, I just ambled through the castle, admiring the furnishings upstairs, as grimy as they were.

Now I drew in a deep breath, letting the flowers' sharp, sweet spearmint scent wash away the sour, bitter thoughts of my mother. I moved away from the child-size doorway, although the memories kept replaying inside, caught in the endless loop of my mind and my magic.

I tugged on some other doors, but they remained firmly locked, like always. Eventually, I reached a door in the back center of the room—*the Door*, as I thought of it, since it was different from all the others.

Blue flowers and black vines snaked up the wall and curled around this archway, forming a crude trellis over it. Unlike most of the other doors, which were plain and featureless, this one was quite beautiful, with intricate sigils carved into the dark stone. Sometimes, if I squinted hard enough, I could make out a few of the symbols—crescent moons and stars, mostly—although I had no idea what they meant.

I focused on the Door's centerpiece, a large, upside-down, open eye. Just like all the other eyes, this one also looked like it was made of sapphsidian, and the jewel had always reminded me of a sapphire mixed with a black opal but with far more life and sparkle than just a flat, static gem.

This door didn't have a knob, although somehow I knew the eye was the key to opening it. Every time I came here, I tried to get the eye to move, turn, sink into the stone, or however it actually worked, but I'd never been able to budge it.

I hesitated, wondering if I should try yet again. But what was a little more disappointment in my life? Besides, given what had happened in the Kent Corp conference room, this might be the last time I was ever here before I died—if I wasn't already dead.

I reached for the eye. My fingertips touched the jewel, which went ice-cold against my skin, even as blue and black sparks erupted and showered into the air. I tensed at the new, unexpected sensations, which had never happened before.

After a few seconds, the chill faded away, and the sparks were merely light, so they didn't shock, burn, or otherwise harm me. Surprised, and a little wary, I gripped the jeweled eye and moved my hand to the right, not really expecting anything to happen . . .

The eye turned.

Shock zinged through me, and I froze, wondering if I had just imagined the movement—and especially if I should keep going.

Should I open this door? It would probably just show me another painful memory I would be better off forgetting. But my curiosity got the better of me, and I tightened my grip on the jewel and kept turning, turning, turning the eye, until I heard the distinctive *click* of a lock opening—

A shoulder bumped into mine, and the sour stench of sweat, vomit, and piss filled my nose, shattering my connection to my magic. My mindscape vanished, and I was jolted back to the real world.

My eyes snapped open, and I saw . . . metal walls.

For a moment, I thought I was still at Kent Corp, but that shoulder bumped into mine again. A loud, obnoxious snore blasted into my ear, and a man swayed closer to me, rancid breath puffing out of his mouth. I couldn't tell if he was asleep, drugged, or some other form of unconscious, but I shoved him away. The man swayed to the other side, and his head and torso flopped down onto the metal bench we were both sitting on.

I eyed the man, who let out another snore and mumbled something incoherent. Since he couldn't tell me where I was or what was going on, I glanced around, searching for someone who could. I'd been right before. Those were metal walls in the distance, only I wasn't in some Kent Corp conference room or holding cell.

I was in an enormous docking bay on board a massive space cruiser.

The docking bay was at least a mile wide, and smooth gray metal stretched out as far as I could see, from the floor under my feet to the wall behind me and then across the soaring ceiling high above to the opposite wall far in the distance.

Several ships were docked inside the bay, their ramps down so that hoverpallets loaded with weapons, armor, and other cargo could be floated on board. The ships had been built by a variety of corporations, but most were shaped like spears, massive triangular heads with multiple decks attached to long rectangular bodies. The typical shape for military cruisers, designed to move soldiers and supplies in and out of battle zones, areas affected by natural disasters, and other dangerous places. All the ships had boastful names like *Valiant* and *Courageous*, as though they were warriors about to fly into battle.

That's because they *were* about to fly into battle.

All the cruisers were fitted with cannons capable of blasting holes in just about anything, including enemy ships. Domes, satellite dishes, and antennas stuck out at odd angles from the ships, each one serving a different purpose, from providing energy shields to absorb and deflect cannon fire, to scanning planets for weather and seismic activity, to calculating coordinates for pinpoint travel from one side of the galaxy to the other.

Workers in light blue coveralls clustered around the cruisers like ants running around a nest. Some were dangling in harnesses along the sides of the ships, their eyes covered with protective goggles as they used laser torches to fix broken domes, dishes, and antennas. Below, on the ground, other workers were rooting around in open hatches, yanking on wires, and causing blue, red, and green sparks to fly in all directions. Conversations, shouted orders, and the clanging of tools hitting metal droned through the air like swarms of bees.

". . . hope the shields hold up in the heat . . ."

". . . getting ready for the assault . . ."

". . . better make sure the conscripts get their obligatory blasters . . ."

Every word chilled me to the bone, despite the hot, dry air

filling the docking bay. My seatmate was still snoring away, so I looked in the opposite direction. More benches lined this section of the wall, and each one held two people, all varying ages, shapes, and sizes. Some folks were dressed in common work clothes like me, while others sported slick suits and fancy gowns. One man was even wearing a pink fedora, a purple feather boa, and a teal loincloth. But no matter who they were or where they might have come from, all the people had one thing in common: they all looked miserable, sullen, and terrified.

I leaned forward, trying to see just how many other people were in this same unfortunate position. A female soldier dressed in a dark red Imperium uniform was standing about fifty feet away, holding a blaster and eyeing the guy in the loincloth as if she was expecting him to cause trouble. Fifty feet past her was another soldier with a blaster and the same tense, watchful stance. No one on the benches was here of their own free will. They were all conscripts, forced into Imperium service—and I was one of them.

In the distance, footsteps sounded in a steady, thumping cadence, and a squad of Imperium soldiers marched through an opening in the back of the docking bay. They sported dark red armor that gleamed like liquid blood under the bright lights, and each one had a blaster strapped to their thigh. The polyplastic armor was another Kent Corp design, as were the blasters. Pretty to look at but pretty inferior at stopping more than a couple of bolts from a blaster, cannon, or other energy weapon.

I struggled to make sense of things. I'd been knocked out in the Kent Corp conference room and had woken up on an Imperium military cruiser. That I could understand. But *why* had Rowena Kent sent me here instead of just letting Hal snap my neck and drop my body into a vat of chemicals in one of the production plants?

Get rid of her. Rowena's voice floated through my mind. *The usual method is fine. Let Holloway think we are still loyal and beholden to his precious Imperium.*

Rowena Kent must have had some deal with Callus Holloway. She sent him all her enemies, and he conscripted them into his army and turned them into cannon fodder, literally. I shuddered, wishing I could return to the comfort of my mindscape and escape this waking nightmare.

My gaze dropped to my hands. The plastic blue eye that had been on my right thumbnail was missing, but the one on my left thumbnail was still shellacked in place, thanks to the glue I'd used. I tried to wiggle the jewel, but it didn't move, indicating that the microdot drive with the *Velorum* files was still hidden underneath it. Bitterness flooded my chest. Not that the information was going to do me any good now.

The squad of Imperium soldiers marched to the center of the docking bay and stopped. Then they split into two sections, spun away from each other, and fell back, forming two separate units. Everyone stopped what they were doing and turned in that direction, and a hush dropped over the entire area. Even the workers snuffed out their laser torches and raised their goggles to peer that way.

More footsteps sounded. These thumps were much quicker and softer, but somehow that made them far more sinister. A shiver swept down my spine, and a strange tension filled my body.

A man walked through the open space between the two sections of soldiers. He was tall, with a quick, purposeful, arrogant stride that indicated he was used to people getting out of his way in a hurry. He was wearing a short, fitted, long-sleeved jacket over a tight tactical shirt, cargo pants, and knee-high boots. At first glance, the garments seemed a dull, flat black, but then the light hit them, bringing out their true deep blue color. A silver bandolier studded with a variety of small objects sliced across his chest. A blaster was strapped to his right thigh, while a silver sword dangled from his belt. A dark helmet covered his head, hiding his features, but I didn't need to see his face.

Even from this distance, I knew *exactly* what he was—an Arrow, one of the elite fighters who reported directly to Callus Holloway.

A soldier clutching a tablet scurried forward. She bowed to the Arrow, then showed him something on the screen. I couldn't hear what, if anything, he said, but for some reason, I couldn't stop staring at him.

For the third time, footsteps sounded, and two more Arrows appeared—another man and a woman. They were dressed the same way as the first Arrow, although they were wearing different colors, pale blue for the man and dark red for the woman.

That sense of dread swept over me, stronger than before, and my gaze darted from one thing to another. Miserable people on benches being watched by armed guards. A docking bay full of ships. A squad of soldiers. Three Arrows. Everyone readying for battle.

My initial assessment had been correct. I had been forcibly conscripted into the Imperium army, and I was most likely going to die within the hour.

Despite my best efforts to remain calm, a scream rose in my throat, but only a puff of air escaped my lips. No sound of any kind, not so much as a whimper. I frowned and tried again, but the result was the same puff of nothingness. Suddenly, I realized that I was scratching my left arm and that blood had soaked into the sleeve of my white lab coat. Suspicion filled me, and I yanked the fabric up.

A small round disk bulged up against the skin on the inside of my left wrist. Gingerly, I pressed down on the bulge, and a bit of blood welled up around the wound. No, not a wound, an injection.

Someone had injected me with a husher.

The round disks were yet another Kent Corp design and often used in prisons and labor camps when the guards got tired of listening to inmates yell, babble, and curse. I opened my mouth and tried to scream again, but I wasn't any more successful than before.

I slumped back against the wall, the enormity of the situation pressing down on my chest like a spaceship about to land and crush my ribs to bits. Rowena Kent had handed me over to the Imperium and was going to let them kill me. Or rather, let them send me into a battle where I was almost certain to be killed.

Still, the longer I stared at the husher bulging up against my skin, the angrier I got. Rowena Kent didn't care about anything but protecting her corporation, wealth, and Regal status. She wouldn't lose any sleep over what she'd done to me, and she had probably already forgotten my name. But it wasn't enough for her to just have me killed. Oh, no. The bitch had wanted me to *suffer* first. She'd wanted me to wake up, realize what was going on, and piss myself, like so many other people languishing on the benches had done.

My anger boiled up, blazing into full-on rage. I might have been conscripted into the Imperium army, but I would *not* die in silence.

That rage scorched through my dread, and I thought about how I could best improve my situation—or at least get the husher out of my arm.

I glanced toward the open end of the docking bay. Judging from the cruiser's slight vibrations and the hot air wafting inside, we were in hover mode, probably several hundred feet off the ground. Too high to jump out without a parachute or glider, which, of course, I didn't have. And given all the guards between here and there, I wouldn't even make it to the opening to try to jump out into whatever landscape was waiting below.

I looked in the opposite direction. My gaze skimmed over the soldiers, maintenance workers, and hoverpallets. Finally, in the back corner, I spotted something useful: a workstation covered with tools.

I considered my choices. Sit still and stay alive until the battle began, or stand up and potentially get shot trying to help myself survive the coming conflict. Just like back at Kent Corp, I had only bad options. Either way, I was still probably going to die, so I might as well go out with a bang, so to speak.

I let out a silenced breath, then surged to my feet. I tensed and glanced around warily, but no one started shooting at me, so I headed toward the workstation.

One of the guards drifted this way, eyeing me with suspicion, but she didn't try to stop me, probably because I wasn't screaming and running away in an obvious escape attempt. The guards were most likely supposed to keep the conscripts in the docking bay, so I was betting they didn't care where we went, so long as we stayed inside the massive space. Besides, from what I could see, there was only one opening on this side of the docking bay, and it was far too close to the squad of soldiers and the three Arrows for my liking. I might be desperate, but I wasn't suicidal.

No one called out to me as I strode over to the workstation. Hammers, pliers, and other tools littered the surface, while several sets of light blue coveralls were hanging on hooks on a nearby wall. My white lab coat was streaked with black grease, probably from the bench I'd been slumped on, and the bloodstains on my left sleeve stood out like splotchy bull's-eyes. Disgusted, I stripped off the coat and tossed it into a nearby recycler.

The guy in the teal loincloth let out a low, appreciative whistle, as though he had never seen a woman in a shirt, cargo pants, and boots before. I flipped him off, which made the female Imperium guard snicker.

I grabbed a set of coveralls, stepped into them, and pulled them up over my hips and shoulders. Maybe the thick fabric would offer some protection from the elements outside the ship if the worst happened and the weather was awful.

I snorted, although no sound came from my lips. Who was I kidding? The worst had already happened, and it was far more horrifying than I had ever imagined.

I zipped up the coveralls, then sorted through the tools on the workstation, but I didn't see anything that would help me remove the husher. At least, not very easily. I was about to pick up a pair of pliers when a glint of metal caught my eye, and I pulled a dagger out from underneath a pile of melted wires.

A bit of hope rose inside me, and I held the dagger up to the light. The weapon was small, with a silver hilt, but the arrow-shaped blade gleamed with a sharp, opalescent edge, something I tested by deliberately pricking my thumb with it. I silently hissed as a drop of blood welled up and trickled down my skin, but I didn't want to start sawing at my own flesh with a dull tool that wouldn't get the job done.

I shoved up my left coverall sleeve, revealing the husher. I grimaced. Even with the dagger, this was still going to hurt—

A shadow fell over me, blocking the light. I shifted to my right, trying to escape the shadow, but it moved with me. I shifted to my left, and the shadow slid that way. Annoyed, I glanced up and opened my mouth, even though my words wouldn't be heard.

An Arrow stood in front of me.

I froze. No one else had paid much attention to me, so why would this Arrow? I stared, but all I could really see was my own reflection in the smooth, shiny surface of the Arrow's helmet.

Tangled hair, wide eyes, pale face. I looked like a ghost who had somehow come back to life—or someone who knew she was about to die in a matter of minutes.

The Arrow shifted on their feet, and I realized it—*he*—was wearing a helmet that was so dark it looked more black than the blue it truly was. I remembered the other times I had seen that sapphsidian color—and him. First on the holoscreen in my apartment and then later on Bodie's terminal in the Kent Corp lab.

Suddenly, I was glad the husher was in my arm. Because without it, I would have spewed enough curses to make even the most hardened soldier blush at their length, breadth, and violence.

Kyrion Caldaren, the most notorious killer in the galaxy, stood in front of me.

FIVE

KYRION

The first thing I noticed about the woman was her lab coat.

The garment covered her from her shoulders all the way down to her knees, and it gleamed like a white beacon against the gray walls. Given the coat, she was probably a scientist of some sort, although she seemed far more disheveled than any scientist I had ever seen. Either way, she was extremely unfortunate that her enemies had dumped her in with the latest round of conscripts.

The Imperium generals called them conscripts, but we all knew what they truly were: prisoners. Most of them were literal prisoners, plucked from labor camps across the galaxy to help fight the Techwave. But some of them, like the woman in the lab coat, came from other places—Houses, corporations, and organizations where they were no longer needed, wanted, or welcome. Places where the people in charge couldn't be bothered to kill their enemies themselves but rather shipped them off to the Imperium to have them die in some painful, pointless way.

Oh, the conscripts served a purpose, albeit an unfair, gruesome one. They were usually sent into battle first to draw fire so that aerial drones could map enemy locations, numbers, and weapons and thus give Imperium captains and generals information about when and where to send in the real soldiers, along with Arrows like me.

Despite their grim fate, these conscripts were the lucky ones. Some people ended up in Imperium labs, to be poked, prodded, and dissected until they either died or went mad from the pain, chemicals, and surgeries. In a way, being conscripted into the army was a small mercy. Most of these people wouldn't survive the coming battle, and so their pain and struggles would quickly, abruptly cease.

Unlike the rest of us, who had to soldier on and on and on with no end to anything in sight. Not the simmering war with the Techwavers, not the ever-fraught relations with the Erztonians, not the Regals and their ridiculous rules, traditions, and demands, and especially not Callus Holloway and his iron-clad grip on the Archipelago Galaxy and especially on me—

"Lord Caldaren!" A captain hurried over and bowed to me. "We're so happy you're here for today's charge! As you can see, we've mapped the refinery again, although so far, the Techwavers have maintained their position on the walls and haven't moved any of their troops . . ."

She thrust her tablet forward, and I dutifully peered down at it. The camera in my helmet would record everything so I could review it later, but the Techwave troop movements didn't really matter. All that did in the heat of battle was killing—and surviving.

The captain finished her briefing, bowed to me again, and scurried away to ready the soldiers.

A flash of movement on the opposite side of the cargo bay caught my eye. The woman in the lab coat had surged to her feet. Thanks to my telempathy, my psionic ability to sense other people's emotions, I could feel the rage blasting off her. Even from here, the force of it was as hard as a sledgehammer cracking against my chest. Apparently, she'd realized exactly where she was and what was happening, and she was not pleased about any of it.

The woman glanced toward the far end of the docking bay, as if she was thinking about running forward and hurling herself out of the opening and into the empty air below. Lots of conscripts did that. For most of them, it was a far more merciful death than what was waiting on the ground.

I watched the woman, wondering what she would choose. Most people who felt such rage often charged at the guards, as if grabbing a single blaster would let them shoot their way out of the docking bay. Fools. All it did was hasten their own death.

To my surprise, the woman spun around and stalked in the opposite direction, heading even deeper into the docking bay.

"What is she doing?" a soft feminine voice murmured beside me.

"No idea," a louder male voice replied. "She's not trying to escape, is she?"

Two Arrows stepped up beside me. They hadn't donned their helmets yet, so their faces were visible. Both were in their late thirties, just like me.

Julieta Delano was petite and slender, although her body was all pure, lean muscle. Her long dark brown hair was pulled back into several braids that were woven together and trailed down her back, disappearing beneath the collar of her bloodred jacket. Her bronze skin gleamed under the lights, as did her golden eyes. She was one of the few seers among the Arrows, with a special talent for knowing exactly when and how to strike out and kill an enemy.

In contrast, Zane Zimmer towered over Julieta, almost a foot taller than her and roughly even with me. Zane had wavy blond hair, ice-blue eyes, and skin that was always perfectly tan, despite the fact that we spent so much time in the blackness of space, traveling from one hot spot to another.

Zane was a psion like me and many of the other Arrows. Abilities could vary wildly between psions, but most of us were capable of telekinesis, telepathy, and telempathy, along with creating mental shields that could block out pain. Many psions could also create electrical shields that would deflect small projectiles and even absorb blaster fire and add that power to our own mental energy. Zane was particularly skilled at telekinesis, which he used to ruthlessly dispatch his enemies. Something much more useful than my telempathy, which often drenched me in other people's annoying emotions.

The three of us watched while the woman stripped off her lab coat and donned a pair of coveralls.

"Well, she's certainly not shy about making herself at home," Julieta drawled, her voice sounding in the air as well as echoing through my helmet.

The three of us were the only Arrows on this mission, and we were all connected by earbuds, both the ones in our actual ears and the other ones embedded in our helmets. Standard operating procedure, along with the trackers in our helmets. Callus Holloway liked to know exactly where his prized weapons were.

The woman zipped up the coveralls, then started rummaging through the junk on a nearby table, as though she was looking for something in particular—like a weapon.

Zane let out a loud, overly dramatic sigh. "She's going to grab something off that table, start screaming, and attack one of the guards."

Julieta shook her head. "No, I think she has something else in mind." Power glimmered in her eyes, making them flare a bright gold. "Although I don't know what that might be."

"You can't see anything about her?" Zane asked.

"I don't see things about every single person I encounter.

Mostly, I just know how to kill them." Julieta's face turned thoughtful. "Although I can't quite see how to kill her. Strange."

The woman's nose crinkled with disgust, as if the table didn't have whatever object she wanted. She started to move away from it, but then she turned back, leaned down, and snatched something out of the mess. The woman held a dagger up to the light and then poked the tip into her thumb. Well, at least she had enough common sense to test its sharpness, rather than trying to attack someone with a blunted blade that wouldn't cut through a piece of plastipaper, much less their clothes and skin.

"And now she has a knife," Zane muttered. "Why does a conscript *always* manage to find a knife? And I just got a new jacket."

He ran his hands down his jacket, which matched his ice-blue eyes. Such a ridiculous color for anyone to wear, but especially an Arrow. The pale, pristine fabric would be stained with blood, gore, smoke, and ash within seconds of Zane stepping off the cruiser. Then again, I had always found Zane Zimmer to be ridiculous. Dangerous but still ridiculous, especially given his unwavering loyalty and devotion to his House and family above all else.

Julieta nudged my elbow. "Actually, it's Kyrion's turn to deal with the conscripts."

Arrows didn't have any authority over the conscripts, so I couldn't have freed or saved any of them, even if I had wanted to, but we were supposed to help the guards keep them in line. Which Julieta knew was one of my least favorite tasks, since it made me feel far too much useless sympathy when all I should be feeling—all I *wanted* to feel—was the icy acceptance that helped me survive.

I glared down at Julieta, but a knowing smile spread across her face.

"We haven't even left the ship yet, and I've already made

Kyrion glower at me. Excellent," she purred. "You know I'm a seer. I can sense your glare even through the helmet covering your face."

"Helmet or not, most people would be pissing themselves if I glowered at them," I grumbled.

"I am made of sterner stuff than most people." Her smile widened. "So go take your fearsome wrath out on the conscript. It will be a good warm-up for the battle."

Zane snickered and made a shooing motion with his hand. This time, my glower was genuine. Even if he could have seen it, he was no more afraid of me than Julieta was. Arrogant fool. The two of us barely tolerated each other, and I would be more than happy to kill him the first chance I got. Zane felt the same way about me, although we had managed to coexist as Arrows for the last several years.

A reckoning was coming soon, though, one he wouldn't survive.

Still, Julieta was right. Like it or not, it was my turn to deal with the conscripts, so I stalked away, my long, quick strides eating up the distance between me and the woman.

The woman was so absorbed in whatever she was doing with the dagger that she didn't sense my approach. I eyed the weapon—a Zimmer dagger, given the short, thin design and lunarium blade. Zane came from a family of spelltechs who were known for making old-fashioned weapons, which they often imbued with psionic power. How had such a quality blade gotten mixed in with the rest of the junk on the table?

I stood there, waiting for the woman to notice me, but she bent her head a little more, singularly focused on whatever she was trying to accomplish. I sighed. I would have to stop her if she tried to cut her wrist or otherwise injure herself.

Oh, I didn't particularly care what happened to her, especially since she would probably be killed as soon as the battle started. I simply didn't want to deal with whatever mess she might make of herself in the meantime. There would be plenty of blood, death, and screaming during the battle, and I selfishly wanted a few more minutes of peace and quiet. I reached for my power to rip the dagger out of her hand—

The woman's head snapped up, and she looked at me. I hadn't been able to see much of her features from across the docking bay, but her wild, wavy hair was a deep, dark brown shot through with a few russet highlights. A large, ugly bruise adorned her left cheekbone like a blue-black flower had bloomed in her pale skin.

She blinked a few times in surprise, and then recognition spread across her face. She probably knew exactly who I was, thanks to all the bloody gossipcasts about the spring ball and my supposed marriage prospects. But she didn't scream, shrink down, or try to run away as many people did when confronted by an Arrow. Instead, her face brightened, as though she was actually happy to see me. And then she did the last thing I expected: she held the dagger out to me.

Even though she couldn't see my face through my helmet, I still frowned. The woman was thrusting the dagger at me as though she was begging me to slit her throat with it. For a moment, I considered doing just that. On rare occasions, I was still capable of mercy.

I reached for the dagger, but the woman yanked it back and shook her head. Then she held the dagger out again and tapped the blade against the inside of her left wrist, as if she wanted me to slice it open. My frown deepened. Why would she want me to do that?

The woman's lips parted. No sound came out, although I got the sense she was huffing in frustration. Curious. People usually regarded me with fear, wariness, and either abject terror or excessive greed—not frustration.

She gave me an annoyed look, as though I should have known exactly what she was demanding. And she *was* demanding something. I could still feel the rage blasting off her. Before, the sensation had been as hot and oozing as the lava bubbling on the Magma planet below, but now the emotion was as cold and hard as a Frozon moon.

The woman's lips opened, and she let out another one of those silent, annoyed huffs. Then she strode around the table and planted herself in front of me. She held her arm up where I could see it, then slowly, deliberately tapped the flat side of the dagger against her wrist a couple of times.

I finally spotted the small round disk creating an odd bulge against her skin. Someone had injected her with a husher, then conscripted her into an Imperium army unit bound for battle. Someone wanted her very, very dead, very, very quickly, although they wanted her to suffer a bit first.

Unwanted sympathy spattered over me like an icy rain. I knew what it was like to have to suffer through something horrible first and then still not be able to escape a terrible end.

So I plucked the dagger out of her hand, then grabbed her wrist. I yanked the woman toward me, and her body bumped up against mine. Her eyes widened in surprise, and she tensed, as though she was going to wrench away. I stifled a laugh. I could shove the dagger into her heart before she could blink.

Once again, I considered doing just that, but the woman had roused my curiosity. Instead of panicking, she had tried to solve the problem of the husher in her wrist. If nothing else, she deserved to live a few more minutes for showing that much spine.

I held her wrist up and dug the dagger into her skin. She tensed again, and I got the impression she was hissing with pain, but I kept going, making a shallow, curving cut. Then I slid the tip of the dagger underneath the husher, pried the disk up, and fished it out of her. I tossed the device onto the table, then released her wrist, wondering what she would do next.

First, she picked up a rag from the table and wrapped it around her wrist to stem the bleeding. Then she leaned past me, plucked the husher off the table, and held it up to the light, studying it. Even more rage blasted off her, burning hot, then cold, and tickling my telempathy in equal measure. Curious. People were usually one or the other, not both, and especially not within a matter of seconds.

The woman shoved the husher into the pocket of her stolen coveralls. I had no idea why she would want to keep such a thing, but I didn't bother taking it away, since the device was harmless now that it was out of her body.

The woman tipped her head up, looking at me. She opened her mouth, but no words came out. Frustration flickered across her face, but she cleared her throat and tried again. "Thank you."

Her voice was soft, and she had a slight drawling accent that indicated she was from one of the Temperate planets, instead of the sharp, crisp tone of Corios or one of the other posh planets where the Regals and other wealthy citizens played, partied, and schemed against each other.

She cleared her throat again, as if trying to reassure herself that the husher was gone and she could, in fact, talk freely. "My name is Vesper."

I didn't care about her name. Now that I knew she wasn't a danger to anyone, I had no further interest in her. I stabbed my finger to the left, pointing at the bench she had been sitting on before. Distaste filled her face, although I thought that had more to do with the man sprawled across the bench than with my order.

I turned to go, but she latched on to my wrist. I slowly pivoted back toward her. The woman—Vesper—grimaced, as if realizing just how far she had overstepped, but instead of releasing me, she tightened her grip and held out her other hand.

"The dagger," she said. "Please."

My eyebrows shot up, causing my forehead to scrape against the inside of my helmet. Her rage had made her quite audacious. Did she really think the dagger was going to help her survive the coming battle? Fewer than one percent of conscripts made it through their first live action. She might not know those odds, but she was railing against them anyway. A small part of me admired her for trying to do everything in her power to survive.

I flipped the dagger over and held it out to her, hilt first. Vesper snatched it away as though she thought I was going to change my mind and stab her with it after all. I probably should have done that. Conscripts like her were always more trouble than they were worth.

"Thank you," she repeated, her voice firmer, stronger, and louder than before.

She released my arm and started to return to the bench, but this time, I grabbed her uninjured wrist.

I wasn't sure what had prompted me to reach for her again, but I yanked her toward me just as I had done a few minutes ago. She tensed, but she didn't duck her head or shrink down.

Whoever she was, wherever she had come from, Vesper had quite a lot of spine, and I was willing to bet that spine was the reason she'd made a powerful enemy who had dumped her here. Fool. Spines were only good until someone stronger came along and snapped them into pieces, something I knew all too well.

We stood there, staring at each other, and I found myself studying her eyes. They were blue but with a surprising depth of color, like a cold, dark moon sprinkled with luminescent silver flecks. Perhaps her vision had been enhanced, hence the odd, striking color.

I drew her even closer. Blood had soaked through her make-shift bandage, which was in danger of falling off completely, so I unwrapped and then rewrapped it. She hissed again, the sound audible this time, as I tightened the bandage around her wrist and tied the ends together, but she didn't pull away. Instead, she just kept watching me, as though I was a Frozon snow wolf and she didn't know whether I was going to leave her alone or rip her to pieces.

I didn't quite know myself.

I finished with the bandage and released her wrist. Wetness coated my skin, and a few drops of her blood stained my fingertips a dark ruby red. Annoyed, I wiped my hand off on the front of my shirt, right over my heart.

She frowned. "You just ruined your shirt."

I shrugged. "It would have been ruined soon enough anyway."

Then I whirled around and strode away to prepare for the coming battle.

SIX

VESPER

Despite my shaking legs, I shoved the dagger into my pocket, then walked over and dropped down onto the bench. I'd just survived an encounter with Kyrion Caldaren. Not only that, but he'd let me keep the dagger, and he'd even bandaged my wrist. Odd—and more than a little disturbing.

He stalked back over to the other two Arrows. The dark-haired woman and the blond man donned their helmets, and they all morphed into the killers they truly were.

"Conscripts! Listen up!" the female guard yelled. "It's your lucky day! You get the honor of serving the Imperium!"

She marched down the line of us, talking about how we could all prove ourselves in battle and potentially earn our freedom, but she obviously didn't believe what she was saying. Being a conscript was nothing but a death sentence, and everyone here knew it.

A couple of other guards followed along behind her, passing out blasters. One of them dumped a weapon into my lap.

Disgust filled me. Another shoddy Kent Corp design. I'd be lucky if it even fired, so I did what I always did.

I figured out how to make the blaster *better*.

To my surprise, the solar magazine was fully charged. Ideally, with a full charge, a Kent Corp blaster was supposed to fire nonstop for twenty-four hours. But like with all their products, the Kents designed the blasters to last only half as long as they advertised, so customers would have to buy replacement magazines and weapons sooner than anticipated and thus make House Kent even more money.

I shoved the magazine back into place, then examined the buttons on the side of the grip. Most blasters were equipped with three settings: stun, kill, and shield. But this blaster only had two buttons: stun and shield. More disgust filled me. Of course, Imperium soldiers wouldn't give conscripts weapons that could be used against them.

Since I couldn't kill anyone with the blaster, I turned off the stun setting and cranked the shielding up to maximum capacity. A soft hum sounded, and a faint electrical field emanated from the weapon, making my skin itch. The blaster's shielding wouldn't stop more than a few energy bolts, but it might buy me some time to figure out how to escape this madness.

The female guard reached the end of the conscripts and finished her spiel. The other guards handed out the last of the blasters, and then we were all ordered to stand up. The guards herded us into a square formation, more or less, in the center of the docking bay.

I was near the middle of the pack, so I didn't see Kyrion Caldaren or the other two Arrows, just hundreds of conscripts flanked by Imperium soldiers clad in dark red armor and clutching blasters and larger hand cannons.

The cruiser picked up speed and then abruptly dropped, and the sudden motion made my stomach swim up into my throat. The landing gear slammed down, rocking the entire ship, and dry heat rushed in through the docking bay opening.

"Go! Go! Go!" the female guard screamed.

More Imperium soldiers came up behind us, and I, along with all the other conscripts, had no choice but to clutch my blaster, run down the metal ramp, and plunge into the battle-field.

Chaos—sheer, utter chaos.

For several seconds, everything was a blur of sound, sensation, and motion, of noise and heat and bodies pressing together all around me. I ran over the rocky, uneven ground, trying to maintain pace with the other conscripts so I wouldn't get pushed down and trampled by the ones coming up behind me.

A red energy bolt shot through the air, straight into the chest of the man in front of me. He screamed and tumbled to the ground. At least, I thought he screamed. Hard to tell over the roar of my heart in my ears. I gritted my teeth, leaped over him, and kept running.

More and more bolts shot out, filling the air with hot, deadly streaks of color—red, blue, green, yellow, purple. The acrid stench of electricity flooded my nose, along with the popping, snapping, and sizzling of burning flesh. Some of the conscripts screamed, while others gasped for breath, frightened or winded or both.

Another man in front of me yelped and tumbled down, also dropped by a bolt to the chest. I tried to leap over him, but I misjudged the distance, and I tripped over his body and hit the ground. Sharp black rocks dug into my knees and elbows, but I managed to hang on to my blaster. A grunt of pain escaped my lips, but it was drowned out by the yelps and shrieks piercing the air.

More conscripts were still running this way. I couldn't get back up onto my feet in time to keep from being trampled, so I reached out, grabbed the dead man, and flung his body over my own.

One foot after another slammed into the man's body and shoved it into me, but the blows were far more muted than they would have been otherwise, and they only bruised my ribs instead of breaking them outright. I wasn't sure how long this went on. Probably only seconds, although it seemed like an eternity. Then the last of the conscripts raced by, and I was able to shove the dead man away, sit up, and get my bearings.

I was in a field of shiny black rocks that jutted up like teeth, as though this was the maw of some enormous dragon that was trying to devour us all. In the distance, shadows scurried along the tops of the outer walls of a sprawling production plant with towers that were belching orange flames into the air. Beyond the plant, mountains also made of shiny black rocks soared up to touch the low, ominous gray clouds.

No, not clouds, smoke. This was a Magma planet, a thin crust of land wrapped around a molten core, and lava shot up out of the tops of the mountains—volcanos—before falling back down like red-hot rain. Soot and ash swirled through the air, and the intense heat blasted over me like I was being roasted alive in a smelter.

I couldn't see everything that was happening through the smoke, soot, and ash, but more energy bolts rained down from the production plant walls, striking the conscripts in front of me. None of them had a chance, and only a few managed to fire their blasters in return. One by one, they dropped to the ground, screaming and sobbing.

In less than two minutes, the last conscript was dead, the blaster fire stopped, and an eerie silence descended over the field. Then, behind me, footsteps thumped out a low, steady beat. Imperium soldiers were streaming down the docking bay ramp, while several blitzers—small, maneuverable fighter ships—were also zooming out of the opening.

Somehow I had ended up on the left side of the field, and my position made it seem like I was watching speed racing or some other sporting event on a screen, instead of seeing, smelling, hearing, and experiencing the battle for myself.

For a moment, everything was relatively quiet, except for the marching footsteps and the soft purr of the blitzers' engines. Then, in the distance, green lights appeared, glowing big and bright. More footsteps sounded, although these clanks were louder, sharper, and more metallic than the soldiers' footsteps, almost like tin cans rattling together. Through the swirling smoke, hundreds of figures appeared, which I recognized from gossipcasts.

The Black Scarabs.

Each Techwave fighter looked the same: a black polymetal suit of plated armor studded with two compound green eyes like those on some massive insect. Many of the Black Scarabs were hollow shells, machines controlled by people in other locations, and their lumbering motions were jerky, slow, and awkward. But several of the Scarabs moved with quick, easy fluidity, indicating that a real person was buried somewhere inside all that shiny black metal.

I'd heard the gossipcast reports about how the Techwave melded men and machines in all sorts of painful, unnatural ways, but seeing it with my own eyes made the horror even more vivid. A shudder rippled through my body, and a hand squeezed tight around my chest, almost as if I had been stuffed into one of those metal suits. Whether they were man or machine, the Black Scarabs all looked like monsters that had risen out of the rocks and taken on the rough outlines of people.

The Black Scarabs halted, as did the Imperium soldiers, and the two groups faced each other, with the open, rocky expanse of the field stretching out between them. Smoke, soot, and ash swirled through the air, and the tension grew and grew as each side waited for the other to make the first move.

Suddenly, one of the Imperium blitzers swooped down to fire on the Techwavers, but the orange flare of a laser cannon shot through the sky, cutting off the blitzer's charge. The pilot avoided the blast, but they banked too hard, and the blitzer spiraled down toward the ground. The pilot managed to pull out of the spin and make a rough landing on the far edge of the field, although the blitzer looked like a toy that a child had tossed aside in a tantrum, along with the bodies of all the dead conscripts.

More blitzers swooped down, and more cannon fire cut through the air, adding an electric orange tinge to the thick clouds of smoke. A few seconds later, several Techwave ships appeared overhead, and the battle began in earnest. Bolt after bolt streaked through the sky like colorful lightning. A few bolts even slammed into the Imperium cruiser behind me, although the ship's energy shield easily absorbed the blasts.

A dull roar filled my ears. For a moment, I thought it was the booming echoes of the cannon fire, but it was the sound of the Black Scarabs advancing across the field. Unlike my cheap polyplastic blaster, their weapons were sleek, shiny silver, and they fired bolt after bolt with unerring precision.

The first line of Imperium soldiers dropped to the ground, smoking black holes punched into their helmets and breast-plates. A few of the Black Scarabs also dropped, but not nearly as many, given their superior armor. More shouts, shrieks, and sobs tore through the air, and the sizzle of fried flesh grew stronger and stronger, forcing its way down my nose and throat and making me want to vomit.

The Techwavers pressed their advantage, rushing across the field and firing shot after shot at the Imperium cruiser, trying to break through its energy shield. Even more Imperium soldiers dropped to the ground. Some died from blaster wounds, while others were picked up by the Black Scarabs, who used the enhanced strength of their armored suits to break the soldiers' backs. A few particularly vicious Scarabs tore off arms and legs and then tossed the rest of the bleeding, screaming soldiers aside.

It was the most horrific thing I had ever seen.

The Black Scarabs quickly advanced across the field. Just before they would have cut through the final knot of Imperium soldiers, those men and women scattered, revealing the secret weapons hidden inside their ranks: Kyrion Caldaren and the other two Arrows.

The female Arrow leaped forward and swung her sword at the closest Techwaver. The blade glimmered like liquid gold and easily sheared the Scarab's head from the rest of its body. Sparks shot out of both pieces as they toppled to the ground, indicating that it was just a machine and not an actual person.

The male Arrow stepped up beside her and waved his hand. Telekinetic power rolled off him, causing the ground to ripple like water, and the ominous wave zoomed straight toward the Black Scarabs. The instant it reached them, the male Arrow snapped his hand into a tight fist, and the wave erupted like a grenade, spewing razor-sharp rocks everywhere and skewering several Scarabs. The male Arrow calmly walked in that direction, sending out more telekinetic ripples, while the female Arrow cut down enemies beside him.

I finally had the presence of mind to quit gawking and get up off my ass. I was still clutching the blaster, which I shoved into my coveralls pocket. No reason to hold it, since I wasn't going to fire it at anyone. I just hoped the shielding would keep me safe until I figured out some way off the battlefield.

I glanced back over my shoulder, but the faint blue energy shield was still up around the Imperium cruiser. Not only would it block blaster and cannon fire, but the barrier would also electrocute anyone who tried to physically breach it and charge up the docking bay ramp.

I cursed, although my voice was lost in the shouting and shrieking. Still, I kept glancing around, searching for some way to escape this madness.

A faint silver glow caught my eye. The blitzer that had gone down in the opening salvo was still sitting at the edge of the field, somehow untouched by all the fighting. The longer I stared at it, the brighter the silver glow became. Hope flared in my chest, and in that moment, I appreciated the scraps of my seer magic more than I ever had before. If I could get to that ship, I could get out of here.

I knew it—I just *knew* it.

But even if my magic hadn't shown me what to do, the blitzer was still my only option. Sooner or later, one of the Black Scarabs would spot me, march over, and break my back.

Too bad I didn't have a way to actually *get* to the blitzer. It was on the opposite side of the field, and Imperium soldiers and Techwave troops were fighting in the space in between. Blaster bolts and cannon fire were still zinging through the air like colored streaks of lightning, both down here on the ground and in the skies above between the enemy ships.

My only chance was to start running and hope I could reach the blitzer before I got clipped by too many energy bolts or a Black Scarab got their armored hands on me. But maybe my magic could help with that. Worth a shot, anyway. So I drew in a breath and reached out with my power. Well, as much as I could ever reach out with it.

Nothing happened.

No more silver glows flared, and no safe path through the chaos suddenly appeared. Frustrated, I tried again and again, with the same useless results as before—

A blaze of blue erupted on this side of the field, only about a hundred feet away from my current position. My head snapped in that direction, and I spotted someone I had almost forgotten about.

Kyrion Caldaren.

A sword was glowing a dark, deadly blue in his hand, and he walked steadily forward, completely unafraid, despite the overwhelming number of enemies converging on his position. Even though he was wearing a helmet and I could see nothing of his face, I could have sworn that his smile filled my mind—a cold, vicious expression that revealed how eager he was to unleash the rage that was always simmering inside him.

The first Black Scarab reached him, and Kyrion casually waved his hand, using telekinetic power to send that one crashing back into the others. Another Scarab came up on Kyrion's right side, and he swung his sword out in a quick arc. The glowing blue blade cut through the Techwaver's armor like it was made of plastipaper instead of polymetal. Another enemy approached him on the left, and Kyrion spun around and chopped that man's head off his shoulders. All the while, he kept moving forward, never breaking stride, not even for an instant.

For the first time, I realized why he was called an Arrow. Because that's what he *was*. Kyrion Caldaren was an arrow, a projectile, a weapon pure and simple, and once fired, he would inevitably seek out whatever target he was aimed at—and destroy it.

He maintained that steady, deadly pace, lashing out with his sword over and over again. Every time he struck, flashes of fire and shards of ice shot out of the blade, along with sharp crackles of wind that I could somehow hear above all the other noise. My eyes widened, and my breath caught in my throat.

Kyrion Caldaren had a *real* stormsword.

A stormsword could be used by anyone, since it was a weapon just like any other. But supposedly, the lunarium blades greatly amplified psionic abilities and could even transform a psion's mental energy into physical elements, so only a powerful psion could wield a stormsword to its fullest potential. In

Kyrion's case, that potential included burning, freezing, and blowing away the enemies he didn't cut down with the actual blade itself.

Despite the danger, I itched to get my hands on the stormsword, to study it and see exactly how it worked. But I had as much chance of that happening as I did of getting across the field to the blitzer without getting killed. Unless . . .

My gaze locked onto Kyrion Caldaren again. Unless I had some help.

I might not have much magic, but over the years, I'd learned to listen to all the odd thoughts, ideas, and instincts that came along with my seer power. Before I could think about how reckless I was being and how I was probably going to die at any second, I sucked down a breath and ran toward the Arrow.

The Imperium soldiers and Techwave troops were still engaged in an intense battle, and more than once, I had to dodge a blaster bolt, spin away from a grasping hand, or leap over a smoking corpse. But I reached out with my magic and kept my gaze focused on Kyrion Caldaren as much as possible. Sure enough, a silver glow appeared around his body, rippling and flowing right alongside his stormsword and killing strikes. The harder and longer I homed in on that glow, the brighter it became, and the easier it was for me to maneuver around all the deadly obstacles between us.

My arms pumped by my sides, and my boots slapped against the rocks. I was seventy-five feet away from him.

Fifty . . .

Twenty-five . . .

Fifteen . . . ten . . . five . . .

Kyrion waded deeper and deeper into the Black Scarabs, cutting down enemy after enemy. I'd lost track of the other two Arrows, and I didn't see their colored clothing among the crush of bodies and energy bolts still zipping through the air.

When I got close enough, I slowed down, not wanting Kyrion to whirl around and attack me. Instead, I simply followed along behind him, staying as close as I dared, although keeping up with his smooth strides was far more difficult than I'd expected. Why did he have to be so tall and have such long legs?

Out of the corner of my eye, I spotted a Black Scarab running toward me. My gaze dropped to the ground, and I snatched up the first blaster I saw. Then I whipped around and pulled the trigger.

Pew! Pew! Pew!

I put three bolts into the Scarab's chest, and they dropped to the ground. I lifted the blaster up where I could see it. Sleek silver, compact design, and plenty of power. This Techwave weapon was far superior to the cheap Kent blaster that was still tucked into my coveralls pocket. Even better, it was set to kill. Excellent.

With my new blaster in hand, I trailed along in Kyrion Caldaren's deadly wake. More Techwavers took notice of me, and I fired the blaster over and over again, dropping every enemy who charged at me.

All Kent Corp employees were taught rudimentary self-defense, but negotiators like Tivona were given far more training, since they were often the targets of kidnapping attempts, given all the sensitive corporate files and information they could access. Tivona had gone through some advanced self-defense and weapons training a few weeks ago, and she had insisted I come along. She claimed my being there would make it more fun, but mostly, she'd been trying to take my mind off Conrad. I sent a silent thank-you to my friend. As much as I had hated the training back then, especially all the resulting bruises and sore muscles, those lessons were saving my life right now.

Kyrion kept striding forward, although he was veering off the course I wanted him to take and moving away from the grounded blitzer. I hesitated, torn between sticking close to him, which was the safest place in the battle to be, or making a break for the ship. I glanced back and forth between the two, but that telltale silver glow remained strong and steady on both Kyrion *and* the blitzer. Each was a viable option, but I had to do what gave me the best chance of surviving, and that was clearly getting to the ship.

I had turned toward the blitzer, getting ready to sprint toward it, when a bright flare caught my eye. On the edge of the battle, an intense green glow appeared through the smoke, soot, and ash, larger and brighter than the blaster fire still slicing through the air.

The glow kept growing larger and larger, brighter and brighter, as though some sort of weapon was charging up for a massive strike—

An enormous energy bolt shot out and zipped across the battlefield straight toward Kyrion Caldaren.

"Look out!" I screamed.

Kyrion jerked back, as though he'd heard my yell above the continued chaos and pain-filled screams. The air shimmered and rippled around his body, and even from here, I could feel the cold, crackling strength of his psionic shield. He whipped around and stretched out his hand, as if to deflect the energy bolt with his telekinesis—

The bolt cut right through his shield and slammed into his left side. The blast knocked Kyrion back, and he went down on one knee.

I hissed and clutched my own side. For some reason, pain spiked through my body in the exact same spot, stealing my breath. I also lost my grip on the Techwave blaster, which slipped through my fingers and tumbled away across the rocks. Perhaps the mystery weapon had some sort of psionic echo or aftershock.

Another green bolt of energy zipped across the field. Kyrion snapped up his weapon in defense, and the bolt hit the stormsword's glowing blue blade and bounced away, slamming into a group of Black Scarabs. Something exploded, and the entire group dropped to the ground, green flames licking at their plated armor.

In the distance, that green glow appeared yet again, as the weapon, whatever it was, revved up for a third strike. Kyrion Caldaren staggered upright, clutching his side. He might be an Arrow, might be a powerful psion, but that weapon had badly wounded him.

My gaze snapped back and forth between him and the blitzer. The silver glow on the ship remained bright and steady, but the one around Kyrion flickered and dimmed, right along with his strength—and his life.

"Fuck," I muttered, and changed direction.

I raced over to Kyrion and clamped my hand around his wrist, just as he'd done to me in the docking bay earlier. He whirled around and started to jerk away, but then he hesitated, as if confused by my presence.

Across the field, that green glow intensified, and another bolt shot out, heading straight for the two of us. Instinct took over. There was no time to dart out of the way, so I lunged in front of Kyrion, hoping, hoping, hoping the blaster in my pocket had enough juice to shield us from that weapon—

The energy slammed into me.

The eerie, electrified green bolt lit up my entire field of vision, as though I was standing in front of a bomb and watching it explode in slow motion. The blaster's invisible shield sizzled, then fizzled out, and the green bolt streaked toward my heart—

Kyrion snapped up his free hand and used his telekinesis to fling the bolt away, sending it spinning right back at whoever had fired it.

The bolt hit something, and the opposite side of the field lit up, revealing a figure crouching down on one knee, as though they had ducked the blast. I squinted, but given the thick clouds of smoke, I couldn't make out who or what the figure might be, just that they were holding some sort of hand cannon.

The shadowy figure surged to their feet, spun around, and vanished into the smoke. Their smooth motions indicated that they were a real person, instead of just an empty suit of armor. Wait. Were they even wearing armor? Their quick response was far more fluid than the other Techwavers, and they seemed much thinner, as if they weren't encased in a metal suit.

Before I could puzzle it out, that green glow appeared yet again. I tensed, knowing we wouldn't survive another blast. But instead of zooming toward us, this bolt shot downward and slammed into the ground.

Once again, the eerie, electrified green glow filled my eyes and, even worse, the field underneath my feet. The energy zipped through the rocks, lighting up the crevices like they were veins full of poisonous blood. The energy faded away as quickly as it had appeared, but a few seconds later, the ground began to quake violently.

And then it cracked open.

One stream of lava appeared, then another, then another. In an instant, all I could see were those growing streams of lava, and all I could feel was the oppressive volcanic heat blasting over my body and threatening to melt my skin and bones.

"Let's go! Let's go! Let's go!" I yelled.

Kyrion hesitated, as though he was going to dig in his heels and wrench away, but I tightened my grip on his wrist and yanked him to the side. My sheer determination overpowered his greater size and strength, and he stumbled after me.

After a few seconds, Kyrion regained his balance. This time, he did dig in his heels, stopping me, although I kept my death grip on his wrist. He shoved his sword into a slot on his belt and veered toward the left, back toward the Imperium cruiser.

"Not that way!" I yelled.

He ignored me and kept going in that direction. Despite his

injury, he was still bigger and stronger than I was, and this time, I had to dig in my own heels to keep from being yanked along behind him. All of my magic and instincts were screaming that going back toward the Imperium ship was a bad idea—

The ground in front of Kyrion split apart with a thunderous roar, and a geyser of lava arced up into the sky before spattering back down like crimson raindrops. Horrified, I stared at the oozing red mass and smoking rocks. If we'd taken just ten more steps forward, we both would have been scalded alive.

This was the first time my seer magic had ever saved my life, but there was no time to wonder about that—there was only time to run.

Dozens of cracks opened all around us, and both the Imperium soldiers and the Techwave troops fled, abandoning all pretense of fighting. Most of them didn't make it very far, and more than one soldier and suit of armor dropped into a new stream of lava that suddenly surged up.

I gritted my teeth and sucked in a breath. Even with my O2 enhancement, the intense heat still scorched my throat and dried out my lungs. I swayed on my feet, but a firm, strong body kept me from falling.

I blinked in surprise. Kyrion Caldaren was still right beside me, only now my right arm was wrapped around his waist, while his left one was slung across my shoulders. I stared at him, seeing my wild, desperate face reflected in his dark blue helmet. He nodded at me.

Together, with one thought, we whirled around and staggered away from the lava as quickly as we could.

SEVEN

KYRION

The woman—Vesper—dragged me forward. Or maybe we dragged each other forward. I couldn't quite tell.

At first, I didn't think about where we were going. But the farther we moved from the Imperium cruiser, the more I realized she was actually heading *toward* something, rather than just away from the lava. Weariness swept over me, and I didn't even try to stop her.

Any second now, I fully expected a chasm to appear below our feet and for us both to be boiled alive by the lava, which was now bubbling, spewing, and flowing everywhere. But Vesper looked straight ahead, her jaw locked, her eyes fixed on . . . something. All I saw were ever-thickening clouds of smoke and ash. I coughed, but that only increased the burn in my lungs. If the lava didn't kill me, then the smoke would, despite the filtration system in my helmet.

Since I couldn't see where we were going, I looked down at Vesper. Perhaps it was my imagination or the pain of my injury, but her eyes seemed both darker and brighter than before, the blue more intense and the silver flecks more vivid. Even more telling, psionic power surged off her, the sensation somehow cool and soothing, despite the intense heat surrounding us.

Who in the bloody stars *was* this woman?

"Kyrion! Kyrion! Come in!" Julieta's voice echoed through my helmet, although it sounded weak and far away. "Where are you? We have to go! Now! Kyrion—"

Her voice abruptly cut off, and static filled my helmet, along with my earbud. Julieta's voice didn't sound again, and neither did Zane's. Of course not. He would love for me to be killed so he could take over as the leader of the Arrows. I thought of the shadowy figure who'd fired those green energy bolts at me. Perhaps Zane had grabbed a Techwave weapon and finally decided to take matters into his own hands. He wouldn't be the first Arrow to try to settle a score under the cover of battle. If so, he couldn't have picked a better spot. This Magma field was literally melting down.

But I kept plodding along and clutching Vesper for support. I didn't know who she was or what her agenda might be, but for right now, I needed her, even though I still had no idea where she thought we were going.

Some of the smoke rolled away, and I spotted a blitzer in the distance. So that's where she was heading. Smart.

All around us, more and more cracks opened wide, and plumes of lava shot up into the air like red-hot fountains, but Vesper's gaze remained locked on the ship. More than once, I veered to the left, trying to take a more direct route to the blitzer, but Vesper tightened her grip and steered me back onto the path she wanted. Somehow she knew *exactly* where to put her feet and when to zig instead of zag, and she kept us away from the worst of the lava, although I still felt as though I was seconds—and inches—away from melting into a puddle of skin and bones.

Suspicion filled me about who and what Vesper was, but I

had no way of proving my theory. Besides, it wasn't important right now.

Eventually, we made it to the blitzer, but the cargo bay was closed, which meant we had no easy way to get on board.

"Dammit!" Vesper snarled.

She released me and moved forward, trying to find another way onto the ship. I reached out with my power, scanning the blitzer. The image of a green button popped into my mind, and I punched my fist forward, as though I was standing in front of that button and hitting it with my actual hand, even though it was on the interior of the ship.

A light on the side of the blitzer flashed green, and the cargo bay ramp descended.

Vesper whirled around to me. "How did you do that?"

I had always been good at opening doors and the like, even when I couldn't physically see or touch them. But I didn't feel like explaining the finer points of my psionic abilities, so I ignored her and staggered forward.

Vesper darted in front of me. "Come on!" she yelled. "Move faster!"

I growled in response, but I churned my legs a little faster and plodded up the ramp. Vesper was already inside. The second I stepped into the cargo bay, she slapped the green button, and the ramp began to close.

"Wait!" someone yelled. "Wait for me!"

A Techwaver was running in this direction, moving as fast as their black-armored legs would carry them. Vesper's hand hovered over the button, as though she was going to make the ramp descend again.

I reached down, plucked my blaster from its thigh holster, and shot the Black Scarab in the head. They dropped to the ground, and the lava quickly covered their body.

Vesper gaped at me, but I ignored her shock. Instead, I glanced around the cargo bay, searching for enemies, but the pilot must have fled when the ship crashed, because I didn't see or sense anyone else on board.

I looked over at Vesper, and my finger tightened on the blaster trigger. She stared at me, her body tense and still, as if she knew exactly what I was thinking about doing. Maybe she did, given her power. Either way, she was a conscript who would most likely kill me the second I passed out, which was going to happen sooner rather than later. Even now, I was teetering on the edge of unconsciousness. Better to kill her now rather than wait for her to betray me the way Francesca had—

The blitzer rocked violently from side to side. I stumbled up against the cargo bay wall, and the blaster slipped out of my hand. I cursed, but I was too weak to bend down and retrieve it.

Vesper rushed past me, sprinted to the front of the ship, and dropped into the pilot's seat. She glanced over the console, her gaze flicking from one button to another. After a few seconds, her face brightened, as though she'd just solved a complicated puzzle.

"A ZMR43. Excellent," she said, a satisfied purr in her voice.

She leaned forward and started hitting buttons. The thrusters engaged, the blitzer jerked up off the ground, and I slammed into the wall again. The ship hovered in midair, rocking from side to side, as though it had been damaged by the crash and wasn't quite sure it had the energy to take off.

Vesper kept hitting buttons. "Come on, ship," she muttered. "You can do it. You can get us out of here . . ."

She kept muttering, cursing and encouraging the ship in equal measures as though it was a living thing and not just a hunk of metal and wires welded together.

With a reluctant groan, the blitzer lifted a little higher. Vesper threw a lever forward, pushing the thrusters to maximum capacity. Then, with another, even louder and more reluctant groan, the ship zoomed through the sky, leaving the exploding lava field behind.

When the ship quit shaking and the ride smoothed out, I pushed away from the wall and stumbled over to some observation windows located in the middle of the vessel between the pilot's seat in the front and the cargo bay in the back.

Down below, all the cracks and chasms had widened exponentially, and lava had completely consumed the battlefield—bodies, blasters, and all. The gelatinous mass looked like a red sun that had lost its shape and was oozing everywhere.

As an Arrow, I had been through countless battles, but the sight of all that lava made my gut twist. Fire was always a bad way to go. Not that there were any *good* ways, as my parents had proven. Whether it was slow and drawn-out like my mother's, or quick and surprising like my father's, death was still death, and there was no coming back from it.

The ship rocked from side to side again, and Vesper muttered something about volcanic eruptions and unstable air currents. Since she seemed to know what she was doing, at least with the autopilot's help, I moved away from the windows and stumbled back toward the cargo bay.

The blitzer was shaped like an old-fashioned arrow, an older Zimmer model that was larger and more powerful and comfortable than the newer, smaller, inferior Kent ships. The pilot and copilot chairs and controls were at the tip of the arrow on this top main deck, then came a long, shaftlike corridor with several rooms branching off it, and finally the cargo bay fanned out like a tuft of feathers on the end.

I stuck my head into each area I passed, and lights automatically clicked on. Sleeping quarters with beds that could be folded up into the walls. A bathroom with a toilet, sink, and shower. A small kitchen. A slightly larger dining area. The lower decks would be more of the same, albeit with maintenance and storage areas.

Nothing unusual or noteworthy, so I kept going toward the cargo bay, my eyes locked on the freestanding waist-high medtable in the center of the open space. I always carried a couple of injectors filled with skinbonds on my bandolier, but they didn't have enough meds to stabilize me. Not this time.

The pain in my side was increasing by the second, the burning and stabbing sensations so intense that they were slowly slicing through the mental shield I'd used to block off the agony of the injury from the rest of my mind. Black stars flashed in my eyes, a warning that I was very close to passing out, but I hit a button on the side of the medtable, and the surface lit up with a blue-white light.

"Welcome," a female voice chimed. "Please lie down to begin a diagnostic scan."

I ripped off my helmet, yanked the earbud out of my ear, and tossed them both onto the nearest counter. Then I pitched down and forward and rolled onto my back, so that I was lying on the table. That blue-white light flared again, enveloping me in its soft glow.

"Severe damage to left side. Immediate action necessary to prevent death. Treatment will begin in five seconds . . ." The medtable kept talking, the mechanized feminine voice bright and cheerful, as though she was reciting a weather report instead of my many internal injuries.

Something hissed, and a clear panel popped out of a hidden compartment in the side of the table. The flexible panel arched up and then closed over me as though I was a mammoth butterfly trapped in a cocoon just waiting to be free.

If only things were that easy.

The panel transformed the table into a makeshift hyperbaric chamber. Pure oxygen flooded the enclosed space, and I breathed in deeply, letting the air cleanse my lungs. Strangely enough, it smelled like vanilla, and I welcomed the slightly sweet taste. Despite the filtered air in my helmet, I still felt like I had inhaled half the smoke that had billowed over the lava field. How had Vesper survived it? She should have been coughing, choking, and gasping for breath, but she had seemed fine when we'd boarded the ship. Yet another mystery surrounding her.

"Starting repair work," the table chirped again in that annoyingly cheerful voice. "Please remain still in order to avoid further damage."

Several sharp pricks stabbed into my back, and I ground my teeth to keep from snarling. In addition to the oxygen tube, medtables were also equipped with robotic needles filled with antibiotics, along with skinbonds and other chemicals that promoted bone, muscle, and tissue regeneration. The dull, numbing sensation of a local anesthetic flooded my side.

The first wave of needles retracted, but they were replaced by a second round that sank even deeper into my skin, suturing my muscles, tendons, and everything else back together. Despite the anesthetic, I could still feel every tug and pull and yank and stitch, and I ground my teeth again. The medtable treatment certainly wasn't pleasant, but it was a necessary evil—like so many other things in my life.

A few seconds later, the rest of the meds kicked in, and I . . . floated outside myself. One moment, I was trying not to snarl and silently cursing the person who'd shot me. The next, I was staring up at the ceiling, the pain in my side completely gone.

"Treatment complete. Life saved," the table intoned in a smug, satisfied purr.

The needles retracted, and the flexible panel hissed open and slid back down into its hiding spot. Weariness flooded my body, even stronger than the meds, but I couldn't rest. Not while the woman was on board. I couldn't afford to show any sign of weakness, not even to a stranger.

If she was actually a stranger. She could always be a plant by one of my enemies to kill me or, worse, trap me.

I forced myself to sit up and swing my legs over the side of the table. My mind spun around, but I drew in several deep breaths, and the dizziness slowly faded away. I wasn't steady enough to stand yet, so I studied my surroundings. The cargo bay took up the back third of the ship, although the medtable was toward the front, close to where the wide space narrowed and flowed into the long corridor that formed the center of the blitzer.

Some plastic crates were lashed to the cargo bay walls, but other than that, the area was empty. I couldn't tell what weapons or supplies might be in the metal cabinets that lined the walls, but I doubted they contained much, since this type of blitzer was designed to get Imperium soldiers in and out of hostile zones as quickly as possible.

A shower of blue sparks erupted, and vicious cursing sounded. Vesper was sitting on the corridor floor right outside the cargo bay. A metal panel was lying beside her, and she was peering at an exposed nest of wires in one of the walls.

"What's wrong?" I asked, then frowned. "Why aren't we moving?"

The low, steady hum and faint rocking sensation of the thrusters had vanished, indicating that we were just drifting along through space, rather than being propelled by the ship's engines.

"Oh, good," she drawled, sarcasm rippling through her voice. "You're awake."

"Why aren't we moving?" I repeated.

"The thrusters overheated, probably due to all the lava," Vesper replied in a distracted voice, yanking a handful of wires out of the open panel. "Who decided to fight a battle on a Magma planet?"

I could have told her that the Techwavers didn't care how

many troops they sacrificed—whether they were merely machines or men stuffed inside metal shells—so long as they achieved their objectives, but I kept my mouth shut. She didn't need to know mission details or the fact that no one seemed to know what the Techwavers had been so eager to steal from the metal refinery.

"How long was I out?"

Vesper shrugged. "I don't know. Fifteen minutes? I've been a little busy trying to fix the thrusters."

She still had the dagger she'd grabbed off the table in the Imperium cruiser, and she used the blade to strip the plastic casings off the wires. Then she twisted some of the metallic strands together. A few more sparks shot out, but she kept right on stripping off casings and twisting wires together in intricate patterns.

"Where are we?"

Vesper shrugged again. "We made it up past the volcanoes, and then the pinpoint drive shot us around to the back side of the Magma planet before the thrusters crapped out, and everything stopped. We've been skating along the top of the atmosphere ever since, hence all the jerking and shaking. So far, there's been no sign of the Techwavers. I don't know where your Imperium buddies are either."

I opened my mouth to ask another question, but she cut me off.

"And before you glower at me again, you should know the communication system is also fried," she said. "In fact, pretty much *everything* is fried. The blitzer was sitting on the lava field for way too long. It's a wonder it didn't just melt away—"

The ship rocked from side to side. Vesper pitched forward, then hissed and jerked back. She was still clutching the dagger, but the blade had slipped and sliced into her left palm, leaving behind a long, bloody gash.

A small sting of pain bloomed in my own hand. Startled,

I glanced down. A shallow cut had appeared across my left palm, exactly where Vesper had sliced her own hand, although my wound wasn't nearly as deep. Icy tendrils of dread slithered around my heart and squeezed it tight.

No, it couldn't be. Not this. *Anything* but this.

Another shower of sparks erupted out of the open panel. One landed on Vesper's palm, right beside the cut. She cursed and flung the spark off, causing it to wink out.

Once again, an answering burn erupted in my own hand, along with a small red dot where the spark had landed. My dread vanished, replaced by rage.

I'd been right before. She *was* an enemy plant. Only she had done something much, much worse than simply trying to kill me.

I surged up off the medtable and stormed in her direction. She must have heard my footsteps, but she kept her gaze on her injury. I had to hand it to her—she was very good at playing innocent.

"Hey, will you find me a rag so I can wipe this blood off—"

I leaned down, dug my hand into the back of her coveralls, and hauled her to her feet.

Vesper staggered away. "Hey! What was that for?"

My fingers clenched into fists, then flexed wide again. I was going to get some answers—and then I was going to kill her.

EIGHT

VESPER

Kyrion Caldaren glared at me with a cold, furious expression that made a shiver zip down my spine.

Kill her . . .

The words rasped through my mind, startling me. Was that . . . *his* thought . . . about *me*? But why would I be hearing his voice in my head? I was a seer, not a psion like he was.

"Who are you?" he demanded. "Who sent you? Who told you to do this to me?"

"Do what?" The way he was growling, you would think I'd just shot him in the back with a blaster.

His fingers curled into fists, and he stalked toward me, his long legs eating up the distance between us. It took me several precious seconds to realize what was happening.

Kyrion Caldaren had morphed back into Arrow mode and was sweeping toward me like a wave of death.

I had saved him from the lava field, so why would he want to hurt me now? What did he think I had done to him? And why was he so determined to kill me for it?

He snarled and lunged forward. I darted away and accidentally banged into one of the walls. A button poked into my back, making me hiss.

He stopped and hunched down, as though he'd felt the same pain in his back that had just spiked through mine. But after a few seconds, he straightened up, his eyes as dark and merciless as a black hole. Whatever discomfort he'd experienced had further angered him.

"Tell me who you're working for," he said. "And I'll let you live."

Let me live? Who did he think he was? Rage roared through me, burning as hot and bright as an exploding star. I hadn't survived a horrific battle and saved this ungrateful bastard's life just to let him accuse me of . . . Well, I had no idea what he thought I'd done.

My fingers tightened around the dagger still in my hand, and I pointed the weapon at him. Kyrion huffed, almost in amusement, and flicked his fingers. Telekinetic power punched the dagger out of my hand, and it tumbled across the floor, well out of my reach.

"Who was it?" Kyrion demanded again. "How much did they pay you to do this to me?"

"I have no idea what you're talking about!"

He huffed again, this time sounding more derisive than amused, and reached for me. I dodged him, although I felt like a butterfly flitting around a cement block. He was several inches taller than me, with a body that was all hard, solid muscle, and sooner or later, he was going to latch on to me and crush my wings.

I needed some sort of weapon if I had any chance of getting away from him, so I ran my hands along the wall behind me, but my searching fingers only encountered smooth metal. Frustration filled me. I needed to find something to defend myself with—right now.

The ship rocked from side to side again. Kyrion lurched backward, and his head smacked into the wall. He didn't even flinch, but strangely enough, I felt as though I'd just cracked my own head against the metal, and I couldn't help but wince.

"You feel it too," he muttered, his words a bit slurred. "That's why I have to stop it, stop *you*, before it goes any further."

Stop what? What nonsense was he spouting?

Another violent, jerking motion sent me staggering forward, and I slammed up against his chest. Yep, Kyrion Caldaren was most definitely a cement block—cold, hard, and utterly unfeeling. I put my hand down to push myself away from him, and my fingers brushed up against something on his belt. What was that?

The answer popped into my mind. His stormsword.

Determination surged through me, and I shoved my hand down. Once, twice, my fingers slipped off the sword's silver hilt. A frustrated growl tumbled from my lips. Kyrion listed from side to side and blinked several times, clearly trying to shake off his daze.

The ship rocked yet again, forcing me even closer to him. This time, I managed to wrap my fingers around the hilt, and I tore the weapon off his belt.

The sword's hilt was heavy and solid, like a hammer in my hand, so I snapped it up and punched it into his face. Kyrion snarled, and pain exploded in my own cheek, but I gritted my teeth and hit him again.

And then again, and again, even though each blow made an answering pain spike through my own body.

I slammed the hilt into his face yet again, and this time, a cut opened up high on his right cheek. Blood trickled down his skin, and a small sting zipped through my own face. What was happening? Why were we mirroring each other's injuries?

Kyrion reached for me, but I brought my left hand up between us and shoved myself away from him. I flew across the corridor, banged into the opposite wall, and bounced off. My ass hit the floor, and the sword slipped out of my fingers, but I managed to scramble back to my feet.

The ship shuddered violently, throwing us both off-balance. Kyrion staggered all the way back into the cargo bay and bumped up against the medtable, while I latched on to a counter bolted to the corridor wall. My gaze snagged on a blue button close to the cargo bay entrance, the same button I'd hit earlier when he'd stalked toward me.

An image of a ZMR43 blitzer schematic popped into my mind. I'd studied them ad nauseam at the Imperium university and then at my various jobs, learned every single inch of that ship and dozens of others, so I knew exactly what that button did. I slid my hands along the edge of the counter, using it to pull myself in that direction.

The ship's course leveled out again. More rage filled Kyrion's face, and he pushed away from the medtable. I wouldn't be able to escape him a second time, so I rushed forward and slapped the button on the wall, even though that put me far too close to him.

Nothing happened.

Kyrion swayed on his feet, trying to get his balance.

"Come on," I growled. "Come on! Come on!"

I slapped the button again. No response.

Kyrion snarled and headed toward me.

Desperation filled me, and I surged forward and slammed all my body weight onto that button, holding it down, down, down—

A blue light flashed on the wall, and a clear sheet of glass dropped down from the ceiling right between me and Kyrion Caldaren, saving my life—for now.

I sagged against the wall, sucking down one relieved breath after another. My O2 enhancement helped smooth out the worst of the adrenaline rush, and I felt much more like myself again. A battered, bruised version of myself, but at least I was still alive.

Kyrion Caldaren growled, then lashed out and punched his fist against the clear barrier. I flinched, but it didn't even shake. He tried again and again, battering at the barrier with his fist, but he didn't so much as chip the glass.

"Don't be an idiot," I snapped. "It's permaglass. The good stuff. Not even a psion like you can punch through it."

His eyes narrowed to slits. His gaze was as hot as the lava that had almost incinerated us both on the battlefield, and I had to grind my teeth to keep from shivering.

Kyrion paced back and forth on the other side of the glass like a Tropics tiger trapped in a zoo. For the first time, I noticed he had removed his helmet and that I was seeing his actual face. I wasn't sure what I'd been expecting, but once I started looking at him, I couldn't make myself stop.

He was around my age, late thirties, and his midnight-black hair was a bit wavy and a touch on the long side, as though he didn't get it cut often enough. His skin was pale, probably from all the time he spent in space, and he had high cheekbones, a straight nose, and a strong chin.

At first, I thought his eyes were a dead, flat black, but on closer inspection, I realized they were a dark, inky blue. Strangely enough, the color reminded me of the sapphsidian eyes in my mindscape. Ugh. I shoved that thought away. I didn't want to have any connection to a man who had just threatened me, not even something as trivial as that.

Kyrion Caldaren wasn't what I would consider to be gorgeous. Not even handsome. But there was something . . . *striking* about his face. Something that captured your attention, as though his features held some sort of optical illusion, and you could figure out the puzzle if only you studied him long and hard enough.

I shook off my strange thoughts. He wasn't a puzzle. He was a cold-blooded killer, and he'd been ready to hurt me to get whatever answers he thought I had. More rage roared through me, and I stalked over to the barrier and glared at him.

"I saved your life on the lava field! Why did you attack me?"

He gave me a disgusted look. "No doubt, that small kindness was all part of your master plan. As was your little performance in the docking bay on the Imperium cruiser. I'll admit, it was a clever way to attract my attention and start the process. When did you dose me with the first chemical? What did you use?"

Every word he said only confused me more. "What are you talking about? I didn't do anything to you! All I've been doing ever since I woke up on that Imperium ship is trying to survive."

"I don't believe you."

"Are you kidding me? Do you think I *wanted* to be attacked, drugged, and conscripted into the Imperium army? Do you think I *wanted* to watch all those conscripts die? Or be burned alive by lava myself? Or trapped on a ship with a man who has suddenly decided I'm his most hated enemy for no apparent reason?" I threw my hands up in frustration. "I didn't want *any* of this! Not one damn bit of it!"

He kept staring at me, but the rage dimmed in his eyes, and his features turned more thoughtful than angry. "And yet here you are with me, despite all those odds and obstacles."

I threw my hands up again. "What is that supposed to mean?"

"We're bonded." He growled the words as though they were the most horrific thing in the entire galaxy.

For a moment, I wasn't certain I'd heard him correctly. But his tight, serious expression indicated that, yes, I had heard him correctly.

I couldn't help myself. I laughed.

The chuckles flew past my lips one after another, and the

force of them shook my body from head to toe. It was just so
. . . *laughable*. Out of all the things he could have said, out of
all the reasons he could have come after me, the fact that he
thought we were bonded was insane. *He* was insane. Perhaps
the Techwave weapon had scrambled his brains as much as it
had scrambled his insides.

"I don't know what drugs the medtable dosed you with, but
you are out of your mind. There is no way that we are *bonded*."
I flapped my hand back and forth, indicating the two of us.
"You're a Regal lord, an Arrow, and the most notorious killer
in the galaxy. I don't even like to kill the spiders that sneak into
my apartment. I always catch the spiders in a jar and take them
outside to the nearest park . . ."

I was babbling, but I just couldn't stop the random, ram-
bling thoughts from rushing out of my mouth in a nonsensical,
unstoppable stream of idiocy. It took a while, thanks to my O2
enhancement, but I finally ran out of breath, and I bit down on
my tongue to keep from letting loose another stream of babble.

Kyrion gave me a cold, flat look, then glanced around the
cargo bay. He marched over, opened one of the cabinets, and
rummaged around inside. A few seconds later, he shut the
cabinet door and flipped open a small tactical knife. He held
the knife out where I could see it, then slashed it across his left
palm.

Pain erupted in my own hand. I hissed and glanced down.
A shallow slice now cut across my palm in the exact same spot
where he had slashed himself. Kyrion stalked back over to the
barrier and held up his hand. His gash was much deeper and
oozing blood, whereas mine was as thin as a plastipaper cut,
but there was no denying the two injuries were mirror images
of each other.

Shock zipped through me. My legs trembled and threatened
to buckle, and I had to brace my hand against the barrier for
support.

"No," I whispered. "This can't be . . ." My voice trailed off, and all words, thought, and reason failed me.

"Do you believe me now?" Kyrion growled. "Or do I have to cut us both to pieces to convince you?"

He held the knife over his hand again.

"No!" I yelled. "Stop, you idiot! I believe you. Okay? I believe you."

He lowered the knife, although he kept eyeing me with suspicion and hostility.

This time, I was the one who paced back and forth in front of the barrier. "How did this happen? When? Why?"

The questions tumbled out of my mouth, but I didn't have any answers. For someone who spent her life figuring out how things worked, I couldn't quite grasp the chain of unexpected and unfortunate events that had led me to this place and this moment.

"Who *are* you?" Kyrion demanded. "Who sent you? Who told you to do this to me? How did you trigger the bond? What chemicals did you use?"

I kept right on pacing. "No one sent me, and I have no idea how this happened—" I stopped and whirled around to him. "Wait. What chemicals?"

He gave me a disbelieving look. "Surely you know about chembonds."

"Of course I know about chembonds," I snapped.

Chembonds were just what their name implied, bonds that were induced by certain chemicals. Two people took the same cocktail, and as soon as the drugs started circulating through their bodies, the bond formed.

Basically, a chembond connected two people—for a while.

High-level, military-grade chembonds let soldiers share physical traits, like strength, speed, and combat skills, while other, less restricted, more cerebral chembonds allowed academics and scientists to share thoughts, theories, and knowledge. And of course, there were the common chembonds that were available to everyone and used mostly for sex. Find a willing partner, have a bartender mix the right cocktail, drink up, and you would supposedly have the best sex of your life.

Some chembonds only lasted a couple of hours, while others could linger for a couple of weeks or longer. But once a person's body started metabolizing the chemicals, the bond would start to fade. And the stronger the initial chembond, or the more you used them, the greater the danger involved. Even with a short, common chembond, the withdrawal could still be as bad as an alcohol-induced hangover—or worse. And with the military and academic chembonds, well, more than one person had gone mad from them, which was why chembonds were mostly used for brief recreational fun.

Conrad had sweet-talked me into trying a chembond once, a few weeks before he'd dumped me. I'd gotten sick within five minutes of taking it and had spent the rest of the night vomiting, while he'd gotten bored and gone out clubbing with his friends. I should have realized then what a selfish dick he was.

Still, all this talk of chembonds made my mind start churning. "Maybe it was something in the lava field. Maybe the Techwavers saturated the air with some chemicals from the production plant before the battle began. That could explain why we're bonded."

Kyrion shook his head. "I don't think so. My helmet didn't pick up any chemical readings from the refinery itself, only smoke and natural gases from the volcanic activity. Also, certain things don't happen with chembonds."

"What things?"

He held up his cut hand. "Things like this."

I frowned. "Okay, so what do *you* think it is?"

"Well, if it's not a chembond, then it has to be . . ." His voice trailed off, and uncertainty filled his face.

"What?"

He drew in a breath, then sighed, as though he was going to confess some deep, dark secret. "If it's not a chembond, then it has to be a truebond."

I couldn't help myself. I laughed again.

My chuckles were even louder and stronger than before, and the force of them shook my entire body and made my ribs ache even more than they already did from our earlier fight and being slung around the ship.

Kyrion gave me a sour look, and my chuckles faded away.

"That's the most ridiculous thing I've ever heard." I flapped my hand back and forth again. "There's no way that *we* have a truebond. Besides, such things don't really exist. Truebonds are just fairy tales people tell themselves to justify their actions."

An image of Conrad and Sabine flickered through my mind, but I shoved it away.

Kyrion's eyebrows drew together. "What do you mean?"

I clasped my hands to my chest, batted my eyelashes, and let out a loud, overly dramatic sigh. "Even though I'm married, I'm going to cheat on my partner because I have a truebond with someone else. A truebond is true love! It's our *destiny*!" I dropped my hands to my sides. "Bah! Truebonds are just an excuse people use to do something they know is wrong."

Kyrion snorted, almost as if he agreed with me. "Despite what most people think, truebonds aren't always romantic in nature. They can form between friends, relatives, even complete strangers who despise each other."

Given what had just happened, the two of us definitely fell into that last category.

"But no matter their origin or nature, truebonds aren't about *feelings*," he continued, a derisive sneer creeping into his voice.

"Then what are they about?"

He shrugged. "Magic."

For the third time, I started laughing. Kyrion quirked his

head to the side. No doubt, he could hear the desperate hysteria in my chuckles.

"You *do* have magic? Some sort of psionic ability?" he asked when my laughter finally died down again.

The arrogance in his voice rankled me. Condescending Regal lord. I opened my mouth to snap back, but he stabbed his finger at me.

"You *do* have magic," he said, making it a statement rather than a question. "I sensed it when you were dragging me across the lava field."

"I don't know what you sensed. Perhaps you were just light-headed from the heat and blood loss and killing people and not feeling very steady."

He peered down his nose at me. "I can assure you that I am quite *steady* when it comes to battle, and I have never, *ever* killed anyone I didn't intend to."

The memory of him slicing through the heavily armored Techwavers like they were as harmless as wisps of black smoke filled my mind, and I had to hold back a shudder.

"What kind of magic do you have?" Kyrion asked. "My guess is that you're a seer, given what you did earlier."

"What was that?"

"You knew *exactly* how to get across the field without running into any of the lava streams. Even with all my psion power, I couldn't have managed that. But a seer could have."

He was right. I *had* used my seer magic to get us across the field, something I was still trying to wrap my mind around.

"So what family, what House do you belong to?" he asked. "Takahashi? Gonzalo? Park?"

He rattled off the names of several famous seer families among the Regals that I recognized from the gossipcasts.

I shook my head. "My name is Vesper Quill, and I don't come from any fancy Regal family. I only have a bit of magic. Nothing particularly grand or exciting."

His mouth turned down, as though he was disappointed. He wasn't the only one. "What, exactly, can you do with your power?"

I gestured over at the mass of wires still hanging out of the open panel. "I see how things work. How to fix things and make them better—stronger, faster, more efficient."

"But that's not what you did on the lava field," he countered. "There was nothing to fix there."

I turned his words over in my mind, thinking about how to explain my magic. "I also see . . . possibilities. Sometimes I get these . . . instincts, and I see these . . . flares of light. They're almost like silver arrows pointing me in one direction or another, although it's up to me to figure out what they mean. But that's the extent of my magic, such as it is."

I didn't mention the beautiful, dilapidated castle that filled my mindscape or the round room with doors I couldn't open. He didn't need to know about any of that, especially since I had never been sure what to make of it myself.

"How do you know so much about truebonds?" I asked.

His jaw clenched, but after a few seconds, he answered me. "My parents had a truebond."

Ah, yes, that was right, and something else I should have remembered from the gossipcasts. Chauncey and Desdemona Caldaren had had one of the most famous romances in the Archipelago Galaxy, every aspect of which had been breathlessly covered by the media. The gossipcasts had absolutely adored the epic tale of the poor farmgirl who had joined the Arrows and caught the dashing lord's eye.

For years, right up to their deaths, Chauncey and Desdemona had been held up as a bright, shining example of what a truebond could be, what it *should* be. Even now, the gossipcasts still mentioned their bond, especially on the anniversary of Desdemona's death.

I'd thought it had been another fairy tale spun by the Regals to make their wealth, power, and excess seem more palatable to everyone who had less than they did. I'd thought the Caldarens—or anyone else—having a truebond was about as likely as my suddenly sprouting wings and flying around like a giant ice owl.

"Maybe it's genetic," I said, still trying to find an explanation other than, well, *magic*. "Maybe you're more predisposed to have a truebond because your parents did. Maybe there's something in your blood . . ."

My voice trailed off, and I thought of how he'd gotten my blood on his fingers when he'd sliced the husher out of my wrist on the Imperium ship. And I'd gotten his blood on me too. First, when I'd dragged him across the lava field, and then just a few minutes ago, when I'd opened that cut on his cheek.

"If blood were a trigger, then I would have bonded with someone long ago," Kyrion said. "I've been exposed to more blood than you can possibly imagine."

This time, I couldn't hide the shudder that rippled through my body.

Kyrion's eyes narrowed in thought. "Besides, none of your half-baked theories explains why *I* would form a truebond with *you*."

I stiffened. "What is that supposed to mean?"

Disgust filled his face, and his gaze trailed down my body, reminding me of how grimy and disheveled I was. "Look at you. Vesper Quill. You come from no Regal family, and you obviously have no connections, wealth, or influence. Not much common sense either, or you wouldn't have ended up as a conscript. I doubt you've had any training, either combat or psionic, which means you probably don't even know how to properly use the few scraps of power you have. You're like a child flailing around in the dark, searching for a light switch. So very . . . *inferior*."

The unmitigated arrogance, the sheer audacity, the smug

condescension . . . More rage flared up inside me, and I stalked over to the glass so that I was standing right in front of him. "*Me?* I'm inferior? Please. If one of us is inferior, then it is most definitely *you*."

He cocked a black eyebrow. "Explain."

"First of all, your arrogance knows no bounds. It's a wonder your ego hasn't already used up all the oxygen and suffocated us both. Second, why in all the stars would *I* want to be bonded to *you?* Everyone in the galaxy knows that Kyrion Caldaren is a stone-cold killer. People fear and hate you. Why, some folks even say that you—" I cut off my words.

His eyebrow arched a little higher. "That I killed my own father," he finished in a toneless voice. He leaned a little closer, his blue gaze as cold and hard as the barrier between us. "Those people are right. I *did* kill my father. I shoved a stormsword into his heart and watched the light die in his eyes."

His words punched me in the chest, and all the air whooshed out of my lungs. Kyrion Caldaren had killed—*murdered*—his own father, and now he was claiming we had this . . . this *connection*. I wasn't going to dignify it by calling it a bond, especially not a truebond.

I rubbed my aching head. Nervous energy surged through me, as though I had touched a live wire, and I started pacing back and forth again. "This is *not* happening. This cannot *be* happening. My karma could not possibly be *this* bad."

"Oh, I doubt your karma has anything to do with it," Kyrion drawled. "Although perhaps whatever gods are left in the galaxy are playing a cruel joke. If so, I hope they are getting a good, long laugh at my expense."

His expense? What about *my* expense? But I ignored his snide words and kept pacing, trying to work through the problem the way I had so many times in the R&D lab. There was always a solution. I just had to be clever enough to think of it.

"Tell me about the truebond. Explain how it works."

Kyrion gave another arrogant, careless shrug, a motion I was rapidly coming to despise. "It's the same general principle as a chembond. The two people involved can share strength, speed, skills, thoughts, and the like. Although with a truebond, the connection is deeper, far more intense, and much more . . . intimate. It makes both people incredibly strong *and* exceedingly vulnerable."

He sounded particularly unhappy about that last part.

"What do you mean, *vulnerable*?"

Kyrion held up his cut hand again, then gestured at my own. "This is how it starts. One person is injured, and the other person feels the sting of that pain—literally. It's a warning that the bond is there, that it is forming. As the bond strengthens and deepens, the physical wounds vanish, but if I were to be injured, then you would feel my pain as if it were your own, and vice versa. That's one of the reasons truebonds usually only occur between psions. Because our mental shields are the only ones strong enough to absorb those psychic blows, while our ability to compartmentalize and block out pain lets us sense an injury without being crippled by it."

"So what are you saying? That if you die, then I . . . die?" My stomach churned.

Another annoying shrug. "That's one theory. The more foolish, romantic notion is that the second person dies of a broken heart."

I huffed at the ridiculousness of that idea, but my gaze locked onto the bloody gash in his hand. If he cut himself again, would I feel that wound too? Probably.

"But if you knew that you were going to experience the same pain as I did and suffer some version of the same injuries, then why did you attack me?"

"To get some answers," Kyrion replied. "The separation is usually survivable in the initial stages, and since our bond seems to have formed sometime over the past few hours, it was worth potentially injuring myself to see just how deep it goes."

There was no heat, no real anger or emotion in his voice, just a calm, clinical recitation of facts, which made his words even more chilling. He hated truebonds so much that he'd been willing to hurt me, hurt *himself*, to escape it. Another shudder rippled through my body.

Still, I turned his words over in my mind again, searching for flaws, gaps, and mistakes, the same way I would examine a faulty brewmaker in the R&D lab. "But the bond *can* be broken. How?"

"The quickest and easiest way to sever a truebond is for one of us to die," he said in that same cold, clinical voice. "And that person will *not* be me."

More and more horror shot through my body, much the same way the lava had rushed into all those cracks and fissures in the battlefield, and the enormity of the situation dropped on me like a meteor plummeting from the sky.

I was trapped on a broken ship with a man who wanted to kill me more than anything.

NINE

KYRION

I watched Vesper carefully, wondering how she would react to my words. The growing horror creeping across her face was oddly satisfying. At least, the severity of our situation had finally penetrated her stubbornness.

She started pacing yet again, muttering some rather colorful curses. After the better part of a minute, she stopped and whirled toward me again. "You said the quickest and easiest way to sever the bond is through death. That indicates there are *other*, less violent and fatal ways to get rid of it. How?"

I shrugged. "Some people believe the right chembond can overwrite and break a truebond. There are other theories, but I have no idea if any of them actually work."

Her face scrunched up in thought. "But your parents had a truebond. What happened to them?"

And there it was, the question that always haunted me, that always made me want to shove my sword through a person's chest when they so carelessly, thoughtlessly, rudely asked what had ended my parents' tremendous love story.

"My mother died," I said in a flat, toneless voice. "And no, I didn't kill her. She . . . succumbed to an illness."

"I'm sorry," Vesper replied, sincerity softening her voice. "It must have been difficult to lose her that way."

It had been one of the most difficult things of my life, especially since I had only been thirteen at the time and little more than a boy myself. But what had come after my mother's death had been far worse.

My father had been . . . *worse*.

Even now, I could see Chauncey slumped in a chair in the family library, a bottle of bourbon in his hand and a vacant look on his gaunt face as he stared into the fireplace at nothing, as he did nothing but drink and sigh and brood about what he had lost . . .

"What a fucking OBO," Vesper muttered.

Her voice jolted me out of my dark memories. "What is an OBO?"

"Something my cousin Liesl used to say. When you're stuck in a situation with only bad options—an OBO."

Well, that sentiment certainly applied to this situation.

Vesper resumed her pacing and muttering. I tuned out her babble and peered past her, searching for my stormsword. It had landed on the floor on her side of the glass. Perhaps that was for the best. Vesper might think the barrier would protect her from me, but that was a mere illusion. Even from here, I could reach out with my telekinesis, grab my sword, and use it to attack.

But first, I needed to know more about her—*everything* about her. After seeing what had happened to my parents, I had vowed that I would *never* be bonded to anyone. Not so much as the briefest, most harmless chembond. I needed to figure out what had triggered this unwanted connection so I could ensure it never happened again.

Plus, I still wanted to know exactly what Vesper Quill had done and whom she had pissed off enough to get conscripted onto an Imperium ship, especially one that had been at the forefront of the latest battle with the Techwave.

I also wanted to know what, if anything, she had to do with the person who'd fired that cannon at me. The weapon had cut through my psionic shield like it wasn't even there and had cracked the ground open like it was a fragile egg instead of solid rock. If the Techwavers had more weapons like that, then things were even more dire than I'd thought.

Although if the Techwavers did manage to kill me the next time I faced them, then I wouldn't have to worry about being bonded to Vesper Quill. A silver lining in a galaxy of death and darkness.

Then again, all I had known for the last twenty-five years were death and darkness. I didn't mind it, though. Things were simpler, easier in the dark, especially when no monster was worse than the one that lurked inside you. Sometimes I thought that was what my psion power was—the monster that let me survive. But apparently, my monster had a twisted sense of humor to saddle me with someone as unsuitable as Vesper Quill.

She stopped pacing and cracked her neck from side to side. Then she sat down on the floor beside the open panel.

"What are you doing?" I asked.

She grabbed a handful of wires. "I'm going to fix the thrusters so I can fly this ship to the nearest planet, one that isn't made of boiling lava."

"And what are you going to do with me?" I held my arms out wide. "Now that you have me trapped in here?"

Vesper gave me a thoughtful look. "Well, since you're in the cargo bay, I could open the ramp. You might survive the cold for a few minutes, but the oxygen would quickly run out. Then, when you were dead, I could tilt the ship up and let gravity roll you down the ramp and out into space."

Her matter-of-fact tone and simple but effective plan to murder me dramatically raised my estimation of her. I flexed my fingers, ready to summon my stormsword if she made good on her threat.

"But that's only a last resort," she continued. "Unlike you, *I* don't go around attacking people who have helped me."

"When did I ever help you?"

"You cut the husher out of my arm on the Imperium ship. You didn't have to do that, but you did. Why?"

I couldn't come up with a satisfactory answer, so I went for the simplest version of the truth. "I wanted to see what you were up to. If I'd known this would happen, I would have left it in you."

She snorted. "Of course you would have. Not the sentimental sort, are you?"

"And you are?"

"I used to be. Sometimes I still am, even though nothing good ever comes of it. Just like nothing good ever comes out of trusting other people or relying on them to help when you need it the most."

Waves of pain and sadness washed off her, along with a strong undercurrent of bitterness. I couldn't tell if my telempathy was letting me sense her turbulent emotions or if it was part of the bond between us.

"But back to the husher. I could have gotten it out on my own, but it would have been much more painful." She paused. "So thank you for that, at least."

Once again, a satisfactory response eluded me, so this time, I remained silent. After a few seconds, Vesper focused on the wires again. All I could do was stand there and wonder why her path had crossed mine—and how I could break the bond between us without killing myself in the process.

About five minutes later, Vesper let out a loud whoop of delight.

The engines hummed again, and the thrusters reengaged.

"Good-bye, boiling lava planet of doom!" she crowed, heading up to the pilot's chair.

I didn't bother asking what course she was setting. I doubted she would tell me, and it didn't matter anyway. If she decided on a planet too far from Corios, then I would summon my sword, bring down the barrier, and end the illusion of her safety. Besides, I was curious about what option she would choose, especially since she'd said that only bad ones were available to her.

You could learn a lot about a person when they thought they were in complete control. Most people turned exceedingly cruel, like Callus Holloway and so many of the Regals I had dealt with over the years. And Vesper was capable of that cruelty too, given her proposed plan to suffocate me and then dump my body out of the cargo bay.

But for now, I returned to my own work and kept searching the cabinets, drawers, and other storage areas inside the cargo bay. I even pried the tops off the crates, which contained bottles of clean water, along with purification tablets to make more, and a box of vacuum-sealed strawberry protein bars. Not my favorite, but I needed calories to replace what I'd lost during the battle and then the fight with Vesper, so I tore open a wrapper with my teeth and downed a bar, plus two others.

A movement caught my eye, and I looked up to find Vesper on the other side of the glass, staring longingly at the box of protein bars on the counter. Her stomach rumbled, further confirming her hunger.

I picked up a protein bar and waggled it at her. "What? Is there no food on your side of the ship? Pity."

She glared at me. "You really are a sadistic bastard."

For some reason, I found myself grinning at her. "You have no idea."

Her gaze grew even brighter, the silver flecks burning like

pinprick stars in her dark blue eyes, and more of that icy-hot rage blasted off her. Vesper Quill's power might be weak, but her emotions were not.

I waggled the protein bar at her again. "You could always lower the barrier, come over here, and get one for yourself."

She snorted. "And have you kill me before I took the first bite? Hard pass."

"It's nothing personal."

"It felt very *personal* to me."

She gingerly probed a bruise on her right cheek, the same spot where she had cut my face by hitting me with the stormsword hilt. That bruise was especially vivid, as though a puffy blue butterfly was trapped underneath her skin. I had been so *certain* Vesper was an enemy plant, and so *angry* that she had tricked and trapped me into the bond, that I had been willing to do whatever it took to break that connection, even kill an innocent person.

I truly was the monster everyone said I was.

A dim spark of unexpected remorse flickered in my chest, but I snuffed it out. Most people might dream about having a truebond, but it was nothing but a death trap for both of us. Something Vesper would realize if we were forced to spend any length of time together.

She glared at me a moment longer, then spun around and started searching the cabinets and drawers in the corridor on her side of the ship, as well as the adjoining rooms. She found several blasters but no food and no water, not even in the bathroom.

"It seems you chose poorly when you locked me in the cargo bay." I took a long, deliberate gulp of water.

Vesper's left eye twitched, and her fingers flexed, as though she wanted to strangle me. Couldn't blame her for that. If I'd been in her position, I would have already followed through with her plan to suffocate me.

"How long has it been since you've had some water?" I asked. "I would guess several hours. You won't last more than a few days without it."

"I know that," she snapped back. "But we'll reach another planet by then, and I can have all the water I want, without fear of being murdered the second I take a drink."

"Touché."

She huffed in annoyance and continued her search, but she didn't find anything edible, not so much as a pack of protein crackers. That silver lining was slowly growing larger and brighter. I wouldn't even have to kill Vesper. Her own stubbornness was going to be the death of her, along with dehydration.

Another one of those annoying sparks of regret flickered inside my chest, but I snuffed it out just as I had snuffed out the other one. You either used people or they used you. There was no real give and take, no true partnerships in the galaxy. Not in my experience.

Vesper slapped her hands on her hips and looked over her supplies, such as they were, which she had laid out a counter. She glanced around as though she had forgotten something, and her gaze landed on my sword, which was still lying on the floor. She scurried over and scooped it up. Her hand curled around the hilt, and my chest tightened, as though she was wrapping her fingers around my heart.

Every muscle in my body tensed. "Don't touch that."

"Relax. I'm not going to break it. I just want to look at it." She held the sword up to the light, then turned it around and around, studying the weapon from all angles.

Compared to others, my stormsword was rather plain, with only a single sapphsidian jewel shaped like an arrow set into the silver hilt. The crossguard was a bit fancier, with curls of silver that stretched out in opposite directions, as well as others that arced up and cupped the base of the lunarium blade.

Vesper waved the sword through the air, and the lunarium's

silvery, opalescent sheen took on a pale blue tinge, hinting at her psionic abilities. The sword also began to hum, like a cat purring in response to a welcome touch, although the sound was so soft that she didn't seem to hear it.

"A *real* stormsword," she breathed in a reverent voice. "It's so beautiful. Sleek and light and perfectly balanced. Nothing like that clunky version we have in the R&D lab."

So she was a lab rat. Well, that explained the white coat she'd been wearing on the Imperium ship, although it didn't tell me whom she worked for. Just about every House and corporation was trying to mass-produce some version of a stormsword, along with cracking the genetic code of psionic abilities.

Vesper squinted at the hilt. "What are these sigils? They look like spearheads . . . and eyes." A frown creased her face, as though she found that last revelation particularly troubling.

"Those are arrows, not spearheads. They are the sigil for House Caldaren. And they're nothing important. Just decorations."

She shot me a disbelieving look, but I wasn't about to reveal that those sigils had appeared the first time I had touched the stormsword, when the lunarium's innate power had bonded with my own psionic abilities. The arrow symbolism had always been obvious, since my parents were Arrows and they had given me the weapon for my thirteenth birthday, but I'd never known what to make of the eyes. Even my parents had been puzzled by the eyes.

"Put it down," I growled.

Vesper rolled her eyes, but to my surprise, she laid the weapon on the counter. Those tight fingers clutching my heart retreated, and my muscles relaxed.

She went to the other end of the counter and picked up one of the blasters. She quickly, expertly disassembled the blaster, then did the same thing to two more weapons. Just as quickly, she put the disparate pieces together, her fingers flying over the parts as skillfully as a musician playing a pianotronic as she bound them together with some wire.

Vesper held up her creation, a new, larger blaster that was far more than the sum of its previous parts, and gave it a critical once-over.

"What did you do to those blasters?" I asked.

By this point, I'd eaten my fill of protein bars and had propped myself up against the bottom of the medtable, with my legs stretched out on the floor in front of me. With all the food and water on my side, I was content to wait and watch— for now.

"I took the solar magazines from the two Kent blasters and hot-wired them to the one in the Takahashi blaster to give it more juice," she replied. "I need a better weapon to defend myself, so I made one."

She shot me a nasty look. Ah, she was referring to my murderous tendencies.

"Going to shoot me the second you get the chance?" I murmured. "Not a bad plan, but it's still destined to fail."

Vesper sat down on the floor opposite me, cradling the supposedly better blaster in her hands. "And why is that?"

I shrugged. "Because I'm a psion. Most energy blasts are no more bothersome than static electricity to us."

"Really? Because that green energy blast on the lava field cut through your psionic shield and then your side like you were a toy soldier." Vesper jerked her chin at me. "That energy blast was specifically meant for *you*. Lots of Black Scarabs attacked you during the battle, but that person waited until you were alone, exposed, without any other Arrows or Imperium soldiers around—and *then* they shot you."

I sat up a little straighter. "Did you see who fired the blast?"

"No, there was too much smoke for me to get a good look at them. Although . . ."

"What?"

She shook her head. "They didn't seem to be wearing any Techwave armor. In fact, if I had to guess, I would say they weren't wearing any armor at all." Her gaze drifted over to my helmet, which was still sitting on a counter on my side of the ship. "Just a helmet."

Understanding sliced through my gut, the sharp sensation as familiar as it was sickening. It was exceedingly likely that Zane Zimmer had tried to eliminate me. The two of us had never gotten along, and House Zimmer had always been a rival to House Caldaren, especially back when my parents had still been alive. But I couldn't discount Julieta Delano either. Despite her cheerful, friendly demeanor, she was a killer, just like I was, just like all the Arrows were.

"You don't seem surprised that one of your own people might have tried to murder you," Vesper said.

I shrugged again, as though the knowledge didn't bother me, even though it did. "It's one of the many hazards of being me."

"The dark prince of the galaxy," she murmured.

"Someone's been watching too many gossipcasts."

A bit of pink flooded her cheeks. "My roommate loves to follow the Regal gossip. Tivona had a program on this morning, and the gossipcaster was talking about the spring ball before . . ." Her voice trailed off.

"Before you did the supremely stupid thing that got you conscripted onto an Imperium ship?"

"It wasn't stupid," Vesper said in a defensive tone.

"Then what was it?"

She sighed. "I don't know. I tried to do the right thing, but I also tried to make money doing it, mostly so I could run if things got dangerous. I tried to be noble and selfish at the same time, and I failed miserably at both."

I glanced at the blaster pieces strewn all over the counter

and thought about how easily she'd taken them apart, especially the Kent models. "You worked for Kent Corp. In the R&D lab, right?"

Vesper jerked back, clearly surprised, but then her features settled into that stubborn look I was coming to know all too well. "Why do you care? If you have your way, I'll never get off this ship alive. So what does it matter where I worked or what I did?"

"Just making conversation. It helps to pass the time."

She snorted. "Please. People like you never *just* make conversation, and I doubt you care anything about passing the time either. You're trying to pump me for information."

"Wow, you must be a truly powerful seer to come up with such a smart deduction."

Her hot glare zeroed in on me again, and a genuine laugh escaped from my lips. Which, of course, only pissed her off more.

She was right. I never *just* made conversation with anyone, but Vesper Quill was far more intelligent, witty, and entertaining company than most. It was odd and a bit . . . *refreshing* to talk to someone who wasn't afraid of me or planning to use me in some way. I'd almost forgotten what it was like to speak to someone without worrying about their true agenda, since both of ours were crystal-clear—kill the other person before they killed us.

Suddenly, a siren blared to life. "Warning, warning," the same mechanized female voice from the medtable rang out. "Ship approaching. Warning, warning, ship approaching . . ."

Vesper scrambled to her feet, and I did the same. We both hurried over and peered out the observation windows on our respective sides of the ship. In the distance, a blitzer zoomed in our direction, closing fast.

"Fuck," Vesper muttered. "That's a Kent Corp ship. How did they even track me here . . ."

Her voice trailed off. She dug into the pocket on the front of her coveralls and yanked out the bloodstained husher I had cut out of her arm.

"Dammit!" she snarled.

She dropped the husher on the floor and stomped it to pieces. Too little, too late, although I could appreciate her angry sentiment.

"Friends of yours?" I drawled.

"They're here to interrogate and torture me—before they murder me."

"Ah, so you're a thief. You stole something from the Kents, and now they want it back."

"Technically, I didn't steal anything, since I had access to all the files," she replied. "But yes, Rowena Kent most definitely wants me dead."

Vesper checked the blaster, her fingers flying over her odd creation as if she could will it to work just by touching every single part of it. Maybe she could if her psion power was more tactile then visually based. When she was satisfied, Vesper peered out the window at the other blitzer again.

"That's an RK blitzer, and it's already too close to outrun, especially with our thrusters threatening to conk out again at any moment," she muttered, although I got the impression she was talking more to herself than to me. "Most RK blitzers can hold a crew of at least five. Oh, who am I kidding? There's no crew on board, just Kent Corp mercenaries."

She curled her finger around the trigger of her improvised blaster. "I can kill them. I can kill five mercenaries. I killed more people than that on the lava field . . ."

Vesper kept muttering similar sentiments, psyching herself up, while the other blitzer zoomed closer and closer. Whoever was on that ship was determined to catch up to this one, and if they found me locked in the cargo bay, well, I wasn't sure what they would do. I might persuade the mercs to free me—for a hefty price—or they might decide to turn me over to Rowena Kent.

Either way, someone was going to die, and it wasn't going to be me.

"Let me out of here," I said, interrupting Vesper's monologue. "I have no alliance with the Kents. I could easily dispatch whatever mercs they've sent after you."

"And then kill me the second you get the chance? How stupid do you think I am?" Vesper scoffed and flicked her fingers at me, dismissing my offer.

She was right. I would still do whatever it took to break the bond between us. Still, something about her dismissive motions reminded me of . . . someone, although I couldn't quite remember who.

We fell silent, watching as the other blitzer glided into position alongside our ship.

"Docking initiated," the female voice intoned.

Vesper cursed again, but she took up a position in front of the boarding doors, her jaw clenched, her blaster up and ready, and her finger curled around the trigger as she waited for the Kent mercs to board the ship.

TEN

VESPER

I tightened my grip on the blaster and faced the docking doors. Of course, the doors were on *my* side of the ship. If the doors had been in the cargo bay where Kyrion was, then I could have gone through with my original plan to suck all the oxygen out of that part of the ship and suffocate him, along with the mercenaries. Although knowing my luck, the Kent mercenaries had the same O2 enhancement as I did and wouldn't be so easily dispatched.

I silently cursed this latest bit of bad luck, even as I wondered if this would be the thing that finally killed me. Either way, there was no place to hide, so I had no choice but to face the mercenaries and hope that I could kill them before they captured me.

On the other side of the glass, Kyrion Caldaren grabbed his helmet, which was sitting next to those protein bars and bottles of water he had mocked and tempted me with earlier. On the bright side, the mercenaries murdering me would be a much quicker way to die than by dehydration, although the torture they would inflict would be far more painful.

Kyrion leaned against a counter, holding his helmet in his hand, completely calm and relaxed. "Last chance," he called out. "I could kill them all in less than a minute."

He was actually trying to blackmail me into freeing him, just so he could turn around and kill me himself. Arrogant jackass.

A thin red seam appeared in the center of the boarding doors, and the acrid stench of melting metal filled the air. The mercenaries were using a laser torch to cut through the doors.

I might be trapped on this ship like a worm in a can of fish food, but I wasn't going to make it easy for them to capture me. My best chance—my only chance—was to start firing and take them by surprise.

Once again, I was in a situation where I had only bad options. Sometimes I thought that was the sad story of my life. No good, easy, simple choices, only those that ranged from bad to worse to catastrophic. I firmed up my shooting stance. Well, let's see how catastrophic I could make someone else's day.

The red seam grew wider, longer, and hotter, and a shower of sparks appeared, winking like the fireflies that sometimes braved the polluted evening air on Temperate 42. The distinctive *clink* of a lock breaking sounded.

Then . . . silence.

The sparks vanished, but the red seam remained, slowly growing dimmer. The mercenaries had put away their laser torch and were getting ready to board. I drew in a deep breath, then slowly let it out, steadying myself.

A large metal spike punched through the molten seam in the middle of the doors, making me flinch. The two halves of the spike split apart, turning into a hydraulic spreader. Then, with a loud, ear-splitting *screech*, the doors zipped apart, and the first mercenary rushed on board.

I shot him in the throat, above his protective breastplate and below the clear visor that covered his face. He gurgled something unintelligible, then toppled to the floor. Behind him, a curse sounded, but I pulled the blaster trigger again and again and again.

Blue bolts zinged through the dark opening. A few more muffled curses rang out, although I couldn't see whom I was shooting at.

"Return fire! Return fire!" someone yelled.

Bolts streaked in my direction, but I kept firing my own blaster in return. If the other mercenaries managed to get on board the ship, then I was dead.

A bolt zipped out of the opening and slammed into my body, right above my left hip. Red-hot pain erupted in my side, and the force of the blow punched all the air from my lungs and threw me back. I ground my teeth to keep from screaming, raised my blaster, and fired again.

And then again . . . and again . . .

No more bolts came shooting out of the opening. I stopped firing, straining to listen over the roar of my heart in my ears—

A black-clad figure erupted out of the darkness. He must have had a speed enhancement, because he closed the distance between us before I could get off another shot. He shoved me back, then grabbed my right arm and banged it into the wall. Painful tingles zipped through my hand, and the blaster slipped from my nerveless fingers and hit the floor. I lunged after it, but the mercenary dug his hand into my hair and yanked my head back.

"No use fighting anymore, Vesper," Hal Allaston hissed. "You're going to tell us exactly what you did with those files you stole."

He released my hair and punched me. Pain exploded in my jaw, but I braced my legs and managed to stay upright. Slowly, I blinked the world back into focus.

Four men were now standing in front of me. Three of them had blasters aimed at my chest, while Hal was cracking his knuckles in a clear attempt to intimidate me. I wasn't afraid, though.

I was *angry*.

I was angry that I'd gotten shot. Angry that Kyrion Caldaren had attacked me after I had saved his life. Angry that Rowena Kent had dumped me on an Imperium ship. That she thought it was okay to play games with my life when she was the one putting innocent people in danger.

And my anger went back even further than that. I was angry that Conrad had stolen my work, my ideas, and the promotion that should have been mine. That he had cheated on me with Sabine Kent. That he had just bided his time with me until someone richer and more powerful had come along.

And I was especially angry about my mother abandoning me and never looking back, that Nerezza had cared more about becoming a Regal with wealth and power than she had ever cared about me. I was angry that my father—whoever he was—didn't know that I existed and probably wouldn't care even if he did.

I was angry about all of that—so fucking *angry*.

But most of all, I was angry that I was going to die on this ship, surrounded by men who saw me as just another piece of trash they would dispose of as soon as they got what they wanted.

Hal cracked his knuckles again and gave me the same toothy, predatory smile he'd given me in the R&D lab this morning when he'd propositioned me. Even more anger surged through me. Lecherous bastard.

"I'm impressed, Vesper," Hal said, his voice deceptively calm and pleasant. "I didn't think you would survive being conscripted. Then again, I didn't think you would be clever enough to download all those files either. But you're just full of surprises, aren't you?"

I gritted my teeth, trying to ignore the pain pounding in my side.

Hal gave me a speculative look. "What were you going to do with the files, Vesper? Send them to a gossipcast and hope they would run some exposé?" He clucked his tongue in mock sympathy. "I thought you were smarter than that."

"I *was* smarter than that," I snapped. "I was going to sell the files, take the money, and disappear."

"Sell them, huh? Yeah, I can see that. At least a dozen gossipcasts would have paid you handsomely for the information, not to mention some of the other Regal families. It might be enough to ruin the Kents if it got out, especially once Callus Holloway learned about it." Hal's face hardened. "But that's never going to happen. Do you understand me, Vesper? Your little escapade is *over*. All that's left is for you to decide how much more you want it to hurt before I kill you."

More anger bubbled up inside me, along with frustration. He was right. This was over. Given the severe wound in my side, I would bleed out soon if I didn't get some help—and no one on this ship was going to help me. The mercenaries would spend whatever time I had left torturing me. If they were especially smart and vicious, they would heal me just enough so they could hurt me again. A process they could repeat over and over until I spilled all my secrets and was begging them to kill me.

I had never felt so completely helpless, so utterly *useless*, as I did in this moment, which made my anger boil up into full-on rage.

Hal slapped me across the face. "Pay attention, Vesper. I'm only going to ask these questions once. Then I'll let my friends work on you, and they won't be nearly as nice and gentle as I am. Understand?"

I was too busy blinking the stars out of my eyes to respond. Hal's blow had spun me sideways, and I found myself staring through the glass barrier into the cargo bay.

Kyrion was still leaning against the counter. The mercenaries were so focused on me that they hadn't spotted him yet. Kyrion stared at me, his face blank and unreadable, although his fingers tightened around his helmet, as if he wanted to use it as a weapon—as if he wanted to do something to help me.

If I'd had the breath for it, I would have laughed at the absurdity of that idea. Kyrion Caldaren didn't want to help me. He was probably just bored waiting for the mercenaries to finish killing me.

Hal dug his hand into my hair and yanked me back. I banged into a wall, causing more pain to ripple through my body. Tears streamed down my face, but I swallowed the screams that kept bubbling up in my mouth like acid.

He gave me a cold, dispassionate look. "We know you downloaded the *Velorum* files. We searched your workstation and your apartment, but we didn't find them. So what did you do with the files, Vesper? Where did you hide the drive? Is it on you right now?"

His gaze slid down my body. I stiffened, and I had to stifle another scream as he stepped forward and pinned me up against the wall.

Hal quickly, ruthlessly searched me from head to toe, patting me down with the practiced efficiency of a professional who knew exactly what he was searching for and was determined to find it. I was too weak to try to stop him, and the other three mercenaries kept their blasters aimed at my head in a clear warning not to fight back.

Hal finished with my body, then ran his hands through my smoky, tangled hair, as though he was a lover about to draw me in for a passionate kiss. I shuddered at the intimate touch, and my nose crinkled as his hot, rancid breath washed over my face.

He yanked his fingers out of my hair, then looked me over again, even more carefully than before. His gaze fell to my hands, and I couldn't stop myself from tensing.

"What do we have here?" Hal murmured.

He latched on to my left hand and held it up where he could see it better. Despite all the heat and chaos of the lava field, the blue eye had stayed attached to my thumbnail. He peeled off the plastic jewel, then grabbed the microdot drive hidden underneath.

Hal let out a low whistle of appreciation. "So that's how you got the files past our scanners. Clever, Vesper. Truly clever."

He grinned at me, then dropped the microdot drive onto the floor and crunched it under the toe of his boot. All I could do was slump against the wall and watch him destroy the one tiny piece of leverage I had.

"Now what?" one of the other mercenaries asked.

Hal turned to answer him, but a cold voice cut him off.

"Now you're all going to die."

All four mercenaries whipped around, and my head snapped to the right.

Kyrion Caldaren pushed away from the counter and stalked over to the glass barrier. He was still clutching his helmet, like a kid about to go ride a hoverbike.

Hal and the other mercenaries froze, and one of them let out a low, muttered curse. They all knew exactly who and what he was.

Hal's gaze flicked back over to me. "What are you doing hanging out with an Arrow, Vesper? Rowena Kent will not be pleased about this. Why, she'll probably want to question you herself about what you've told him."

His lips split into another cruel grin. "And then, of course, we'll have to question him ourselves. He should put up much more of a fight than you did. I've always wanted to get my hands on an Arrow and see if they're really as tough as every-one claims."

Kyrion shrugged. "Given the wound in her side, Vesper will be dead in a matter of minutes, unless you decide to heal her.

Which you can't do without either bringing her in here and putting her on the medtable or taking her to the one on your own ship. But given how quickly you got here, I'm guessing your ship is equipped more for speed, rather than to deal with severe injuries, especially the amount of trauma Vesper has suffered."

He spoke in that calm, clinical voice, as though the pain pounding through my body was no more concerning than the distant stars glimmering outside the ship. I wondered if he could sense my pain through the truebond. If so, how did it feel to him? Because I felt like someone was slamming a red-hot hammer into my side. But if my injury was bothering him through the bond, then he wasn't letting his discomfort show.

"If Vesper dies, you won't be questioning her about any-thing," Kyrion continued. "As for me, well, you do not want to *get your hands on me*, as you so ineloquently put it. Because I will chop them off with my sword, feed them to you, and watch you choke on your own bloody fingers."

His voice remained cold and clinical, but anticipation glimmered in his dark blue eyes, as though he was looking forward to keeping his deadly promise. If I hadn't already realized exactly how dangerous Kyrion Caldaren was, those words would have driven the point home. For all his bluster, bravado, and enhancements, even Hal looked concerned by the Arrow's calm threat of dismemberment, torture, and forced self-cannibalism.

"Forget about questioning them," one of the mercenaries piped up in a high, nervous tone. "Let's kill the woman and be done with her. Then we can suck all the air out of the cargo bay and get rid of the Arrow."

He gestured at the red button on the wall that controlled the oxygen level in the cargo bay. The mercenary's fingers twitched, as though he wanted to lunge forward and push the button before Kyrion could deliver another threat. Smart man.

A razor-thin smile curved Kyrion's lips, revealing just a hint of his white teeth. It was one of the most chilling expressions I had ever seen. "Ah, yes. Vesper had a similar plan. Suffocate me, then dump my body out of the cargo bay. But it's not going to work for you any more than it would have worked for her."

"Why is that?" Hal asked, a sneer in his voice.

Kyrion's smile grew a little wider and sharper. "Because my stormsword is still on your side of the glass."

He pointed to the left, and we all looked in that direction. His sword was sitting on the counter, looking like a random piece of silver among all the parts I'd cannibalized from the blasters to make my own supercharged weapon.

Hal laughed, then turned back to the glass and spread his arms out wide. "How does your little toy being on this side hurt us? You're the one who's trapped without a weapon."

Kyrion's eyes glittered with more of that eerie anticipation. "I *am* the weapon."

The mercenaries stared at him with tense, watchful expressions, and even Hal fell silent. Idiots. They should have been *doing* something, not just standing around and waiting for Kyrion Caldaren to kill them. If I'd had the strength for it, I would have staggered over and pushed that red button myself.

Hal opened his mouth, probably to spew another stupid, pointless insult, but Kyrion waved his hand. His body might be trapped behind the permaglass, but his magic rippled through the barrier like it wasn't even there. I blinked, wondering if he had shattered the glass with his power, but it looked as stable and solid as before—

Kyrion's stormsword flew up off the counter, zipped through the air, and slammed hilt-first into the blue button on the wall.

Hiss.

The glass barrier shot back up into the ceiling. Hal and the three mercenaries had turned their heads to track the sword, but I looked at Kyrion, who was standing in the same spot as before, still clutching his helmet.

He waved his hand again, and the stormsword zipped back and forth through the air like an angry bee. The hilt slammed into the face of first one mercenary, then another, then another, stinging them all in equal measure.

The sword zoomed toward Hal, who growled and slapped it away, but Kyrion was already moving forward. He didn't run so much as he *glided*, his movements as smooth as water rippling in a pond. One second, he was still in the cargo bay. The next, he was right in front of Hal.

The mercenary fumbled for the blaster on his belt, but Kyrion smashed his helmet into Hal's face. An audible *crack* sounded as Hal's nose broke, and he yelped and stumbled back.

The three other mercenaries whirled around and aimed their blasters. Kyrion tossed his helmet at one, then stretched out his hand. Telekinetic power rolled off him, strong and smooth. His sword zipped up off the floor, spun through the air, and settled into his hand. The second his fingers closed around it, the blade pulsed with power.

One, two, three . . .

Four, five, six . . .

Seven, eight, nine . . .

Kyrion moved back and forth between the three mercenaries at a dizzying speed, slicing his sword across their stomachs, their chests, and finally their throats, as though they were rungs on a ladder of death he was climbing.

The three men barely had time to scream before he killed them, although they all hung in midair for a second, as though their brains hadn't received the messages that they were dead and were still telling their legs to prop them up.

Another second ticked by, so quick and yet so curiously slow at the same time, and the three mercenaries toppled to the floor.

Hal's mouth gaped. For once, he actually did the smart

thing—he ran, trying to get back to the open boarding doors so he could flee into his own ship.

No one was paying any attention to me, so I scooped up one of the mercenaries' blasters from the floor. A fresh wave of pain exploded in my side, but I gritted my teeth, aimed the blaster at the fleeing Hal, and pulled the trigger. He yelped, but he didn't go down, so I pulled the trigger again. This bolt clipped his shoulder and spun him back around toward me.

Hal snarled and reached for the blaster on his belt, but I pulled the trigger again, and this bolt blasted straight into his face, charring his features. He too hung in midair for a second before crumpling to the floor.

An eerie silence descended over the ship, and the only sound was the continued popping, cracking, and sizzling of Hal's melting face. The stench of his fried flesh filled my nose, but it didn't bother me. The bastard had gotten exactly what he deserved.

I glared at him another moment, then turned my attention to Kyrion. The Arrow was standing amid the three dead mercenaries, blood and guts oozing on the floor all around him, but he was strangely untouched by all the death he'd just dealt out.

He stared at me, his sword still glowing in his hand. The shimmering blade matched his eyes, a dark, inky blue that bordered on utter blackness. Another one of those razor-thin smiles curved his lips, and he opened his mouth, probably to tell me how much he was going to enjoy killing me the same way he had the mercenaries.

I snapped up my blaster and pulled the trigger.

Click.

Click-click.

Click.

A sick sense of dread flooded my stomach. The blaster was empty. Of course it was. Cheap piece of Kent tech. I snarled and hurled it at Kyrion, who calmly swatted it away with his sword. The lunarium blade easily sliced through the blaster, and the resulting pieces clattered to the floor, landing in the mess around the three mercenaries.

I tensed, fully expecting Kyrion to wave his hand and toss the blaster bits back at me, to pelt me with them the same way he'd slammed his helmet into Hal's face. But instead, he just stood there, his lips puckered in thought, as though debating the slowest, most painful way to kill me.

Kyrion stared at me, his gaze cold and unreadable. When we'd been talking earlier, I had almost thought he was enjoying our conversation, snarky and threatening though it was. But now he had morphed back into full Arrow mode, and he had just killed those mercenaries without batting an eye. Why, he wasn't even breathing hard. Arrogant, deadly bastard.

Me? I felt like I was back in the lava field. Only the lava was inside my veins, and it was quickly boiling me alive. I had to push down another wave of pain before I could speak. "Well, you're going to get your wish."

"What's that?" he murmured.

I gestured down at my side, trying not to notice how much blood was coating my hand. "You're not even going to have to bother with killing me. I'm going to die, and the bond will be broken."

He didn't respond, although he kept staring at me with that inscrutable expression. It suddenly occurred to me that his face was going to be the last thing I ever saw—

My legs buckled, my ass hit the floor, and blackness crashed over me, blotting out everything, including Kyrion Caldaren.

ELEVEN

KYRION

Vesper was right. Blood was already pooling under her body, and the wound in her side would kill her in a matter of minutes.

Unless I did something supremely stupid.

Unless I broke the vow I had made to myself twenty-five years ago when I'd killed my father.

Unless I saved her.

I studied the three dead mercenaries crumpled around my feet. I'd heard everything they'd said, and the story wasn't hard to follow. Vesper worked at Kent Corp, and she'd been assigned to figure out why the *Velorum* had crashed. Even Callus Holloway had been concerned about the crash, especially since the *Velorum* was a prototype for all the military cruisers, blitzers, and other ships he had ordered to help fight the growing threat of the Techwave.

According to the chatty mercs, Rowena Kent had sent them to retrieve the information Vesper had stolen and then kill her. You didn't do that if your new spaceship had crashed because of pilot error, like Kent Corp was claiming.

I stepped over the dead mercs, crouched down, pressed my index finger to the floor, and then held it up. The remains of the broken microdot drive clung to my fingertip. It was smashed beyond repair, so I flicked it aside, straightened up, and went to the flight deck.

I punched a few buttons on the console, but all the scans came up negative. The mercs had come alone, and no other ships were nearby. Good. That gave me time to consider my options.

I returned to where Vesper was still sprawled across the floor. Now that she was unconscious, I didn't sense the pain of her wound quite so vividly, but it still ground into my side like shards of hot glass slowly being shoved deeper and deeper into my flesh. If I lifted my shirt, I would probably find a vicious burn on my own skin.

Given such a painful, debilitating injury, I was surprised— and impressed—that Vesper had stayed on her feet so long and that she had grabbed a blaster and killed the last merc. I was less pleased that she'd tried to kill me with the same blaster, but I couldn't fault her for it. She'd thought I was going to attack her again.

I had actually been debating the best way to propose a truce when she'd fired the blaster and then thrown the empty weapon at me. Even when faced with her own death, Vesper was still full of rage.

It was . . . *She* was . . . intriguing.

I set that troubling thought aside and focused on what was important: discovering what House Kent was so desperate to cover up. And like it or not, the quickest, easiest way to do that was by healing Vesper now and then questioning her later.

That was the only reason I was thinking about saving her. This had nothing to do with our unwanted connection. I might feel her injuries as if they were my own, but the truebond couldn't influence my thinking, emotions, and decisions. It couldn't make me give up my independence, my free will, or any semblance of my own self the way my father had for my mother.

Not yet.

And if it ever did, then I would eliminate Vesper anyway, information or no information, and regardless of the possibly fatal consequences to myself.

I shoved my sword onto my belt, bent down, and scooped Vesper up into my arms. The instant I touched her, the bond stirred to life deep inside me, a thin, fragile ribbon anchoring me to her. That ribbon, that thread of connection, of awareness, vibrated in warning, wanting me to share my strength, my power with her, wanting me to *help* her.

I gritted my teeth, carried her into the cargo bay, and dumped her onto the medtable. Vesper didn't make a sound, and another one of those annoying sparks of regret flared in my chest for treating her so roughly. She hadn't deserved that.

"Critical wound detected," the ship's female voice intoned. "Immediate action needed to prevent loss of life . . ."

The ship kept talking, listing everything that was wrong with Vesper and estimating that she had less than five minutes to live.

I hesitated, once again wondering if I should really do this, if I should save her, and risk the bond growing stronger and deeper between us. But she had information about the Kents, information I needed to protect myself, along with the rest of the Arrows.

It was worth the risk—for now.

I punched a button on the side of the table. The flexible panel shot out of its hiding place and closed over Vesper. A moment later, her body jerked as the needles embedded in the medtable punched into her back, flooding her system with skinbonds and repairing all the damage to her side.

A hundred phantom needles pricked my own body, as I once again felt her pain, and I could have sworn a larger, sharper one stabbed deep into my heart, for reasons unknown.

PART TWO

RUMORS AND REGALS

TWELVE

VESPER

I was having the dream again. Beautiful but dilapidated castle, staircase spiraling downward, round room full of flowers, eyes, and doors.

But this time, my dream—my mindscape—was different.

Instead of being closed like before, some of the doors were now standing wide open, with memories clearly visible on the other side. I peered in through one of the newly opened doors and watched Kyrion cut the husher out of my wrist on the Imperium ship. Another door showed me dragging him across the lava field. And of course, a third door showed Kyrion chasing me around the blitzer and me desperately trying to avoid him. I shuddered and turned away from that memory.

More doors were also embedded in the walls than before, dozens and dozens of new doors, as if my mindscape had somehow doubled or even tripled in size. I tugged on a few of the new, closed doors, but they didn't budge, making me even more curious about what might be lurking behind them. More old memories I would rather forget? Or awful new memories I hadn't yet made?

But perhaps the strangest things were the eyes, which were all open now. Some of them had migrated from the walls to the doors, but even more unnerving was the fact that they all kept staring at me curiously, as though they didn't know what to make of me.

I shivered and moved over to the Door in the back of the room. The beautiful sapphsidian eye was once again upside down in the dark stone, and the Door was tightly shut. The last time I was here, right before I had woken up on the Imperium ship, I'd turned the eye, and the Door had seemed like it was about to open. So why was it closed again?

Curious, I pressed my palm up against the jeweled eye, which burned like an ice-cold brand about to crystallize my skin. I grimaced at the painful sensation and started to remove my hand, but that curiosity welled up inside me again, so I ignored the chill, tightened my grip on the jewel, and moved my hand to the right. To my surprise, the eye turned easily. A soft *click* sounded as it settled into a right-side-up position, and then . . .

The Door popped open.

Startled, I dropped my hand and scuttled back, wondering what new memory might appear. But the Door remained as it was, neither fully open nor closed. My curiosity overpowered my common sense, and I stepped forward, grasped the edge of the Door, and pulled it back to reveal . . .

Darkness—absolute, utter, unrelenting darkness.

A few wisps of black smoke curled out of the opening, and the sharp, sweet scent of spearmint tickled my nose. Well, at least it didn't have the sulfuric stench of the lava field. I waved the smoke away and peered through the archway, but all I could see was blackness, as though I was staring into the heart of a shadow. Still, despite the lack of light, I could sense *something* waiting inside the darkness, something cold, cruel, and calculating, like a monster lurking just out of sight that would devour me if I ever walked through the opening.

I chewed on my lower lip. Why wasn't a memory waiting behind this door? What was so different or special about this spot?

"So this is what seer magic is like," a familiar voice drawled.

I whirled around. Kyrion Caldaren was standing off to one side of the room, as though he'd somehow stepped through the open door behind him and strolled right into my mindscape.

"What are *you* doing here?" I hissed, my hands balling into fists.

"No idea. The last thing I knew, I was resting on the ship. I felt a sort of . . . tug in my mind, and suddenly, I find myself in here with you." He gave me a thoughtful look. "Apparently, your power is quite strong, if you can drag other, unwilling people into your dream world."

"This is *not* my dream world," I hissed again. "Because if it was, then you would most definitely not be here."

"I didn't mean dream as in *ideal*. But seers often have vivid dreams, such as the vision we are both experiencing right now. What do they call these things?"

Before I could answer, he snapped his fingers.

"Ah, yes. Mindscapes." Kyrion glanced around. "The eyes are certainly interesting, albeit extremely creepy. Do they actually *do* anything? Or do they just stare at you?"

He leaned forward to poke one of the eyes with his finger.

"Don't touch that!" I snapped.

Kyrion arched an eyebrow, but he dropped his hand. I hoped he would go back to . . . wherever he'd come from, but instead, he clasped his hands behind his back and strolled around, as though he was ambling through a museum and studying all the art on display.

I watched him warily. Had he come here to try to kill me in

my own mindscape? Probably. Even though I had only known him for a few hours, Kyrion Caldaren struck me as exceptionally thorough, especially when it came to eliminating his enemies.

He stopped and peered through one of the doors at the memory playing out on the other side. I crept up behind him, wondering if I could somehow kill him instead. I glanced around, but there were no weapons in here, just all those jeweled eyes staring at me, along with the pale blue flowers that were flooding the room with their sharp, sweet spearmint scent.

"Is this you as a child?" Kyrion murmured. "Adorable. I love the pigtails."

I glanced through the opening, which showed a different angle of the memory I'd seen the last time I'd been in here. I was hiding at the top of the stairs, peering between the slats of the banister railing, and watching my mother argue with Liesl below. The words *useless child* floated up the steps, and the seven-year-old version of myself flinched and clutched a book to my chest as though it would shield me from my mother's caustic words.

I had already lived through that once, and I had no desire to repeat the experience—or let Kyrion Caldaren watch it for his own amusement. So I stepped between Kyrion and the opening, drawing his gaze back to me.

"Do you enjoy being a voyeur?" I snarked. "Do you like watching other people's pain? Because this is the day my mother abandoned me."

"Why?"

The truth tumbled from my lips before I could stop it. "The Imperium academy instructors said my magic was weak and that I wasn't worth training. My mother's own magic had seemingly fizzled out, and she'd been hoping to use mine to claw her way back up the Regal ladder. She left in the middle of the night and went back to Corios. She never returned."

For the first time since I'd known him, a bit of sympathy softened Kyrion's features. "Parents truly don't realize the power they have to shape us, hurt us—even destroy us."

That was by far the kindest thing he had said to me, but I got the impression it wasn't *only* about me. His lips puckered in thought, and his eyes grew dark and distant, as though he was thinking about his own parents. Once again, I wondered why he had killed his father, especially since, from all accounts, Chauncey Caldaren had been one of the more honorable and decent Regals.

Kyrion shook off his thought, whatever it was, and strolled over to the next door, which featured eight-year-old me assembling my first blaster out of spare parts. It was a harmless memory, so I let him watch it, even as I glanced around again, still searching for something to hurt him with—or some way to wake myself up from this dream world that was rapidly morphing into a nightmare, thanks to his unwanted presence.

The memory ended with me accidentally shooting a hole in the classroom wall. Kyrion chuckled at the instructor's outraged screams, then walked over to another door.

Through this opening, Conrad launched into his speech about how we just weren't right for each other, and the rest of the sad scene quickly unspooled, along with Conrad showing up to work hanging on to Sabine Kent's arm the next day.

My heart twisted, and I darted forward, grabbed the door, and slammed it shut. Kyrion being here was bad enough. He didn't get to see my humiliation too.

He stared at the closed door, but he didn't make any comment. I wasn't sure what I would have done if he'd said something. Probably screamed and tried to punch his smug, arrogant face, even though I knew how pointless that would be. Even here, he could still easily defend himself and subdue—kill—me.

Kyrion strolled on and eventually wound up at the Door,

the one seemingly filled with nothing but darkness. He studied the curls of black smoke snaking out of the opening. "What's in there?"

"This is the first time I've ever opened that door, so I don't know what, if anything, has ever been inside it." A thought popped into my mind. "Perhaps that's where *you* came from. The imagery certainly fits—darkness that will suck you in and swallow you whole."

A wry smile curved the corner of his lips. "I've never heard my villainy described in such grandiose terms before. You, Vesper Quill, are quite the poet."

Kyrion stretched out his hand, as though he was going to reach through the opening and touch the darkness waiting beyond. I grabbed his wrist and yanked his arm back.

"Stop that!" I snapped again. "I don't want you poking around in my mindscape, in my *brain*, like a child with a new toy he is determined to break. I have no desire to spend the rest of my life as a drooling vegetable."

"You're the one who dragged me in here with your power, so don't get upset if I want to learn everything I can about it," he replied in a mild voice.

He was *infuriating*, so infuriating that I darted forward to shove him away, to try to get rid of him however I could. But of course, Kyrion easily avoided my lunge. To make matters worse, I tripped over my own feet, and the floor rushed up to meet my face—

Hands clamped around my body, jerking me to a stop. My brain sloshed around inside my skull, then settled back into place. I stared up at Kyrion, who was looming over me, with one hand under the small of my back and the other clamped around my right forearm, as though he had dipped me as part of some fancy Regal waltz. His fingers flexed and dug a little deeper into my back, and the heat of his hand soaked all the way through my thick coveralls.

"You seem to be inordinately fond of putting your hands on people without their permission," I snarked.

He arched an eyebrow again. "As you wish."

He dropped me. One second, Kyrion was holding me upright. The next, he had removed his hands and stepped back, his movements smooth and fluid. My ass hit the floor, and pain spiked up my back. Kyrion winced, as if he'd also felt the jarring impact. I hoped he had. Arrogant bastard.

"Just as I thought," he said. "You have no self-defense skills whatsoever."

I scrambled back onto my feet. "I didn't need such skills until—"

"Until you stole valuable information from Kent Corp? Oh, yes. I heard your conversation with the mercenaries. It was most enlightening."

I thought back, reviewing everything Hal had said. The mercenary hadn't revealed much, but Kyrion was smart enough to read between the lines.

"What really caused the *Velorum* crash?" he asked. "And what does it have to do with the new ships House Kent is handing over to the Imperium during the spring ball?"

I crossed my arms over my chest. Let him figure out what Rowena Kent was up to himself. Perhaps he would even be on one of those doomed Imperium ships the day its navigation sensor malfunctioned and it crashed. The thought warmed my heart.

"Why are you smiling?" he asked.

"Just picturing your death."

At my words, a door flung itself open, and an image appeared on the other side: Kyrion standing on the observation deck of an Imperium cruiser that was plummeting toward the ground.

I blinked, and the door abruptly slammed shut. I stared at the eye embedded in the stone, which stared right back at me.

"What . . . what was that?" I whispered.

"Your seer magic," Kyrion drawled. "Although it's hard to tell if that was just the death you are currently wishing for me or something that might actually happen in the future."

"I don't see the *future*," I growled. "I told you before, I just see possibilities and how things work."

He gave another one of those annoying shrugs. "I'm starting to think you are severely underestimating your power."

"Better than overestimating it, like you do."

"How do I overestimate my power?"

"Well, you weren't able to kill me, for starters. I would think a mighty Arrow such as yourself wouldn't have had so much trouble eliminating me."

Kyrion stiffened. "I had just been severely wounded, and you took me by surprise. Those things happen, even to the best, most skilled warrior."

More anger bubbled up inside me. He couldn't even admit when he'd lost. Arrogant, insufferable jackass.

"Why are you here? Why don't you just go away and leave me alone?" I flapped my hand at him.

Amusement crinkled his face. "I'm not a butterfly you can just shoo away anytime you like. The bond won't let either one of us do that to the other, no matter how much we might want to."

"*You* can believe whatever you want." I stabbed a finger at myself. "But *I* prefer to put my faith in things I can see, hear, smell, taste, and touch. Not some magical, mystical connection we may or may not have."

"Do I need to remind you about how your injuries are mimicking mine and vice versa?"

I huffed. "You didn't seem too hampered by my injuries when you were killing those three mercenaries."

"You misunderstand. Your injuries won't cripple me, just as mine won't cripple you. Not yet, anyway." His face darkened as he muttered the last few words.

"Stop speaking in riddles, and just say what you really mean."

Kyrion gave me another cool look. "You tell me what you know about Kent Corp and why the *Velorum* crashed, and I'll tell you everything I know about truebonds."

"Hard pass. Besides, it's all moot anyway."

"What do you mean?"

I gestured at the wisps of black smoke still drifting out through the Door. "Well, if you didn't come through that door, then given how injured I am, I'm guessing it leads to the great beyond or the afterlife or whatever term you want to use to pretty up death. So whatever I know about Kent Corp is going to die with me. And since I'll be dead, the supposed bond between us won't matter anymore either."

"You're being very pragmatic," he replied. "Most people would be screaming and weeping and beating their fists on the wall at the thought of their own impending death."

He was right. I was being strangely pragmatic. But even more than that, I was just . . . tired—so *tired*. I was tired of sneaking around and looking over my shoulder and constantly worrying if my plan to expose the *Velorum* crash cover-up was going to be discovered. At least, that was all over with now, although I was still royally pissed that Rowena and Sabine Kent had gotten the better of me.

I wondered what Conrad would think when he learned that I'd been killed. He probably wouldn't care, except to scheme how he could best use my death to his own advantage. A familiar mixture of anger, sadness, and bitterness washed through me at how wrong I'd been about him.

"What are you thinking about?" Kyrion asked. "You look . . . troubled."

"Nothing," I muttered. "Just leave me alone and let me die in peace."

I spun around, marched over, and sat down on the floor,

close to the open door that was still spitting out curls of darkness. I leaned my back against the wall and tilted my head up, staring at the clusters of eyes and flowers adorning the ceiling. After a few seconds, I sighed and dropped my head.

Kyrion Caldaren was gone.

I jerked upright, but he was nowhere in sight. Beside me, curls of darkness kept wisping out through the Door. He hadn't walked through the opening, so where had he gone?

My gaze locked onto a closed door on the other side of the open one. Instead of another eye, a glittering sapphsidian arrow was embedded in the stone—the same sigil that adorned the hilt of Kyrion's stormsword.

The stalk of the arrow rose, then split apart and curved out and down in two opposing directions before flowing back up, joining together, and ending in one razor-sharp tip. A spearhead, a leaf, a spade from an old-fashioned tarot or playing card. Every time I blinked, I saw something different. For some reason, the symbol also reminded me of an upside-down heart.

I blinked again, and the shape solidified into an arrow, a House Caldaren arrow, just like Kyrion had said it was. I frowned. I had never seen that sigil in here before. Had he gone through there? Was that *his* door into my mind, my magic? More proof of the truebond between us?

I shivered and drew my knees up to my chest, as if that simple gesture would protect me from whatever unwanted connection I had to Kyrion Caldaren.

Another wave of tiredness crashed over me, and I dropped down onto my side and rested my cheek against the cool stone. More black smoke was creeping out through the open door and snaking in this direction, but I wasn't afraid of it. The first bit of darkness touched my face even as my eyes slid shut.

I was already dead, so there was no use being afraid of anything anymore.

Sometime later, my eyes fluttered open, and a stone ceiling swam into view. Weird. Was I back in my mindscape again?

I drew in a breath and was surprised at how smoothly the air filled my lungs. And the pain in my side had completely vanished.

I sat up. Instead of being on the blitzer or even in my dream world, as Kyrion had so mockingly dubbed it, I was lying on a massive bed with four large posts that loomed up into the air like wooden spears. Six people could have easily slept side by side in this monstrosity, but I was alone, on top of the covers, with pillows piled all around me, as though to prevent me from rolling off the side.

Even stranger, I was wearing a uniform—socks, cargo pants, and a long-sleeved tactical shirt, all in a blue so dark it almost looked black. Sapphsidian blue, as I was coming to think of the color. A sigil had been stitched on the shirt, right over my heart—the House Caldaren arrow.

I rubbed the bottom of the shirt between my fingers. Despite the thin, soft material, I wasn't cold, indicating that the shirt was made of tempered silk, which automatically adjusted to the wearer's body heat, along with the environment. Expensive, and not something I had ever owned on my lab rat's salary.

Where *was* I?

I glanced around the rest of the room. A nightstand squatted beside the bed, while a dressing screen stood in the corner next to a walk-in closet. Despite the sparse furnishings, everything was made of real wood instead of the much cheaper composite wood that I was used to.

I swatted the pillows away, scooted over, and swung my legs over the side of the bed. A pair of knee-high boots were sitting there, so I slid my feet into them. They fit perfectly, as did the rest of the uniform. Creepy.

A shimmer of silver caught my eye, along with a pop of pink. The dagger that I'd swiped from the Imperium cruiser was lying on the nightstand, right next to some bottles of water and several strawberry protein bars, the same kind Kyrion had mocked me with on the blitzer.

So Kyrion Caldaren had a sense of humor. Wonderful.

I glared at the items, wishing I could chuck one of the bottles at his head. Then my stomach rumbled, reminding me how long it had been since I'd eaten anything, so I ripped open a protein bar and sank my teeth into it. Despite the fake strawberry flavor and chalky texture, it was one of the best things I had ever tasted.

I quickly polished off that bar, then two more, and drank two bottles of water. Everything else could wait, especially since I didn't know when I might get the chance to eat again. I also slid the dagger into a slot on my belt.

Between bites and drinks, I searched the room, but the nightstand drawers were all empty, as was the closet, except for more uniforms like the one I was wearing. Well, since there weren't any answers in here, I would have to seek them out, along with Kyrion.

He was here, right now, in this building. I could *feel* him, like a cobweb clinging to a corner of my mind. I tried to brush the sensation away—tried to brush *him* away—but it stuck to my fingers, stuck to my mind and magic, just like a real cobweb would. Even worse, the light, thin, fragile strands were far stronger and much more stubborn and annoying than they seemed at first touch.

So this was what a truebond felt like. Ugh. No wonder Kyrion had been so desperate to break it. I wondered if he could sense me the same way I could sense him. Probably. What did my presence feel like to him? Probably a Frozen bear trap sinking its sharp, giant metal teeth deep into his leg. Ugh.

But brooding in here was not helping my situation, so I marched over to the door—also real wood—on the opposite side of the room. To my surprise, the knob turned easily, and I cautiously opened the door.

A dark stone corridor greeted me, its walls blank and featureless, and it had even less personality than the spartan bedroom. Curious, I stepped out into the corridor and headed toward a flight of stairs at the far end. As I walked along, I rapped my knuckles on the wall, but it was most definitely solid stone and not some hologram or hallucination. Well, this was a marked improvement from being conscripted on the Imperium ship.

Still, I couldn't help but wonder *why* Kyrion Caldaren had saved my life instead of letting me die. What did he want? Maybe he had to kill me himself to sever the truebond. I shivered and walked faster, my curiosity replaced by growing unease.

I went down the stairs and pushed through a door at the bottom. An alarm pinged, as though this was an emergency exit, but I kept going.

The door opened into a large garden filled with flowers, trees, and vegetables. Normally, I would have stopped to admire everything, but unease drove me forward. I hurried along a stone path, shoved through a black wrought-iron gate, and careened around a corner.

I stopped in my tracks, my eyes widening in surprise. An enormous terrace rolled out like a stone carpet in front of me. Several sets of wide, flat steps were set at equal distances in the terrace, and they all led down to a broad cobblestone boulevard below—*the Boulevard*, as the gossipcasts called it.

People strolled along the sidewalks, many of them clutching parasols, as if the sheer bubbles of lace would truly shield their skin from the bright morning sun. Out on the Boulevard itself, folks were sitting in open-air carriages that were propelled by servants pedaling old-fashioned bicycles. Several loud *clop-clop-clop-clops* rang out, and my eyes widened again as a white horse with a violet mane trotted by, pulling a carriage behind it. I had never seen a real, live, actual horse before.

More horses and carriages appeared, and the clopping hooves and creaking wheels hummed through the air like a pleasant symphony that was nothing like the coughing rumbles of transport engines and the screams of spaceships I was used to on Temperate 42.

The stone structure looming up behind me took up this entire end of the Boulevard, with smaller structures lining the rest of the rectangular thoroughfare. Some of the buildings were short and squat, like mushrooms growing in the shade of the larger, wider structures, but they all featured towers and turrets, and they were all painted in rich, vibrant colors—ice blue, plum purple, mint green, sunset orange, even flamingo pink.

I glanced up. The hulking structure behind me also boasted a plethora of towers and turrets, although it wasn't painted. The raw stone was a dark blue that bordered on black, and it resembled a dull lump of coal squatting among the brighter, more whimsical buildings. Of course it did. I doubted Kyrion Caldaren cared about something as mundane as fitting in with the rest of his Regal neighborhood.

On the far side of the busy Boulevard, an enormous park—Promenade Park—stretched out like a green pool of water set into the center of the surrounding streets. Grassy lawns rolled up and down, while bushes and trees arched up into the air, their limbs bursting with white, purple, and yellow blossoms. Dozens of people were strolling along pink cobblestone paths that wound through the park, their clothing as colorful as the Boulevard castles, while other folks were seated on blankets, enjoying early-morning picnics. The air was pleasantly warm and smelled of spring, or at least what I had always imagined an unpolluted spring would smell like: fresh, green, and bursting with new life and possibilities.

I'd only wanted to escape from Kyrion, but I felt as though I had stepped into some old-fashioned painting that depicted another time, another place, another galaxy, where everything was clean and bright and shining, not shrouded in a smoggy haze of exhaust.

A blitzer zipped by overhead, shattering the pastoral tranquility, and headed for a structure on the far side of the park. Unlike the candy-colored stone castles along the Boulevard, this structure was made of chrome and glass, and it glimmered like a metallic diamond. Blitzers, cruisers, and transports hovered around the slender, needle-like towers that jutted several miles into the air like bees dancing around a sharp, pointed flower.

I recognized the structure—Crownpoint, the home of Callus Holloway, ruler of the Regals and ostensibly the galaxy, although the Techwavers and Erztonians would disagree with that assessment.

For the first time, I realized exactly where I was, but the knowledge didn't fill me with awe. Instead, a sense of dread crashed over me. I had been on this planet once before, when I was twelve and had foolishly come looking for my mother. After that disastrous trip, I had vowed never to return.

I was on Corios, the heart of the Imperium.

THIRTEEN

VESPER

I stood on the terrace, gaping at the view and wondering how I had gotten here. But that was easy enough to guess. After he'd used the blitzer's medtable to heal me, Kyrion had flown us to Corios.

But why? Back on the ship, Kyrion had been determined to sever the bond between us, even if that meant killing me. But here I was, still alive, despite the best efforts of Hal and the other mercenaries. I thought back to how Kyrion had appeared in my mindscape, how he'd claimed that I had somehow pulled him in there.

Determination flared in me. Well, I might have inadvertently dragged him into my dream world, but I didn't have to stay in his *actual* world. I squared my shoulders and headed toward the closest set of steps. I didn't know where I was going, but I'd figure things out. I always did.

"There you are!" a voice called out. "I thought you'd darted off like a scared rabbit."

I spun around. A thirty-something man strode in my direction. He was a couple of inches taller than me, with a lean, muscled body, short black hair, dark brown eyes, and golden skin. He was wearing the same uniform as mine—a dark blue long-sleeved shirt, cargo pants, and knee-high boots—although he made the outfit seem sleek and official, rather than merely functional.

He thrust a tablet at me. "I need a palm print in order to give you access to the secure areas."

I started to protest, but he shoved the tablet at me again, so I placed my palm on the screen. A light flashed, and a soft voice chimed out. "Print recorded. Access granted. Welcome, Vesper Quill."

I jerked my hand back, startled by the sound of my own name.

The man tapped on the tablet, then nodded, apparently satisfied. He looked at me again, his lips puckering as though he were a general who wasn't impressed with the lowly soldier in front of him. I resisted the urge to stand up straighter.

"I am Daichi Hirano, the chief of staff for Lord Caldaren. According to him, you are his new . . . weapons consultant."

I stifled a laugh. He obviously didn't believe the lie Kyrion had told him. Still, I supposed *weapons consultant* was better than *kidnap victim*. "Nice to meet you, Daichi."

He sniffed, then spun around on his boot heel and walked away. I eyed the terrace steps, wondering if I could still make a break for it.

Daichi stopped and glanced over his shoulder at me. "Are you coming?"

"Um . . . sure."

I might not know what was going on, but Daichi certainly seemed confident, so I fell in step beside the chief of staff. He marched right back through the garden, opened a side door, and moved along a wide hallway. Only a few tables and chairs populated the space, along with some tapestries and paintings.

Despite the spartan furnishings, I had the strangest sense of déjà vu, as though I had been here before. Weird.

I peered into every room we passed, but I didn't see anyone else. "Where is everyone? Shouldn't people be polishing knickknacks and whatnot?"

A muscle ticked in Daichi's jaw. "Lord Kyrion prefers to keep a small staff."

"How small? As in just you?"

"Me and a few kitchen workers."

Well, that explained the empty, abandoned feel to the building, as well as the dust and cobwebs clinging to many of the ceilings.

Daichi cleared his throat as though the confession had left a bad taste in his mouth. "Lord Kyrion asked me to program your tablet, so keep up. I have a hundred things to accomplish today, and I don't have time to explain things more than once. Understand?"

"Sure." That seemed like the safest thing to say.

Daichi gave me a sharp look, as though he thought I was mocking him, but I merely grinned in return.

"Your room was to your liking?" he asked.

"Sure." I had a feeling I was going to be saying that a lot around him.

Daichi kept going. He didn't seem to be one for idle chitchat, and he radiated a crisp professionalism that I envied. I wondered how long he'd been the chief of staff and why he was the only one who seemed to work for Kyrion. Most Regal Houses had hundreds, if not thousands, of staff members.

As we walked along, Daichi pointed out various rooms, although he never slowed down, and I only managed to get brief glimpses of them. Still, the deeper we went into the building, the more familiar it seemed, which rekindled my unease.

Eventually, Daichi strode through an open door. Unlike all the other rooms, which were sparsely furnished, bordering on straight-up empty, someone actually worked in this area. Real papers and folders were piled on a large desk in neat stacks, and clear bins held gelpens and other office equipment. Tivona would have loved it. A pang of longing shot through me. If I hadn't thought it would put her in danger, I would have contacted my friend and let her know I was okay . . . more or less.

"Sit." Daichi stabbed his finger at a much smaller, empty desk that was perched across from the larger one.

I dropped down into the chair, which was surprisingly comfortable. Certainly much more comfortable than the rickety stool I'd had at Kent Corp.

Daichi placed his tablet on a charging station, then marched over to a cabinet covered by a metal grate. He laid his palm on the scanner, a green light flashed, and the grate buzzed open. He plucked out a tablet from a row of them, then came over to my desk and set the device down in front of me.

I perked up. "Oh, the new Wazaki tablet! I've been itching to get my hands on one of these."

Daichi rolled his eyes, as though enthusiasm was beneath him, but he barked out the directions that let me activate the tablet.

"This should go without saying, but I will say it anyway. The tablet is for your consulting work only," he said in a stern voice. "It is *not* to be used for shopping or gaming or whatever other frivolous thing you engage in to pass the time. Understand?"

"Sure."

A dark look clouded his face, and I found myself grinning back at him. Working for Daichi—or whatever I was really doing here—might actually be fun. If nothing else, trying to crack his cool composure would be an amusing challenge.

"Let me set you up in the rest of the House Caldaren system," he muttered.

For the next hour, Daichi made scans of my palms, fingers, and retinas and took several blood and DNA samples. If he could have, I imagined he would have compiled a digital record of my entire body, from each strand of hair on my head to the tips of my toes.

"Lord Kyrion said you are here to consult on security and other matters related to the upcoming ball," Daichi said, sounding extremely unenthusiastic about my presence. "You will keep your tablet with you at all times, and you will report to either Lord Kyrion or myself, no one else. Understand?"

Daichi glared at me, as if daring me to say *sure* again.

"Sure," I chirped in a bright tone. I never could resist a challenge.

By this point, he looked like he wanted to grab a gelpen from his desk and stab me with it. He settled for smoothing his hand down his shirt, as if the small, simple motion kept his murderous urges in check. Maybe he should share that calming technique with his boss.

"Come." Daichi picked up his tablet and swept out of the office.

I grabbed my own device and followed him.

Daichi led me even deeper into the building, and every single door required either a palm print or a retinal scan before it would open. I wondered if the paranoia was on Kyrion's orders or if Daichi perpetrated it himself.

Eventually, Daichi reached a large door set into a particularly thick wall. Unlike all the others, which were plain, this door featured a House Caldaren arrow streaking upward through a cluster of stars in the dark stone, just like the door Kyrion had seemingly stepped through in my mindscape. A shiver skittered down my spine at the odd, eerie similarity.

This time, Daichi scanned both his palm and his retina and punched in a code for good measure. A faint *click* sounded, and the door swung open. He stepped through to the other side. I followed him, and the door swung shut and locked behind me.

We went down a short, dark hallway, then stepped out onto a balcony.

"This is the training ring," Daichi said. "Where Lord Kyrion spends much of his time."

A large rectangular space lay below us. Several stone benches lined the area, along with racks and cabinets filled with weapons—blasters, cannons, swords, spears, even a few long wooden staffs. In the center of the space, a man and a woman were fighting with swords, and each clash, crash, and bang of metal on metal made me flinch.

"That's it, Jules! Chop his bloody head off!"

Another man standing by one of the benches clapped his hands, encouraging the woman in the ring. I recognized him as one of the Arrows who had been on the Imperium ship.

"The Arrows always train here, at Lord Kyrion's ring, since he is their leader," Daichi said.

He pointed out first one Arrow, then another, saying their names, including Julieta Delano, whom I also recognized from the Imperium ship. I already knew most of the other Arrows from Tivona's gossipcasts. Despite the fact that they were all ruthless killers, in some ways, the Arrows and their murderous exploits were even more popular than the Regals, and the gossipcasts endlessly speculated about the Arrows' romantic lives and various tensions within the group.

The fight ended with Julieta slapping the sword out of the male Arrow's hand and then pressing her own blade up against his throat. A polite round of applause rang out, and the two Arrows retreated to their respective benches to grab towels and wipe the sweat off their faces.

"Come," Daichi said. "Lord Kyrion has requested your presence."

"I'll just bet he has," I muttered.

He gave me a sharp look, but I plastered a bland smile on my face and followed him down the stairs and over to the training ring.

A few of the Arrows nodded their heads in greeting to Dai-chi, who returned the gestures.

"Next up, Zane and Kyrion!" Julieta announced.

The two men strutted out from separate corners. Zane Zim-mer was stripped to the waist, his tan chest bare and glistening with oil. His tight pants hugged his thighs, while his feet were bare. His blond hair flowed around his face, and his sculpted physique made him look like an ancient god whose perfect form had been made flesh. Zane held his arms out wide and turned around in a slow circle, letting everyone admire him. According to the gossipcasts, he was an attention seeker who loved the Regal spotlight, something this display seemed to confirm.

In contrast, Kyrion glided into the ring as silent as a shadow. He too was stripped to the waist, although his chest was miss-ing the coating of oil. Kyrion was also wearing tight pants that left little to the imagination. My mouth went dry, and I forced myself to focus on his bare feet. No one ever had attractive feet . . . except for him. Drat. The man had tried to hurt me. I should *not* be thinking about how hard and solid his chest looked or how his muscles rippled with every step he took . . .

Daichi jabbed his elbow into my side. "You're here to work, not ogle the Arrows."

He had a point, so I dragged my gaze away from Kyrion's impressive form.

The two men faced each other in the center of the ring. Neither one tilted his head or showed any sign of deference to the other.

"Begin!" Julieta barked out.

Zane and Kyrion flew at each other. In an instant, they were fully engaged, using their fists, fingers, elbows, knees, and feet to punch, hit, and kick each other. Every time one of them landed a blow, the other man would absorb it and retaliate with his own equally vicious attack.

And I felt every single punch that Kyrion took.

At first, I wasn't sure what was happening. Pain twinged in my left ribs. Then my right ribs. My right hip. My left thigh. Every time Zane landed a blow, it jolted through Kyrion and moved right through me too.

Daichi shot me a curious look, clearly wondering why I was flinching so much, but I ground my teeth and kept quiet, despite the fact that I felt like Zane was using my body as a remote punching bag.

Zane and Kyrion exchanged another round of blows, then whirled away from each other. Each Arrow snapped his right arm out wide, and energy exploded in their hands, flaring bright and hot before abruptly gelling into pulsing weapons, a pale blue hammer for Zane and a dark blue sword for Kyrion.

Awe filled me. "What are those?" I whispered.

"Psionic blades," Daichi replied in a hushed voice. "Many psions can form shields around themselves, but some particularly strong psions can also shape their mental energy into physical weapons and other objects. It's quite draining, though, which is why most psions use stormswords and the like. It's a similar level of power but without the added mental and physical strain of forming a psi-blade yourself."

It didn't seem to be draining to the two of them, and Zane and Kyrion attacked each other with the psionic weapons just as viciously as they had with their fists, elbows, knees, and feet. But neither man could land a debilitating blow, and after about a minute, the psi-blades flickered and vanished, and the two Arrows started swinging their fists again.

Zane dropped his guard, just for an instant, and Kyrion pounced. His fist connected with Zane's jaw, and the other Arrow tumbled to the ground.

"Winner!" Julieta called out.

Kyrion loomed over Zane, giving the other man a cold look. Zane glared up at him, then spat out a mouthful of blood and climbed to his feet.

Kyrion turned around, and his gaze locked with mine. He took in my uniform, just as I took in his body again. Somehow the sheen of sweat covering his chiseled chest made him even more attractive.

I quickly squashed that thought, not wanting to add any more fuel to our supposed bond, however it might work. Or maybe it was the bond itself that was making me notice how gloriously defined Kyrion's abs were. Yes, I decided, that would be my strategy going forward.

Blame the bond for everything.

Kyrion drifted in this direction, then abruptly stopped, as though he wasn't supposed to approach me for some reason. Zane swaggered up beside him and looked me over, his eyes lighting up with interest.

I tensed. Had he recognized me from the Imperium ship? Did he know how much I didn't belong here?

"And who might you be?" he asked, a low purr in his voice.

Apparently not. Then again, I doubted Zane Zimmer noticed anything that didn't directly impact him in some way.

"This is Vesper," Kyrion replied in a clipped tone. "She's my new weapons consultant."

"Consultant?" Zane drawled. "Are you sure you don't mean *conquest*?"

Kyrion didn't react, but I could have sworn anger surged off him. No, I decided. That was just the emotion scorching through my own chest.

"I am no one's *conquest*," I snapped, my voice ringing out far louder than I had intended.

Everyone stopped what they were doing to look at me, and Daichi was shaking his head, as though I should have known better than to insult an Arrow. Yeah, he was probably right about that.

Zane let out a low, appreciative whistle. "Well, this one certainly has a mouth on her. I hope you're putting it to good use, Kyrion."

Chuckles rang out among the Arrows, although they quickly faded away. Everyone looked at me again, waiting to see how I would react to Zane's insult, including Kyrion. Despite the fact that he had brought me here, he wasn't going to help me. But I didn't need—or want—his help. I had been dealing with smug jackasses like Zane Zimmer ever since I had started working at Kent Corp, and long before that, at my other jobs and even at the Imperium university.

I stepped into the training ring, and a mocking grin spread across Zane's face.

"Would you like to wrestle?" he purred again, holding his arms out wide. "I'd be happy to spar with you, Vesper."

I ignored his suggestive words and marched over to one of the weapons lockers. I slapped my palm up against the scanner, and the locker opened. I eyed the assortment of blasters inside, then pulled out three different ones. I took the weapons over to a bench, sat down, plucked the dagger off my belt, and went to work.

My fingers flew over the parts and pieces, and a strange calm settled over me. In that moment, I could have put my creation together blindfolded, as crazy as that seemed. Or maybe it wasn't crazy at all, if my seer magic was as strong as Kyrion claimed.

Either way, in less than a minute, I had assembled a new and improved blaster. Oh, it didn't look improved. In fact, the whole thing looked like it would fall apart if you dared to pull the trigger, but I knew what the weapon—what I—was capable of.

I slid the dagger back onto my belt, then picked up the blaster and got to my feet. Everyone was still staring at me, including Zane, Kyrion, Daichi, and Julieta. I glanced around the training ring, and my gaze landed on a pale blue bag embroidered with two large interlocking *Z*'s. Perfect.

"What are you going to do with that?" Zane called out. "It looks like a kid's science fair project."

I snapped up the blaster and fired it at his bag.

Whoosh!

A blue energy bolt slammed into the bag, knocking it off the bench and down to the floor. Even better, the fabric ignited, and hot sparks and blue smoke spewed up into the air.

"Hey! My clothes were in there!" Zane yelled.

"Oops," I purred.

I spun the blaster around in my hand and shoved it into a slot on my belt. Zane kept staring at me, although his disbelief quickly boiled up into anger. He opened his mouth, probably to curse me, but Kyrion stepped up beside me. Zane snapped his lips shut, but he shot me another angry glare, then whirled around and stalked out of the ring, leaving his burning bag of clothes behind.

Julieta stopped long enough to wink at me before hurrying after him. She didn't seem to recognize me either.

"Leave us," Kyrion ordered.

The other Arrows gathered up their things and exited the training ring. Kyrion said something to Daichi in a low voice, and the other man gestured at me.

"Come," Daichi said. "Some refreshments are waiting for you, Vesper."

My stomach rumbled at the word *refreshments*. I glanced over at Kyrion, who shook his head the tiniest bit, indicating that he hadn't told Daichi who and what I really was. I stared at Kyrion a moment longer, wondering what game he was playing, then followed Daichi out of the training ring.

Daichi led me back through the corridors, scanned his palm on another reader, and opened a door. "This is Lord Kyrion's private library."

I stepped into the room and stopped cold. Because it wasn't just Kyrion's library. It was also *my* library. The one I always saw in my mindscape.

Floor-to-ceiling shelves filled with real paper books, two cushioned chairs with a low table squatting between them, a fireplace embedded in one wall. The furnishings were *exactly* the same as in my mindscape. I glanced back out into the hallway, and I finally realized what the rest of the building reminded me of—*my* castle, the one I had been wandering through in my dreams for as long as I could remember.

My stomach clenched with worry, dread, and more than a little fear. How was this possible? I had *never* been in this library before, had never seen it on a gossipcast or anywhere else. So why had I been dreaming about it for years?

Daichi was saying that Kyrion would be here soon, but his voice was a dull buzz in the back of my mind. My legs propelled me forward, and I crossed the library and stopped, staring up at the portrait over the fireplace. For the first time, I could see it clearly. A man and a woman smiling wide, their hands resting on the shoulders of the boy between them.

The man was quite handsome, with black hair, black eyes, and tan skin, while the woman was stunningly beautiful, with blond hair, blue eyes, and pale skin. The boy was a mixture of the two of them, black hair over dark blue eyes and pale skin.

The three of them were clearly a family, but the man and woman were staring at each other as though they were lost in their own world, leaving the boy to stare sourly at the artist.

Not just a random boy but Kyrion.

Daichi stepped up beside me, not seeming to notice my shock. "The Caldarens were a lovely couple."

He sighed. "Such a shame that Lady Desdesmona took ill.

And that Lord Chauncey died soon after."

"When Kyrion killed him," I said.

Daichi stiffened, and anger glimmered in his dark brown eyes. "Lord Kyrion invited you here to work, not insult him. Something you would do well to remember. Or I will throw you out of the castle myself."

"Why are you here when no one else is? Given your obvious skills, you could work for any Regal House you choose. So what do you owe Kyrion?"

Daichi peered down his nose at me. For a moment, I thought he wasn't going to answer, but then a single, clipped word escaped his lips. "Everything."

Before I could ask any more questions, Daichi jerked his head to the left. "The kitchen staff has set out the refreshments. I have other matters to handle."

He gave me another angry glare, then spun around and strode out of the library.

I studied the portrait of Kyrion and his parents again. I'd been wrong before. Kyrion didn't look sour so much as he looked . . . sad. Curiosity filled me. He'd been part of what looked like a loving family. So why did he seem so miserable? And why had I been seeing the painting in my mindscape for all these years?

I shivered and turned away from the portrait. I didn't want to look at it anymore—or think about how I might have been connected to Kyrion Caldaren for far longer than either one of us had realized.

The rest of the library also reminded me of my mindscape, so I walked over to the one thing in here I had never seen in my dreams before: a long table filled with food.

Cubes of cheese, piles of fresh fruit, large squares of bread that had been cut into bite-size sandwiches. My stomach rumbled again, and I snatched up a piece of cheese and bit into it.

Instead of the chalky paste and yellow dust of most

cheese-flavored products, a burst of pure, real, genuine cheddar filled my mouth. A moan escaped my lips at how good it was, and I quickly downed another cube.

I wandered along the table, shoving one thing after another into my mouth—sweet grapes, grainy figs, juicy apricots, toasted breads heaped with roast chicken and beef and slathered with sweet and spicy sauces. The delicious blend of flavors made me hum with happiness.

At the far end, chilled crystal pitchers held a variety of drinks, and I poured a dark blue liquid into a glass. I cautiously sipped it, and the sweet, floral flavors of blueberries and hibiscus tickled my tongue. I hummed again and drained the rest of the liquid. The fruity iced tea was a hundred times better than anything Tivona had ever made in our apartment brewmaker.

I kept eating and drinking until the sharpest edges of my hunger and thirst had dulled. Then I forced myself to slow down, take smaller bites, and really savor everything.

Fruits and vegetables were quite plentiful on Temperate 42, thanks to its moderate climate, but most produce had been genetically engineered so many times that it simply didn't have any *taste*. Sometimes I thought tomatoes, carrots, and broccoli were just colorful mush that people ate to make themselves feel better about all the processed sugar and other chemicals they willingly ingested on a regular basis. But given the glorious cavalcade of flavors filling my mouth now, I was betting that all the food here was purely organic and probably artisanal to boot.

Behind me, a door creaked open, and Kyrion stepped into the library. I couldn't see him from this angle, but I could *feel* him. That little cobweb in my mind had suddenly grown much larger and was now fully encasing me in its sticky yet silky threads.

He walked over to me. "The refreshments look like they've been ravaged by wolves."

Amusement colored his voice. I rolled my eyes and ate another cheese cube.

Kyrion grabbed a grape and popped it into his mouth. The motion made his bicep bulge against the tight fabric of his shirt. My mouth went dry again, and I resisted the urge to grab a pitcher and down all the liquid inside. What was *wrong* with me? This man had thought about *killing* me. I should absolutely *not* be thinking about how chiseled his arms were, along with the rest of him.

Kyrion ate another grape, then went over and dropped into a chair in front of the fireplace. He gestured at the opposite chair. "Please. Sit."

I eyed him warily, but I had no real reason to protest—yet. So I piled more cheese and fruit onto a plate, poured myself another glass of iced tea, and set everything down on the low table between us.

Kyrion relaxed back in his seat. "You did well in the training ring. I've never seen anyone render Zane Zimmer speechless before. Well done, Vesper. Truly."

"Perhaps if you'd hit him harder in the ring, he wouldn't have been so inclined to run his mouth out of it," I retorted.

"You sound more upset with me than with Zane."

Anger boiled up in my veins, and I squished a grape between my fingers. It was too good to waste, so I ate it anyway. "Why did you bring me *here*?"

His black eyebrows drew together in confusion. "What's wrong with *here*?"

My gaze strayed up to the Caldaren family portrait, then drifted past the fireplace and over to the wall where a door always appeared that led downstairs to my mindscape. But of course, that was only in my dream world, and the wall here was solid stone.

"Nothing," I muttered. "It's just . . . unexpected. But why save me? Why not just let me die on the blitzer?"

Kyrion peered down his nose at me. "Because I decided you can be useful, especially when it comes to what you know about Kent Corp and the real reason the *Velorum* crashed."

Ah, so that was what he wanted. Well, at least he was honest.

"But what about the bond?" I asked. "You were worried enough about it on the ship to try to kill me. So what's changed?"

He straightened up and cleared his throat, as though he was about to say something unpleasant. "I was a bit . . . hasty before. I thought you were an enemy, and I reacted badly."

Surprise rippled through me. "Are you *apologizing*?"

Kyrion shrugged one shoulder in an uncomfortable motion. Well, this was certainly unexpected, although his apology could use some work.

He cleared his throat again. "Anyway, I've had some time to think since we were on the blitzer."

"About what?"

He gestured at the blaster that was holstered to my hip. "How you can help me figure out what Techwave weapon wounded me and how I can defend myself against it."

I bristled. "So now you want to use me. Fantastic."

"Your sarcasm is unnecessary. What I'm proposing is more of a . . . limited-time arrangement."

I snorted. "In other words, you'll keep me around until you get all the information you want, and *then* you'll kill me in order to sever the bond, which you definitely do not want."

Kyrion shook his head. "No. As distasteful as I find the idea of a truebond, it's not your fault. As I said before, I reacted badly due to my own prejudices. I will not make that mistake again."

Maybe it was foolish, but I actually believed him, especially since the sticky cobweb in my mind pulsed with sincerity.

A wry smile flickered across his face. "Besides, you are much too smart—and far too stubborn—to fall for such an obvious trick. So instead, I am proposing a partnership."

"What sort of *partnership*?"

Kyrion shrugged again. "You tell me everything you know about the Kents and study the battle footage relating to the Techwavers' new weapon."

"And once I do that?"

"I will set you up with a new identity and enough credits to live an extremely comfortable life on any planet you choose. Daichi is already working out the details." He gestured around at the library. "As you can see, I am not without resources."

No, he was not. The thousands of credits' worth of fresh food I had just inhaled cost more than I made in two weeks as a lab rat.

"And what about the bond?"

Kyrion's eyes glittered. "We break it."

Wariness filled me. "But you said the only way to break a truebond was for one of us to die."

"I said that's the quickest and easiest way to break a truebond, especially a long-standing one."

"So there *are* other ways to break it. How?"

Kyrion fell silent, and this time, his gaze drifted up to the family portrait hanging above the fireplace. After a few seconds, he looked at me again. "I told you before on the blitzer. Some people believe a combination of chemicals can break a truebond, especially if both people take the same cocktail at the same time. It's just a theory, though. It didn't work before."

My eyes narrowed. "When did you try it before? Who else have you bonded with? What happened to them?"

Something flickered across his face. It almost looked like regret, but it vanished in an instant, replaced by the cold disdain he wore like a suit of armor. "That's none of your concern."

Once again, I felt like sloppy seconds, and this time was even worse than it had been with Conrad. Looking back, I could see all the warning signs that should have clued me in to the fact that Conrad was a money-grubbing, Regal ladder-climbing, cheating scumbag. But all the stories made truebonds out to be these magical, mystical things. They were supposed to be *special*, a once-in-a-lifetime connection. But to think that Kyrion had bonded with someone else . . . Well, it upset me far more than I'd thought possible. And the other, more important part of his statement also pissed me off.

"So you knew of a possible way to break the bond, and yet you still decided to try to kill me first? What a gentleman lord you are. Truly."

"As I said before, I was a bit hasty on the blitzer," he replied. "I thought someone had put you in my path, had deliberately sent you to trap me into the bond."

Confusion filled me. "Who would do that?"

"I have many enemies, among both the Techwavers and the Regals. Many people would love to see me fall." Kyrion hesitated, and when he spoke again, his voice was pitched much lower than before. "And there are some who would dearly love to see me bonded to another so they could use the connection to their own advantage."

"The whole I-die-you-probably-die-too thing?"

"Something like that."

More frustration surged through me at his vague answers. He was dancing around the truth instead of just revealing it to me.

"Regardless, my offer remains the same. Tell me what the Kents are doing, and see if you can figure out the new Techwave weapon. In return, you get a comfortable new life, far, far away on any planet you like."

"What aren't you telling me?"

He tilted his head to the side. "Why do you think I'm not telling you everything?"

I shrugged. "It's hard to describe, exactly. Just a feeling."

That sticky cobweb in my mind bristled with anger, and a

muscle ticked in his jaw, matching the motion. "Do us both a favor. Try not to have any more *feelings*."

His words stung, and I snapped right back at him. "Then try not to be such an obnoxious, overbearing, arrogant, secretive jackass."

He glared at me. Somehow I resisted the urge to toss a cheese cube at him.

"Where are these chemicals?" I asked. "When can we take them?"

"My contact here on Corios is already working on obtaining the chemicals. He should have them in a few days."

"I suppose I can endure your company for a few more days." I leaned forward and stabbed my finger at him. "But I want your word that you won't try to kill me again, whether we break the bond or not."

His face hardened. "This isn't a negotiation."

A bitter laugh escaped my lips. "*Everything* is a negotiation. Especially among the Regals."

He looked skyward, as though he was running out of the patience to deal with me. "Very well. I promise that I won't try to hurt you ever again."

I waited, but he didn't ask me to promise not to try to hurt him in return. His dismissal sharpened the edges of my anger and made me want to punch him. Perhaps he was smart not to ask for a promise I doubted I could keep.

"All right. You won't hurt me, and I'll try to get the answers you want." I hesitated. "But what if I can't find those answers?"

What if we can't break the bond? I didn't say the words, but they hung in the air between us anyway, like a noose binding us together and slowly tightening around both our necks.

"Let's not resign ourselves to failure right from the start," Kyrion replied, which was another one of those nonanswers I was rapidly coming to despise.

"Fine." I ground out the word. "Then we have a deal."

I held out my hand to shake, but he stared at it like I'd offered him a poisonous sand scorpion.

"Any sort of physical contact can potentially strengthen the bond," he said. "So I'll keep my hands to myself, and I suggest that you do the same."

My hand plummeted to my lap. "Very well."

"Good. Then we are agreed."

Kyrion surged to his feet, marched over to a cabinet, and drew a couple of wooden swords out of the dark depths. He kept one sword for himself, then tossed the other one over to me. It landed on my lap, making me flinch.

"What's this for?" I asked.

He twirled his sword around in his hand. "Corios might seem bright and whimsical and fun, but it's one of the most dangerous cities and planets in the galaxy. If anyone were to even suspect we are bonded, however tenuously, then my enemies would stop at nothing to capture or kill you. I'm not going to be injured—or worse—just because you don't know how to defend yourself. So in addition to your consulting work, you will also train with me every single day until I'm satisfied you can fend off an attack."

"I fended you off, didn't I?" I sniped back.

"You got lucky. I'm not going to bet my life on you getting lucky again."

Kyrion took up a fighting stance in the middle of the library, clearly meaning to start training me right this very second. I sighed, got to my feet, and raised my own sword.

Our partnership had barely started, and I was already wishing for it to end.

FOURTEEN

KYRION

Bringing Vesper here had been a mistake—probably a fatal one.

But whether that would be for her or for me remain- ed to be seen.

I slapped the practice sword out of her hand. She growled in frustration and watched the weapon sail across the library, even as I moved forward and pressed my own sword up against her throat.

"And you are dead—*again*. You didn't even last a minute that time."

Vesper shoved the blade away. She glowered at the wood as if she could ignite it with the sheer force of her gaze, and anger surged off her, twinging the soft, velvet ribbon of her in my mind.

"That's because you're a ruthless killer who has been fighting people for years," she said, turning her hot glower to me. "The only experience I've had swinging a sword was in a renaissance fair Kent Corp sponsored for its workers back on Temperate 42. To say we are mismatched is an understatement."

In every sense of the word. I didn't voice the thought, but Vesper gave me a sour look anyway, as though she could hear the telepathic echoes of it through the bond. Maybe she could. I certainly felt more attuned to her moods and thoughts with every passing hour.

And once again, I wondered, why her?

There were plenty of women—men too—on Corios whom I could have bonded with. Over the years, more than one Regal had thrust their offspring at me during a ball, hoping the person in question would somehow enchant me and make me forget all logic and common sense. All those people—parents and offspring alike—had been left disappointed by my lack of interest, attraction, and desire.

Oh, every now and then, I indulged in a discreet dalliance, but only when I was away on an undercover mission on a distant planet with someone who didn't recognize me and whom I would never see again.

I would never forget my vow, and I would never let myself be willingly bonded to anyone, not even through a chembond that would burn out in a few hours. Most people had grand, romantic notions about a truebond, but it was nothing but a ticking bomb, a certain death wrapped in a tempting ball of feelings that would explode when you least expected.

My parents had taught me that.

Chauncey and Desdemona had been so in love, so connected, so attuned to each other, that there was never much space for me in their lives—or especially in their hearts. This had been reinforced when my mother had died, and my father had alternated between being almost comatose and then mad with grief. I had no desire to experience such suffering myself or inflict it on some random person whose power arbitrarily decided that it was the perfect complement to my own psionic abilities.

For the last twenty-five years, I had successfully kept every-one at arm's length—until Vesper Quill had crossed my path.

After I'd put her on the medtable in the blitzer, I had ducked into the Kent mercenaries' ship and used it to fly both vessels to Corios. I'd been dozing in the pilot's chair when I'd sudden-ly found myself in that round room with all the eyes, doors, and flowers. Not much unsettled me, but the truebond pulling me into Vesper's dream world, her mindscape, the heart of her psion power, had shaken me far more than I would ever admit, especially to her.

It was proof that the bond was deepening, despite all our mutual efforts to kill each other.

After I'd woken up, I'd stayed in the mercs' ship to keep as much distance between us as possible. Some people claimed a truebond could fade away, given enough time and space, although I feared it was already too late for such a simple solution between Vesper and myself. My parents' bond had certainly never faded, not the smallest bit, no matter how long or how far apart they'd been separated on their Arrow missions, and I'd watched my mother and father pine for each other whenever they were separated for more than a few days.

In a way, it had been amazing to see their love, to know such real, pure, intense emotion, concern, and caring could exist between two people. But in so many other ways, it had been deeply disturbing. A weakness, a vulnerability, and a risk I never wanted to take—especially not after my relationship with Francesca had ended so badly.

Once I'd engaged the pinpoint drive in the mercs' ship, it hadn't taken us long to reach Corios, and I'd docked both ships at my private spaceport late last night. Daichi had been waiting there, and I'd told him that I'd rescued Vesper from the Techwavers as part of my latest mission. Daichi had eyed me in obvious disbelief, but he hadn't asked any questions. He was a good chief of staff, and an even better friend, that way.

Daichi helped me load Vesper onto a hoverpallet and sneak her out of the spaceport. Once we'd reached Castle Caldaren, Daichi had gotten Vesper cleaned up, while I'd injected her with some much-needed fluids. I'd set out the water and protein bars, and then I'd left, putting some distance between us again.

But I'd known the second she woke up this morning. I could *feel* it—feel *her*—through the bond. Vesper hadn't been frightened, just wary, and more than a little curious. That lack of fear made me . . . Well, I wouldn't say *like* her, as I rarely liked anyone, but it further raised my estimation of her.

Now Vesper limped over, leaned down, and grabbed her sword off the floor. A groan escaped her lips, and I found myself staring at the lines of her body. I wondered if she would make the same sort of groan if I touched her, if I ran my fingers up the curve of her back to the nape of her neck . . .

I smashed that thought to pieces, as it could only hasten my downfall and destruction. Besides, any attraction I felt for her wasn't *real*. It was just another product of the bond, of our psionic powers and pheromones and body chemistries and whatever else was striving to make us come together.

I had never needed anyone to complement, much less complete me, and I didn't need Vesper Quill either. I would rather die than be bonded to someone for the rest of my life. Because a truebond was no life at all but rather a half-life you were forced to share with someone else, one that could be snuffed out at any moment.

Vesper straightened up and faced me again. Her weariness washed over me, along with the dull aches of the many bruises I'd inflicted on her while we'd been sparring. The unwanted sensations only made me angrier, and I struggled to contain my own emotions instead of mirroring hers.

That was the other problem with the bond. It made me feel too bloody *much*, when all I wanted was to drown myself in the coldness, the numbness, the darkness that had been part of me ever since I had killed my father in this very library. There was no sorrow in that deep, dark cavern of coldness, no regrets in that icy numbness, just clear, calm acceptance of what I had done—and all the things I would do to keep surviving.

Vesper looked past me, her gaze focusing on the wall beside the fireplace. She'd peered at that same spot more than a dozen times, almost as if she could see what had happened there. Maybe she could sense that was the spot where I'd shoved my sword into my father's heart, finally stopping the treacherous organ.

"Is there . . ." Her voice trailed off, and she wet her lips. "Is there a door behind that wall?"

"No. It's solid stone. Why do you ask?"

"I just thought there might be . . . a secret passageway. Maybe even a set of stairs that led down into the bottom of the castle."

I frowned. "What, in all the stars, would be in the bottom of my castle?"

"Nothing," she muttered. "Forget it."

Vesper raised her sword, and I smirked and crooked my finger. Her eyes narrowed at the mocking gesture, and she gave in to her anger and charged at me. I easily sidestepped her, but when I whirled back around, her sword whistled toward my chest, and I had to snap up my own weapon to block her attack.

Vesper blinked, clearly as surprised as I was that she had managed to engage me. A smile spread across her face, and the silver flecks in her blue eyes sparked with warmth. She really did have lovely eyes.

Someone cleared his throat. Vesper glanced over at Daichi, who was standing just inside the library doors, but my gaze remained on her.

Daichi cleared his throat again. "Lord Kyrion has been summoned by Callus Holloway, along with the rest of the Arrows. Holloway wants an in-person briefing about the latest battle with the Techwave."

I bit back a curse. The last thing I wanted right now was to see Holloway, but it couldn't be avoided. If I didn't go, Zane would take the opportunity to ingratiate himself even further with Holloway, not knowing what a dangerous, undesirable place that was to be. Arrogant fool. Sometimes I thought I should just give in and let Zane take over the Arrows the way he wanted to. Let someone else be the focus of Holloway's twisted attention for a while.

But I couldn't do that. I had thrown my lot in with Holloway long ago, and I had no choice but to keep the bastard happy or suffer the consequences. Besides, the monster in me had too much pride to give up a single scrap of power without a fight.

"Tell his staff I'm on my way."

Daichi tapped on his tablet, relaying the message. Vesper gave me a curious look, and those silver flecks in her eyes brightened again, even as her magic swirled around us. I wondered what, if anything, she was seeing with her power, but I didn't ask.

Somehow I knew I wouldn't like the answer.

I left Vesper in Daichi's reluctant care and returned to my chambers, where I dressed in one of my Arrow uniforms—a dark blue jacket over a matching shirt, cargo pants, and knee-high boots. I also threw my silver bandolier of supplies across my chest. My stormsword was hooked to my belt like usual, while my blaster was nestled in its thigh holster. I carried my helmet in the crook of my elbow, even though it had malfunctioned during the Techwave battle.

I used one of the castle's back exits, then hopped into a waiting transport. Many Regals preferred to swan about in open-air carriages, but Holloway expected those he summoned, especially me, to arrive in a timely manner.

My transport was cleared for flight within the city, and it rose above the castle, then zipped over the Boulevard and Promenade Park toward Crownpoint. The massive, sprawling structure quickly loomed larger and larger, the miles-high towers casting the transport in deep shadow, despite the late-morning sun.

While the transport sailed toward the palace, I pulled up all the reports from the Techwave battle on my tablet. I swiped through one document after another, skimming through Zane's and Julieta's accounts, as well as those of various Imperium officers. No one else mentioned the Techwavers' new weapon, but the consensus that the battle had been a draw, at best, made more tension gather in my shoulders. During their retreat off-planet, the Techwavers had also bombed and destroyed the metal refinery, so it would be days, maybe even weeks, before we learned exactly what tech, minerals, or other materials they'd stolen.

Given the heavy losses we'd suffered, Holloway would be looking for someone to blame, and he would most likely blame me, even though I had been a last-minute addition to the mission. I had been raiding a Techwave base on a nearby planet when I'd gotten the call to join Zane and Julieta.

I wondered what would have happened if I hadn't been on the Imperium ship. If I had never seen Vesper in the docking bay. If I had never approached her.

Would our paths still have crossed? Impossible to say, and I pushed all thoughts of her aside. I needed to be cold, calm, and detached when facing Holloway, lest he leech something off me that I didn't want him to know.

Then again, the bastard would probably do that anyway. He always had, ever since I was a boy. Even when he didn't home in on my thoughts and emotions, Holloway always found a few more screws to turn to hurt, humiliate, and manipulate me. He had trapped my parents with their truebond, and he had used it to trap me too, yet more reasons I was so determined to break my connection to Vesper.

Callus Holloway would *not* use me the way he had used my parents, no matter what I had to do to myself—or to Vesper—to prevent that from happening.

The transport flew through an open docking bay about half-way up one of the towers. The vehicle glided to a stop, and the door slid back. I shoved my tablet into my pocket and got out, still carrying my helmet in the crook of my elbow.

All around the docking bay, the other Arrows who were currently on-planet were climbing out of their own transports. They all had their uniforms on, their weapons of choice on their belts and thighs, and their helmets tucked under one arm. Everyone always associated death with the color black, but it was much better represented in the rainbow hues of the Arrows. Our uniforms might mirror the colors of our Houses, as well as the actual castles that lined the Boulevard, but each one of us was a ruthless killer, including myself.

Zane stalked by, wearing the ice blue of House Zimmer, and shot me a hot glare. I smirked back at him. Few things had amused me more than watching Vesper blasting his bag in the training ring earlier this morning.

"Don't mind him," Julieta chirped in a cheerful voice as she fell in step beside me. "He's just pissed your friend set his clothes on fire."

"Then maybe he shouldn't have insulted her," I replied. "And she's not my friend. Merely a consultant."

"Whatever you say."

Julieta shrugged, as though the matter was closed, and tugged down the sleeves of her jacket. She wasn't Regal-born, and she didn't belong to any House, so her uniform was the standard bloodred of an Imperium soldier. I'd told her long ago that she could wear any color she liked, but Julieta had refused, saying she looked good in red.

As we walked along, Julieta kept sneaking glances at me. Despite her lack of Regal title and House affiliation, she was still a strong seer. Even without her power, she was good at reading people, including me.

"Although I do find it strange that you disappeared in the middle of the Techwave battle, then reappeared here on Corios a day later with some weapons consultant no one's ever heard of," Julieta said.

Zane was too self-absorbed to remember Vesper from the Imperium cruiser, but I'd wondered if Julieta might recognize her, which was one reason I'd had Daichi bring Vesper to the training ring. But Julieta was acting as though she had never seen Vesper before this morning. Good. Still, if Julieta, Zane, or anyone else decided to dig into Vesper, all they would find was information on Vesper Quinlan, which was the fake identity I'd asked Daichi to create for her.

"I told you before, I got separated from you and Zane when the lava field started exploding. I hopped onto the first ship I came to and got off-planet, but my comms were fried. I returned to Corios as fast as I could."

"That still doesn't explain where the weapons consultant came from," she pointed out. "We're all curious about that."

"It's classified."

Julieta snorted. "That's just a polite way of saying you don't want to tell me."

She was right. I couldn't afford for her to realize the real reason I'd brought Vesper to Corios. Because if anyone—*anyone*—suspected that we were bonded, then both Vesper and I would be in even more danger from my supposed allies than we already were from her enemies.

Julieta and I reached an elevator. Zane was already inside, and he shot me another nasty look that I returned in kind.

"Boys, boys," Julieta chided. "Try to be civil in front of the big boss. He won't like his two favorite toy soldiers squabbling with each other."

She was right, but that didn't lessen my dislike of Zane, or his of me. Once upon a time, Zane Zimmer and I had been mirror images of each other, Regal heirs born to rich, powerful Houses with surprisingly loving families. As children, we'd always been rivals—in the academy, on the playground, and especially in all the schemes the Houses hatched against one another. That was just the nature of our Regal birthrights.

The difference between us now was that Zane still had all those things—his House, his loving family, and his exalted standing among the Regals as the hero of the Arrows. Whereas I was a House of one, or two, if you included Daichi. My family was dead, and I was the evil leader and clear-cut villain of the Arrows, more feared and despised than respected and admired.

Sometimes I didn't know whether I was angry at Zane for his constant scheming and insubordination or simply jealous that his life was still so perfectly golden, while mine was a black hole from which there was no escape.

The three of us rode in silence to the top level of the tower. The elevator floated to a stop, and the doors opened with a deceptively cheery *ping* that made me grind my teeth.

I headed forward, with Julieta and Zane walking beside me. All around us, more elevators opened, and the other Arrows filed out. I took the lead, as I always did, and we walked en masse down a wide corridor made of white marble. Our boots cracked against the stone, the echoes bouncing back and rippling into one low, ominous drumbeat. The air was thin this many miles up, so vents in the walls hissed out a steady stream of supplemental oxygen. Our footsteps and the circulating air combined to form an odd sort of white noise, but instead of soothing me, the innocent sounds made my gut twist with dread.

No matter how many times I made this walk, it never got

any easier. Or perhaps that was because I knew the gentle words and harsh judgments that were waiting at the end.

We reached two double doors that rose more than a hundred feet into the air. At our approach, six guards, three for each door, took hold of bronze rings and tugged the monstrosities open. More guards were stationed along the wall on either side of the doors. Their polymetal armor was the same bloodred as Julieta's uniform, and a large bronze-colored hand glimmered over each of their hearts.

The Arrows might be some of the best warriors in the galaxy, but these soldiers, the Bronze Hands, were just as dangerous. Perhaps even more so, since they were Holloway's personal protection detail and obeyed only him.

I wondered if any of them felt as trapped and suffocated as I did. Probably not. Holloway chose his guards for their absolute, unwavering loyalty, not for their brains and especially not for their feelings.

As I waited for the doors to finish moving, I tamped down my emotions and wrapped myself in the cloak of coldness that had shrouded my shoulders ever since the day my mother had died. Only when it was firmly locked in place did I stride forward.

The doors opened into a massive throne room that took up most of this level of the palace. Just like the corridor outside, the throne room was made of white marble, although thin seams of red shimmered here and there in the stone, like veins of blood running through pale skin. I'd never figured out if the red veins were a natural part of the marble or if the blood of all the enemies Holloway had executed in here had somehow seeped into the stone.

Either way, the effect made me uncomfortable. I always felt . . . *drained* after being in the throne room, as though the marble itself was leeching something vital out of me. Maybe it was. Anything was possible when dealing with Holloway.

More Bronze Hand guards stood at attention around the room, each one wearing bronze-colored mesh gloves and holding a long bronze spear with a glowing diamond-shaped tip. No stun blasters or shock batons here. The spears were designed to kill immediately, either with their actual, razor-sharp points or with the deadly amount of electricity they could emit. Callus Holloway had scores of enemies among the Regals, Techwavers, and Erztonians, and he was paranoid about his own safety. I counted myself as one of those enemies, even though I had been doing his bidding for the last twenty-five years.

Orange-red flames flickered inside round glass hoverglobes that gently bobbed up and down in midair like oversize fireflies. Thick pieces of gleaming copper had been twisted into grasping hands and other patterns and adorned the walls like abstract sculptures, while matching chandeliers dangled from the ceiling, looking like bulbous spiders about to drop down and skitter across the floor. Most folks probably would have thought the sculptures and chandeliers quite beautiful, but I knew their true purpose: to thwart any attempts to spy or eavesdrop. Copper was excellent at blocking electronic signals from cameras and listening devices.

I crossed the floor, my feet growing heavier with each step. I always felt this way whenever I approached Holloway, although I had never determined if it was the horrible things I'd done on his behalf weighing me down or his power trying to latch on to mine and then leech it away. As a siphon, someone who could draw energy from other people and objects and transform it into whatever they wanted, Callus Holloway was quite possibly the most powerful person in the Archipelago Galaxy, and his psionic abilities were one of the many things that had let him hold on to the Imperium throne for so long.

I was simply another deadly weapon in his arsenal.

At the back of the room, three wide, flat steps led up to an enormous dais with a throne also made of red-veined white marble. Spikes of stone jutted up from both arms, and the back of the throne was a mirror image of the Crownpoint towers. Another reminder of where I was and who controlled me.

The throne was empty. Holloway might have ordered us to arrive as quickly as possible, but he had no problem making us wait. Petty bastard.

I stopped a few feet away from the dais and went down on one knee. On either side of me, Julieta and Zane did the same thing, as did the other Arrows behind us. We all bowed our heads, and silence dropped over the throne room.

A minute later, a shadow appeared on the floor in front of me, oozing across the stone as silently as a cloud of smoke. The heaviness in my body intensified, as though a yoke was strung across my shoulders and I was struggling to rise against the massive weights that were hanging off it. Sometimes I thought those weights were the bodies of my mother and father, the specters that haunted me so, along with all the dark deeds I had performed for Holloway, things that he never, ever let me forget.

"Rise," a soft, silky voice commanded.

I rose to my feet, as did Julieta, Zane, and the other Arrows.

Lord Callus Holloway was now sitting on the throne. He was a few inches short of six feet, although his long, flowing red robe made him seem much taller, like a crimson-colored viper curled up on the cold stone throne. His wavy hair was a dark brown, shot through with only a few strands of silver, despite the fact he was in his mid-sixties. His skin was surprisingly tan, given that he rarely left the palace, and I had often wondered if he could soak up energy from the sun as easily as he could from the people and objects around him. In contrast, his eyes were a rich, glimmering bronze that was the same color as the spears his Bronze Hand guards wielded with such brutal, deadly efficiency.

"Mission report," Holloway said.

I stepped forward, along with Julieta and Zane, and we recapped what had happened on the Magma planet—more or less, since I left out everything having to do with Vesper. We finished, and silence descended over the throne room again.

"I have reviewed your reports, along with the footage," Holloway said, his voice deceptively pleasant. "This latest battle ended in yet another stalemate, just as the last several skirmishes have. Such failures embolden the Techwavers. They grow more brazen in their destruction of Regal facilities, as well as their propaganda about their supposed desire to bring *change* to the galaxy."

He spat out the word *change* as though it was a bitter poison in his mouth. No doubt, it was. Holloway had been in power for more than thirty years, and with his siphon abilities, he could easily squat there for another thirty years—or longer.

Sometimes I wished the Techwave would succeed in toppling the Imperium, if only to knock the bastard down off his precious throne. But the Techwavers weren't any better than Holloway, especially when it came to their horrific experiments melding men and machines. They craved power just as much as Holloway did, and their methods to obtain it were just as brutal.

Then again, most people would say the same thing about me.

Holloway snapped his fingers. Servants dressed in light gray uniforms carried a large holoscreen table into the room and set it down in front of the dais.

"Take your positions," Holloway ordered.

I moved forward, as did the other Arrows, and we all gathered around the table. Julieta, Zane, and I each placed our helmets down on our assigned spots, and the audio and video footage automatically started downloading. An unnecessary, repetitive activity, since our helmets had fed the same things in real time out to both the Imperium general manning the cruiser and Holloway, safely tucked away here in Crownpoint. But this exercise was yet another reminder that he was the ruler of the galaxy, including us.

Holloway got to his feet, glided down the dais steps, and stood between Zane and me. Zane smirked at me, thinking that being by Holloway's side was a place of honor. Fool. It was nothing but a sly, clever trap, just like everything else Holloway did.

Holloway waved his hand, and several displays popped up and hovered over the table, showing different aspects of the battle, from the aerial attacks to the ground assault to all the Techwavers that Zane, Julieta, and I had killed. Normally, the audio and video would have been crystal-clear, but the smoke and heat from the volcanic activity had scrambled everything. The footage showed little more than a foggy haze lit up by blaster and cannon fire, while most of the audio was loud crackles of static.

Relief washed through me. I'd checked the footage from my own helmet earlier, and I was glad neither Zane nor Julieta had caught Vesper dragging me across the lava field. That would have prompted Holloway to ask all sorts of questions I didn't want to answer.

For the next two hours, we reviewed the footage, as well as everything that had happened before, during, and after the battle. I also spun my story about how I'd been separated from the other two Arrows, made my way to the downed blitzer, and used it to escape.

Holloway stared at me, his bronze eyes sharp and searching, but I kept my voice steady and even, and I didn't say anything that was technically a lie, not even the smallest embellishment. Perhaps it was some flicker of deceit he could sense through his siphon power, but Holloway had an uncanny ability to tell when someone was lying, and I'd learned long ago to only say things that were true in his presence.

I finished speaking, and then Zane recounted how he and Julieta had also been separated.

"Although *we* managed to send the Techies running before the lava field exploded," he said, shooting me a smug look. "And *we* made it back to the Imperium ship in plenty of time to escape."

I ignored his pointed insults, even as I made a mental note to check Zane's story against the audio and video footage and figure out exactly where he had been during the battle. Julieta too.

"Well, Kyrion was injured," Julieta piped up, rising to my defense the way she so often did. "I saw the blast from the weapon myself."

"What weapon?" Holloway asked in a sharp voice.

"The Techwavers had some sort of new hand cannon," I replied.

I described the intense green glow, as well as the blast of power cutting right through my psionic shield, along with my body. I also described how the weapon had set off a chain reaction that had triggered the lava eruption. The only thing I didn't mention was my suspicion that Zane had taken the cannon from a dead Techwaver and tried to kill me with it. Once I had confirmation, I would handle the matter myself—permanently.

When I finished, silence dropped over the throne room again, and the only sound was the steady tapping of Holloway's index finger on the holoscreen. The motion made the images flicker over and over again.

"Do you think the weapon was powered by lunarium?" he asked.

Lunarium was a rare mineral that had only been found on a handful of planets and moons, although Holloway was always sending out expeditions to search for more of it, as were the Techwavers and the Erztonians. For the last several months, we had been chasing the Techwavers from one planet to another, all of which were rumored to be rich in lunarium deposits, although so far, we hadn't discovered any signs of it.

My hand dropped to my stormsword, which had a lunarium blade. "There's no way to tell," I replied, answering Holloway's question. "I didn't get a clear look at the weapon or who fired it."

Holloway's lips puckered in disappointment. Despite his own considerable psion power and the millions of soldiers and servants at his command, he would still do anything to get more lunarium. I wasn't quite sure why. He probably wanted to turn it into a weapon, just like the Techwave did. Then again, Holloway was always chasing *more*—more lunarium, more weapons, more artifacts and other treasures that famous spelltechs had made centuries ago and supposedly hidden away on distant planets. Holloway didn't care what the object was, where it was located, or how hard it was to obtain, as long as he got his hands on it and it increased his own power.

"I want a full report on this new weapon," Holloway ordered. "If the Techwavers have concocted some device that can blast through psionic shields, then we need to figure out exactly what it is and how to counteract it."

"Maybe Kyrion's new weapons consultant can help with that," Zane piped up in a snide voice.

Holloway's gaze landed on me like an anvil. "What new consultant?"

"Someone I picked up on my way home. She's supposed to be quite talented at figuring things out. After getting blasted by the Techwavers' weapon, I thought it wise to call in an expert."

Holloway nodded, although a sly, speculative gleam filled his eyes. "Yes, of course."

Talk turned back to the Techwavers and what Regal facilities we thought they might target next. But no one had any actionable intelligence, and Holloway dismissed us.

Servants rushed forward to remove the holoscreen table,

and the other Arrows drifted away to follow up on their own leads. Holloway crooked his finger at me.

"Walk with me, Kyrion." His voice might have oozed gentle suggestion, but a clear command rippled through his words.

Zane shot me a jealous look, while Julieta gave me an encouraging nod. Holloway waited for them to leave before striding around behind the dais. I grabbed my helmet off the table and followed him.

Holloway waved his hand over a scanner, and a metal door embedded in the back of the dais opened. He stepped inside the elevator, then crooked his finger at me again. I moved forward.

"Garden level," he barked out.

The elevator chimed and then descended. The first sudden, jolting drop made my stomach whoosh up into my throat. The motion always reminded me of the first time I'd ridden in this elevator—the night I'd killed my father.

Back then, House Caldaren had been among the most powerful Regal families. Until a servant had walked into the library and found me standing over my father, my bloody stormsword clutched in my hand and him dead on the floor. She'd run away screaming and had alerted the rest of the staff. Several Imperium soldiers had been summoned, along with a few Arrows, and I had been dragged in front of Holloway and the rest of the Regals.

I'd expected to be executed for killing my father, and part of me had felt relieved at the prospect. At least then there would be no more tears or pleading or wondering why Chauncey couldn't rouse himself out of his grief to do all the things that needed to be done to save our House—and especially why he couldn't even summon up the energy to be a father to me.

Even back then, I'd realized I was being petty and selfish. My parents had loved each other, and my father had been drowning in his grief, so much so that he hadn't seen how much I was hurting too, how much I missed my mother, and how much I needed him. But even today, part of me was still pissed at my father and especially at the truebond—or, rather, the loss of it—that had warped him so and set me onto this dark, dangerous path.

The elevator's chime interrupted my thoughts. The door slid back, and Holloway strode forward. I swallowed the anger and bitterness in my throat and followed him.

At this level, a conservatory covered with a glass dome bulged out from the rest of the palace like an enormous eye. Green solar seams ribboning through the glass captured the sun's energy and used that power to run the sprinkler system. The cool, misting sprays of water ensured that the flowers, trees, and other plants didn't bake like bugs trapped under a massive magnifying glass.

Holloway strolled along one of the paths. The Crownpoint gardens were open to the public, and people bowed and curtsied as he walked by. Holloway smiled and waved at the more important Regals, playing the part of the kind, benevolent ruler. He'd done it for so long that even I would have believed the illusion if I didn't know better.

We reached a pond in the middle of the gardens, and Holloway set off on the path that curved around the clear, aquamarine water.

"Tell me about this weapons consultant," he said. "You didn't pick her up on your way back to Corios."

"No," I replied, choosing my words carefully. "She was on the Magma battlefield."

"Was she working for the Techwavers?" Holloway asked, a sour note creeping into his voice.

"No. She was trying to escape them."

It was the truth, more or less. I wondered if he realized just how much I was parsing my words, but he nodded, telling me to continue.

I explained how I'd been hit by the mysterious Techwave

weapon and how Vesper had helped me reach the Imperium blitzer so that we could escape from the lava field. I also mentioned the mercenaries who had tracked her down afterward, although I didn't reveal that they had worked for Rowena Kent. Instead, I painted them as Techwavers who were eager to recover their prisoner. I kept strictly to the facts, although I left many things deliberately vague. I also kept my sentences short and to the point, not wanting to give Holloway any chance to find a crack and pry more information out of me. The less he knew about Vesper, the better off she and I would both be.

"Do you think she helped the Techwave build the new weapon?" Holloway asked.

"I don't know," I replied, still choosing my words carefully. "I brought her to Corios and offered her shelter and refuge so I can figure out exactly why the Techwavers wanted her back so badly."

"Very well. Keep me informed." Holloway stopped and speared me with a hard look. "But if she won't talk willingly, use whatever methods you like to ensure she does. I want to *crush* these bastards before they become any more of a threat. Every facility they attack is a reflection on me, and some Regals are starting to grumble about my leadership. As if any of those idiots would do any better."

He let out a loud, derisive snort, but a thin thread of worry snaked through his words. We'd both heard the rumors that some of the stupider Regals were thinking about assassinating him and trying to claim the Imperium throne for themselves. Fools. Holloway would *never* let that happen, and he would kill every Regal who opposed him, along with every single family member, servant, and worker associated with their House, including the children.

"Of course," I replied. "I'll start questioning her as soon as I return to Castle Caldaren. She'll tell me everything she knows."

Holloway nodded again, and we continued our walk. Out in the pond, two mammoth butterflies flitted back and forth over the water. The creatures were among the largest known butterflies in the galaxy, wider than my arm was long. Big, but fragile, like so many things in the Imperium. Their wings were a shiny, iridescent black, although each one featured dark blue spots that reminded me of the jeweled eyes in Vesper's dream world.

"It is time for you to marry," Holloway said without any preamble or warning as we watched the two creatures perform their mating dance. "Several of the palace seers agree with me."

In addition to his Bronze Hand guards, Holloway also had his own private group of seers, who were tasked with only one mission: having visions of the future that kept him on the throne. A fresh dagger of dread twisted in my gut. If the seers had told Holloway such a thing, then one of them must have sensed the bond forming between Vesper and me, which was even more reason to break it as quickly as possible.

"I hardly think now is the appropriate time to take a spouse," I replied, striving to keep the anger out of my voice. "Especially with the Techwave bombing Regal facilities and killing Imperium soldiers right and left."

Holloway waved his hand, dismissing my concerns. "The Techwavers are a minor annoyance, nothing more. You and the rest of the Arrows will deal with them just as you've dealt with all my enemies over the years. I am much more concerned about *you*, my boy."

My fingers clenched around the edge of my helmet so hard that the polyplastic creaked in protest. Somehow I resisted the urge to smash it into his face. *My boy* had been my parents' endearment. After I'd killed my father, Holloway had slyly used the term to convince me that he truly cared about me and that I had no choice but to join him.

"After all, you're almost forty," he continued. "It's time for you to continue the Caldaren family line."

Eagerness colored his voice, and that speculative gleam filled his eyes again. Holloway had been pressuring me to marry for the last five years, but he had become much more insistent over the past few months. My producing an heir to House Caldaren was extremely important to Holloway, since he could further control and manipulate me through my child.

Despite all the years I'd worked for him, Holloway had never tried to siphon off the smallest bit of my psion power, but only because he had a far grander prize in mind—the fervent hope that I would form a truebond with someone, and he could leech magic from two people instead of just one.

Just as he had done to my parents.

But he wouldn't be content with that. Not for long. Eventually, Holloway would take my power the same way he had taken my mother's magic—and he would kill me just as he had killed her.

Rage rose inside me, like a roaring monster demanding to be unleashed, but I pushed it down and smothered it with all the cold detachment I could muster. "You know how difficult it has been with the Regals. No one wants to marry their daughter to a man who murdered his own father."

"Bah!" Holloway waved his hand again. "That is ancient history, a childish mistake, and everyone knows it. Besides, you have far too much psion power and far too vast a fortune for every Regal to turn their nose up at you."

Unfortunately, he was right. As the years had gone by, the horror of what I'd done had faded from some people's minds, and more than one Regal parent had shoved their daughters at me, sons too, saying what a wonderful conversationalist they were or how well they played the pianotronic or some other nonsense. As if I cared about such things. Then again, all the other Regals truly cared about was getting their hands on

Castle Caldaren and my fortune. Why, I would be lucky to find a wife who wouldn't poison me the first chance she got.

"As you have been so busy fighting the Techwave recently, I have made inquiries on your behalf, as any good, concerned godfather would," Holloway continued in that deceptively benign voice.

More rage threatened to crack through my cold façade. Holloway had appointed himself as my guardian after I'd killed my father. All the better to keep me close and convince me that I needed his protection. I had been such a bloody fool back then.

"Who has responded to your inquiries?" I replied in a bland tone.

"The Colliers," he replied. "One of the ruling families of the Erzton. Lady Asterin Armas, the stepdaughter of Lord Aldrich Collier, is quite beautiful from the holograms I've seen. Plus, she is in excellent health, and the palace seers say she should easily produce multiple heirs."

I had never met Asterin Armas, but a bit of sympathy for her flickered through me. So much of Imperium business was transactional, especially when dealing with the Erzton and all the planets and minerals the rival group controlled.

"You wouldn't care if Lady Asterin had a hunched back and warts all over her body," I replied in a flat voice. "What's the real reason you're so interested in her?"

Holloway let out a hearty chuckle, as though I had caught him with his hand in a jar of sweets, and not maneuvering me around like a bloody pawn on his game board.

"Lady Asterin controls the mineral rights to Frozon 3," he replied. "And she has recently opened a new mining facility there."

Frozon 3 was one of the few moons known to have large deposits of lunarium. Holloway was selling me to the highest bidder, and that bidder just happened to have the rare resource he wanted.

199 ONLY BAD OPTIONS

"What do Asterin Armas and the Colliers get in return?" I asked.

"Over the past year, the Techwave has targeted several Erzton mining facilities, killed their workers, stolen their tech, minerals, and equipment, all the usual annoyances. Verona Collier, Asterin's mother, has proposed a joint task force between the Erzton and the Imperium to eliminate the Techwave once and for all. I suggested that a marriage between an Erzton family and a Regal one would further strengthen such an alliance."

I held back my snort of derision. Verona Collier might think she was marrying off her daughter to defeat the Techwavers, but whatever peace the Erztonians gained would be short-lived. No doubt, Holloway was already planning to turn the lunarium on Frozon 3 into weapons he could use against both the Techwave *and* the Erzton.

A sly, sinister smile spread across his face. "Asterin's mother and stepfather have a truebond, and the seers have high hopes that you two will form one as well."

Equal amounts of rage and dread rushed through me. Not only had Holloway found someone to give him more lunarium, but he'd also discovered a woman whose family had a history of truebonds. Even though both my parents had been Arrows, Holloway had always kept one of them by his side, even as he had sent the other into battle. He would do the same thing to me and Asterin, along with whatever children we might have.

I was nothing more than a fucking *battery*, a force to fuel the engine of Holloway's reign, something that made me sick to my bones.

I'd thought about killing the bastard so many times, but I could never figure out a way to actually *do it*, much less survive afterward. Given his seers, Holloway would most likely be tipped off to any assassination attempt I might make. Then either his Bronze Hand guards would cut me down or, worse, they would capture me, and I would end up in one of the palace labs, to be experimented on, dissected, and discarded when my psion power, my strength, and my mind were broken and exhausted.

Holloway clapped me on the shoulder, his touch burning like a red-hot brand through my jacket. "I've made all the arrangements. Lady Asterin is already on Corios, and the two of you will be introduced during the spring ball. After that, well, perhaps nature will take its course, and we'll have an engagement *and* a truebond to announce to the gossipcasts."

He winked at me. As much as I wanted to grab my sword and ram it through his eye, I nodded back at him.

Despite Holloway's manipulations, no truebond would ever form between Asterin and me, not as long as Vesper was alive. Which was even more reason to keep her as far away from Holloway as possible. If he were even to *suspect* the two of us were bonded, however tenuously, he would use Vesper to try to control me. I might be a monster, might be a killer, might be a villain through and through, but I would never subject anyone to the same cruel fate my mother had suffered.

"Come," Holloway said, taking my silence as acceptance of his scheme. "I have a few more matters to discuss regarding the Techwave."

As we continued around the pond, I reviewed my choices, such as they were. Marry someone I would never bond with, or remain bonded to a woman who wanted nothing to do with me.

Vesper was right.

There were only bad options.

FIFTEEN

VESPER

I spent the rest of the afternoon working in the office with Daichi watching my every move. Every time I hit a key or swiped through a screen on my tablet, he eyed me with open suspicion, as though I was up to no good.

He was right about that.

Instead of figuring out what kind of weapon the would-be assassin had used on Kyrion, I called up all the information I could find about his castle. I wasn't nearly as good at hacking as I was at fixing things, so I couldn't get past any of the internal House Caldaren firewalls, which were quite impressive given that only Daichi and a few other people worked here. But since Daichi had entered me into the system, I was still able to access the castle's security feeds.

I made a mental map of the structure in my mind, including all the entrances and exits. It seemed like a prudent thing to do, given all the mysterious enemies Kyrion kept mentioning. I didn't want to be trapped like a rat in a maze if someone decided to hurt me in order to get to him or if Rowena Kent sent more mercenaries to kill me. I also searched for any secret doors or staircases that led downward, but I didn't find any.

When that was done, I called up some gossipcasts that covered Temperate 42, but none of them mentioned anything unusual or noteworthy going on at Kent Corp. Of course not. I was just a lowly lab rat, and no one would even notice I was missing, except for Tivona. My friend had to be worried sick, but it was far too risky to contact her. Given that Hal and the other mercenaries hadn't returned, Rowena Kent had to realize I was most likely still alive.

I changed my search parameters and pulled up info on the Kents, who were featured in several gossipcasts related to their new line of space cruisers. The stories included the usual House and corporate bullshit about how excited Rowena and Sabine were about the ships, how many improvements had been made to the pinpoint drive technology, how the vessels were so much faster and more maneuverable than the previous models, and blah, blah, blah, blah.

The latest story mentioned that the Kents were to officially launch the new cruiser line here on Corios. A ceremony was scheduled to take place during the upcoming spring ball, with some of the ships on display so that Callus Holloway and the other Regals could tour them.

I rocked back in my chair, making it squeak in protest, which earned me another suspicious look from Daichi. There was no way the Kents had had time to fix the faulty navigation sensors, but they were proceeding as though nothing was wrong and their fancy new spaceships weren't death traps just waiting to plummet from the sky and kill hundreds of thousands of people. Curious and alarming.

Since I hadn't found any new public information, I pulled up the Kent Corp website and clicked on the employee login section. I hesitated, wondering if I should risk accessing the system, but Kyrion wanted answers, and I doubted he would accept any more silence from me when he returned from his meeting with Callus Holloway. So I used another one of the fake employee logins I had created, making sure to mask my location through a virtual private network, then accessed the system.

Despite my fake credentials, all the pages and databases popped up as normal, and I scrolled and clicked through dozens of documents, taking a circuitous route to get to what I really wanted—the *Velorum* crash files.

I skimmed through one document after another. They were all the same as before, with one notable exception. My name, work, experiments, reports, and conclusions had been scrubbed from every single document. A sinking sensation flooded my stomach, but I kept clicking, scrolling, and reading.

I had been totally excised from the *Velorum* files, and there was no record of my ever having worked at Kent Corp. I was a faulty part, and an invisible hand had plucked all the tiny pieces of me out of the system so that the Kent machine could run smoothly again. No, it was worse than that. It was like I had never even *existed*.

Anger flared in my chest, and my fingers itched with the urge to smash the tablet against the desk, to break something, just like the Kents had broken me. Instead, I forced myself to take deep breaths and keep looking through the information.

Rowena's and Sabine's names were on all the files, and they had both certified that the *Velorum* crash had been due to pilot error. Conrad's name also appeared on the documents but in a much more minor capacity—

Beep. Beep-beep. Beep.

My heart leaped into my throat, and the tablet slipped through my fingers and clattered onto the workstation. Had the Kents realized I'd used a back door to access their system? Were they tracking my location even now, despite the precautions I'd taken?

"Stupid machine!" Daichi growled, and slapped his hand on top of the brewmaker on a table in the corner.

The machine burped out a loud, plaintive beep at the abuse. Daichi glared at it, and his hand twitched, as though he was thinking about slapping it again. A relieved breath hissed out between my teeth.

I logged out of the Kent Corp site and called up one of the gossipcasts I had been watching earlier to hide what I'd been doing. Then I got to my feet and went over to him. "I can take a look at the brewmaker if you like."

Daichi glared at the machine again. "What can you do? I've had three House Kent repair techs come look at this thing, and it just keeps malfunctioning—and burning my honey-ginseng green tea. I didn't even *know* you could burn tea, but somehow this piece of junk excels at it."

My nose twitched at the faint, acrid stench in the air. "I'm good at fixing things. Trust me."

He gave me another suspicious look, but he stepped aside. The brewmaker was the same model Tivona had in our apartment, the same one I'd helped Conrad design, so it was child's play for me to pop off the top, tweak the settings and sensors inside, and put it back together.

I gestured at Daichi. "Try it again."

He hit a couple of buttons, and the machine whirred to life. Within seconds, he was holding a cup of steaming tea.

Daichi took a sip of his tea and hummed in appreciation. "You fixed it."

"Oh, Vesper is good at fixing all sorts of things," a familiar voice drawled behind me.

Kyrion entered the office. Daichi dipped his head to the other man, but I remained straight, tall, and stubborn. Despite my current situation, Kyrion Caldaren was *not* my lord and commander. Amusement flickered across his face at my petty defiance, but he nodded back at Daichi.

"Vesper and I have some things to discuss," Kyrion said. "Please leave us."

Daichi nodded, then grabbed his tea and tablet and left the office, shutting the door behind him.

Kyrion leaned his right hip against my workstation and crossed his arms over his chest. His pose was confident, but his shoulders were high and tight, and the sticky cobweb of him in my mind pulsed with a combination of anger, frustration, and weariness.

"I assume by now you've accessed the Kent Corp mainframe," he said.

"How do you know that?"

"It's what I would have done. Besides, they're the ones who tried to kill you."

I arched an eyebrow at him.

"They're the ones who tried to kill you first," he corrected. "I'm guessing you are much more interested in exacting your revenge on the Kents than in helping me figure out the Techwave's new weapon. So what did you discover?"

I hesitated, wondering how much I should reveal, but we had made a deal, and I intended to honor my part of it. All I could do was hope he would do the same.

"Nothing," I muttered. "I didn't discover anything in the Kent Corp mainframe, because there's nothing *to* discover. They wiped all my notes, work, and research from the system and all my personnel records from the employee files. It's like I never even existed, much less worked at Kent Corp for the last five years."

Kyrion nodded. "Standard operating procedure among all the Regal Houses. If you can't fully eliminate a problem, then destroy as much of the evidence as possible. What about the *Velorum* crash? Are you finally going to tell me what caused it?"

I hesitated again, but I couldn't go any further on my own,

and Kyrion Caldaren had resources I didn't—wealth, influence, contacts, access. I might have been planning to sell the crash information, but I didn't want innocent people to die because I'd withheld it.

"There's a design flaw, a safety hazard, in the new line of Kent ships. That's why the *Velorum* crashed, not because of pilot error."

Surprise filled his face. "What kind of safety hazard?"

A whiteboard was standing in the corner, so I dragged it over and plucked the blue gelpen off the shelf at the bottom. I explained what I'd found during the crash investigation and sketched out one of the new Kent cruisers, using an X to mark the spot where the faulty navigation sensor was located.

"See? The navigation sensor is right under the observation deck windows. Normally, those sensors are housed in a protective casing, and their tolerance for heat and light is much higher than the one on the *Velorum*. I don't know why the Kents manufactured these sensors to be so different and made their settings so much weaker."

Kyrion tilted his head to the side and studied my drawing. "Maybe it's not a flaw. Maybe the ship was deliberately designed that way."

"What do you mean?" I asked.

"The Kents are set to deliver fighter ships to the Imperium just as the Techwave has created a new weapon. You saw what that green energy blast did to me and the lava field. A weapon like that could potentially bring down each one of these new military cruisers and all the Imperium soldiers on board."

The new cruiser line was your idea, your design, and you were so bloody pleased *with your own brilliance you didn't even consider that someone else might notice the modifications.* Rowena Kent's voice growled in my mind. *Arrogant fool. Your carelessness could have set our plans back years, if not scuttled them altogether.*

She'd said that in the conference room, right before Hal had attacked me. Her words, combined with Kyrion's, added up to one sinister conclusion.

"You think the Kents are secretly working with the Techwavers."

Kyrion nodded again. "It makes sense. Rowena Kent and Callus Holloway have been bitter enemies for years. She only got the contract for the new ships because her bid was so much lower than everyone else's. Even then, Holloway didn't want to give it to her, but the other Regals approved the deal, so he had no choice. Rowena deliberately sabotaging the ships would be one way to thumb her nose at Holloway and severely weaken his grasp on the Imperium throne."

His words clicked like a key unlocking a door in my mind. An image suddenly flickered in the air beside Kyrion—one of *another* Kyrion.

I blinked, wondering if I was seeing double for some reason. In a way, I was. Because the original Kyrion remained leaning against the workstation, his arms still crossed over his chest, while the second Kyrion stood on the observation deck of a cruiser, beating his fists against the windows as the ship plummeted toward the ground.

"Vesper?" Kyrion's deep voice cut through my vision. "What are you seeing?"

I shook my head, and the second Kyrion vanished, along with the doomed ship. "How do you know I saw anything?"

"The silver flecks in your eyes glow when you're using your seer magic. Plus, I can bloody *feel* your power, like a bowstring drawing tight in my chest and about to release an arrow."

He grimaced and rubbed his chest, right over his heart, as though the psionic echoes of my magic physically pained him. For some strange reason, his expression made me want to reach out and comfort him, but I squashed the notion.

"Remember that image we saw in my mindscape? The one of you dying in a spaceship crash?"

"Yes. So what?"

"So that's what I saw just now." I started pacing back and forth in front of the whiteboard. "Maybe . . . maybe you're right about my seer magic being stronger than I realized. And maybe my vision wasn't about the death I wished for you. Maybe it was about your *actual* death. Or at least the *possibility* of your death."

Kyrion huffed. "I am much too dangerous to die in a common ship crash."

I rolled my eyes. "Your unmitigated arrogance truly knows no bounds."

At my snarky words, a grin spread across his face, softening his sharp features and warming his eyes. In an instant, he went from a stone-cold killer to someone much more approachable—and attractive.

I spun away from him and gestured at the whiteboard again. "So the Kents roll out their new ships, and everything is fine, until the next time the Techwave attacks. Then you and your fellow Arrows would most likely be deployed on the new ships, right?"

He nodded. "We would be spread out on various missions across the galaxy, like usual, but yes. The plan is for some of the Arrows to take the new military cruisers and hunt down the Techwavers before they attack another Regal facility, as well as find and destroy their home base. Right now, the base's location remains a mystery, as do the identities of much of the upper Techwave leadership."

"But if the Techwavers were *waiting* for you on the ground like they were on Magma 7, they could fire their new cannons at the faulty navigation sensors, crash your ships, and kill off any survivors, Imperium soldiers and Arrows alike."

As soon as I said the words, as soon as I gave voice to the

thought, I could *see* it all playing out in the air in front of me, as though I was watching an action movie on a holoscreen. Kyrion standing on the observation deck of a cruiser, a legion of Techwavers firing cannons at the vessel, the sensor overheating, and the ship plummeting in a deadly dive. The thunderous roar of the crash boomed in my ears, the aftershock jolted my body, and the acrid smell of cannon fire and charred flesh flooded my nose.

I shook my head again, and the images vanished, along with the phantom noise, vibration, and stench. "What would happen if you and some of the other Arrows were killed?"

Kyrion shrugged. "It would be a serious blow to Holloway and would probably shake the other Regals' confidence in his rule, but he still has the Bronze Hands, his own personal guards, to defend him. Rowena Kent wouldn't be able to wrest the throne away from him or even kill him."

"But it would definitely hurt Holloway, help Rowena, and embolden the Techwave."

He nodded. "Yes."

I started pacing again, thinking back over everything that had happened. All the time I'd spent at the *Velorum* crash site, all the experiments I'd conducted, all the reports I'd filed. This whole time, I'd thought I was just doing my job, pointing out a mistake, a flaw, an error, when I had really been threatening a massive conspiracy that had been years in the making. No wonder Rowena Kent had been so determined to get rid of me.

"The *Velorum* crash wasn't an accident," I said. "It was a *test run*, a proof of concept to whomever Rowena is working with inside the Techwave."

Kyrion nodded again. "I think you're right."

"I know I'm right." My seer magic was screaming it at me. I stopped pacing and raked a hand through my hair. "I went to the *Velorum* crash site, along with everyone else in the R&D department at Kent Corp. We got there about three hours after the ship went down. I had seen the aftermath of other crashes on gossipcasts, but witnessing it in person . . . The sheer size of it. The twisted, crumpled metal. The stench of polyplastic and other materials burning in the air. The hands and feet and other body parts sticking up out of the rubble. And the people crying and screaming, not just those who were injured but the folks who had rushed to the crash site, not knowing if their loved ones were alive or dead and buried in the debris . . ."

I remembered my own sick doubt, after I had seen the passenger manifest and realized I too had known someone who'd been on the ship, even though I hadn't seen her in years. Next had come the dwindling hope that she was still alive and then the cold confirmation that she was dead, along with all the other passengers. My grief had been a shallow slice compared to others' deep heartache, but it had still been a terrible way to lose someone, especially since the crash had been deliberate sabotage instead of a tragic accident.

I swallowed the hard knot of emotion clogging my throat. "If there's a door in my mindscape that leads to that memory, I *never* want to open it."

"Was it worse than the lava field battle?" Kyrion asked.

"Yes, because the conscripts and soldiers at least knew what was happening, what was going on, and why they were there. The people on the *Velorum* had no idea they were in danger, that they were test subjects for Rowena Kent."

"Just like you had no idea Rowena Kent was going to ignore your conclusions, delete your work, and conscript you onto an Imperium ship," Kyrion pointed out in a soft voice.

I flinched at the reminder. More anger surged through me, and I kicked the bottom of the whiteboard, which slid back a few feet. The action wasn't nearly as satisfying as I'd hoped.

"So now what?" I asked. "You tell Callus Holloway what we suspect?"

"No."

"*No?* Why not?"

His lips puckered, as though he had bitten into something rotten. "Holloway doesn't care about accusations, only proof. Especially when it involves one of the richest and most powerful Regal families like the Kents."

I threw my arms out wide. "Aren't I proof enough?"

He arched an eyebrow. "Do you really want to go before Holloway and tell your story?"

My arms plummeted to my sides.

"I didn't think so," Kyrion replied. "Besides, it would be your word against Rowena Kent's, and she could easily paint you as a disgruntled employee and spin the whole thing as a revenge plot on your part. Or worse, she could claim the faulty sensors were *your* idea and that *you* have been secretly working with the Techwavers. Holloway despises the Techwave, and he would not treat you kindly. You would be lucky to be executed immediately."

Another shudder rippled through my body, along with more than a little fresh anger. "Regals and their stupid games."

Kyrion didn't respond. I wondered how many Regal games he had been involved in and how badly he had been hurt by them, but I didn't ask. I doubted he would tell me, and I didn't want to start thinking of him as anything more than a conven-ient, temporary ally. I didn't want to . . . *feel* anything for him and inadvertently deepen the bond between us.

I started pacing yet again, thinking about where we might get some proof. My gaze fell to my tablet, which was still silently playing the gossipcast about the upcoming ship launch. "Some of the Kent cruisers will be on display during the spring ball, right? Here on Corios?"

"Yes. So what?"

"So that's how we get our proof. All we have to do is sneak on board one of the ships and access the mainframe."

"How will that help?" Kyrion asked.

"We should be able to download the programming that tells the navigation sensor to overheat and sends the ship into a steep dive."

"And if we can't?"

I shrugged. "Then I'll take you up on that offer of a new life and let you deal with the Kents. Either way, I will have done my best to stop them, and my conscience will be clear."

I doubted that, given how the memories of the *Velorum* crash site already haunted me, but I didn't mention that to Kyrion. I imagined he had more than his fair share of haunting memories too.

I wondered if I would be another one of those ghosts when our uneasy partnership came to its inevitable end.

SIXTEEN

VESPER

Despite my wariness about, well, everything, the next few days passed without incident.

During the mornings, I stayed inside the castle, mostly in Daichi's office. I kept scouring the Kent Corp mainframe for information about the potential ship sabotage, but I didn't find so much as a stray memo about Rowena Kent's plan. I also reviewed all the footage from the Magma 7 battle, and I did my best to sketch the hand cannon the Techwaver—or whoever it had been—had fired at Kyrion.

Given the limited angles and grainy, foggy footage, I didn't have the design quite right, but based on the simulations I ran, the cannon, and any like it, had more than enough power to bring down any Kent spaceship equipped with the faulty sensor. But perhaps the strangest thing was that the cannon's design seemed very familiar, as though I had seen it somewhere other than on the Magma battlefield.

At lunchtime, I put on a cloak, threw the hood up to hide my features, and explored the city of Corios. All the surrounding streets and buildings were as bright, whimsical, and colorful as the ones on the Boulevard, while the shops sold the finest goods I had ever seen: furniture crafted from real wood, stone, and glass; clothing made of soft, supple silk, cashmere, and leather; jewelry set with gemstones, crystals, and rare minerals that sparkled more brightly than the twin blue moons and stars in the night sky.

Corios was the most beautiful and lavish place I had ever been. For the first time, I could understand why my mother had been so desperate to return here. I'd had a good, comfortable life on Temperate 42, but everything there seemed dull, dim, and drab compared to Corios.

And the food, oh, the food was *amazing*. Everything was fresh, organic, and utterly delightful, whether it was sugar-crusted strawberries served with vanilla-bean whipped cream or blueberry scones dripping with honey-lemon syrup or any of the other dozens of delectable treats I tried on my walkabouts. The first half of the Kent Corp whistleblower payment from the gossipcast was still in my anonymous account, and I enjoyed every single delicious, high-priced bite it bought me.

And for the first time, I could appreciate why Tivona had been so addicted to the gossipcasts. Not only was who courting whom interesting fodder for the rumor mill, but it also revealed so much about the constant jockeying for power between the Regal Houses. Daichi and I often watched the gossipcasts in his office, me for entertainment and him for taking copious notes about how various couples' burgeoning—or disintegrating—relationships might affect Kyrion, the Arrows, and Holloway's grip on the Imperium throne.

Despite his prickly demeanor, I quickly grew to like Daichi, who was serious, professional, and exceptionally good at his job. Being chief of staff and running a House, even one with a skeleton staff, was no small feat, and he was constantly dealing with food suppliers, couriers, and workers from the other Houses.

In fact, Daichi was so good at his job that I wondered why he was working for Kyrion instead of one of the larger and more prominent Houses, but I didn't want to be rude and ask. Daichi clearly felt he owed Kyrion something, and being chief of staff and making sure that Kyrion's House ran smoothly was his way of repaying that debt, whatever it was.

In the afternoons, Daichi would escort me to the training ring, where Kyrion would toss me a wooden sword and proceed to spend the next two hours whacking my knuckles, arms, chest, and legs, while barking out everything I was doing wrong. He also ruthlessly knocked me down on my ass more times than I cared to remember.

Oh, occasionally, I could land a few blows, but then Kyrion would amp up his intensity and mock-kill me again within seconds. Try as I might, I simply couldn't mimic all the moves he showed me with any cohesion or regularity. It was a puzzle I couldn't solve, and it was driving me crazy.

Just like he was.

Kyrion usually remained cool, calm, and utterly aloof, but sometimes when we were sparring, his eyes almost gleamed with . . . appreciation, as though he was proud of the progress I was making, small and slow as it was. Then he would kick my ass again, and I would go right back to despising him with every atom of my being.

After we were done sparring, Kyrion would disappear into his library to do whatever Regal lords did, leaving me to amuse myself. At first, I simply wandered around the castle and admired the fine furnishings. But the more I looked at them, the more I realized how many of them were broken.

So I fixed them.

A grandfather clock that no longer chimed the hour. Crystal figurines with arms and legs that had been cracked off. Tables that listed to one side. Solar chandeliers that shot out sparks every time you switched them on. I repaired all those items and others. The work helped keep my mind off my many, many worries.

As for my magic, well, that took a turn too. Every night, I dreamed of my mindscape. And every single night, the round room was bigger than the night before, with more and more doors embedded in the walls. Several doors opened up into my own memories, for better or worse. A few showed me people, places, and things I had never seen or heard of before, while others remained tightly, frustratingly locked, including the door with the jeweled sapphsidian arrow—Kyrion's door, as I had come to think of it.

Every single night, I also studied the Door in the back of the room, but it always remained the same, and only wisps of black smoke curled out of the dark opening. Sometimes I wondered if the Door was my truebond with Kyrion, if his darkness was trying to merge with my magic, or however the bond worked. But so far, I hadn't summoned the courage to do more than peer into the blackness, even though I could see nothing inside it. Then I would wake up and stare at the ceiling, wondering what, if anything, the darkness in my mind truly meant.

Finally, the night of the spring ball arrived, and I boarded a transport, along with Daichi and the few other House Caldaren members. We were all dressed alike in short, formal, fitted jackets over matching shirts, tight pants, and knee-high boots. The uniforms were much nicer and fancier than what we usually wore, and they were all that dark blue bordering on black that signified we belonged to House Caldaren. The sapphsidian color was everywhere I went these days, and it seemed like an omen, although of what I couldn't say.

As we neared Crownpoint, the transport lifted off the ground and floated up, up, up, until I thought we were going to drift away like a weather balloon in the atmosphere. Eventually, the transport landed in a docking bay, and we stepped outside.

Kyrion wasn't with us, but that sticky cobweb pulsed in my mind. He was already here . . . somewhere. Over the past few days, we'd come up with a simple plan. Kyrion and I would meet up later, slip out of the ball, and sneak onto one of the Kent ships. Once on board, I would download the information from the faulty sensor that would prove the Kents were deliberately sabotaging the new Imperium ships.

After that, well, I wasn't sure what would happen. Most likely, I would take Kyrion's money, along with the new identity he had promised me, board a shuttle to some distant corner of the galaxy, and start over on a planet where no one knew who I was—or wanted to kill me.

"Try not to get into any trouble tonight, Vesper," Daichi said in a mild voice.

I clutched a hand to my chest in mock horror. "*Me?* Get into *trouble*? Surely, you jest, good sir."

He lifted his chin a bit higher. "I never jest about trouble, and neither should you."

I grinned and followed him across the docking bay.

Crownpoint Palace looked the same in person as it had on various gossipcasts that Tivona had made me watch. Real wood, stone, and glass furnishings were juxtaposed with silver chrome, painted polyplastic, and thick sheets of permaglass, creating a discordant mishmash that I found particularly ugly after the clean, simple, understated elegance of Castle Caldaren.

The soft whir of security cameras sounded, along with the steady hiss of supplemental oxygen. Guards were stationed along every corridor, many dressed in dark red armor and clutching long bronze spears with glowing white tips. The Bronze Hands, Holloway's personal guards. Bronze helmets covered their faces like sheets of pebbled glass, although the faint glitter of their eyes was visible through the wide horizontal slits in the metal. Their blurry, distorted features made them even more intimidating.

Daichi and I entered the throne room. The area was huge, easily the size of a docking bay, and had been decorated to match the ball's spring theme. Hundreds of thousands of roses, orchids, and lilies sprouted up out of real dirt gardens that had been set into the white marble floor, along with ponds filled with silver koi and other bright, glimmering fish. Mammoth butterflies lazily flapped their blue-black wings inside netted areas, while hummingbirds darted to and fro over glass fountains filled with sugar water. Thick pink and purple vines snaked along the walls and dropped down from the ceiling, along with copper lanterns shaped like stars, moons, and planets.

I had seen similar scenes on various gossipcasts, but no holoscreen could capture the vibrant colors or the floral perfumes that filled the air, and I had to stop myself from gaping in wonder.

Some people were already dancing in the middle of the throne room, whirling around to some old-fashioned but fast-paced waltz, while other folks sampled the fresh fruits, cheeses, chocolates, and other treats that were arranged in the shapes of flowers, butterflies, and birds on glass tables. Sparkling liquids shot out of metal spigots in the walls and streamed down into crystal bowls before being funneled into dainty flutes, as though the drinks were complicated science experiments.

All put together, it was like something out of an old fairy tale. Once again, part of me could understand how difficult it must have been for my mother to see all of this and then have the Regals say she didn't have enough magic and worth to remain among their glitz and glamour. No wonder she had been so determined to prove them wrong.

Despite the overwhelming opulence, I could still see the cracks in the elegant, charming façade. Everyone was smiling just a little too widely and laughing just a little too loudly and dancing, eating, and drinking just a little too quickly. The Regals might be spoiled, but they realized this could all be destroyed, especially if the Techwavers continued their reign of terror. According to Kyrion, the Arrows and Imperium generals were still no closer to tracking down the Techwave's home base or whoever was ultimately behind the organization.

Daichi and the other House Caldaren workers drifted away, searching for their friends, but I remained rooted in place. Thousands of people were in the throne room, but the space still felt empty and cavernous, and I kept expecting some dragon to erupt from behind the rows of columns and swallow us all whole. I shivered, trying to push my unease aside, but with little success.

To distract myself, I went over to the refreshment area and filled a plate with food, while a servant handed me a crystal flute with a sparkling pink liquid that tasted like lemons, strawberries, and summer sunshine. I took up a position in an out-of-the-way spot, content to watch the lords and ladies waltz around the dance floor while others engaged in the more mental dancing, gossiping, and sparring that was going on in different cliques.

Tivona could have told me who each person was, which House and family they belonged to, and more. My friend would have loved being here, and a pang of longing shot through my chest. My life on Temperate 42 might not have been perfect, but I had been comfortable there. Here? I was decidedly uncomfortable.

In addition to the Regals, staff members dressed in the colors of their respective Houses were also in attendance. Some were chatting in small groups, while others were cozying up to lords and ladies, proving that the derogatory *climber* nickname was quite apt. I didn't need my seer magic to know that many people here would do whatever it took to improve their own positions and prospects. I supposed in some ways I was a climber too, because I had no compunction about taking the money Kyrion had offered me and getting as far away from the Kents as possible.

Trumpets blared, and Lord Callus Holloway swept into the throne room. Dark brown hair with a few silver strands, tan skin, bronze eyes, pleasant features, benign smile. I had seen him on many gossipcasts, but he was far more vibrant, charismatic, and distinguished in person, and the wide bronze circlet on his head, along with his long red coat, made him look every inch the Imperium ruler he was.

Still, the longer I stared at Holloway, the more the air around him shuddered and darkened. Holloway smiled and shook hands with several people, but with every person he touched, the blackness around him grew larger and larger, and the shadow he cast grew wider and wider, as though he was a black hole devouring all the light, warmth, and energy in the room.

A collective murmur rippled through the crowd, and a beautiful woman appeared on the far side of the throne room. She was about my age, late thirties, with a strong, curvy, muscled body. Her long silver gown flowed around her like water, while dozens of tiny jagged colored stones glittered in her flowing skirt. My eyes narrowed. Not merely stones but bits of raw ore. Lunarium, if I had to guess. More bits of ore were embedded in the silver tiara on her head, making it sparkle like a ring of stars.

Her glossy black hair had been pulled up high and then braided, with the different strands coiling back around each other like a web of ribbons. Black shadow outlined her silver eyes, her lips were stained a deep, dark purple, and a faint dusting of shimmering silver powder brought out her pale skin. Another bit of opalescent lunarium glimmered on the thin silver chain around her neck, while other larger colored pieces were embedded in the silver rings and bangles that adorned her fingers and wrists.

Asterin Armas stopped and lifted her chin, striking a pretty pose. The gossipcasts had been talking about the wealthy Erzton lady nonstop for the last few days, speculating about what she would wear, how her hair would be done, and, of course, whom she might favor with a dance during the ball. She was one of the loveliest women I had ever seen, truly breathtaking, a mythical, magical, ethereal goddess come to life and walking among us lowly mortals.

Still, I could see the cracks in her façade just as I had with the Regals. Her smile was too wide, as though she was grinding her teeth to hold the expression in place, while her fingers plucked at the ore on her skirt, as if she wanted to rip off the stones, hurl them at the Regals, and flee from the throne room.

Lady Asterin turned to the side and held out her arm, each movement steady and graceful. Just like everyone else, I craned my neck, eager to see who her companion was—

Kyrion stepped into view and took her hand.

I froze, my plate of food forgotten, along with the drink in my other hand.

The Arrow looked like a violent storm, a dark force of nature compared to Lady Asterin's softer, more colorful shimmer. Kyrion was wearing a short formal blue-black jacket with silver buttons shaped like arrows running down the front, along with tight pants and knee-high boots. His longish black hair had been brushed back to better show off his features, and his eyes glittered like blue-black stars above his high cheekbones. His stormsword dangled from his belt like usual, a visual reminder of who and what he was, as if anyone here could ever forget.

Kyrion and Asterin made a stunning couple, a distinguished lord and a dazzling lady, and an unexpected dagger of jealousy stabbed deep into my heart. Sure, Kyrion was smart and witty and had a dry sense of humor I quite enjoyed, but he didn't want to be bonded to me any more than I wanted to be connected to him. Although judging from the tight press of his lips, Kyrion wasn't pleased to be paired with Lady Asterin either.

Callus Holloway also didn't seem pleased by the sight of them together. Holloway watched them with narrowed eyes, as if he were waiting for something momentous to happen and was annoyed it hadn't manifested yet.

Kyrion led Asterin out onto the dance floor, and everyone fell back to watch them spin around and around. The longer I studied them, the more that telltale silver glow appeared around them both, as though they were two pieces of a puzzle that fit together perfectly. I wasn't sure what my seer magic was trying to tell me, but the sight of it gilding them like two mirrors made me want to break something.

"They make a lovely couple, don't they?" a low voice murmured.

I glanced over at the man standing beside me. He was at least twenty years older than me, in his late fifties or early sixties, with a mane of blond hair shot through with silver. His pale blue eyes stood out brightly against his tan skin, and he too was dressed in a formal jacket, marking him as a Regal lord.

I thought back, trying to remember every face I'd seen on the gossipcasts over the past few days. Ah, yes. He was Wendell Zimmer, a spelltech from House Zimmer.

I was still clutching the plate and glass, so I settled for dipping my head to him instead of attempting an awkward bow and dropping the dishes. "You're right, my lord. They do make a lovely couple."

"It's a pity Lady Asterin has traveled all this way for nothing."

"What do you mean?"

He shrugged. "Kyrion will never marry her, no matter what Holloway wants—or orders—him to do."

He said the words casually, as though they were a foregone conclusion. Did he have seer magic as well? Hard to tell, as were his motives for speaking to me. I might not have been on

Corios long, but even I knew that lords didn't just wander up to random people dressed as House workers.

Wariness filled me. "Why are you telling me this?"

Wendell Zimmer shrugged again, although mischief twinkled in his eyes. "Ah, you caught me. I'll admit that my conversation was not entirely benign. My son has told me quite a lot about you in recent days, and I wanted to see you for myself."

Son? What son? Who had been talking about me to a lord?

"Father! There you are!" A familiar voice boomed out, and Zane Zimmer strode over to us.

Side by side, the resemblance between the two men was obvious. Same blond hair, same tan skin, same pale eyes.

Zane did a double take, then peered down his nose at me, as though I was part of the floor, necessary to stand on but unremarkable in every other way.

"Father, I see you've met . . ." His voice trailed off, as though he'd forgotten my name.

"Vesper," I replied. "Hello, Zane. Nice to see you again. I'm so glad you found a proper change of clothes."

I deliberately trailed my gaze down his light blue jacket, which matched the one his father was wearing.

To my surprise, Wendell chuckled. "So I was right. This is the woman who burned your clothes. She is just as delightful as you described."

"Oh, I doubt he used the word *delightful*," I drawled.

Zane bared his teeth at me. "You're right. The word I used was *destructive*."

Wendell's face brightened. "Yes! Zane said you rigged three blasters together to make one weapon. You must tell me exactly how you did it."

"You do realize she could have killed me with her little toy?" Zane cut in.

Wendell waved away his son's petulant concern. "Yes, yes,

of course. She took you by surprise. But I still want to know exactly how she did it. Did you use only the solar magazines? Or did you also wire the sparkers together for maximum effect?"

Zane huffed. "Of course, you would want all the technical details about how she almost blasted a hole in my chest."

I gave him a sweet, poisonous smile. "If I'd been aiming for your chest, you'd still be laid out on a medtable."

Zane glowered at me, but Wendell plucked a small notebook made of real paper from the inside of his jacket, along with an old-fashioned ink pen. "But back to your modified blaster."

Zane sighed, although grudging affection rippled through the sound. "Forgive my father. He can't help himself. As the House Zimmer spelltech, he's always looking for new and better ways to do things."

"I don't mind," I replied, and I truly didn't.

Talking about blasters was far preferable to watching Kyrion and Asterin whirl around the dance floor.

For the next few minutes, Wendell Zimmer peppered me with questions about which blaster parts I'd used from which models and exactly how I'd assembled them to make a single more powerful weapon. To my surprise, I actually enjoyed our conversation. It was so nice to talk to someone who was genuinely interested in my creations and not just listening with half an ear, like Conrad had so often done.

Zane stood nearby, sipping a drink and flirting with every woman who gave him a second look. Even as I answered the lord's questions, I kept one eye on the Arrow, wondering if he would be as hostile and insulting as he had been in the training ring a few days ago, but Zane ignored me.

"Really, Wendell. Quit badgering the poor woman. This is a ball, not a demonstration in your workshop."

A woman walked over to us. Her hair was completely silver, but she had the same straight nose and high cheekbones as Wendell, although her skin was more rosy than tan. And just like Wendell and Zane, she had the striking pale blue eyes that were the hallmark of the Zimmer family. The woman, who looked to be in her eighties, was resplendent in a blue silk gown, and an impressive array of blue opals and other gemstones glimmered in her silver hair, as well as in the chandelier earrings that brushed the tops of her shoulders.

"May I present my mother, Dowager Beatrice Zimmer," Wendell said in a formal tone. "Mother, this is Vesper, a weapons consultant for Kyrion Caldaren."

"Vesper? What an unusual name," she murmured.

"Thank you. I picked it for myself as a child."

"How . . . progressive of you."

Despite her polite but clearly bored tone, Beatrice's gaze drifted over me from top to bottom. Her silent, continued scrutiny made me want to shift on my feet, like a child who had been caught doing something naughty. As the silence dragged on, a faint silver glow flared around Beatrice, before spreading over to Wendell and then to Zane. My eyes narrowed, but I couldn't determine what my seer magic was trying to tell me. Probably how dangerous the Zimmers were, despite their nice manners and polished veneers.

A loud trill of laughter cut through the air, and my gaze skipped past Beatrice and landed on another lady sweeping in this direction.

Rowena Kent.

Black hair, green eyes, smooth and ageless complexion. Rowena looked the same as the last time I had seen her in the Kent Corp conference room, although she had traded in her sleek suit for an equally sleek gown that was the same scarlet as her glossy lipstick.

Sabine was by her mother's side, and she looked even more gorgeous than usual in a puffy pink gown. Conrad was clad in a matching pink suit and hovering by Sabine's elbow like a dog waiting to perform a trick for its master.

I had been keeping an eye out for them, since Kyrion and I planned to slip out of the ball once we knew the Kents were here in the throne room and not on one of their ships. I also hadn't wanted one of them to accidentally spot me and realize I was on Corios, although given my House Caldaren worker's uniform, I doubted any of them would give me a second glance.

Anger and disgust rolled through me at the three of them talking, drinking, and laughing as though they weren't actively engineering the deaths of hundreds of thousands of people.

Rowena stopped and waved to someone, and another person joined their group.

This woman was quite striking, with dark brown hair, dark blue eyes, and pale, flawless skin that made her look much younger than her fifty-something years. Her sequined midnight-blue gown clung to her toned body like a viper's skin and slinked from side to side with every step she took. She was clutching a glass of fizzing red liquid that matched the color of her short, square nails.

My heart froze, and my blood ran cold. Even if I hadn't seen her on the gossipcasts over the years, I still would have known exactly who this woman was. I had never been able to forget her, no matter how hard I had tried.

Lady Nerezza Blackwell, current head of House Blackwell—and my mother.

SEVENTEEN

VESPER

Wendell kept chattering about blasters, but all I could hear was my frozen heart, which cracked open and started pounding in my ears. Sweat slicked my palms, my chest tightened, and my stomach did a series of somersaults that would have made even the most skilled blitzer pilot proud.

Zane shot me a curious look, as if he'd picked up on my mental distress with his magic, but thankfully, he didn't comment on it or, worse, point it out to the others.

What was my mother even doing here? According to the gossipcasts, she was busy with House Blackwell business on another planet and wouldn't be attending the ball. I hadn't expected to see her, and I certainly hadn't . . . *braced* myself for it. But I should have realized that Nerezza would never miss such an important social event. Once again, I had been a stupid, hopeful fool when it came to her.

Rowena laid her hand on Nerezza's arm, and the two women laughed merrily. Then they strolled in my direction.

I should have mumbled an excuse and hurried away, but my body was locked in place and coiled as tightly as a metal spring inside a brewmaker. The last thing I wanted was for Rowena to spot me, but I couldn't look away from my mother, whom I hadn't seen in person in more than twenty years.

Not since I'd come to Corios to find her when I was twelve and had gone home with a thoroughly crushed heart for my troubles.

Rowena caught sight of the Zimmers, and she glided in this direction, with Nerezza trailing along behind her.

My numb body finally caught up with my panicked brain, and I backed up to whirl around and dart away. A group of people was standing behind me, blocking any chance I had of slipping away unseen, so I ducked my head and squeezed into the sliver of space behind Wendell Zimmer. He too gave me a curious look, just as Zane had done, but he didn't comment on my sudden shyness.

Rowena stopped beside Zane, although her gaze was focused on Beatrice. "Lady Beatrice," she said. "Wendell. Zane."

Nerezza didn't say anything, although she dipped her head one tiny inch to Beatrice, who stepped forward, putting herself at the front of the Zimmer family, literally and figuratively. Behind her, Wendell maintained a neutral expression, but Zane eyed Nerezza like she was a sand scorpion about to strike. Perhaps he was smarter than I'd realized.

"Rowena. Nerezza." Beatrice's voice was polite and yet ice-cold at the same time.

"Mother!" Sabine called out and waved her hand.

Rowena murmured an excuse and headed toward her daughter. She hadn't spotted me.

A soft sigh of relief escaped my lips, and the sound drew Nerezza's attention. I froze again. She studied my House Caldaren uniform, then focused on my face. I stared right back at her, my heart still hammering in my chest, waiting for her to recognize me.

Would she be shocked? Angry? Scornful? Worried? After all, I was her dirty little secret, the unwanted, illegitimate daughter she had abandoned long ago. Not the sort of baggage any Regal lady wanted to carry around, much less be confronted with during a ball.

But no recognition sparked in my mother's eyes, and no emotion flitted across her face. After a few seconds, she dismissed me as unimportant, just another lowly worker cog in the Regal machine, and turned to Beatrice again.

"Lady Beatrice, you're looking well," Nerezza said.

Even though I hadn't heard her voice in person in more than twenty years, it still stirred twin pangs of familiarity and longing deep inside me. In an instant, my heart quit pounding and froze over yet again, although the chill was as thin as a layer of ice on a pond in the winter, with all my conflicting emotions still churning beneath that cold, crystalline crust.

No silver glow gilded Nerezza's body, but my magic surged up all the same. Even though I wasn't asleep or unconscious, I could suddenly see the round room of my mindscape, and one of those doors opened beside my mother—the memory of the day she'd abandoned me.

I was having the same eerie double vision of Nerezza that I'd had of Kyrion a few days ago when we'd been talking about the Kent ships potentially crashing. It was as though I was looking at two holoscreens side by side, each of them playing a different scene—Lady Nerezza Blackwell standing in front of me in the here and now and my mother calling me useless back in Liesl's tiny apartment.

I didn't know which vision was worse.

"Nerezza." Beatrice's voice was even colder than before. "I see your mourning period is over. And so quickly. My, how time flies."

Nerezza smoothed her hands down her gown, and the sequins slyly winked at me like evil eyes that could see all my secrets. "Yes, well, Giorgio wouldn't have wanted me to wear black for long. He always said I shone best and brightest in blue."

"Indeed you do," Beatrice replied, although it wasn't a compliment.

The two women stared at each other, while Wendell, Zane, and I looked on.

Try as I might to avoid hearing anything about my mother, thanks to Tivona's love of gossipcasts, I had inadvertently seen more than one story about Nerezza over the years. Tivona had always chalked up my avoidance of the gossipcasts as disinterest, and I had never told my friend how much it hurt to see my mother swanning about at the Regal balls.

But why would Nerezza be wearing black? I thought back, trying to recall everything I'd heard about Nerezza recently. Ah, yes. I remembered now. A few months ago, the Regals had been rocked by the sudden, unexpected death of her husband, Giorgio Blackwell. The lord had been a renowned pilot, and he'd been in an experimental new blitzer that had crashed. According to the reports, Lord Giorgio been killed on impact.

But that was just the beginning of the gossip surrounding them.

Giorgio had been a longtime bachelor before he'd married Nerezza, and his death had made her the de facto head of House Blackwell, although from what the gossipcasts insinuated, Giorgio's nieces and nephews were pushing back against Nerezza's iron grip on the family fortune. I wished them well, although I doubted the other Blackwells would ever wrest any wealth, power, or control back from Nerezza. I knew better than anyone the lengths my mother would go to in order to get what she wanted.

And Nerezza had gotten *exactly* what she had wanted all

those years ago. Here she was, in the middle of a Regal ball, with the wealth, power, and status of a major House behind her, even though she didn't seemingly have any magic herself.

My mother had flourished in all the years she'd been gone, and here I was, forced to stare at her shining brilliance as though part of it hadn't come at my own expense and heartbreak.

"Anyway, I should go make the rounds," Nerezza said. "I haven't greeted Callus yet."

Beatrice let out a low, mocking chuckle. "Ah, so that's who you have your sights set on now. Good luck with that, Nerezza. You might think you are a shark swimming among the clueless minnows, but Callus Holloway is another beast entirely."

Nerezza smiled at the older woman, although her expression was more bared teeth than genteel nonchalance. "I am *much* more than a mere shark, Beatrice. I always have been. As for Callus . . ." Her toothy smile widened. "Well, we're old friends, and we've always enjoyed each other's company, ever since I first came to Corios."

"Mmm." Beatrice made a noncommittal sound that was full of derision.

Nerezza glided away without another word, and that eerie, unwanted double vision filled my eyes again. Lady Nerezza Blackwell crossed the throne room, her steps perfectly in sync with the memory of her storming out of Liesl's apartment when I was a child that hovered in the air beside her.

Nerezza skirted around a couple of people and vanished from view. As soon as she disappeared, so did my memory of her. No tears pricked my eyes, as I had cried all of those long ago, but bitterness and weariness flooded my heart, which was still beating hard and fast.

"My dear, are you all right?" Wendell asked in a concerned voice. "You look rather pale."

Zane and Beatrice stared at me too, and I forced myself to smile at the Zimmers.

"I just need some air. It's quite warm in here."

I dipped my head to them, then turned and fled from the throne room.

Well, I didn't actually flee from the throne room. There were far too many people for such a quick, easy escape. Still clutching my plate and glass, I darted through the first opening in the crowd I saw.

All around me, people kept talking, laughing, eating, and drinking. I ducked my head and mumbled excuses to everyone I bumped into, but no one paid any attention. Of course not. My own mother hadn't wanted me. Why would anyone else care about me?

I finally made it to an open space along the edge of the room. Daichi was standing several feet away, flirting with a handsome man wearing House Zimmer colors. Daichi caught sight of me. A frown creased his face, and he stepped in my direction, as if he was going to come and check on me, but I shook my head. No need to ruin his evening with my melodrama. Daichi hesitated, but his companion said something, drawing his attention again.

The second Daichi looked away, I slid behind a column and moved into the shadows—

I collided with a woman moving around the opposite side of the column. "Oh! Excuse me!"

Asterin Armas stepped back into a patch of light that illuminated her beautiful face, along with the bits of ore glimmering on her gown. I stifled a groan. Could this night get any worse?

Instead of snapping at me for bumping into her, Asterin gave me a small, tentative smile.

"Glad to know I'm not the only one in dire need of refreshments," she said, lifting the plate in her own hand. "Dancing is exhausting work."

Her words were polite, although filled with more than a little dry sarcasm.

"Absolutely," I agreed. "Especially since you have to be so careful not to step on anyone else's ego, much less their toes."

Asterin stared at me, and I wondered if I'd misjudged the situation. But then a smile spread across her face, and a laugh tumbled from her lips. "Indeed. Egos are strewn about in here like mines on a battlefield."

And just like that, I liked her.

We stood there in companionable silence. Asterin wolfed down the food on her plate and cast a longing glance at the refreshment tables.

"Would you like some of my food? I haven't eaten any of it. I'm Vesper, by the way."

"Yes, please. Thank you. And please call me Asterin."

She flashed me a grateful smile and took my plate. I polished off my pink drink, while she gobbled down the food. We both set our empty dishes on a nearby table, although we remained in the shadows.

Asterin let out a satisfied sigh. "Despite the lovely gift baskets of fruits, cheeses, and chocolates in my suite, my handler insisted I fast all day. Sometimes I think the preparations for the balls are just as torturous as the actual events themselves."

I gestured over at the refreshment tables. "You mean, why do the workers put out all that wonderful food if everyone can't enjoy it without any guilt?"

Asterin's silver eyes brightened. "Exactly! And yet my handler ordered me not to eat a single bite, lest I commit the grave sin of splitting the seams of my gown or getting something stuck in my teeth and detracting from my appeal." She rolled her eyes, playing it off as a joke, but bitterness colored her voice.

Unexpected sympathy flooded my heart. "It must be hard, to come to a strange planet and city and have everyone look at you. To try to live up to their expectations when they know nothing about you."

"No one's expectations are greater than those of my own family." More bitterness colored her voice.

"I'm sorry."

She shrugged. "It is what it is. What about your family?"

My gaze flicked over to Nerezza, who was chatting up Callus Holloway in the middle of the throne room. "I don't have any family." My voice came out just as bitter as hers.

Asterin winced. "I'm sorry."

"It is what it is."

She laid a sympathetic hand on my arm. I nodded back at her.

We stood there in silence for several more minutes, watching the crowd. Then Asterin tensed.

"I see my handler searching for me. Apparently, it's time for another dance."

Another dance with Kyrion, most likely. The thought twinged my heart, but I smiled at her again. "Good luck, Asterin."

"The same to you, Vesper."

She winked at me, then lifted her chin and stepped out of the shadows. A man waved at her, and she joined the group of people surrounding Holloway. Asterin smiled and nodded at Nerezza, who beamed back at her.

More bitterness and weariness flooded my heart. I slipped through the shadows, and this time, I was finally able to leave the throne room. But try as I might, I couldn't escape the happy images of my mother living the grand Regal life she had always wanted—without me.

EIGHTEEN

KYRION

Something was wrong with Vesper.

Even though I couldn't see her among the crush of people in the throne room, thanks to the bond, I could still feel the worry and dread surging off her. That velvet ribbon of awareness, of connection, vibrated in my mind over and over again, like someone was plucking a bowstring inside my brain. My chest also tightened, but it wasn't from any longing or attraction, despite the fact that I was dancing with Asterin Armas for the third time. No, I recognized this familiar emotion for what it was: heartache.

Why was Vesper so upset? Had someone hurt her?

I turned my head from side to side, trying to find Vesper in the crowd, but it was useless. Even more alarming was the fact that her presence waned ever so slightly, as though she had left the ball.

"Is something wrong, Lord Kyrion?" Asterin asked. "You seem distracted."

I focused on the woman in front of me, the one I was holding in my arms, and not the one who was magically stuck in my mind. "Of course not."

"Mmm." Asterin's noncommittal response made it clear she didn't believe my lie.

I wouldn't have believed me either. I might be a monster, but I had never been particularly good at lying.

The music ended, and our steps slowed and stopped. A hearty round of applause rang out from the other Regals, which I acknowledged with a forced smile of gritted teeth. Asterin swept down into a graceful curtsy before rising again, her smile seeming just as forced as mine.

She truly was beautiful, but even more impressive was how smart and perceptive she was. When we'd been introduced outside the throne room prior to the ball, Asterin had looked me up and down, taking my measure. I'd done the same thing to her, although I'd gotten the sense that she had seen much more about me than I had about her. Another indicator of how intelligent she was, along with the smooth, confident way she had conversed with everyone about a variety of subjects, including all the mines and minerals her family and the rest of the Erztonians controlled.

"Ah, there are my two shining stars of the evening," Holloway said, approaching us.

I didn't respond, but Asterin dropped into an even deeper curtsy than before.

Holloway glanced back and forth between us. Despite his smile, his slightly narrowed eyes indicated he was pissed that a truebond hadn't sparked between us yet.

Despite his hopes for a union between the two of us, I could already tell it wasn't going to work. Asterin put on a good show, but she was as bored with me as I was with her, although of course, neither one of us could admit that to the other. At least, not here and now, with Holloway and everyone else watching.

Asterin gave Holloway a bright smile and engaged him in

conversation. I finally saw a chance to escape, so I asked if anyone wanted a drink. Asterin and Holloway both declined, but I announced I was getting one for myself. Several more people joined the two of them, including Rowena and Sabine Kent, and I was quickly elbowed aside and forgotten, which was fine by me.

No one paid any attention as I headed toward the refreshment tables. Everyone was still involved in their conversations, so I walked right on by the food and drinks and headed for the closest exit.

I needed to find Vesper. Now that the Kents were here and the ball was in full swing, it was time to sneak on board one of the new Imperium ships. I was just following our plan. I wasn't concerned about her at all.

Oh, yes. I wasn't particularly good at lying, not even to myself.

I left the throne room, grabbed the ribbon that connected me to Vesper, and gently tugged on it.

She was over . . . there. Somewhere . . . above me.

I veered to my right and climbed a set of stairs that spiraled upward. Vesper was sitting on the floor of a small balcony, her shoulder propped up against the stone, staring down through the railing slats at the people in the throne room below. A sad, pensive look filled her face, and her harsh, twangy heartache intensified through our bond.

She didn't look at me as I walked over and sat down across from her. I peered through the slats and tracked her gaze over to Holloway, who was talking to Nerezza Blackwell again. Disgust shot through me. I despised Nerezza almost as much as I despised Holloway.

Vesper kept staring at the lady, as though Nerezza was a

painting she found utterly fascinating. More heartache surged off her, plucking that ribbon in my mind again.

Suspicion filled me. "Why are you so interested in Nerezza Blackwell?"

"Why do you say it like that?"

"I have my reasons."

Vesper glanced over at me. "What reasons?"

"You said that your friend Tivona is a fan of the gossipcasts. So you probably know about Lady Nerezza's reputation."

Vesper snorted. "You mean how she flits from person to person and House to House until she gets what she wants out of one of them? Or the fact that she's been married four times now, including to Giorgio Blackwell, and that each of her husbands has been wealthier and more powerful than the last?"

"So you have heard of her."

Vesper shrugged, but that sad, pensive look remained on her face.

I cleared my throat, wondering if I should share this secret, but it was a relatively harmless one, as far as these things went. "Nerezza tried to seduce my father on more than one occasion."

Vesper barked out a laugh. "Of course she did."

"You're not surprised?"

"*Nothing* Nerezza would do to better her own position would surprise me," she replied. "But why would she ever try to seduce your father? Surely, she knew about the bond between him and your mother."

"Truebonds don't mean that the people involved can't have other partners in whatever ways they like—as friends, as business associates, even as lovers. Just that the bond will keep drawing those two people together whether they like it or not."

My gaze drifted back down to Nerezza. "In my parents' case, in addition to the bond, my father loved my mother, so he was never interested in Nerezza's charms, such as they were. But after my mother died, Nerezza decided to try again, and she visited the castle late one night when my father was alone in the library. She had practically stripped herself naked and crawled into his lap when I found them. I ordered the servants to remove her immediately. She didn't like that."

Even now, her screeches of outrage and promises of revenge echoed in my ears.

"What did she do to you?" Vesper asked.

I cleared my throat again. Perhaps this secret was more damning than I'd realized, but I'd already told too much of it not to reveal the rest. "After I killed my father, many Regals called for my execution, but Nerezza was the most vocal and vehement. I'd kept her from getting something she wanted, and she was determined to punish me for it."

Vesper nodded. "That sounds about right."

She stared back down at Nerezza again, and another wave of heartache washed off her and surged through the bond.

"What did she do to *you*?" I asked.

Vesper hesitated for several seconds. When she answered, her voice was barely above a whisper. "She's my mother."

Shock sliced through me. "Nerezza Blackwell is your *mother*?"

"Yes, she is my biological mother. When I was seven, she left me with her cousin Liesl, who in turn shipped me off to an Imperium academy."

Suddenly, I remembered the image of two women arguing that I'd seen through the open doorway in Vesper's mindscape. I hadn't recognized Lady Nerezza at the time, but now I could see the resemblance between her and Vesper. They both had the same dark brown hair and pale skin, although Vesper was much warmer and lovelier than Nerezza's cold, immaculate beauty.

"What happened?"

Vesper drew in a breath, and the words spilled out of her mouth one after another. How her mother had possessed great psionic potential and attended a prestigious academy on

Corios. How Nerezza's power had seemingly vanished, and she had returned to her home Temperate planet pregnant with Vesper. All the fights she'd had with Liesl and then, finally, Nerezza abandoning her daughter and never looking back.

The longer and faster Vesper talked, the more I could *see* everything that had happened, as though it were battle footage unspooling on a holoscreen right before my eyes. Vesper's seer magic was reaching out to my own power. They might be her memories, but my psion power was conjuring the images in my own mind.

"I shouldn't have been surprised that my mother left me," Vesper said. "She didn't even name me, not really."

I started to ask how a parent couldn't name her own child, but instead, I went with a more benign question. "What do you mean?"

"Every child born on an Imperium planet is given an iden-tification code. Well, mine starts with G. Whenever my mother wanted something, she would call me G, although most of the time, she would just snap her fingers and refer to me as *girl*. Not even *my girl*, just . . . *girl*. I *hate* that fucking word."

Vesper sighed, her shoulders drooping and her body curling in on itself. "The day after my mother left, Liesl told me that I should pick a real name for myself since I was starting a brand-new life. She tried to make it fun, but I could tell she pitied me. I had just read a storybook about Vesper, a beautiful space princess who saved the galaxy, so that's the name I chose for myself."

Vesper finally wound down, and her words and story ended. With difficulty, I shoved the memories away, along with her continued heartache.

"Why didn't you mention any of this before?" I asked.

"Because I never thought you would bring me to Corios, much less that I would see her again." She hesitated. "I haven't seen my mother in person since I was twelve."

"What happened then?"

Vesper drew in another deep breath, then exhaled. "Liesl tried to explain why my mother left. She tried to be kind about it, but that just made things worse. Because I started thinking that if only I was *good* enough, *smart* enough, then my mother would come back. So I read and studied and did everything I could to be at the top of my class. When I was twelve, I won an award for making a blaster from spare parts, and I was so damn *proud* of it. I was so certain *this* was the thing that would finally impress my mother enough to lure her back home or at least let me be part of her life."

"What did you do?"

"I worked odd jobs around the academy. When I had enough credits saved, I told my instructors I was visiting Liesl for the weekend and booked passage on a cruiser to Corios."

"What happened there?" I asked, careful to keep my voice neutral.

"I knew from the gossipcasts which House my mother currently belonged to, so when I landed on Corios, I went there. Looking back, it was a small House, befitting a minor lord. It wasn't even on the Boulevard, but at the time, I thought it was the most elegant place I had ever seen. I waited outside for a couple of hours, trying to figure out how to sneak inside. I overheard one of the servants say that Lady Nerezza was in Promenade Park, so I went there."

Vesper dropped her gaze and traced her finger over a thin vein of red in the white marble floor, as though the motion could somehow soothe her pain and make her memories easier to bear. "I saw my mother in the park. She was even more beautiful than I remembered, far more beautiful than the images I had seen on the gossipcasts, and I was so stupidly *proud* that this lovely, graceful creature was my mother. That she had achieved what she had set out to do and was now a member of the Regals, even if it had come at my expense."

She traced her finger over another vein of red. "I ducked behind some trees and got close enough to eavesdrop. My mother was picnicking with some other ladies, and they started talking about their children. I kept hoping she would mention me, but of course, she didn't. Eventually, the Regals started gossiping about some other lady who'd had an affair with one of her servants and had gotten pregnant. It was quite the scandal. Someone asked my mother if she'd ever had an affair, and she got all coy and vaguely mentioned a few men she had dallied with, despite being married at the time."

Vesper's hand froze, and her entire body tensed. She drew in yet another deep breath, then let it out, along with another rush of words. "And then my mother said the key to having affairs was to always be smart enough *not* to get burdened with a low-born brat like this other woman had. All the other ladies thought she meant she was careful enough never to have gotten pregnant herself, and they all started laughing in agreement. But I knew the truth, and it just . . . devastated me."

More memories flickered off Vesper and crowded into my own mind. The ladies sitting on a picnic blanket, gossiping over refreshments. Nerezza holding court in the center of the group, a sly smile on her face and a mocking sneer in her voice. Vesper flinching at her mother's words, which sliced into her heart as deeply and easily as the sharpest stormsword.

"Part of me wanted to leap out of my hiding place and confront my mother with the truth of my own existence." Vesper sighed. "But I just . . . couldn't do it. One of the servants spotted me and asked what I was doing, and I ran away like a coward. I ran through the park, and I kept right on running until I reached the nearest spaceport. A lady there took pity on me and put me on the first shuttle back to my home planet, where Liesl was waiting. She knew what I'd done and exactly how badly it had gone, but she didn't punish me. Liesl already knew that seeing my mother had been punishment enough."

"I'm sorry," I said, surprised by how much I meant it. "That must have been difficult."

Vesper gave me a sad smile. She didn't say anything else, but she didn't need to, given how clearly I could feel her churning emotions through our bond. I should have been alarmed by this new development, especially by how much I wanted to reach out and touch her, comfort her, in whatever small way I could. My hand was already creeping across the floor toward hers, and I clenched my fingers into a tight fist to stop the unwanted motion.

"What about Liesl?" I asked. "You said she cared for you after your mother left?"

Vesper nodded. "Liesl was young, like my mother. She had no idea how to raise a child, but she somehow got enough money to send me to an Imperium academy so I would at least get an education and learn some skills. It wasn't so bad. Lots of the other kids didn't have parents either, so I fit right in. And Liesl came to visit me sometimes, although I hadn't seen her in about ten years when . . ."

"What?" I asked. "What happened to her?"

Vesper blew out a breath. "Liesl was on board the *Velorum* when it crashed."

Suddenly, Vesper's determination to expose the real cause of the crash made perfect sense. Liesl might not have been her biological mother, but she had cared for Vesper in her own way, and Vesper wanted to honor that.

That made me think of the other side of Vesper's story, such as it was. "If Nerezza is your mother, and she got pregnant with you while on Corios, then who is your father?"

She shrugged. "No idea."

"None at all?"

Vesper shook her head. "No. I asked Liesl, more than once, but she said Nerezza never told her anything about my father. Just that his family didn't approve of her and that they'd paid her off to disappear, along with me. Nerezza took all the money when she left us."

My gaze swept over the people below. Vesper's father could be any lord in the crowd, or one of the guards, or one of the servants, or someone else entirely. No way to know for certain without running her DNA against the genetic profiles in the Regal archives, which would trigger all sorts of alerts and unwanted scrutiny. Still, I found myself wanting to take those risks, to give her some more answers about her past, even if they wouldn't ease her pain.

"Knowing my luck, my father is just as awful as my mother." Vesper jerked her head at Nerezza, who was still talking to Holloway. "It's probably someone like Callus Holloway. Nerezza bragged to the Zimmers earlier about how much she and Holloway have *enjoyed* each other's company."

She shuddered, as though the thought disgusted her. Yeah, me too. "So I'm probably much better off not knowing who my biological father is."

"But aren't you curious?"

Vesper glanced down at the people talking, drinking, laughing, and dancing below. Her heartache vanished, replaced by a hard, bitter coldness that sank deep into my own bones. The familiar sensation made my own monster hum and stir in appreciation.

"No. My mother abandoned me for all of *this*. I have no desire to weasel my way into some Regal family who would always treat me like the outsider I am. The Regals can keep their balls and rules and scandals. I want no part of it—or any of *them*."

Icy rage surged off her, adding to that chill in my bones. Most people would have taken advantage of the situation, but not Vesper Quill. I admired her for that—and many other things.

Too many things, as the growing bond between us suggested.

I got to my feet. "Come. We should go now, while everyone is distracted."

I hesitated, then leaned down and offered my hand to her. Surprise flickered across her face. Vesper also hesitated, then reached out and clasped my fingers.

The instant her warm, soft skin touched mine, a jolt of . . . *something* shot through me. Anticipation, maybe, perhaps even a spike of attraction, desire, coupled with the tiniest spark of . . . longing.

I dropped her hand and stepped back. Vesper glanced down at her mother one last time, then followed me off the balcony.

NINETEEN

VESPER

I couldn't believe I had spilled my guts to Kyrion. I should have kept my mouth shut about my mother and how much she'd hurt me, but he'd been there, cool and calm as always, and I couldn't stop the words from spewing out like vomit.

But strangely enough, talking to him had soothed my heartache in a way that talking to Liesl never had. Maybe because in this respect, we were eerily similar. Kyrion had had his own issues with his parents, particularly his father, and I had mine with my mother.

No, with *Nerezza*. She wasn't my *mother*. She had *never* been my mother, not in any way that truly mattered, and it was long past time I stopped thinking of her in a role she had never wanted.

Oh, I wasn't the first person who'd been abandoned by one or both of their parents. Mine was an all-too-familiar story. I might have even made peace with it, might have put Nerezza out of my thoughts entirely, if only I hadn't been forced to watch her on the gossipcasts and realize she had never missed me, not for one single second.

Nerezza wasn't worth missing, much less thinking about any longer, so I shoved her out of my mind and focused on the mission at hand.

Kyrion moved from one corridor to another, and I bowed my head and followed along behind him, playing the part of the dutiful servant. All the guards nodded respectfully to him and paid no attention to me, and we quickly moved through the palace. Still, the longer we walked, the more I felt as though we were being watched and followed, but every time I glanced behind us, all I saw were the guards stationed along the corridors. I shivered and faced front again.

Eventually, we stepped into an elevator. The door slid shut with a whisper, and the car dropped. Kyrion's face remained calm, but his hand curled around the hilt of his sword, betraying his tension.

The elevator floated to a stop, and the door slid back, revealing another corridor. Kyrion strode forward, pushed through a glass door, and stepped out onto a wide terrace lined with columns. We were on the ground level of the palace, which featured a wide, grassy lawn that flowed into the adjoining Promenade Park. The cool night air gusted across my face, bringing a wave of pollen that forced me to scrunch up my nose to keep from sneezing.

Three Kent ships were parked on the grass, a large military cruiser and two smaller blitzers, all outlined with strings of white lights that made them twinkle, as though they were precious gems and not potential instruments of death and destruction.

Three guards were stationed around the ships, although they were chatting while they studied their tablets. Music blared from the devices, indicating that the guards were watching the gossipcast coverage of the ball hundreds of stories above their heads.

Kyrion and I slipped into the shadows behind one of the columns.

"How are you going to get rid of the guards?" I whispered.

He stretched out his hand and flicked his fingers. Telekinetic power rolled off him, and several small rocks skittered across the terrace, drawing the guards' attention.

"What was that?" a guard muttered.

Kyrion flicked his fingers again, and more rocks skittered off in the distance.

"Let's go check it out," another guard said.

All three guards shoved their tablets into their pockets, yanked the blasters from their holsters, and headed in that direction, disappearing into the dark. Kyrion grinned at me, then sprinted toward the closest ship, the cruiser. I rolled my eyes and followed him.

The docking bay ramp was down in anticipation of the Regals touring the ship later, so we were able to easily creep on board. Kyrion started toward the flight deck, but I pointed to a ladder that led downward.

"The navigation system is on the lower deck."

I took hold of the ladder and started climbing down, and he followed me. The only sounds were the soft pings of our boots on the rungs and then the resulting thumps of us hitting the floor of the lower deck. Only a few emergency lights broke up the darkness down here, so I pulled out my tablet and activated the flashlight feature, painting the corridor in a faint white glow.

"This way," I said.

I had been on prototype cruiser decks in the Kent Corp production plants dozens of times before, and finally seeing the finished product gave me an odd feeling of déjà vu. Despite the Kents' deliberate sabotage, a sense of pride filled me. Conrad might have taken credit for my work, but several of my suggestions had been incorporated into the final design, like the wider access corridor that let Kyrion walk beside me instead of behind me.

I stopped at a terminal near the front of the cruiser. The main flight deck was on the level directly above us. The navigation sensor was mounted on the outside of the ship, right below the observation windows, which were always a tempting and obvious target for any enemy vessel. In addition to overheating the navigation sensor, the Techwave's new hand cannon might even be powerful enough to punch through the permaglass windows, something else that would result in a catastrophic crash. I shivered at the thought.

I hit some keys, and a login prompt appeared on the terminal's screen. I hesitated, then entered one of the many fake IDs and passwords I had used to sneak into the Kent Corp mainframe over the past few days. It was accepted, and I breathed a sigh of relief.

The first thing I did was access the ship's security system, switch off the cameras, and erase the footage of Kyrion and me creeping on board. Next, I inserted a thumb drive I'd gotten from Daichi's office supplies into one of the terminal slots, then pulled up the cruiser's navigation system, along with the sensor in question.

Status: Armed.

I blinked at the message. Was I looking at the right thing? I exited the system and went back in again, but the message remained the same.

Status: Armed.

I clicked on a few more screens. Horror filled me. Not only had the Kents screwed with the sensor's settings, but they had rigged it to immediately activate the fatal dive protocol the second it overheated. They'd essentially turned the sensor into a bomb, one that would take down the entire ship when it detonated.

I showed the information to Kyrion. "Looks like you were right about the Kents deliberately sabotaging the Imperium ships."

His eyes narrowed in thought. "So Rowena Kent is either

making a play for the Imperium throne herself, or she's thrown in with the Techwave. Either way, she's going to get them to do her dirty work."

I hit a few more keys, and the files started downloading onto the thumb drive. One percent, two, three . . .

The number kept climbing. I willed the files to download faster, but of course, they didn't. No matter how new, shiny, and sophisticated they were, terminals always had minds of their own.

As the download chugged along, I was all too aware of Kyrion standing beside me, the monitor's white glow highlighting the sharp planes of his face. He had moved as far away as the small space permitted, but he was still too close, too tall, too *everything*.

He shifted on his feet, and I tensed yet again.

"Don't worry," he drawled. "I'm not going to skewer you with my sword as soon as the download is complete."

"Well, at the very least, you should do the smart thing and make sure the data aren't corrupted before you try again," I replied, my voice as dry and sardonic as his.

But I wasn't worried about him hurting me. At least, not physically. No, sometime over the last few days, that fear had completely vanished. Instead, it had been replaced by something far worse, this growing and unwanted attraction I had for him.

Objectively speaking, most people probably would have found him at least moderately attractive. Kyrion was fit and muscled, and I could have written a very detailed report about how his moods made his eyes shift from sapphsidian blue to midnight black and back again. For science, of course.

But even more appealing than his physical appearance was the fact that I actually *liked* him.

Oh, he was still an arrogant jackass and a stone-cold killer, but he was also thoughtful and generous and kind in his own way, like when he had listened to me on the balcony earlier.

Kyrion had *really* listened to me, not just nodded along with half an ear the way Liesl always had whenever she had visited me at the Imperium academy. And then, when he'd offered me his hand, when he'd helped me to my feet . . . Well, his warm, strong, callused fingers pressing against mine had sent tingles of awareness zipping through my body, as though I'd touched a live wire and gotten a sizzling shock.

Despite all that, I still wondered how much, if anything, of what I felt for him was *real*. Was I attracted to him just because of the truebond? Was the bond the same reason my feelings toward him had softened? Or was I genuinely drawn to him of my own volition? I had no way of knowing, and it was driving me crazy.

"You and Lady Asterin looked cozy earlier," I said, trying to distract myself.

"It's all part of the game," Kyrion replied, his voice cold, clipped, and remote. "Dancing, smiling, laughing. A true Regal would *never* let anyone know that they were unhappy in the slightest way. And especially not during a ball with all the gossipcast crews in attendance. No one wants to be beamed across the galaxy looking anything less than ecstatic."

"Well, according to those gossipcasts, you and Asterin make a splendid couple," I said, striving to make my tone as cool as his. "I watched some of the coverage on my tablet before you found me on the balcony. The reporters are already picking out your wedding china. House Kruger porcelain trimmed with gold leaf and the colors of both your Houses."

Kyrion snorted. "They've probably already decided how many children we're going to have as well."

"The oddsmakers currently have that at two children, born a few years apart. Several people are betting on twins, while a few extreme gamblers are predicting triplets."

He snorted again. I checked the download. Twenty-five percent and climbing . . .

"I'm not going to marry Asterin Armas," Kyrion said. "So House Kruger and the oddsmakers and everyone else are going to be sorely disappointed."

"Why not? The two of you made a lovely couple on the dance floor. Truly." Jealousy aside, even I could admit that.

His jaw clenched. "Despite what many Regals think, you need more than a couple of smooth waltzes to bind two people for life."

He'd barely finished speaking when the soft thumps of footsteps sounded.

"Let's check down here," one of the guards called out. "I thought I saw someone sneaking on board earlier."

Several distinctive pings rang out, indicating that the guards were climbing down the ladder to this deck. At the far end of the corridor, a light appeared, slowly but steadily bobbing in this direction.

I glanced at the terminal. Thirty-seven percent.

"Leave it," Kyrion whispered. "We have to hide. Now!"

I slapped off the terminal monitor and hoped the guards wouldn't notice the drive sticking out of one of the slots. Then I brushed past Kyrion and rounded a corner, heading to the right. A few feet away, I stopped at a door and keyed in a code—5368, which spelled out KENT.

The Kents always set all the codes on their new ships to that sequence, leaving it up to the owners to change the numbers, although few folks ever bothered to do that. The door unlocked, and I yanked it open and stepped into the dark space inside.

"What is this?" Kyrion whispered.

"A supply closet. Maybe they won't think to check in here."

He remained in the corridor, an uncertain look on his face.

"Unless you can make yourself invisible with your magic, the guards are going to see you!" I hissed. "So come here! Now!"

He muttered a curse but stepped into the closet and pulled

the door almost shut behind him. The closet was empty, its shelves bare of supplies, but the space was only big enough for one person to occupy comfortably. My back was pressed up against a metal rack, while Kyrion was plastered up against me.

Arms, chests, hips, thighs. I was painfully aware of every single part of him pressing up against every single part of me. I'd always thought him too tall, but now I realized he was just the perfect height for me to lean forward and rest my chin on his shoulder if I wanted to.

And I *wanted* to.

"Will you stop looming over me?" I snapped. "I'm not some enemy you're trying to intimidate."

"Where else am I supposed to loom in here?" he snapped right back at me.

I glared at him, or at least what I could see of him in the semidarkness. A sliver of light crept in through the cracked door, gilding his black hair and making the tips of his locks look like tiny silver swords. The same light cast most of his face in shadow, except for his eyes, which gleamed like blue stars. I sucked in a breath, and the scent of his soap flooded my nose, sharp but faintly sweet at the same time, like spearmint.

I shifted on my feet, trying to put some distance between us, but my shoulder banged up against the metal rack, and I was effectively trapped by it—and by his body.

"Stop squirming," he hissed.

"*You* stop squirming," I hissed right back at him.

More footsteps sounded, growing louder and closer, and the glow of light increased, as did the sound of the guards' chatter. Kyrion and I both froze.

"Are you sure there's someone down here?"

"I didn't see anything."

"Could have sworn I saw a couple of people dart on board."

Through the crack in the door, I could see the three guards

sweeping the small flashlights mounted on their blasters back and forth. The lights sliced across my face, stabbing into my eyes, and I resisted the urge to snarl like an alley cat flushed out of the dark.

In front of me, Kyrion remained as still as a statue—a very warm, extremely muscular statue. Instead of looking back over his shoulder, he tipped forward, as though he was trying to shield me from the guards' lights with his own body. A noble impulse but one that brought him into even closer contact with me. Once again, I resisted the urge to snarl, this time with frustration, and to lean into his tempting warmth. How could someone so cold and detached radiate such delicious heat? It truly was one of the galaxy's greatest mysteries.

"I don't see anything," the first guard said, an annoyed note in his voice.

"There's no one down here," the second guard chimed in. "Let's get back outside."

"Fine," the third guard muttered.

The flashlights vanished. More footsteps rang out, but they quickly faded away. I waited a few more seconds to be sure the guards were gone, then turned my head.

Kyrion was right there, his face looming over mine just as his body was still doing.

I stared into his eyes, mesmerized by their dark, glittering beauty. His head dipped a little lower, and I wet my lips and tilted my head to the side. His gaze dropped to my lips, then flicked back up to my eyes. He slowly tilted his head to the other side, and I mirrored the movement, as though we were performing a slow, seductive dance.

Our lips were inches apart, and our raspy breaths mixed and mingled in the semidarkness. His spearmint scent flooded my nose again, even stronger than before, and I wanted to lean forward, bury my face in his neck, and drink in the clean, heady smell of him—

Kyrion drew back, wrenched the door open, and stepped out into the corridor. I had to lock my legs to keep from staggering forward into the suddenly cold, empty space in front of me.

"Let's go," he said in a tense voice.

I opened my mouth, but no words came out. I didn't know what to say. My heart was pounding, and my fingers were itching with the urge to reach out, snag his jacket, and yank him back into the dark with me. The sticky cobweb of him vibrated in the corner of my mind, as though he was battling the same urges I was. The odd sensation was strangely comforting, even as it increased my own desire.

This was crazy, ridiculous, foolish. This man had considered killing me, and I had considered killing him. And now here I was, wanting to forget about everything that had happened between us, everything that was at stake, just so I could melt into him for a few minutes.

"Vesper." Kyrion's voice came out as a low rasp, although I couldn't tell if he was pleading for me to step out of the darkness or drag him back in here with me.

I opened my mouth again, although I still didn't know what to say—

Beep.

"The download is finished," I said, my voice as hoarse and raspy as his.

Kyrion jerked his head in acknowledgment, then headed down the corridor.

I blew out a breath, stepped out of the supply closet, shut the door behind me, and followed him. That precipitous beep might have saved me this time, but I was still in danger of doing something supremely stupid where he was concerned.

I rounded the corner, plucked the drive out of the terminal, and passed it over to Kyrion, who slipped it into his jacket pocket. We climbed the ladder up to the main deck, then made our way to the docking bay ramp. The three guards had resumed their positions around the ships, but Kyrion waved his hand, and more rocks skittered in the darkness, drawing their attention again.

As soon as the guards went to investigate, we hurried down the ramp and disappeared into the shadows around the columns on the terrace.

Kyrion stopped and faced me. He cleared his throat and straightened up, once again towering over me, although this time, there was a healthy amount of distance between us. "I'm sorry about before. In the supply closet. That was inappropriate. I shouldn't have . . . *loomed* like I did."

"We were hiding. There's no need to apologize."

He let out a bitter laugh. "Hiding. Right."

His harsh tone cut into something deep inside me, something I hadn't even realized was there until this very moment: longing.

"I just thought . . ."

"What?" he growled.

I hesitated, wondering if I should give voice to the thought rattling around in my mind. But if I didn't say it now, I knew I would regret it later, just as I regretted not confronting my mother when I had come to Corios all those years ago.

"I just thought it would be nice to be connected to someone," I confessed in a low voice. "If only for a few minutes."

Surprise flared in Kyrion's eyes, along with some other emotion I couldn't quite identify. It might have been hunger, but just as quickly as it dawned, that emotion vanished, and cold, familiar anger filled his face.

"We are not *connected*," he spat out the word. "We are being unwillingly subjected to some arcane quirk of magic.

Nothing more, nothing less. Whatever tenuous . . . *attraction* might exist between us isn't *real*. It's just the product of the bloody truebond."

Even though I'd had similar thoughts, the venom in his voice still made me flinch. "Would it really be so terrible to be bonded to me?"

Kyrion drew himself up to his full height and peered down his nose at me. In an instant, he had morphed back into a ruthless Arrow. "I will *never* be willingly bonded to you or anyone else."

I started to ask why, but then the answer came to me. "Your parents. You didn't like their bond. That's why you're so determined to get rid of ours."

To get rid of me. I didn't say the words, but they echoed in the air between us anyway.

Another laugh spewed out of his lips, this one even more bitter. "When I was very young, I loved their bond. I thought it was the strongest, purest, most magical thing in the entire galaxy. What could be better or more perfect than a truebond between two people who loved each other more than anything else?"

"But?" I challenged.

He blew out a harsh breath. "But as I grew older, I realized their bond was *their* bond—and that there wasn't any room in it for *me*."

My magic surged, and suddenly, I was back in my mindscape. One of the doors swung open, and a barrage of images, memories, flooded my mind.

A young Kyrion watching his parents smile at each other and dance with each other and talk and laugh and generally be lost in each other. He was always watching them, always hovering on the fringes, always on the outside looking in at their closeness, their happiness. Icy fingers of loneliness emanated from him, wrapped around my own heart, and squeezed it tight. Suddenly, I could understand his conflicting feelings about his parents' truebond.

Kyrion started pacing back and forth. "Even when one of my parents was away on an Arrow mission, the other one wasn't there with me. Not really. My father was always waiting for my mother to return home, and vice versa. As soon as she got close, he would stop whatever he was doing and go wait for her at the front door like a dog yearning to see its master. One time, he got up in the middle of the story he was reading to me, even though my mother didn't arrive home for three more hours. It was like his need to see her and hers to see him were so strong they just forgot about everything else, including me."

More bitterness colored his voice, and more memories flickered through my mind, including one of Chauncey Caldaren staring at a door with a pensive, wistful expression.

"But the worst part was when my mother got sick," Kyrion continued, his voice even lower and more strained than before. "My father tried everything to heal her. He even gave her some of his own psion power through their bond."

Memories kept flickering through that open door in my mind. Kyrion's mother, pale and thin and propped up against pillows in a bed, while his father clutched her hand, pleading with her to wake up, to open her eyes, and especially not to leave him.

"But she died anyway," Kyrion said in a flat, toneless voice. "I didn't think things could get worse after that, but they did."

"How?" I whispered.

He stopped pacing. "My father didn't want to live without my mother. The second she died, it was like all the life drained right out of him as well. He just . . . gave up."

Yet more memories appeared in the doorway, including Chauncey sitting in a chair, staring blankly into the library fireplace, while Kyrion begged and pleaded with him to eat and drink.

"Things completely fell apart for House Caldaren," Kyrion continued. "The other Regals saw what was happening to my father, and they took advantage of it. The other Houses started reneging on contracts and not paying the bills they owed us. I handled it all the best I could, but no one was intimidated by me the way they had been by my father."

"Your father was grieving," I said in a soft voice.

Kyrion sighed. "Of course he was. Me too. I loved my mother dearly, and him too. But he couldn't even function, and it was all because of their bloody bond."

Once again, the venom in his voice slapped me across the face.

"I *needed* him," Kyrion said, his voice sad, tired, and bitter. "I was thirteen years old, and I had just lost my mother. I needed my father, but he couldn't rouse himself out of his own grief. He just wanted to be with my mother again more than anything else."

Every word he said was like another puzzle piece sliding into place in my mind and giving me a much clearer picture of Kyrion and the awful choice he'd made.

"That's why you killed him," I whispered, a sick sensation twisting my stomach. "You didn't murder your father because you wanted to be Lord Caldaren like the gossipcasts claimed. He *asked* you to kill him."

Kyrion gave me a short, sharp nod, so much pain and emotion packed into that one small motion. "He *begged* me to do it. For *weeks*. He said if I didn't kill him, he would go on a mission with the other Arrows and let one of his enemies do it. The way he was talking . . . he didn't care what happened to him or anyone around him. Not the other Arrows or the Imperium soldiers or even the other members of House Caldaren."

He gave me a small, humorless smile. "My father was rather like the navigation sensors on the Kent ships, a safety hazard to everyone around him."

"What happened?" I asked.

"We were in the library. I told my father he needed help and that I was going to summon some of his friends among the Arrows. My father had been drinking heavily, and he flew into a rage. Despite everything that had happened, I never thought . . ." His voice trailed off.

"Never thought what?"

Kyrion's gaze locked with mine, then skittered away. "That he would attack me."

Horror filled me. "But he did."

He jerked his head in acknowledgment. "My father hit me, and it was like that first blow added even more fuel to his grief and rage. He started talking about how we could both be with my mother again, and I knew that he wasn't going to stop until we were both dead. He hit me several times, but I finally shoved him away, and he fell back against the wall by the fireplace. I grabbed my sword. I only meant to use it to fend him off . . ."

Kyrion drew in a breath, then let it out. "But my father charged at me again, and I stabbed him in the heart."

He fell silent, but memories kept surging off him and filling that open door in my mind. I didn't tell him what I was seeing, though. I didn't want to add to his pain.

Kyrion cleared his throat again. "One of the servants came in, realized what I'd done, and ran off screaming. Despite my obvious injuries and the extenuating circumstances, all the other Regals wanted to execute me for killing my father. Except for the Zimmers and Callus Holloway."

"Holloway saved you from the other Regals?"

Kyrion gave me another short, sharp nod. "Yes. He told everyone that I had been overcome with emotion and lashed out in a moment of haste and that it would never happen again. Holloway offered to act as my guardian, and I had no choice but to let him. It was either that or be executed. I had already lost so much to the bond, and I was damned if it was going to get me too. I started training to join the Arrows the next day."

"And Holloway has been using you as his own personal assassin ever since," I finished.

Another thin, humorless smile split Kyrion's lips, as though he was a statue slowly cracking apart. "Turns out Holloway was right about one thing. I am very good at killing. And if people are going to treat you as a monster, then you might as well become one. Even the mighty Regals are afraid of a monster like me."

My heart ached for him, for everything he had been through. Even though Nerezza had abandoned me, I'd still had someone who cared about me, even if Liesl had left me at the Imperium academy and gone on to live her own life and we had fallen out of touch over the years. But Kyrion had lost both his parents and then been used and manipulated by Holloway. No one had ever had his best interests at heart, and he'd gone from one bad situation, one bad option, to another.

"Why don't you leave the Arrows?" I asked. "You're just as strong in your magic as Holloway is. You could break free of him."

Kyrion let out a derisive snort. "And go where? And do what? As you so succinctly pointed out back on the blitzer, I'm one of the most hated, most notorious people in the galaxy, responsible for the deaths of thousands. And not just Techwavers. I've killed other people on Holloway's orders, Regals, Erztonians, and common folks alike. Eliminated them without giving it a second thought. There is no *breaking free* of what I've done. Not even if I could somehow figure out a way to kill Holloway and escape from Corios."

He sighed, all the pain and anger draining out of him with that one soft, resigned sound. "Like it or not, I'm trapped in Holloway's web, but he won't be satisfied until he's snared me as tightly as possible."

"How so?"

"Even before my parents died, Holloway was studying truebonds. He's obsessed with figuring out how and why they form so that he can replicate them at will," Kyrion replied. "Holloway and his scientists have never been successful, but ever since my parents have been gone, he's pinned his hopes on me. And he's not the only one."

"What do you mean?" I asked.

"Over the years, several Regals have tried to forcibly bond with me."

Horror shot through me, and I sucked in a startled breath.

"Oh, yes," Kyrion said. "I might be a murderer, might be a monster, but many people covet the Caldaren fortune. They've put chemicals into my drinks at balls and tried to do the same with the food at my castle. One of them even succeeded. Her name was Francesca Balor."

Another memory appeared through that open door in my mind: Kyrion beaming at a beautiful woman with blond hair, brown eyes, and rosy skin.

"Francesca was from a small House, but her ambition more than made up for her limited resources, and she was far more clever than most. She dosed her perfume with a chembond, then danced with me during a series of balls, dosing me with a little more of the chembond every time. I thought I was in love with her, until I found the perfume bottle in her things."

Anger and bitterness surged off him, shattering the memory in my mind.

"So that's why you attacked me on the blitzer," I said. "You thought I was trying to trick you like Francesca did."

He nodded. "And that is why I will do whatever is necessary to break the bond between us. I will *not* let some quirk of magic dictate my fate, and I will *never* let another person have that much power, control, and influence over me. Especially someone as—"

He bit off his words, but I remembered what he had said on the blitzer.

"Especially someone as *inferior* as me?" I snapped. "The unwanted daughter of a greedy Regal climber and whatever man she dallied with. Is that what you were going to say?"

"Something like that."

Kyrion's face was as hard as stone, his eyes utterly devoid of emotion. Even that sticky cobweb in my mind was cold, still, and silent. He might not be feeling anything, but anger rose in me just like all that lava had erupted on Magma 7. Anger at his arrogance, his stubbornness, and especially his small, insulting, utterly wrong opinion of me.

Kyrion was right about one thing, though. A truebond was nothing more than a pretty, romantic trap, and I would not let myself be caught up in it any longer.

"Then let's end this. Right now." My voice came out just as cold and harsh as his.

"And how do we do that?"

I forced myself to give him a nonchalant shrug. "We have proof that the Kents are deliberately sabotaging the Imperium ships. You can expose them now, and I can take your money and disappear into the bright, shiny new life that's waiting for me. Our partnership is officially at an end. So it's time to break the bond as well, before it's too late."

Kyrion looked at me, and I clenched my jaw, trying not to let any emotion show. I must have done a better job than I thought, because he jerked his head in agreement.

"Follow me."

TWENTY

KYRION

I was finally getting exactly what I wanted, so why was I so conflicted about it?

Vesper agreeing to try to sever the bond was the best thing that could have happened, especially given our disastrous encounter in the supply closet. Just those few minutes alone in the dark with her had increased the bond exponentially, at least for me. Even now, I wanted to draw her into my arms and kiss her senseless. To see if her lips were as soft and her skin as smooth as I imagined. To see exactly how well her body molded against my own.

But it was just the bloody bond working its magic. It wasn't real, it wasn't genuine, and it wasn't anything born of my own free will, which made it all the more insidious.

At least, that's what I kept telling myself, not wanting to admit that, bond or not, I found Vesper's intelligence, wit, strength, and sarcasm highly appealing. That she challenged me in a way no one had in a long time, perhaps ever. That I liked, respected, and admired her. That I had even become a bit . . . concerned about making sure she escaped to her new life unscathed.

Those turbulent, disturbing thoughts swirled through my mind as I slid through the shadows around the palace, keeping away from the many guards and cameras. Vesper followed me, and eventually we made it into Promenade Park. I stopped long enough to send a message on my tablet, then cut through the grass, came out on the Boulevard, and hailed a transport.

I sat on one side of the transport, with Vesper across from me. She stared out the window, her body tense and her lips pressed into a tight line. Only a couple of feet separated us, but it might as well have been an ocean.

A few minutes later, the transport glided to a stop. I paid the fare, and we got out.

Vesper glanced around curiously. "This is a far cry from the Boulevard."

Instead of a smooth, wide thoroughfare lined with castles, this street was dark and narrow, with cracked cobblestones that were gray and grimy with transport exhaust. The low, uneven buildings leaned against each other for support, as though they were made of paper playing cards that would collapse the next time a stiff breeze gusted over them.

"I've seen this area on the gossipcasts," Vesper said. "This is the industrial part of the city, where the commoners and workers live and where the Regals come when they want to walk on the wild side."

"Among other things."

I set off down the street, with Vesper following me. I took a circuitous route, making sure no one was following us and sticking to the streets that were devoid of traffic and other cameras. Even though it was creeping up on midnight, throngs of people were out and about. Neon signs flashed over restaurants, while loud, thumping music spilled out of nightclubs. The Regals might be having their spring ball, but the other citizens of Corios were celebrating too.

Ten minutes later, I navigated the twists and turns of a crooked alley that was just wide enough for one person to walk through. At the end of the alley, I knocked on a metal door that was as gray with grime as everything else in this part of the city.

The holoscreen embedded in the wall beside the door flickered to life. "Who is it?" a gruff voice demanded.

"You know exactly who it is. I sent you a message, and you can see me on your screen."

A dry chuckle rasped out. "You never do waste any time. I like that about you."

The screen went dark, and the door buzzed open. I yanked on it and stepped through to the other side, with Vesper still following me.

I walked down a short, dark corridor and emerged into a cramped, well, I suppose you could call it a *workshop* if you were feeling generous. Really, though, it was a repository for all the junk someone had collected over the years, a place where things came to die, if objects had any sort of life or awareness. Piles of wires, scraps of metal, buckets of bolts, and every other kind of odds and ends you could think of clustered on uneven wooden shelves that stretched all the way up to the low ceiling, which was less than three feet above my head. The air smelled of wet paper and dry rust, two things that should not have existed in the same space but seemed perfectly in sync here.

"In the back!" a voice called out.

I maneuvered around a half-built transport engine that was squatting on the floor, but Vesper paused, and her fingers flexed as if she'd spotted something on the engine that needed fixing. I cleared my throat. She shot the engine a wistful look, then followed me.

The workshop zigged and zagged, much like the alley

outside, but eventually, the narrow area opened up into a much larger room that was crammed with even more junk. I stopped in front of a long table that was one of the few clean, relatively clear spaces.

Behind the table, a man was perched on a stool, using a laser torch to solder two pieces of wire together to make . . . something. The object could have been anything from a blaster to an engine to an artistic sculpture. The man was in his seventies, with a thick tuft of white hair that stood straight up over his forehead as though he'd crossed the wrong wires together and had gotten a violent shock. Dark gray coveralls strained to cover his barrel chest, along with the rest of his short, stocky body.

Touma Hirano glanced up at the sound of our footsteps, the clear goggles on his face making his dark brown eyes look as big and round as suns in his golden skin. He turned off the laser torch and set it aside.

"Ah, Kyrion! Right on time." His gaze flicked past me and landed on Vesper. "Is this the lucky lady in question?"

"More like *unlucky lady*," she muttered.

As far as insults went, it was rather mild, but her words still stung, which was another reason I needed to break the bond. There was no place for any emotions in my life, especially not the dim sparks of regret that kept flickering in my chest about what I was here to do.

Touma laughed and slapped his knee. He grinned at Vesper, then looked at me. "Are you sure you want to do this? I like her."

I ignored his question. "Are you ready?"

"As ready as I'll ever be. I received the last batch of chemicals earlier this evening." He got to his feet, rounded the table, and stuck his gloved hand out to Vesper. "Touma Hirano, renowned spelltech, at your service."

She blinked in surprise. "As in Daichi Hirano?"

"Ah, you've met my nephew. Don't worry. I am far more relaxed, much more handsome, and infinitely more charming than Daichi is." Touma winked at her.

A laugh tumbled from her lips, and she shook his hand. "Vesper Quill. Unwitting victim of a truebond."

Touma chuckled, then released her hand.

"What are you working on?" Vesper nodded at the pieces of metal on the table.

He waved his hand. "Bah! I'm trying to rewire an engine so that it feeds more power to the thrusters on an old transport I have out back, but I can't get it to work."

Vesper brightened. "Oh, it's simple, really."

She went around behind the table and plopped down on the stool. She touched one of the wires with her fingertip, making sure it was cool enough to handle, then grabbed it, along with the other one.

"Pliers?" she called out in a distracted voice.

Touma frowned, but he handed over the pair from his tool belt. Vesper stripped the plastic casings off some of the surrounding wires, then started humming as she wrapped the wires around each other and attached them to the hunk of metal I now recognized as an engine. A minute later, she leaned over and pushed a button on the side of the engine, which smoothly rumbled to life.

Touma stared at Vesper, an awestruck expression on his face. "How did you do that?"

She grinned, laid the pliers down on the table, and got to her feet. "I'm good at fixing things."

Yes, she was, given the grandfather clock, the uneven tables, and all the other items she had repaired around Castle Caldaren over the past few days. Even Daichi had been impressed by Vesper's skills, but it was her thoughtfulness that I appreciated, far more than was wise, given the bond.

Touma studied her a little more closely. "Ah, yes. I can

sense it now. Seer magic, right? Perhaps mixed with a touch of something else?"

She shifted on her feet, as though suddenly uncomfortable. "Something like that."

Touma glanced over at me, but I shrugged in return.

"Well, since you fixed my engine, the least I can do is try to break your bond," he said. "Let's get started."

Touma fished out a handheld biometric scanner, which he ran up and down my body and Vesper's, recording everything from our heart rates to our oxygen levels to how many times we blinked per minute. He fed all that information into an ancient terminal I had mistaken for another piece of junk, then questioned us about when the bond had formed and why. Of course, neither one of us knew the answers, but Touma typed in our responses anyway.

A few minutes later, a printer spat out a formula, and Touma started mixing the chemicals.

He pulled one glass vial after another off the shelves. Blue, pink, purple, green. I didn't know what chemicals the vials contained, and frankly, I didn't *want* to know. Touma poured a cup of this into a beaker and added a drop of something else. A soft *bang* rang out. Vesper and I both flinched, but Touma waited for the smoke to clear, then added something else from yet another vial.

I didn't dare rush him, but every minute he worked made me even more impatient. By this point, Holloway was sure to have realized I had left the ball, and I wasn't looking forward to facing his cold wrath. But Vesper was interested in everything Touma did, and she asked him question after question about the scanning, the chemicals, and everything else he knew about truebonds.

"Of course, the longer a bond goes on, the harder it is to break," Touma said. "That's why I couldn't help Lord Chauncey. You can't erase a lifetime of love and memories with a few chemicals. That's just not how psionic connections work, especially when it comes to truebonds."

Vesper glanced over at me. "You tried to break the bond between your father and mother?" Realization dawned on her face. "After she died, right?"

Somehow I kept my features calm, even as my gut roiled at the memory. "Yes. I thought it might . . . help my father, but it didn't. Nothing did."

"I used to do quite a bit of work for Lord Chauncey and the other Regals, mixing chemicals and the like, back when I had my shop just off the Boulevard," Touma continued, a wistful note creeping into his voice. "Until I discovered one of the lords was using my chembonds on his unwilling servants."

Vesper recoiled in horror. "What happened?"

"I gave the lord a taste of his own medicine—a chembond that paralyzed him for a week and let his servants take their revenge." Touma shrugged. "The other Regals didn't like that. They would have executed me if not for Kyrion's intervention."

Vesper glanced at me again. "So that's why Daichi works for you."

I shifted on my feet. "He's trying to repay a debt that was paid long ago."

Touma huffed. "My nephew has always been stubborn that way, but it all worked out for the best. Now, instead of dealing with all those stuffy Regals, all I have to do is keep Kyrion happy and keep his secrets, especially when it comes to truebonds."

Vesper frowned. "Why is this a secret?"

He added a drop of blue liquid to the beaker. "Don't you know? Among the Regals, it's a crime to try to break a true-bond. Punishable by death."

"I thought that was just a rumor the gossipcasts had made up."

"Oh, no," Touma replied. "The law is quite real, although

there is rarely cause to enforce it. But any couple even suspected of having a truebond is supposed to be brought before Callus Holloway so he can verify the validity of it."

"How does he do that?" Vesper asked.

Touma's gaze slid over to me. "Holloway usually calls a court session with all the Regals in attendance. Then he has an Arrow cut the hand of one person. If the same wound appears on the other person's hand, then a truebond is declared."

Vesper's gaze dropped to her own hand. She traced her index finger over the spot where that shallow slice had appeared after I had deliberately cut my own palm on the blitzer to prove the bond's existence. She glanced over at my hand, which still showed the healing gash.

"What happens to the people after the truebond is declared?" she asked.

Touma shrugged. "Well, in the old days, most of them were put to work in the palace in some capacity, depending on their station or House. But I don't know what would happen to them now. A truebond was discovered between two Regals several years ago, but there hasn't been a new one found since then."

Vesper's forehead crinkled in confusion. "Why is Holloway so interested in truebonded pairs? What does he get out of it?"

Touma snorted with obvious derision. "Their magic, of course."

She jerked back in shock.

"Everyone knows that Callus Holloway is a siphon," Touma continued, adding a drop of black liquid to the beaker. "That he can draw magic, power, energy from whomever and whatever he likes—people, machines, even the weather, if you believe some of the rumors. But nothing is more attractive to a siphon than a truebonded pair."

"Why?" Vesper asked.

"Siphons can draw power from other people and objects, but they experience withdrawal symptoms the same way that you and I would from using a chembond—headaches, nausea, light sensitivity, and the like. Of course, the stronger the siphon, the less the withdrawal bothers them, but even someone as powerful as Holloway would still feel the ill effects, if he drew enough energy from someone or something at once."

Vesper shook her head. "I still don't understand what that has to do with truebonds."

"Siphons don't experience any withdrawal when they drain magic from a truebonded pair. It's one of the purest, strongest kinds of psionic power there is, able to traverse time and space and sometimes even death itself. That's why some people refer to a truebond as a galactic bond."

"And the truebonded pair have no say in this?" Vesper demanded, anger sharpening her voice. "They just have to stay at the palace and let Holloway take their magic?"

Touma shrugged again. "He's painted it as a high honor, and the Regals have wholeheartedly bought into the idea. It's far easier to stomach that way than the truth."

"That Holloway is a greedy leech," Vesper snarled. "Adding to his own power by taking it from others."

"Something like that," Touma agreed.

She looked at me. "No wonder you think it's a death sentence."

It was far worse than that. Because the couple wouldn't die. Not until Holloway had drained every last drop of power out of them that he could.

I had never wanted that to happen to me, which was why I'd fought so hard against ever bonding with anyone. But now, strangely enough, I didn't want that to happen to Vesper either. It would be like watching my mother sicken and slowly deteriorate all over again. No, it would be *worse* than that, because at least my mother had loved my father. She had known exactly what Callus Holloway was, what he would do to her, and she'd stayed with my father anyway. I might have been born—trapped—into this life, but Vesper hadn't asked for any of this.

"There," Touma said, studying the mixture in the beaker with a critical gaze. "That should do it. If you two are still determined to go through with this? A truebond is not without its perils, but it's nothing to just throw away either."

Vesper and I looked at each other, our eyes locked together.

"I won't risk being Callus Holloway's or anyone else's puppet," she said.

"Neither will I."

Vesper nodded, and I returned the gesture. Those pesky sparks of regret flared in my chest again, but I snuffed them out the same way I had before. This truly was for the best. Even if we had both wanted the bond, even if it cemented into something real, something genuine, we would only be in more danger. From my enemies, from hers, from Holloway, from the Techwave. A truebonded pair could be useful in all sorts of unpleasant ways.

"If you will both sit." Touma gestured at two reclining chairs in the corner.

Vesper looked at me a moment longer, then walked over and sat down, leaning back against the light blue cushion, a rare clean spot among the workshop's dust, rust, and clutter. I sat in the other chair, while Touma pulled up a short rolling stool and perched in the space between us.

He divided the liquid equally into two glass vials, then handed one to each of us. The liquid was light blue and filled with shimmering flecks—silver, dark blue, black. Strangely enough, the colors reminded me of the eyes in Vesper's dream world.

"Well, I suppose this is it," Vesper said in a low voice. "Cheers."

"Cheers," I murmured.

She held her vial out to me, and I clinked mine against hers.

That one soft sound echoed through the workshop like a bell tolling out the end of . . . whatever this had been between us.

"You must both drink at the same time," Touma said. "On three. One . . . two . . . three!"

Still staring at each other, Vesper and I lifted our vials to our lips and drained them dry.

The chemicals hit my tongue in a cold rush, as though I was a child who had eaten too much ice cream and was about to have a massive headache. The headache didn't materialize, but the tasteless chill coated the inside of my mouth, then dripped down my throat and plunged into my stomach like an icy brick. That brick shattered, and cold shards shot out into my veins. Within seconds, my body was chilled from head to toe, as though I had been transported to a Frozon moon.

"I . . . feel . . . numb." Vesper's voice was soft and slow, as though she was having trouble forming words, and her breath frosted in the air. "Is this normal?"

"Yes," Touma replied, watching both of us with avid interest, even as he swept his biometric scanner back and forth between our bodies. "The bond is warm, strong, alive, just like the two of you are, just like your respective powers are. To be severed, it must become cold, frozen, and still. Then, with any luck, it will break, and the two of you will be free of each other."

"You didn't say anything about the chemicals stabbing our insides like icy swords," I grumbled.

Touma gave me a smug, slightly evil smile. "You didn't ask."

Vesper barked out a laugh, which ended with her teeth chattering. Her lips had turned blue, and she swiped her tongue out over them, as if she couldn't feel them anymore. I did the same thing to my own lips. Nope, I couldn't feel them.

And so we sat there, shivering and hugging our arms around ourselves in a vain effort to stay warm. Touma grew bored, put down his scanner, and wandered away to tinker with something.

I laid my head back on the cushion and stared upward. Several metal spaceship models dangled from the ceiling like oddly shaped wind chimes. I snorted, my breath streaming out in a cloud of frost. Even the ceiling wasn't immune to Touma's collection of junk . . .

I must have dozed off, because the next thing I knew, those icy swords had vanished, and my body was, well, not warm but at least no longer frigid. I blinked, and the spaceships dangling from the ceiling snapped back into focus. I sat up and had to wait several seconds for my head to stop spinning. Beside me, Vesper also sat up, a dazed, vacant look on her face. She blinked several times, and her eyes slowly sharpened.

She touched the side of her head before smoothing her hand down over her heart. "I think it's . . . gone."

I searched that place in my mind where the bond had been, for the tiny velvet ribbon that connected us, for the soft twinge of awareness and pure, raw emotion that was Vesper, which had been haunting me since the first time I'd seen her on the Imperium cruiser. That space felt . . . *empty*, as though someone had pulled a plug in my mind, and all my awareness of her had drained out, like water leaking out of a bathtub.

"I think it's gone too."

I waited for a sweet rush of relief to hit me, but it didn't come. Instead, all I felt was that jarring emptiness in my mind, as though something vital was missing. I clenched my jaw and ignored the sensation as best I could.

Touma clapped his hands together in delight. "Excellent! It appears my theory was correct that the bond can be broken as long as it hasn't grown and strengthened for any considerable length of time."

Was a week a considerable length of time? That was about how long it had been since I had first met Vesper. In some ways, it seemed like the shortest week of my life; in others, it had been interminably long. Perhaps even more disturbing than the bond was the fact that Vesper had somehow learned every little thing about me in that timespan, no matter how hard I had tried to keep her at arm's length.

"And you're sure it won't . . . return?" I asked.

Touma scratched his chin. "It *shouldn't* return. But just to be on the safe side, perhaps the two of you should stay on different planets for a while. At least a year, maybe longer. I assumed that was your plan anyway?"

Vesper nodded and straightened up in her chair. "Yes, that's right. Now that this is . . . over, I have no reason to stay on Corios. In fact, the sooner I get off this fancy rock, the better."

Her gaze grew dark and distant, and I wondered if she was thinking about her mother, Lady Nerezza, and her absent father, whoever he might be. Vesper shook her head, as if flinging off painful memories.

I studied her closely, but she looked the same as before, and even her lips had returned to their normal color. Whatever chemicals Touma had given us didn't seem to have any ill effects, other than severing the bond.

"I guess we should leave," Vesper said.

We both stood up and stared at each other again. Her body was tense, and purple smudges of exhaustion, worry, and stress stood out like bruises under her eyes. I wondered if I looked as haggard. Probably.

Touma pointedly cleared his throat. "There is still the matter of my fee."

I pulled out my tablet and transferred the credits from one of my untraceable accounts to one of his. The loud, jarring *cha-*

ching! of an old-fashioned cash register rang from Touma's ancient terminal, and he grinned when he checked the balance.

"Always a pleasure doing business with you, Kyrion. Tell Daichi that I'll see him for lunch tomorrow like usual." Touma looked at Vesper again. "And if you ever want a job, come back here. I could use someone with your skills and magic."

She grinned at him, and the warmth of her expression stabbed me in the gut, even as her voice whispered through my mind. *I just thought it would be nice to be connected to someone. If only for a few minutes.*

For the first time, I wondered if I'd made a mistake, if I'd willingly given up something that could have been . . . good, maybe even . . . great.

No, I told myself in a firm voice. No connection was worth the danger a truebond would bring. This was for the best.

Besides, the bond was broken. Even if I'd wanted to fix it, I had no idea how. Even with all her skills and power and ability to figure things out, I doubted Vesper could have fixed it either—or that she would even want to.

Yes, this was most definitely for the best, even if a tiny voice in the back of my mind kept muttering what a fool I had just been.

TWENTY-ONE

VESPER

Kyrion and I left Touma's workshop, found a transport, and returned to the palace.

By this point, the ball had moved from the throne room outside to the lawn where the three new Kent ships were parked. We got back just in time to catch the tail end of Rowena Kent's speech about how Kent Corp's new line of military cruisers and blitzers would help the Imperium finally prevail in the ongoing conflict against the Techwave. She slammed a bottle of pink champagne against the side of the cruiser, officially inducting it into Imperium service.

Everyone cheered, and the party started winding down. More than a few couples stumbled away, their arms wrapped around each other, obviously high on chembonds and determined to make the most of their night together.

Kyrion murmured an excuse and disappeared into the crowd, probably to try to smooth over his disappearance with Callus Holloway. I stared at the three Kent ships a moment longer, then started searching for Daichi. I found him, and together, along with the other House Caldaren workers, we all returned to the castle and wound up in the kitchen.

Everyone was full of food, alcohol, and chembonds, and for once, merriment and laughter filled the castle. I enjoyed the happy sounds, which were another sign that this dangerous adventure was finally coming to an end.

"Vesper! Where are you going?" Daichi said, sipping from a crystal flute.

To my surprise, Daichi—the quiet, stern, responsible chief of staff—had swiped a bottle of champagne from the ball and was pouring a round for the rest of the staff. Tipsy Daichi was quite entertaining, as he had taken to spouting random lines of poetry between sips of champagne. But right now, I just wanted some peace and quiet.

"I have a headache," I lied. "I'm going to bed."

"Going to bed?" Daichi said. "But the ball isn't over yet!"

"It's well past midnight, so yes, the ball is officially over. I'll see you later. And Daichi?"

"Yes?"

"Thanks for everything." I squeezed his arm.

Tears gathered in his dark eyes, and he threw his arms around me. "Thank you for fixing my brewmaker! That's the nicest thing anyone has done for me in a long time!"

I patted his shoulder. Daichi cleared his throat, then pulled back and rejoined the others.

I retreated to my bedroom. I thought about taking a shower and going to bed, but too much restless energy was zinging through my body, so I opened the closet door, intending to pack my things so that I would be ready to leave on the first ship off Corios in a few hours.

A row of House Caldaren uniforms greeted me. Sure, they were all in my size, and I had worn them over the past few days, but nothing in this room truly belonged to me, so I had nothing to pack. Even the dagger on my belt was the one I had swiped off the Imperium ship during my conscription. My regular clothes, tools, books, jewelry, pictures, and everything else I owned were back on Temperate 42, the one place I could never return to. Anger and sadness filled me, and I slammed the closet door shut. Then I marched over, flopped down onto the bed, and stared up at the ceiling.

The events of the last few hours replayed in my mind. Sneaking onto the cruiser, downloading the files that would prove the Kents' guilt and sabotage, having that moment with Kyrion in the supply closet, the cold rush of chemicals flooding my body in Touma's workshop.

Even though the chemical chill was gone, I still felt numb, as though something deep inside my mind, maybe even my heart, had been extinguished. I started to reach out, to see exactly what, if anything, might be left in that hollow space, but I decided not to. I didn't want to reawaken the bond, if I could even do such a thing.

Kyrion had never wanted the truebond, and now that I'd learned what it really entailed—and the danger it would put me in—I wasn't so sure I wanted it either. I might long for a connection to someone, but the price was far too high to pay, especially with Kyrion.

Besides, it would never work out between us. What would we be, anyway? We weren't even friends, much less lovers, and I had no job and no real prospects, other than working for Touma doing all sorts of illegal things that would put me in danger again.

No, the best thing for me was to take Kyrion's money, go somewhere far, far away, and start over, even if the idea hurt my heart far more than I ever imagined it would.

Despite my inner turmoil, I drifted off to sleep and woke

a few hours later, just as the sun was rising over the candy-colored castles along the Boulevard. I stared at Crownpoint in the distance, at the tower where the ball had been held, and an image of Callus Holloway sitting on his throne like a red spider in the center of its white web popped into my mind. Somehow I knew my seer magic was letting me see the siphon as he was at this exact moment. I wasn't sure why I was having a vision of Holloway, but I shuddered and moved away from the window.

I showered and changed into a fresh House Caldaren uniform. It would do well enough until I was off-planet and could buy some new garments, even if I still had no idea where to go, other than far away from Corios.

I slid my dagger onto my belt and headed down to the ground floor. Given the early hour and last night's merriment, I was the only one up, and I ambled through the corridors, studying all the furnishings, including the ones I had fixed. The grandfather clock softly chimed out the hour as I strolled past, bringing a smile to my face.

Eventually, I ended up in the library, and I wandered over to the portrait hanging over the fireplace—Chauncey and Desdemona Caldaren, smiling wide, their hands resting on a young Kyrion's small, thin shoulders. Perhaps it was a quirk of my seer magic, but I could feel their hands on my own shoulders, the pressure of their fingers soft and slight but the combined weight of them dense and heavy.

The painting perfectly captured the truebond dynamic Kyrion had described last night, one that was more exclusive than inclusive. Once again, my heart ached for him, for always feeling so alone, even within his own family. I knew exactly how awful that was.

Liesl had cared about me in her own way, but I had still been an unwanted responsibility that had been dumped in her lap. Even when Liesl came to visit me at the academy, I could tell she would much rather have been doing something else, living her own carefree life, instead of having to clean up the mess Nerezza had left behind in me.

No footsteps sounded, and not so much as a whisper of air stirred, but I could still feel him looming behind me.

"Your mother was very beautiful," I said.

Kyrion moved up to stand beside me. "Yes, she was."

"You have her eyes."

His lips lifted briefly, then plummeted back down. "Yes. Everyone used to say that, especially right after she died. Now no one cares what my eyes look like, only what I can do or who I can kill for them."

I didn't say I was sorry, even though I was. In some ways, Kyrion Caldaren was as trapped in his Regal life as I had been trapped all these years by my hurt, anger, and bitterness over Nerezza's abandonment. My issues with Nerezza were something else I hoped to leave behind on Corios, along with my unexpected feelings for Kyrion.

We stood there in companionable silence, staring at the portrait of his family, for the better part of a minute.

Kyrion cleared his throat. "I transferred the funds to your anonymous account. You can check the balance if you like."

I waved my hand. "I trust you."

He frowned. "You do?"

"Yes."

Surprise flickered across his face, but I meant it. As crazy as it sounded, I *did* trust him, more than I had ever trusted anyone in my entire life. Once again, I thought about reaching out to that cold, numb space in my mind, and once again, I decided against it. This was over, and I needed to move on.

I squared my shoulders. "I guess this is good-bye."

"Where will you go?"

"I haven't decided yet. Although I've always wanted to visit Tropics 33."

He arched an eyebrow. "I wouldn't take you for a lover of

rainforests, humidity, and giant spiders that eat careless tourists."

I rolled my eyes. "Man-eating spiders aside, Tropics 33 is supposed to be quite stunning. Blue sand beaches, purple tide pools, three pink moons lighting up the night sky. But I do like having all four seasons, so sooner or later, I'll probably wind up on one of the Temperate planets."

"And what will you do there?"

"I'm not sure. Perhaps I'll open a small workshop like Touma's and fix things for people, make things better in whatever small way I can." I paused. "But without the mess. I might be a slob, but I'm not *that* much of a slob."

He chuckled at my joke, although his face turned serious again. "Well, wherever you go and whatever you do, I'm sure you'll be a great success." Kyrion hesitated, and when he spoke again, his voice was pitched much lower and softer than before. "You really are quite extraordinary, Vesper."

Despite all the praise I'd received from my instructors and employers over the years, that was, without a doubt, the loveliest, most thoughtful thing anyone had ever said to me. In fact, it was so lovely and thoughtful it robbed me of all coherent thought. I just stood there, staring at him like an idiot, desperately trying to ignore the longing squeezing my heart tight.

"Good-bye, Kyrion."

"Good-bye, Vesper."

I nodded at him, then walked away. I stopped at the doorway and glanced back over my shoulder. Kyrion had his hands clasped behind his back, staring up at the portrait of his parents again.

I drank him in a few seconds longer, then left the library and him behind—for good.

A few people were finally stirring in the castle, but no one paid any attention as I slipped outside and hailed a transport. I settled back in the seat to get one last glimpse of the colorful castles along the Boulevard, but an uneasy feeling swept over me.

Something was wrong.

I glanced out the window, but the Boulevard was empty, except for a few House workers going about their early-morning chores. Three blocks later, I finally puzzled it out.

"We're going the wrong way," I called out to the transport driver. "The spaceport is in the opposite direction."

The driver didn't respond, although he steered the transport over to the right, then turned into a narrow alley and stopped. More unease filled me, and I opened the door and stepped outside. The driver remained inside the vehicle, but I backed away from it. Even without my seer magic, every instinct I had was screaming that I was in danger.

I bumped into someone and whirled around. "Oh, I'm sorry—"

A figure wearing a dark red cloak stood in front of me. I froze, even as one of those doors in my mindscape opened wide. Suddenly, I was seeing two distinct images side by side, just as I had last night when I'd run into Nerezza at the ball.

The figure standing in front of me remained solid and still, but the other figure, the one in my vision, raised a handheld cannon and shot a bolt of green energy that slammed into Kyrion. I blinked, and the two figures merged into the single person before me.

The figure reached up and threw back the hood of their cloak, revealing a familiar face.

Julieta Delano grinned at me. "Hello, Vesper."

Before I could run or scream or try to fight back, the Arrow stepped forward and punched me in the face. Stars exploded in my eyes, and air rushed over my body as I plummeted toward the ground.

Crack.

My head hit the cobblestones, and the world winked to black.

TWENTY-TWO

KYRION

I wasn't sure how long I stood in the library, staring at the portrait of me and my parents. Not for the first time, I yearned to tear it down, toss it into the fireplace, and burn the bloody thing. But the longer I stared at it, the more I noticed the love shining in my parents' eyes, as well as the gentle way their hands rested on my shoulders, subtly drawing me closer to them.

I might not have been a part of their bond, but for the first time, I realized I was the result of it. I wasn't sure what, if anything, that changed. My mother was still dead, and I had still killed my own father. But for the first time in years, sour bitterness didn't churn in my gut when I thought about my parents. They might not have been able to care for me the way they had for each other, but at least they had loved me. Unlike Nerezza Blackwell, who had deserted Vesper just so she could climb the Regal ladder. A common occurrence, but the fact that it had happened to Vesper saddened me more than I would have thought possible.

She deserved better.

A knock sounded on the door, and Daichi stepped into the library. "Zane Zimmer is here," he said in a dry voice.

"You didn't have to announce me," Zane called out, blowing past Daichi and strutting into the library. "As a fellow Arrow, I'm always welcome here. Right, Kyrion?"

"Hardly," I replied, cold venom leeching into my voice.

Daichi raised his eyebrows in a clear question: whether he should forcibly remove Zane from the library. As part of his chief of staff duties, Daichi trained in various self-defense arts, but the two of them fighting would only lead to more problems, so I shook my head. Daichi glared at Zane's back, then left the library.

Zane sauntered over to a table along the wall and poured himself a healthy amount of my father's favorite bourbon. Then he sprawled in one of the chairs by the fireplace and raised his glass, toasting the portrait on the wall.

"Cheers to the Caldarens, the perfect little Regal family," he said in a mocking voice, then drained his bourbon in one long gulp.

Somehow I resisted the urge to draw my sword and pin him to the chair with it like he was a bloody butterfly. "What do you want, Zane?"

He set his empty glass on a nearby table, then settled himself back into the chair again. "I know you don't bother watching the gossipcasts, but everyone was quite taken by your dance routine with Lady Asterin last night. According to some of the chatter, wedding bells will soon be ringing."

I crossed my arms over my chest. "What's your point?"

He ignored my glower. "Even I will admit you gave a good performance with Lady Asterin. You were oh so attentive to her—until you snuck out of the ball with your weapons consultant."

Zane smirked at me. "Looks like I was right about her being

a conquest after all. Good for you, Kyrion. Perhaps fucking around like a normal person will help remove the stick that is perpetually lodged up your ass."

I dug my fingers into my elbows to keep from surging forward and throttling him. "If you call Vesper a conquest one more time, you will not leave this room alive."

Despite my threat, Zane maintained his seemingly lazy, unconcerned pose. "I would be quite happy to kill you, Kyrion, and take my rightful place as the head of the Arrows. A position that should have been mine all along, that *would* have been mine if Holloway hadn't interfered on your behalf."

I sighed, too weary to have this same old argument again. "You have no idea what Holloway has done on my behalf."

Zane's gaze sharpened. "What does that mean?"

"Nothing. Forget it."

He tilted his head to the side, studying me, but he didn't ask any more questions. Despite my dislike of him, Zane wasn't a complete idiot, and he knew there was much more to my relationship with Holloway than a ward trying to repay a guardian for shielding him during a difficult time.

"What do you want?" I asked yet again.

"I want to know why you were sneaking around the Kent cruiser during the ball," he replied. "Or was that just a convenient place for you to fuck your weapons consultant?"

I ground my teeth to keep from cursing. Zane excelled at creeping around and spying on people. All the Arrows spied on each other to some extent, but he was by far the most cunning and skilled at it, and his prowess in that regard easily surpassed my own. I hadn't even sensed him following Vesper and me last night. Then again, I'd never had the patience for such things, preferring to kill my problems rather than wait them out.

For a moment, I thought about telling Zane the truth, just to stop his incessant questions and insults about Vesper, but I quickly discarded the idea. I hadn't told Holloway about the

Kents' sabotage yet, and I needed the information to explain why I'd left the ball and the truebond trap he had so carefully planned for me with Lady Asterin.

Besides, I couldn't trust Zane. I couldn't trust anyone except for Daichi, Touma, and Vesper—

I cut off that thought. The bond was gone, and so was she, and the sooner I stopped thinking about her, the better off we would both be. I had gotten exactly what I wanted, and Vesper was off to enjoy her new life. There was no turning back for either one of us.

"Why does it matter that I snuck onto one of the Kent ships?" I countered.

"Because you're up to something," Zane replied. "You're *always* up to something."

"Like you're not?" I snapped back. "Please. We both know you tried to kill me during the battle with the Techwavers on Magma 7. But unfortunately for you, I managed to survive."

"Yes, unfortunately for me, you always manage to survive—" Zane stopped and frowned, as though he was re-winding my words in his mind. "Wait a second. What did I supposedly do during the battle? As I recall, you were the one who disappeared."

Anger surged through me, and I dropped my hands to my sides and took a menacing step forward. "No more games. I know you're the one who tried to kill me. Just go ahead and admit it. I'm not going to tell Holloway, if that's what you're worried about."

I was going to deal with Zane myself, just as soon as I could figure out a way to make his death look like a somewhat believable accident or an unfortunate battle casualty.

Zane barked out a laugh. "You think *I'm* the one who shot you with that fancy cannon that almost split you in two?"

He laughed again, and I balled my hands into fists to keep from giving in to the urge to throttle him.

"You're denying it?"

Zane's laughter cut off, and he climbed to his feet. A predatory grin split his lips. "Please, Kyrion. You should know me better than that. I'm a lot of things, but a backstabber isn't one of them. If I was going to kill you, I would do it face-to-face. Shove my sword into your gut, twist it around a bit, and watch you die."

His fingers twitched over the hilt of his stormsword, as though he was going to reach for the weapon and attempt to keep his murderous promise.

"That would end very badly for you," I replied in a soft, sinister voice.

Zane's toothy grin widened, and a gleam of anticipation filled his icy eyes. "Want to find out once and for all?"

I had opened my mouth to tell him nothing would give me greater pleasure, when a knock sounded on the door, and Daichi stepped back into the library.

"Sir? We have a situation that requires your immediate attention," he said in a clipped voice.

Zane shook his head. "Saved by your assistant. Truly pathetic, Kyrion. But I'll let you skate away—this time. I have more important things to do today besides staining my boots with your blood."

He smirked at me again, then strode away. Daichi stepped aside, and Zane winked at the other man as he moved into the corridor and disappeared.

I reached out with my power, but Zane's presence quickly faded away. He was gone, for now, so I turned my attention to Daichi. "What is it?"

He hurried over and showed his tablet to me. "Someone is trying to gain remote access to our systems. I'm not sure how they're doing it, but the signal is coming from inside this room." He glanced around. "Did Zane leave some sort of bug behind?"

I glanced over at the chair where he'd been sitting. Zane hadn't made any suspicious movements with his hands, and I didn't see any hiding places where he might have planted a bug. For once, I didn't think Zane Zimmer was the source of my problems.

Vesper had also been inside the library this morning, but she hadn't left anything behind either. So the only other person who could have planted a bug in here was . . . me. But I didn't have my tablet right now. In fact, the only device I had on me was . . .

I froze for a moment, then reached into my pocket and drew out the thumb drive with the Kent files that Vesper had given me last night.

Daichi held his tablet up to the drive, and it let out a sharp warning beep. "That's it. That's the bug. Where did you get that drive?"

I waved my hand. "Don't worry. I'll take care of it. Thank you, Daichi."

He gave me a suspicious look, but he left the library. As soon as he was gone, I went over to the terminal on my father's desk in the corner. I activated an electromagnetic shield so that the bug, virus, or whatever was on the drive couldn't worm its way into the House Caldaren system, then opened the device.

I scanned through the files, which contained the navigation sensor settings Vesper had shown me last night, along with the *Status: Armed* command. The information looked the same as I remembered, except for one thing: Vesper's name was all over the files.

Vesper Quill, Vesper Quill, Vesper Quill . . .

Her name popped up over and over again. I didn't understand all the technical jargon, but Vesper's name suddenly being on Kent Corp files when they had tried so hard to erase all digital and physical traces of her was deeply disturbing.

Something was wrong.

PART THREE

DOORS AND DARKNESS

TWENTY-THREE

VESPER

I was having the dream again.

I was back in my mindscape, back in that round room with flowers twining about all those eyes that were staring at me. And once again, the room had changed since the last time I'd been in here. Now almost all the doors were wide open, and even more of them were crowded in here than before, as though they were multiplying like rabbits whenever I wasn't around to keep, well, an eye on them.

I wandered around the room, peering through the openings. Some contained my memories of the past few days, including my unsuccessful training sessions with Kyrion, while others showed people I had met on Corios—Daichi, Zane, Asterin, Touma. I also saw people and places I had never seen before, at least not in real life.

Including Kyrion's parents.

One of the doors opened into the Crownpoint throne room and showed Kyrion's father, Chauncey, bowing to Holloway, then walking away. Desdemona watched her husband leave, a miserable expression on her face, while Holloway glided over and took her hand in his.

"Now, now, my dear." Holloway's silky voice snaked out of the opening. "Don't fret. He'll be back soon enough. In the meantime, we'll keep each other company, the way we always do."

Holloway started patting Desdemona's hand, like she was a dog he was petting. With every touch, Desdemona's face became a little paler, while Holloway's eyes brightened commensurately. Magic swirled around them, flowing from Desdemona into Holloway, but the sensation felt odd, twisted, and unnatural, like someone was trying to shove a part into an engine where it didn't belong.

Shock spiked through me, even as disgust curdled my stomach. Her husband had been gone for less than a minute, and Holloway was already using his siphon power to leech magic off Desdemona. Greedy, sadistic bastard. I glared at Holloway, but of course, he couldn't see me, since this had happened long ago.

I couldn't stand to watch Desdemona silently suffer, so I moved away from that door. I probably should have tried to rouse myself, tried to wake up, but I was far safer in this room of my magic's own making than I would be out there in the real world with Julieta Delano and whatever horrible thing she was planning to do to me. Every once in a while, a violent motion rocked my body, making me list from side to side, as though I was being moved from one place to another out in the real world, but that was the only thing that disturbed me.

Eventually, I came to the Door in the back of the room. No smoky clouds were wisping out of the opening right now, although the blackness inside seemed even darker and more absolute than before, and the space felt . . . *empty*, as if whatever had lurked in there was long gone.

Did this door lead to my truebond with Kyrion? If so, then

the bond seemed truly dead and broken, just as Touma had claimed it was. I still wasn't sure how I felt about that, about losing something I'd never had a chance to fully explore—

Something pricked my left arm, and a hot rush of chemicals flooded my body. My heart jolted, and my eyes snapped open. For a moment, the world swung back and forth, as though I was on a spaceship rocketing through the atmosphere. I blinked, and the motion stopped, revealing a long wooden table. I was slumped in a chair at the table, and the windows across from me revealed a familiar view of skyscrapers.

My heart sank. I was back in the conference room at Kent Corp headquarters—and I wasn't alone.

Julieta Delano was standing beside me, still clutching the injector she'd jabbed into my arm. She tossed the spent cartridge down onto the table, and it landed beside the dagger I'd had tucked in my belt. I eyed the dagger, wondering if I could lunge forward and grab it, but Julieta dropped her hand to the gold stormsword holstered to her belt, a clear warning that she would cut me down if I did anything she didn't like.

Rowena Kent was here too, sitting at the head of the table and pecking on a tablet. Sabine Kent was typing away on her own tablet, while Conrad was sitting across from me, trying to look cool, confident, and commanding, despite the sheen of sweat coating his forehead. He might be a climber, but he wasn't very good at doing the actual dirty, bloody work of being a Regal—not like Kyrion was.

If the Arrow had been here, he would have made short work of Conrad, along with Sabine and Rowena. Julieta would have been a much more difficult challenge, but he would have eventually killed her too. I could *see* the slaughter happening in my mind's eye—or maybe it wasn't my seer magic at all but rather wishful thinking on my part.

"How lovely. Our special guest is finally awake," Rowena drawled.

She set her tablet down. Sabine and Conrad also focused on me, as did Julieta.

"I should have ordered my men to kill you in this room when I first had the chance," Rowena said. "But I decided to be lenient, to show you some mercy, and this is how you repay me. By trying to destroy my House, my corporation, and everything I've worked so hard to build."

An angry laugh burst out of my lips. "*Mercy?* I woke up conscripted on an Imperium ship and was then thrust into a battle against the Techwave. That wasn't *mercy*. You just wanted to show me how much power you had and especially for me to suffer before I died."

"Yes, well, the conscription was Sabine's idea," Rowena replied. "I will *not* make that mistake again."

Sabine flinched at her mother's words, then glared at me for daring to survive her scheme.

"Why did you bring me here?"

Rowena shrugged. "To fix things, of course."

Suspicion filled me. "What do you mean?"

She tapped her fingers on the holoscreen embedded in the wood, and an image of Kyrion and me sneaking onto the Kent military cruiser last night flickered over the table. My heart sank a little lower. I thought I'd disabled the security cameras and scrubbed the footage, but apparently, I hadn't done as good a job as I'd thought.

Rowena hit another button, and the image shifted to an infrared one of me inserting the thumb drive into the ship's terminal, then Kyrion and me ducking into the supply closet. I held my breath, but she didn't hit any more buttons, and the image skipped forward to a few minutes later, when we snuck out of the closet. I plucked the drive out of the terminal, and Kyrion and I left the ship.

I relaxed a tiny bit. At least she didn't have footage of the two of us crammed into the closet together. I definitely didn't want that on display for my enemies to see.

"Did you really think I wouldn't have backup security measures on my ships?" Rowena asked. "Especially after Hal and his crew didn't return? I knew you were still out there somewhere. I expected you to run away as fast and as far as possible, but you're just not as smart as I thought you were."

Her words sliced into me, but I kept my voice steady. "Since you have that footage, then you know I downloaded all the ship's info, including the *Status: Armed* sensor command. I also know why you didn't fix the design flaw in your new line of ships. Because it's *not* a flaw. You purposefully built that command into the navigation sensors, which means the *Velorum* crash wasn't an accident, more like a preview of things to come. Tell me, did you design the Techwavers' new hand cannon too? The one that has enough power to cut through psionic shields, trigger the sensors, and take down all the new ships you're delivering to the Imperium?"

"I told you she would figure it out," Conrad muttered.

Rowena ignored him. "I might have had a hand in helping design the Techwave's new toys. As did you, Vesper."

I frowned. "How so?"

She tapped another button, and schematics hovered over the table. The design matched the hand cannon I'd seen during the lava field battle, and parts of it were shockingly familiar.

My stomach twisted. "That's *my* work, *my* design. The one I submitted to be transferred out of appliances and over to the weapons lab. The one Conrad told me was too cost-prohibitive to mass-produce when he denied my transfer request."

"Oh, yes." Sabine piped up, grinning at me. "Conrad sent me the specs. Mother and I saw the potential in your design and applied it to our new weapon."

"We were stuck on a few things, and your work let us unlock the cannon's potential," Rowena said. "So you see, Vesper, you also had a hand in creating the Techwave's new weapon, along with several other special projects. Something my friends and I are extremely grateful for."

Special projects? Horror flooded my veins like an icy river. What other weapons had they built using my ideas, my designs?

"Are you sure you want to kill her?" Julieta asked. "We could take her to one of the Techwave bases. Vesper could still be of some use, especially when it comes to creating more weapons to deploy against the Arrows. Why, given the proper motivation, she might even come up with something that will let you kill Callus Holloway outright, instead of him just absorbing an energy blast with his siphon power."

The way Julieta purred the words *proper motivation* chilled me to the bone.

Rowena studied me, her lips puckered in thought. She shook her head. "No. She's already escaped once. I won't risk that happening again. She could still ruin our entire operation."

Anger surged through me, drowning out my horror. "I've already ruined your operation. Kyrion Caldaren has a thumb drive with all the information about your rigged navigation sensor. He's probably showing it to Callus Holloway even as we speak."

A smile spread across Rowena's face. "Ah, yes. The thumb drive. I'll admit I was a bit concerned when I saw the footage of you downloading the information. But then I realized it was actually a marvelous opportunity."

"What sort of *opportunity?*"

"To blame you for everything."

Shock punched me in the chest, and I struggled to remain calm. "How are you going to blame me?"

Before Rowena could answer, Julieta sighed and shook her head. "You should have just let me break into Castle Caldaren and kill her, along with Kyrion. Then we wouldn't be forced to scrap the whole project."

I looked at her, and my magic kicked in, showing me that eerie double vision. Julieta as she was now, standing in the conference room, and a previous version of the Arrow, the mysterious figure firing the Techwave cannon at Kyrion. It was the same vision I'd had on Corios, right before she'd knocked me out, but the implications of it once again made my head spin.

"*You* were the one who shot Kyrion during the lava field battle. You tried to kill him. Why? I thought the two of you were friends."

"Friends?" An ugly, bitter laugh erupted out of Julieta's mouth. "I have *never* been friends with Kyrion Caldaren. Do you know what the difference is between me and Kyrion, Zane, and the rest of the Arrows?"

"No idea."

"They all have Houses and Regal families and proper fucking titles." She spat out the words. "Even though I'm one of the best fighters, I'll *never* be the leader of the Arrows, and I'll never rise any higher in the ranks, because I wasn't born on Corios, my parents weren't Regals, and I don't have enough seer magic for Holloway to siphon off whenever he likes. I hate them all—their arrogance, their archaic societal rules, their pretentions, and especially their psion power that they think makes them better, stronger, and smarter than everyone else."

Rage stained her cheeks a dark red, and the same emotion glittered in her golden eyes, making them burn bright and hot.

"You hate the Regals? Then why are you here with *them*?" I stabbed my finger at Rowena and Sabine. "Because they're Regals, and they have magic and Houses and proper fucking titles. They are everything you hate, so why are you working for them?"

Julieta's nostrils flared. *They're a means to an end. And when they have outlived their usefulness, I will kill them too.*

I blinked. Had I just . . . heard her thoughts? How? With my seer magic? Or . . . something else?

My gaze flicked over to Rowena and Sabine, who were staring at Julieta with curious expressions, as though they hadn't heard her murderous thoughts.

Julieta lifted her chin. "Rowena and Sabine aren't like the other Regals," she said in a deceptively calm voice. "They understand technology is the wave of the future. Not magic, bloodlines, and old, pointless, antiquated rituals about who should marry whom and why. Besides, they barely have enough spelltech power to qualify as psions anymore."

Rowena glowered at the other woman, clearly pissed at her revelation. Sabine also shot Julieta a similar withering look, while Conrad stared at both Rowena and Sabine with a shocked expression. Apparently, they hadn't let him in on their dirty little family secret.

I thought back over everything I knew about the Kents. Supposedly, Rowena and Sabine were spelltechs, like the previous generations of their family, but that sort of magic would be easy enough to fake, especially with the help of advanced technology.

"So that's why you stole my ideas. Because your magic is dwindling, and you couldn't figure the designs out for yourselves," I accused. "That's why you sabotaged the Imperium ships. That's why you want to kill the Arrows and wrest the throne away from Callus Holloway. You *have* to act now, before your magic fades away completely, your lack of power is exposed, and your Regal friends no longer support you."

Rowena shrugged off my words. "After the Arrows are eliminated, it will be open season on Holloway. He might be a powerful siphon, might have his precious Bronze Hand guards for protection, but he won't be able to stand against me and all his other enemies. Some of the other Regals have already joined the Techwave, including a few who are helping to fund the group. Together, we'll get rid of Holloway, one way or another."

"How are you going to do that? Once he knows you sabotaged his ships, Holloway will stop at nothing to eliminate you."

Another sly smile spread across Rowena's face. "And that's where you come in, Vesper. *I* didn't do anything to the ships. *You're* the one who sabotaged them."

A cold fist of dread wrapped around my heart. "What are you talking about?"

She hit a button on the screen, and the footage of Kyrion and me creeping onto the Kent cruiser started playing again. "I have all the proof I need of you sneaking onto one of my ships. And do you know what the best part is? I didn't even have to fake the footage. You boarded the ship willingly so you could upload your virus to the navigation system."

"What virus?"

She smirked at me. "The virus that tells the navigation sensor to execute an immediate, emergency dive that will drive any ship into the ground no matter how skilled the pilot is."

Status: Armed. The command hadn't popped up until *after* I'd inserted the thumb drive into the cruiser's terminal. Accessing the files must have triggered a virus Rowena had planted in the system, a virus that made it look like *I* was the one who had sabotaged the ship, instead of it already being rigged to crash.

Rowena leaned back in her chair and steepled her hands over her stomach. "*You* were among those who worked on the ship's design in the R&D lab, *you* went to investigate the *Velorum* crash, and *you* signed off on pilot error as the cause. But really, the whole thing was a sick, twisted proof of concept to your Techwave friends that you could crash Imperium ships, something they have paid you quite handsomely for."

This time, Sabine hit some buttons, and document after document filled the air. Credit transfers, bank records, and dozens of other pages of damning evidence. And perhaps worst of all, my name was on *everything*, including the final report officially attributing the *Velorum* crash to pilot error.

Nausea surged up in my stomach again, but I forced myself to keep thinking. "What about Kyrion? He knows the truth, and he has the thumb drive with the information proving what you did."

Sabine smirked at me much the same way her mother had. "Thanks to our virus, I was able to remotely access the thumb drive and replace the original files with the new ones related to you, Vesper. All Kyrion Caldaren has is more confirmation of your crimes."

I glanced over at Julieta. "So you're going to kill him too."

"Of course I'm going to kill him too. If Holloway doesn't beat me to it."

"Why would he do that?"

Julieta shrugged. "Holloway made Kyrion the leader of the Arrows because he's one of the best killers in the galaxy. But Holloway has always been much more interested in Kyrion having a truebond and the power he might siphon from such a connection. If Holloway thinks Kyrion betrayed him, then he'll order his Bronze Hand guards to take Kyrion to one of his palace labs. Holloway's doctors and scientists will take Kyrion apart one piece at a time until they figure out exactly how truebonds form and what makes them work."

Horror filled me at the thought of Kyrion being tortured, but I smothered the emotion with my own selfish drive to survive. I had to figure out some way to get out of this room, out of this building, and off this planet.

The sheer enormity of trying to escape threatened to over-whelm me, so I broke it down into the sum of its parts and pictured it as a machine in my mind. My living a few more minutes was just a faulty part in a brewmaker, something I had fixed countless times before. And just like with a faulty brewmaker, all I had to do was take it one step at a time. All I had to do was escape one step at a time.

"I think you've finally rendered her speechless, Mother." Sabine sneered at me again.

I looked at Conrad, who was still sweating, his face tense. "What about Conrad? You promoted him over me, and he was my supervisor through all of this, including the *Velorum* crash. Are you going to kill him too?"

He sucked in a strangled breath, as though he had never realized he was just as expendable as I was. Shortsighted idiot.

"Of course not," Sabine replied in a smooth voice. "Why, Conrad had no idea what you were doing. Of course, he knew you were jealous of his relationship with me, but he never *dreamed* you would go to such extremes just to get some petty revenge on us."

I snorted. "Oh, please. Conrad is not worth the effort of revenge, petty or otherwise."

Julieta chuckled, clearly agreeing with me.

"Regardless, it all ties together quite neatly," Rowena said. "A scorned woman desperate for wealth and power joins the Techwave and sabotages an important Imperium project. I'm actually starting to think you did me a favor by surviving your conscription, Vesper."

"You're right," I agreed. "It does all tie together quite neatly, except for the part where it makes you look grossly incompetent."

Rowena spread her hands out wide. "All the big corporations are riddled with spies. You were just a bit smarter and dug yourself in a little deeper than most. It's true the other Regals might snicker behind my back, but I don't care about them. As long as Callus Holloway considers the matter closed, I will humbly endure whatever slap on the wrist he gives Kent Corp, and all will be well until we can regroup and plan our next move."

My heart plummeted all the way down to my ankles. She was right. Blaming me for everything could work. No, scratch that. It *would* work.

And it pissed me off.

Rowena Kent had stolen my ideas, conscripted me onto an Imperium ship, and erased all traces of me from her corporation. Now she was going to reverse-engineer the whole process and make me the scapegoat for everything, including her alliance with the Techwave and her own plot against Holloway.

Rowena snapped her fingers. "Make it look like she was caught breaking into the building, then kill her."

Julieta grinned. "With pleasure."

She sauntered toward me, and I knew I had to say something *right now* to save my own life—or at least buy myself some more time to try to save my own life.

My gaze locked onto the still-playing footage of me plugging the thumb drive into the terminal, with Kyrion looking on, and an idea popped into my mind. "What are you going to do when Kyrion finds the original files that I downloaded?"

Julieta froze, as did Rowena, Sabine, and Conrad. They all glanced at one another.

"What original files?" Conrad asked.

"The day this all started, I made two copies of the original files. Hal found and destroyed one copy when he caught up with me after the lava field battle. But there's another copy, and Kyrion and I are the only two people who know where it is." I finished my lie and smirked at Conrad. "I guess you were so busy trying to erase me from the Kent Corp system that you didn't check to see how many copies I actually made."

His face paled, and a bead of sweat rolled down his right temple.

"Don't worry," Julieta said. "I can get her to talk."

She drew her stormsword and twirled it around in her hand. The lunarium blade caught the sunlight streaming in through the windows, and a wicked golden glow streaked along the razor-sharp edge. "Tell us where the original files are, Vesper, or I *will* kill you—right here and now."

I lifted my chin in defiance.

Without warning, Julieta lunged forward. I wrapped my hands around the chair arms and forced myself to sit absolutely still—

Her sword stopped three inches from my heart.

The two of us stared at each other. Julieta leaned forward, and her sword crept a little closer to my heart, as though she was going to kill me after all, but I didn't move, didn't waver, didn't even blink.

After a few more long, tense seconds, Julieta lowered her sword and stepped back.

I looked over at Rowena. "You want a scapegoat for your crimes, and I want to get off this planet and never see any of you again. So let's make a deal. The files for my life." I rocked back in my chair, which squeaked in protest. "Or we can just sit here and wait for Kyrion to show up with a bunch of Imperium soldiers to find out what's really going on. Your choice."

Rowena glared at me, as did Sabine. Even Conrad was glaring at me now, as though this situation was all my fault when the three of them were the ones engaged in a deadly conspiracy.

"Is it true?" Rowena asked. "Did she make another copy of the original files?"

Conrad started tapping buttons on the holoscreen. Less than a minute later, his fingers stuttered to a stop, and he sucked in another strangled breath. "She's telling the truth. She *did* make two copies of the original files."

"Told you so," I crowed. "Now, are you going to consider my offer? Because Kyrion is probably on his way here right now to get me *and* the files."

Silence descended over the conference room, and unease flickered across all their faces.

"She's bluffing," Julieta said. "She left Castle Caldaren this morning and was heading to the spaceport when I waylaid her. Kyrion didn't see me grab her on Corios, so he can't possibly know she's here."

She was probably right about that. Perhaps if we had still been bonded, Kyrion would have been able to sense my distress through the connection. Perhaps he would have even tried to rescue me, if only to keep himself from potentially being severely injured. Or perhaps he would have just let me die to finally sever the bond once and for all. No way to tell, and it was pointless to speculate.

Kyrion wasn't here, and I had to save myself.

"Tick-tock," I said in a mocking tone. "Every second you waste is a second Kyrion gets closer to killing all of you."

More silence.

Sabine looked over at Rowena. "Mother, you can't seriously be considering making a deal with this—this *nobody*. We're the Regals, we're the bloody Kents. *We* dictate terms, not the other way around!"

Rowena's cold green gaze settled on me. "It seems Ms. Quill has us at a disadvantage. Very well. We'll trade, the original files for your life. Do we have a deal?"

She leaned forward and held out her hand. I grasped her fingers in mine. As soon as I did, an image popped into my mind of Rowena shooting me in the back with a blaster.

But I smiled and shook her hand as though I hadn't seen a thing and didn't realize that she was going to kill me the second she got what she wanted. "Deal."

TWENTY-FOUR

VESPER

I got to my feet and headed toward the door, but Julieta blocked my path.

"Tell me where the files are, and I'll go get them," she said.

I laughed. "Sorry, but I'm not an idiot like Conrad. I'll get the files, which I will hand over to you. Then, after I am safely off this planet, I'll give you the code to access them."

Julieta glared at me, and I smirked right back at her, not giving any hint that I was lying about the files having an access code.

"Enough," Rowena said, getting to her feet. "Stop wasting time. I want this resolved as quickly as possible, just in case Kyrion Caldaren really is on his way here."

I smirked at Julieta again, and she stepped aside. I moved past her and opened the door. Julieta followed me, along with Rowena, Sabine, and Conrad.

I still couldn't believe I'd talked my way out of the conference room. One escape step down. Now, where could I take them where I might have a chance to get away? Or at least get my hands on a weapon and fight back?

I reached the elevator. A hasty plan formed in my mind, and I hit one of the buttons.

"The research lab?" Julieta asked in an incredulous voice. "You hid the files in the R&D lab?"

"In plain sight," I chirped in a cheerful tone. "It's not my fault Conrad was too stupid to search for them in there."

Conrad shot me a withering glare, which I ignored. I was probably still going to die in this building, but he wouldn't be too far behind me. Sabine might want to keep her lover around, but I was willing to bet both Rowena and Julieta were already plotting the best way to get rid of him.

We all stepped into the elevator, and it dropped down, down, down . . . No one spoke, and I visualized the lab in my mind, thinking about where everything was located and what makeshift weapons I might be able to get my hands on.

I wasn't too worried about Rowena, Sabine, or Conrad. Oh, they would definitely shoot me with a blaster if they got the chance, but Julieta was far and away the biggest threat. The Arrow was still clutching her sword, and she could easily kill me before I took three steps. I had to get away from her long enough to find a weapon of my own.

The elevator slowed, stopped, and chimed out the floor. The door slid back, and we walked over to the lab entrance. Conrad scanned his ID card, the security light flashed green, and the doors buzzed open.

Since it was Sunday, no one was working, and the lab looked the same as when I'd last been here several days ago. Even better, no one had finished their projects yet, and every-thing was still sitting out in the open. My gaze darted from one workstation to another, and I flipped through my mental catalog of all the projects and which ones might help me the most.

"Where are the files?" Julieta demanded, brandishing her sword at me.

My gaze locked onto my own workstation, and another idea popped into my mind. I headed in that direction. "This way."

Perhaps it wasn't the smartest plan to lead my enemies straight to the information they wanted, but this was still my best chance to escape or at least expose the Kents before Julieta killed me. Maybe I could access a terminal long enough to dump the files online and send them to my gossipcast contact. After that, the story would go viral within minutes, and Rowena and Sabine wouldn't be able to hide what they'd done. Oh, I would probably still end up dead, but Callus Holloway would eventually eliminate the Kents. I would settle for that bit of revenge.

As I walked through the lab, Julieta and Conrad flanked me, with Rowena and Sabine following us. The two Kents looked supremely bored by my field trip, and Sabine kept sneaking glances at her tablet, as though her messages were more important than saving her family's corporation and potentially her own life. Self-absorbed diva bitch.

Finally, we reached my workstation, which was just as I'd left it. All my projects were still in the same spots, including the flesh-colored gloves I'd been working on, along with the faulty brewmaker Conrad had dumped on the table the morning this whole thing had started.

"I thought you would have trashed all my stuff by now," I said.

"I've been too busy trying to track you down and clean up the mess you left behind," Conrad snapped.

"Aw, did things not run as smoothly in the lab when you couldn't steal my ideas and I wasn't around to do your work?" I clucked my tongue in mock sympathy. "How awful for you."

"Shut up," Conrad snapped again. "Where are the files? What kind of drive did you put them on?"

My gaze flicked over my workstation. Where was it?

There.

The plastic model of the *Velorum* was still resting on a pile of other models, and it didn't look like it had been touched since I'd first put it there. Excellent.

"Enough stalling," Julieta said. "Where's the drive?"

"Okay, okay, you win." I held my hands up and jerked my head at a plastic cup. "I hid a microdot drive in one of those gelpens. I hollowed out a secret compartment in the pen, then snuck it into the building."

I started to reach for the cup, which also contained a large screwdriver. Julieta brandished her sword again, and I froze.

"Do you think I'm blind?" she said. "Or that I would let you get your hands on a weapon?"

I shrugged. "It was worth a shot."

Julieta huffed in aggravation. "I'm a bloody Arrow, Vesper. I've killed more people in the last year than some generals have in their entire lifetimes."

"Which pen is it?" Conrad asked.

"The blue one."

He frowned, stepped forward, and started sorting through the pens. "They're all blue ones!"

In his eagerness to find the right pen, Conrad shoved me out of the way, sending me staggering to the side of the table, which was exactly where I wanted to be.

"Hey!" I yelped in fake protest, although no one bothered to look at me.

Conrad, Rowena, Sabine, and Julieta were all so focused on finding the gelpen that none of them noticed my hand creeping toward the *Velorum* model. I grabbed the plastic ship, shoved it into the back pocket of my cargo pants, and pulled my House Caldaren jacket down as far as it would go, further hiding the model. Then I flipped the switch on the faulty brewmaker and started counting down the seconds.

Twenty . . . nineteen . . . eighteen . . .

Conrad muttered a vicious curse, then upended the cup and spilled the pens inside all over the table. He frantically dug through them, snapping some of them in two to find that imaginary secret compartment. Sparkling blue gel splattered all over his hands, along with his fancy suit.

Ten . . . nine . . . eight . . .

"Where is it?" he growled.

Rowena's eyes narrowed in thought, and Sabine whirled around to face me.

Five . . . four . . . three . . .

"She's lying!" Sabine hissed. "She didn't hide the drive in any of those pens—"

Whoosh!

Sparks erupted all around the brewmaker.

Rowena, Sabine, and Conrad all shrieked and ducked down, but Julieta was a battle-hardened warrior, and she didn't give the sparking brewmaker a second glance.

"No more tricks," she growled.

The second the sparks winked out, I grabbed the detachable pot, surged forward, and smashed it against the side of the Arrow's head.

Crack!

The sturdy chrome pot made a satisfying noise against Julieta's skull, and she hissed and stumbled away. Conrad lunged at me, but I spun away from his awkward swing and plucked the screwdriver off the workstation. He lunged at me again, and I spun to the other side, then lashed out and stabbed the tool deep into his bicep.

Conrad howled with pain and jerked back. He plowed right into Sabine and Rowena, and the three of them went down in a heap on the floor.

Still clutching the brewmaker pot, I leaped over them and raced toward the front of the lab. All I had to do was get out of here, and step two of my escape would be complete. As for step three, well, I wasn't quite sure what that would be yet, but I would figure it out—

Footsteps pounded behind me, and I glanced back over my shoulder.

Julieta was sprinting toward me, her sword still clutched in her hand. Even worse, she had a speed enhancement, like so many Kent Corp workers did. She would easily catch me before I made it to the exit, so I changed direction, moving through the open doors into the weapons lab. My gaze darted around, as I tried to find something that would help me—

A silver gleam winked at me, and my gaze landed on the stormsword I had been ogling for the last several weeks.

I veered in that direction. I was twenty feet away from the sword. Fifteen feet, ten, five . . .

My magic surged up in warning. I stopped and ducked.

Julieta's sword whizzed through the air where my head had been. I whirled around and lashed out with the brewmaker pot again.

Julieta whipped up her sword, which clanged against the side of the pot, shooting hot sparks everywhere. She blocked my blow, then stepped forward. She could have easily sliced her sword through the container with one strike, but instead, she slowly, deliberately drove the blade through the metal one inch at a time. I tightened my grip on the handle and kept the pot between us.

"I'm going to enjoy cutting you to pieces!" Julieta hissed, her voice matching the eerie hum of the stormsword as it cut through the metal.

She shoved me back against the workstation. I kept my gaze on her and kept the disintegrating pot between us, but I reached out with my right hand, searching, searching, searching for the stormsword, but my fingers only came up with empty plastic.

Desperate, I glanced over at the weapon. My hand was about seven inches short of the hilt, and I couldn't move closer and try to grab it. Not with Julieta and her own sword still bearing down on me.

Come on! I thought, staring at the sword more intently than I had ever looked at anything in my entire life. *Roll toward me! Move in this direction! Seven more inches! That's all I need! Seven more inches—*

The sword flew up off the table and zipped over into my outstretched hand. I was so shocked I almost dropped the weapon, but I quickly wrapped my fingers around the hilt.

A jolt of . . . *something* shot through me, as though the stormsword was a live wire that had sparked against another one buried deep inside me and increased the power flowing through us both. Cold, heat, wind, force. All those sensations and more cascaded through my body before gelling into something hard, strong, and solid that wrapped around my mind and my heart.

Julieta's eyes narrowed. "You're a psion," she snarled. "Another bloody psion, just like Kyrion."

She moved forward. Her sword easily cut through the rest of the brewmaker pot, and the pieces clattered to the floor. At the last second, right before she would have cleaved me in two with the blade, I lurched to the side.

Julieta whirled around. I tightened my grip on the stormsword. The blade was roughly the same size as the wooden one Kyrion had trained me with, but its blue glow was weak and dim, especially compared to the bright magic and fiery gold sparks shooting off Julieta's blade.

"That's not going to save you," she said, twirling her own sword around in her hand.

"Probably not," I agreed.

An evil grin split her lips, and she raised her sword and charged at me.

I blocked her blow with my own weapon, and her sword sizzled up against mine, throwing more gold sparks everywhere, as though we were standing in the middle of a fireworks display. I braced my feet and shoved her away, but Julieta whirled around and attacked me again.

And again and again and again . . .

She drove me across the lab, not giving me any time or space to launch my own counterstrikes. After a few seconds, it became obvious she wasn't trying to kill me. At least, not immediately. No, Julieta was playing with me, just like a cat that had cornered a mouse.

"Holding a sword doesn't mean you know how to use it," she said. "And it certainly doesn't make you an Arrow. I had a vision of Kyrion training you with my seer magic, but he wasn't a very good teacher, was he? Because I'm going to kill you, Vesper."

She'd had a vision of Kyrion and me? A shiver skittered down my spine, but I widened my stance and braced myself for her next attack.

Try as I might, I just couldn't think of any of the things Kyrion had taught me. At least, not enough to go toe to toe with Julieta for any length of time. Why, oh why, couldn't I remember any of those lessons? Kyrion had certainly whacked me enough with that practice sword over the past few days that *some* of those lessons should have sunk into my mind.

Wait a second. Those lessons *were* in my mind—in my mindscape.

My seer magic let me remember everything that happened, everything I saw, did, and experienced, so maybe it would let me remember Kyrion's lessons too.

I thought of all those doors in my mindscape. Usually, I only went to that round room when I was dreaming or if something in the real world triggered a memory or a vision, but I desperately needed to go there right now if I wanted to keep breathing.

I backed away from Julieta. Oh, I could still see her standing in front of me, but at the same time, I was also peering into my mind's eye and searching for the door that led to all the lessons Kyrion had drilled into me over the past few days.

There it was.

I stared through the open door, watching Kyrion lash out at me with his practice sword. I saw every move and countermove. Every strike and pivot. Every attack and defense. Somehow seeing it from this angle, from outside my own body, made the lessons sink in and make sense in a way they never had back when Kyrion had actually been training me.

One by one, all the lessons started clicking in my mind, like keys opening one lock after another. In an odd way, it was like staring at a broken brewmaker. For the first time—the very first time—I could see all the things I had been doing wrong. And more important, how to fix them. How to make myself better.

How to survive.

Julieta twirled her sword around in her hand again, then lunged toward me. This time, instead of scurrying backward, I stepped up and blocked her blow. Surprise flickered across her face, but she whirled around and swung her sword again. This time, I blocked it, then lashed out with my own counterstrike.

More surprise filled her face, and she stepped back, eyeing me with wariness. "Looks like Kyrion taught you a few things after all. But they still won't save you."

I didn't bother responding. I was still too busy peering into that door in my mind and trying to absorb everything I could from Kyrion's lessons.

Julieta came at me again, hammering her sword into mine. I countered her blows, then lashed out with my own, both of us trying to kill each other any way we could.

Snarls and curses erupted from my lips, hers too, and we attacked each other time and time again. Julieta's sword kept throwing off hot gold sparks, which landed on some of the workstations, igniting the plastipapers there and making smoke wisp up into the air. Oddly enough, the curls of smoke reminded me of the ones that always leaked out of that open door of darkness in my mindscape.

Julieta swung at me, missed, and stumbled to the side. I yelled in triumph and rushed forward, thinking I had a chance to finally kill her, but she spun around and kicked out with her foot, catching me square in the chest. The hard motion tossed me back into one of the workstations, and my sword cut a swath through several glass beakers. The chemicals in the containers mixed together and exploded, sending liquid and a noxious cloud of blue gas straight into my face.

Heat seared my eyes, as though I'd rubbed liquid fire straight into them. Tears streamed down my face, but the salty wetness only intensified the burning sensation. I blinked and blinked, but a thick blue film covered my vision, and I could only make out vague, dark blurs.

Something moved. I swung my sword at it, but the weapon only sliced through empty air.

Julieta's low, mocking laughter sounded. "What's the matter, Vesper? Something in your eyes?"

Another blur of movement. I whirled in that direction, but I was too slow, and her sword zipped across my upper left arm, opening up a long, stinging gash.

I hissed and staggered back, still trying to see through the tears and blue film clouding my eyes. I lashed out with my sword again and again, but I didn't even come close to hitting anything, much less Julieta, who moved around me at will.

The Arrow darted in and out, opening up gashes all over my body. My right forearm, my right thigh, my left calf. She was slowly cutting me to pieces, just as she'd promised, and if I didn't find a way to stop her, she was going to kill me.

TWENTY-FIVE

VESPER

Julieta finally stopped attacking me. I still couldn't see her clearly, only the shadowy form of her slowly circling around, once again playing with me the way a cat would play with a mouse.

I *hated* being the mouse.

"I can see why Kyrion decided to train you," she said. "You actually have a modicum of potential. Too bad you won't live long enough to develop it."

Julieta stopped circling. "Although, why *did* he train you? Kyrion isn't known for his generosity. Just his propensity to kill people."

"Maybe he was bored," I said, trying to distract myself from the stinging wounds in my arms and legs. "Who knows why Kyrion Caldaren does anything?"

"Ah, but that's the problem. Kyrion *never* does anything without a reason, usually a very good one. At least, in his mind. So why would he bring a conscript to Corios, pretend you were a weapons consultant, and then start training you? Unless . . ."

Julieta's voice trailed off, but her speculation pulsed in the air between us. "Unless he was worried about your safety. But Kyrion wouldn't care about that. He doesn't care about anyone other than himself, something he's proven time and time again. Unless . . ." Once again, her voice trailed off.

"Unless what?" I ground out the words, still trying to blink the blue film out of my eyes, along with the tears.

"Unless something about your safety impacted his own." Her smug, delighted laugh echoed through the weapons lab. "Of course. I don't know why I didn't figure it out before, why my seer magic didn't clue me in. It finally happened, didn't it? After all these years of trying so desperately to avoid any attachments, Kyrion finally formed a truebond—with you."

A chill slithered down my spine. "I don't know what you're talking about."

Julieta laughed again, and the merry, mocking sound splattered all over me just like those chemicals had exploded in my face. "Oh, please, Vesper. There's no point denying it. I've been around Kyrion long enough to know how he thinks, and there is nothing he fears and dreads more than a truebond. Not that I blame him. A truebond is a truly awful thing."

"I would think you would relish the opportunity to have a truebond," I countered. "To be able to increase your own magic, skills, and strength just by having a connection to another person."

I got the impression Julieta shrugged, although I still couldn't see her clearly.

"I'll admit there are some advantages to a galactic bond," she replied. "I would dearly love to be able to form psionic weapons at will, the way that some truebonded couples supposedly can. But I wouldn't like having to share my magic with someone else. My power is my own. I've worked hard to master it, and it belongs to *me* and me alone."

As much as I hated to admit it, she had a point. Being forced to share your power with someone, rather than choosing to do it of your own free will, would be awful.

Julieta's sword hissed through the air. I tightened my grip on my own weapon and braced myself, expecting her to cut me again, but she must have just been twirling the sword around in her hand in that arrogant, showy motion she loved so much.

"I wonder, if I kill you, will that kill Kyrion too?" she purred, a speculative note in her voice. "That would be an excellent way to eliminate him once and for all."

"Killing me won't let you kill Kyrion too," I snapped back. "Because we are not bonded."

Julieta laughed again. "You're a terrible liar, Vesper."

She was right. I *was* a terrible liar.

"Fine," I admitted. "Kyrion and I were bonded. I think it happened during the battle on the lava field."

"When you saved his life?"

I blinked in surprise, although it didn't improve my eyesight. "How do you know about that?"

"I saw you help him across the lava field and into that downed blitzer," Julieta replied. "Although given the smoke, I couldn't see you clearly. I didn't realize you were the person causing the Kents so many problems until you tripped their ship's security system during the ball and Rowena realized you were on Corios. That's when she asked me to fetch you. But it doesn't surprise me that the bond formed during the Techwave battle. Trauma and stress are both thought to be triggers for truebonds, along with other psionic abilities."

I thought of all those doors in my mindscape, the ones that had never been there before I had met Kyrion. Perhaps Julieta was right. Perhaps all that trauma and stress had increased my own magic, in addition to triggering the truebond. Perhaps Kyrion's power had played a part in it too.

"Once I realized I hadn't killed Kyrion outright with the cannon, I shot the weapon down into the ground," she continued, circling me again. "It released the lava, just like I hoped it would. More cracks kept opening up, and more lava kept spewing up into the air. I fully expected it to incinerate you and Kyrion." She paused. "Which begs the question, how *did* you get past all that lava?"

"Kyrion's magic—"

Julieta snorted, cutting me off. "Please. Don't even try to spin that lie. Kyrion could barely stand without your help. He wasn't the one guiding the two of you across the field. That was all *you*, Vesper. Let me guess. Some little quirk of your magic?"

I ground my teeth again. Trying to see, listen, and lie all at the same time was exhausting. Or perhaps that was just the fatigue and blood loss sweeping through my body.

"Actually, now that I think about it, maybe I shouldn't kill you," Julieta said. "Despite their obsession with technology, the Techwave would *love* to get their hands on a truebonded pair. And if I took you to them, Kyrion would soon follow. Why, I bet the Techies would even put the two of you in adjoining cells so you could watch each other being dissected."

Icy claws of horror dug into my heart. Not just at the thought of myself being tortured but at Kyrion being tortured too. Despite everything that had happened between us, I still . . . cared about him far more than I should have.

"It doesn't matter who did what on the lava field. Just like it doesn't matter whether Kyrion and I bonded there."

"And why is that?" Julieta drawled, amusement coloring her voice.

I straightened up, still holding my sword out in front of me. "Because we're not bonded anymore."

Silence filled the air between us, and the only sounds were the mutual hums and crackles of our swords.

"I don't believe you," Julieta said.

"It's true. Kyrion and I are no longer bonded."

"You can't just *break* a truebond."

I shrugged. "Apparently, you can if the bond is new and hasn't had enough time to solidify. After we snuck off the Kent ship outside the palace, Kyrion and I went to a spelltech who gave us a nasty concoction of chemicals to drink. Bottoms up, and the bond was broken, just like that."

"I don't believe you," Julieta repeated, although a bit of uncertainty had crept into her voice.

"Think about it. I was on my way to the spaceport with a new identity and enough credits to live comfortably for the rest of my life. If Kyrion is as paranoid about truebonds as you say he is, why would he willingly let me out of his sight?"

Silence dropped over the lab again.

"Fuck," Julieta snarled. "You really *did* break the bond."

"Yep," I chirped. "No more bond, no more Kyrion, and no more Regals. Until you came along, kidnapped me, and dragged me back here."

My vision was still as fuzzy as ever, but I could have sworn Julieta was studying me with a thoughtful expression.

"You could always join us," she said.

Once again, I blinked in surprise. "Join the Techwave? Why would I ever do that?"

"Because the Techwave values people for their skills, not their magic and bloodlines and titles," Julieta said, bitterness leaking into her voice.

She sounded like Nerezza always had, pissed that she didn't get what she wanted exactly when she wanted it. Still, Julieta's argument wasn't without merit, and I'd felt the same way when Conrad had gotten the promotion that should have been mine.

"You're right," I replied. "The Regals *should* value people for their skills and smarts and not just for their magic, manners, and wealth, but the Techwavers are worse. They kidnap, torture, and experiment on innocent people and then trap them in metal shells and force them to fight to the death. And for what? So the Techwave higher-ups can get their hands on a few more weapons? Hard pass."

"Your loss," Julieta replied. "Although it's not just weapons the Techies are after. They have quite a few interests."

I started to ask what those interests were, but she cut me off.

"If you won't join us and you're not bonded to Kyrion anymore, then I have no further use for you, Vesper."

"What about the files?" I asked, trying to buy myself some more time. "I wasn't bluffing. I really do have a copy of the original files."

The *Velorum* model was still nestled in the back pocket of my cargo pants, although I had no idea how damaged it—and the microdot drive inside—might be from our fight.

"That's the Kents' problem," Julieta replied. "You're the only problem I need to eliminate, Vesper."

The hiss of her sword slicing through the air was the only warning I had before she attacked me again.

Julieta lashed out with her sword over and over again. I swung my own weapon wildly from side to side, not because I had any hope of hitting her but just to try to keep her from killing me.

To my surprise, it worked—for a little while.

But after about a minute, I got tired of swinging the sword so hard and violently, and I lowered the weapon just a fraction of an inch—

Whoosh!

Julieta's golden sword zipped through the air right in front of my face. I jerked back, but the sharp tip of her blade sliced across my right cheek.

I yelped and stumbled to the side. One of my hips slammed into a workstation. Blindly, I reached out. My fingers closed around a vial, and I tossed it where I thought she was. An instant later, the glass smashed against the floor.

Julieta's mocking laughter drifted over to me. "C'mon, Vesper. Even if you weren't as blind as a swamp bat, you still couldn't beat me. You're nothing but a little lab rat. You've always been a lab rat, and now you're going to die as one too."

Rage exploded in my heart, burning even hotter than the chemicals still stinging my eyes. She was right. For a long time, I had been nothing more than a little lab rat, dutifully going about my job and letting others take credit for my work, my designs, my brilliance.

But I wasn't the same person who had been conscripted onto that Imperium ship. I'd learned so much about myself and my magic over the past several days. I'd come too far and suffered through too much to die now, so I forced myself to do what I always did—take a step back and look at the problem objectively.

Of course, the main issue was that I still couldn't see what I was doing. The blue film in my eyes wasn't going away anytime soon, and blindly swinging my sword at Julieta wasn't working.

But maybe I didn't have to see what I was doing—at least, not with my actual eyes. I was a seer. Maybe it was time to figure out exactly what that meant and just how much I could, well, *see*.

The doors in my mindscape had always shown me things that had happened in the past, but maybe I could do more than that. Maybe I could peer into the present with my power. Maybe I could use my magic to see what my damaged eyes couldn't right now—Julieta and how to defeat her.

I didn't know if it would work, but it was the only chance I had, so I lowered my sword.

"Giving up?" Julieta drawled. "I'm disappointed, Vesper. I thought you had far more fight left in you. It's a good thing you're not bonded to Kyrion anymore. You would have been the death of him . . ."

I ignored her mocking words and went to my mindscape again. Instead of staring through the door where Kyrion was training me, I looked through the others, but they only showed more memories. I needed to see what was happening *right now*, in the present, here in the lab with Julieta.

But how could I do that? How could I open a door to the present if one wasn't already in my mindscape?

Wait. Maybe I didn't have to open a door. Maybe I could *create* the door myself, the same way I would sketch out a design for a new brewmaker.

So I hurried over to a blank space on the wall that was free of the doors, flowers, and eyes that filled so much of the round room. I traced my index finger along the stone, concentrating on the roughness scraping across my skin. I had always been a tactile person, so I dragged my finger along the stone and imagined it was a laser torch that could carve a new door into the wall.

Julieta kept crowing about killing me, but I tuned out her nasty words. They weren't important. All that mattered was creating this door to the present . . .

Slowly, my finger sank deeper and deeper into the stone, and the door began to take shape. Sweat streamed down my face, and my entire body shook with the effort of trying to use my magic this way, of trying to control it, rather than letting it sweep me away like it so often did . . .

I blinked, and from one second to the next, the door solidified in the wall in front of me.

"If you're not going to say anything, then I'm done playing with you, Vesper," Julieta said, annoyance filling her voice.

I flung that door open. Then, before I could think too much about what I was doing, I stepped through to the other side.

It was like free-falling out of a spaceship high in the atmosphere and jolting against the ground. In an instant, my view entirely changed. Instead of a teary, blue smear clouding my eyes, everything snapped into crystal-clear focus, and I could see everything in the lab, including Julieta standing in front of me. But my vision was also different now—sharper, brighter, and drenched in color.

Every single object was tinged with some sort of color, from the palest white shimmers around the workstations to the orange flares of the burning plastipapers to the gold sparks shooting off Julieta's stormsword. The colors flowed into each other, like waves crashing onto a shore and washing back out again, bringing ebbs and flows of energy along with them.

Magic—I was seeing magic itself.

That phantom power, that invisible energy that seers and other psions could tap into. The beautiful swirl of colors reminded me of a comet spinning, dancing, and burning through the galaxy, leaving behind ripples in everything, all the properties that magic controlled—time, space, matter, power, motion.

My eyes widened, and my breath caught in my throat. The colors were so stunningly pure and overwhelmingly beautiful that I wanted to cry.

A bright golden streak slashed toward me. The other colors dimmed, except for the glow of Julieta's sword zooming toward my chest. I snapped up my own weapon, blocking her attack.

Her forehead creased in confusion. "What's wrong with your eyes? Why are they glowing that like?"

I had no idea, and I didn't care right now. All that mattered was killing her.

With our weapons still locked together, I held out my hand and dipped my fingers into those swirling colors, reaching for even more magic, a *different* kind of magic. A vial flew off a nearby table and zipped into my hand. The second my fingers curled around the glass, I slammed it into the side of Julieta's head.

She shrieked in pain and surprise and stumbled away. She whirled back around to me, bits of glass stuck to her skin, as blood flowed down her face and spattered onto the floor. Her eyes narrowed, and her lips drew back into a silent snarl as she attacked me.

Julieta swung her sword at me in a series of fast, furious arcs, but I blocked her blows. Not only did I know what she was going to do, thanks to Kyrion's training, but with my magic, I could also *see* her attacks before she even made them, as though I had skipped a few seconds ahead in a movie and already knew what was going to happen next.

Julieta spun away from me. "How are you doing this?" she yelled. "You're bloody blind! How are you blocking my attacks?"

I didn't know how to put it into words she would understand. I barely understood it myself.

She growled and swung her sword at me again. I blocked her blow but just barely. I might be able to see her now, but she had already cut me several times, and the fatigue and blood loss were creeping up on me with every ragged breath I sucked down.

Julieta pressed her advantage, slicing her sword from side to side. This time, I was the one who staggered back, desperately trying not to get slashed to ribbons.

I took another step back, and my boot slipped on some of the glass littering the floor. I skidded to the side, and Julieta sliced her sword across my left hip.

I screamed and staggered back. I hit one of the workstations, making it rock violently from side to side. I also banged my hand against the edge of the workstation hard enough to make my fingers go numb. The stormsword dropped from my shaky grip, hit the floor, and tumbled away. I started to go after it, but Julieta lunged in front of me.

I jerked back and slammed into another workstation. Before

I could move, Julieta was in front of me, her sword up and ready to strike. I froze.

Then Sabine appeared at the entrance to the weapons lab.

"Forget her! We have to get out of here!" she screamed. "Now!"

She darted away. I didn't see Rowena or Conrad, but no doubt they would be scurrying after her. What had spooked them?

Julieta's eyes narrowed, and she gingerly touched her face. A few drops of blood slid down her chin and spattered onto the front of her red Arrow jacket. "If I had the time, I would slice your skin off one layer at a time," she hissed.

I ignored her threat and slid my hand backward on the table, searching for a vial or whatever else I could find—

Julieta slammed her sword down onto the table, inches away from my fingertips. I jerked my hand back and started to sprint away, but she was quicker, and she brought her sword down onto the other side of the table, forcing me to stand still.

She raised her weapon high overhead. Instead of trying to escape again, I launched myself forward and drove my right shoulder straight into her chest. Julieta's boots skidded on the floor, and she lurched back. This time, she was the one who slammed into a workstation, and her sword dropped from her hand and rolled away.

Julieta shoved me, and I staggered back, clutching my injured hip. Her stormsword spun to a stop right between the two of us. She sprinted toward the weapon, but I turned away from her and stretched my hand out, reaching for the sword I'd dropped earlier.

Air and magic flowed over me, ruffling my hair. Even though my back was to her, in my mind's eye, I could see Julieta grabbing her sword and racing toward me again. I stretched out my own hand and flexed my fingers a little farther and wider than before, focusing on the other stormsword, which was still lying on the floor.

Time seemed to slow to a crawl and yet speed by impossibly fast at the same time. The sword on the floor wiggled its way out of a pile of debris. I took a step forward and reached out with more magic. Behind me, Julieta raised her weapon to deliver a killing strike.

The stormsword flew across the lab and settled into my hand. I gripped the hilt, whirled around, and punched the blade straight into Julieta's heart an instant before she would have stabbed me in the back.

Julieta sucked in a strangled breath, and her golden eyes bulged in pain. She stared at me in shock and disbelief, and a thin trickle of blood spilled out of her mouth and dribbled down her face.

The Arrow toppled forward, straight into me, and we both dropped to the floor.

TWENTY-SIX

KYRION

"**Y**ou are *not* authorized to land here!"

A stern voice blared over the comms system in the blitzer, but I ignored it, just as I had ignored all the other warnings so far. Even the most zealous corporate security stooge would think twice about shooting an Imperium blitzer out of the sky. And even if they tried, the ship's shields would absorb any cannon fire that came this way.

I steered the ship a little lower toward the grassy lawn outside the main Kent Corp building, then engaged the autopilot and set it to landing mode. I got to my feet, drew my sword, and waited for the cargo bay ramp to open.

After I'd realized the thumb drive had received new data, I had given it to Daichi, who had traced the signal back to its source, a House Kent server on Corios. That, combined with the new files with Vesper's name, had confirmed my feeling that something was very, very wrong.

Daichi had hacked into the security and traffic cameras on Corios, and he'd found Vesper's transport heading away from the spaceport instead of toward it. The transport had entered a blindspot, so I hadn't seen who had abducted her, but I knew exactly where they had taken her: Kent Corp headquarters on Temperate 42.

So I'd hopped into a blitzer and left Corios to hunt them down.

"For the tenth time. You are not authorized to land here! Abort! Abort! Or you will be fired upon!" Another warning sounded through the comms system, and yellow cannon fire erupted from the top of the Kent Corp building.

The cannon blast hit the blitzer dead-on, although, thanks to the shields, it merely rocked the ship from side to side. I grabbed a strap hanging down from the ceiling and held on to it while the shields dissipated the blast and absorbed its energy.

"Abort!" the voice demanded again. "Abort now, or you will be fired upon again!"

I didn't give a damn about clearance or procedure or anything else. All that mattered was finding Vesper before it was too late. The blitzer landed, and the cargo bay ramp lowered. I released the strap and straightened up to my full height, my stormsword already glowing a dark, menacing blue in my hand.

The instant the ramp touched the ground, I marched down it.

Kent Corp guards were waiting on the lawn, clutching blasters and shock batons. More than a dozen men and women were spread out in a line about thirty feet away from the ship. I headed straight toward them. During the pinpoint flight to Temperate 42, I'd changed into my uniform, although I hadn't bothered donning a helmet.

"Fuck," one of the guards said. "That's an Imperium Arrow."

"Not just any Arrow," another one chimed in. "Kyrion Caldaren."

Several soft, muttered curses sounded. I grinned. Sometimes being a known monster had its advantages, especially when it came to other people's fear.

"You heard what Rowena Kent said," another guard replied, his voice high and nervous. "No one gets into the building, especially not him."

More muttered curses and uneasy murmurs rang out, but the guards held their positions. I kept striding toward them, wondering which one had the itchiest trigger finger—

A man to my left fired his blaster, but I snapped up my sword and deflected the energy bolt right back at him. The man screamed and crumpled to the ground, smoke rising from the hole the blast had punched into his breastplate. Vesper was right. Kent Corp armor really was cheap junk.

"Fire! Fire! Fire!" the squad commander screamed.

The guards started shooting at me, but I used my sword to deflect all the blasts right back at them. One guard dropped, then another one, then two more. By the time I reached their line, half the guards were already injured or dead, and the caustic stench of blaster fire, along with cooked flesh, filled the air.

A couple of the remaining guards fled, but those who weren't as smart raised their shock batons and charged at me.

I threw myself into the fight, whirling, twirling, spinning back and forth, and wielding my stormsword like the awesome instrument of death it was. I chopped one man's arm off, then took out another one by literally cutting him off at the knees. The guards were all enhanced with strength, speed, and other abilities, but they couldn't withstand my psionic skills, and they were especially no match for my icy fury.

No one was going to stop me from finding Vesper.

No one.

A guard—the last uninjured man—rushed up and jabbed his shock baton into my left side. For some reason, it hurt far more than I expected, and I went down on one knee. The guard pressed his advantage, shoving his baton into my side again.

I braced one hand on the ground, then spun around and lashed out with my right foot, kicking the other man's legs out from under him. The guard landed hard on his back on the ground. I popped upright and reached for my telekinesis. His shock baton flew into my left hand, and I jabbed the weapon straight into his crotch.

The man howled, his entire body jerking and convulsing. I yanked the baton away, but he kept twitching and jerking, moaning between his chattering teeth.

"Where is Vesper Quill?" I snarled.

The guard stared up at me, his eyes wide with fear. I hit the button on the side of the baton, making the end spark with white-hot electricity, and held it right in front of his face.

"Tell me where Vesper is, or I'll put your eyes out one at a time."

I inched the baton toward his left eye, which bulged even wider than before.

"She's—she's in the main building!" he sputtered. "Straight ahead!"

I jabbed the baton into his crotch again. The guard screamed for a few more seconds, then went limp and still. I tossed the baton aside, straightened up, and stepped over him.

Farther out on the campus, people were pointing and staring and using their tablets to film me, along with the blood and bodies now littering the grass, but I didn't care.

All that mattered was getting to Vesper. So I fixed my gaze on the main building and quickened my strides.

Another squad of guards was waiting inside the lobby. These people had been smart enough to take up fortified positions, and, as soon as I stepped through the door, they opened fire, forcing me to scurry to the side and take cover behind one of the large recyclers by the entrance.

Blaster bolts *ping-ping-pinged* off the metal and zipped into the permaglass all around the lobby, scorching the clear finish. I wrapped my cold, crackling power around me like an invisible shield, then stood up and waved my hand. The recycler flew up off the floor, sailed through the air, and crashed right into the center of the main security desk. The motion surprised the guards and made them rush out from behind it like rats desperately fleeing a sinking ship.

I charged into the fray, cutting down first one guard, then another, then another. Screams, whimpers, and pleas for mercy rang out, while the stench of blaster fire once again filled the air, along with the sizzle of singed hair and burned skin. But they were only minor annoyances, things I had seen, heard, and smelled a thousand times before, and no more significant than flies buzzing about my head.

I cut a path through these guards as easily as I had done outside. Soon only one guard was left standing, a woman this time.

I swung my sword, slicing through the end of her blaster. She yelped and dropped the rest of the ruined weapon. Then I reached out, grabbed the front of her uniform, and yanked her toward me.

Her eyes widened, and her mouth gaped in fear. I could see my own faint reflection, along with the dark blue burn of my stormsword, in the clear visor that covered her face.

"Where is Vesper?" I demanded.

"In the—in the lab!" the woman sputtered. "They're in the R&D lab! Downstairs!"

I shoved her aside and headed toward a door marked *Stairs—Emergency Exit* at the far end of the lobby. I pushed through it and sprinted down the steps.

By this point, alarms were blaring in the lobby, and probably throughout the entire building, although the noise faded away as I hurried down the steps.

I didn't encounter any more guards, and I quickly reached the bottom of the steps, which ended at a locked door. A swipe of my sword through a nearby keypad took care of that, and the door cracked open with a weak, disjointed *be-ep*.

I stepped into a long corridor. I moved a bit more slowly and cautiously through this area, expecting to run into more guards—

Footsteps scuffed on the floor, and a man darted out into the corridor in front of me.

He caught sight of me and skidded to a stop. He was clutching several pens, and blue gel stained his hands. I recognized him. Conrad Fawley. The man Vesper had been involved with. The one who had dropped her in favor of Sabine Kent. Fool.

"Wait!" he yelled. "Wait for me!"

Conrad turned and sprinted in the opposite direction. A couple of gelpens dropped from his hands and clattered to the floor. He cursed their loss but kept right on running.

I considered following him, but the guard had said Vesper was in the lab, so I headed in that direction.

I expected some sort of resistance, but there was none, and I quickly reached the lab. The doors were standing wide open, and I tightened my grip on my sword and strode forward, again moving slowly and cautiously.

Rows of clear plastic tables covered with terminals, appliances, and parts stretched out in all directions. Everything was clean, white, and sterile, and the lab was eerily quiet, except for the faint hissing of the air-conditioning system.

I stopped and reached out with my power, searching for Vesper, but I didn't sense her—or anyone else—in the lab. Instead of the velvety ribbon of awareness that had connected us, all I felt now was an icy numbness, the same sensation

I had experienced when I had first drunk Touma's chemical concoction. A frustrated snarl escaped my lips. Even though severing the bond had been the right thing to do, it would have been useful in helping me locate Vesper now.

Sword in hand, I walked through the lab, my gaze sweeping over the tables. Did the Kents make anything besides bloody brewmakers?

Something in the back of the lab caught my eye. A gelpen was sitting on the floor, just like the ones Conrad had been clutching.

I looked over at two nearby tables, which were covered with plastipapers, wires, and tools, along with spaceship models. This had to be Vesper's desk, and the clutter on it suggested that the Kents—or whomever they had employed to do the task—hadn't gotten around to clearing out her things yet.

A grim smile tugged at my lips. Somehow Vesper had convinced the Kents to bring her to the lab, the place where she had spent so much time and which she knew better than anyone else, and she had turned it against them. Smart—very, very smart.

Now I just had to find her.

A sense of urgency swept over me, stronger than before, and I whirled around and headed back toward the front of the lab. I rounded another table, and I finally saw what I'd been searching for all along.

Blood.

Several drops of blood glistened on the floor, spaced far apart, as though someone had been moving fast—or engaged in a vicious fight. I hurried forward, moving into what looked like a weapons bunker filled with experimental blasters and cannons.

In addition to the blood, more debris started appearing. Broken bits of glass. Charred plastipapers. Crushed models and cracked solar batteries. Dread sparked in my chest. I quickened my pace and rounded a table—

A woman was lying on the floor.

My heart did an uncomfortable somersault, even as my gut clenched with worry. I leaned down, grabbed the woman's shoulder, and rolled her over onto her back.

Julieta's sightless eyes stared up at the ceiling.

Relief rushed through me, although it was quickly followed by confusion. What was Julieta doing here? Suddenly, I remembered the shadowy figure that had fired the Techwave cannon at me on Magma 7. Julieta had been working for the Kents and the Techwavers. Of course she had.

So many things made sense now, including how the Techwavers always seemed to know exactly when we were coming and stay one step ahead of us. But I pushed those thoughts aside, along with the dull sting of Julieta's betrayal. I still needed to find Vesper—

A flutter of movement caught my eye, and I surged to my feet and whirled around. Vesper was propped up against a nearby table, and one of the air-conditioning vents was ruffling the bottom of her House Caldaren jacket.

I hurried over and dropped to one knee beside her. "Vesper! Vesper!"

She didn't stir, so I grabbed her shoulder. She was still alive, but she didn't respond to either my voice or my touch. My gaze skimmed over her body, and I studied all the ugly, bloody gashes on her arms and legs, as well as the deeper wound on her left hip. Julieta had sliced her to ribbons. If the other Arrow had still been alive, I would have killed her myself for that.

I set my sword down, plucked a small injector off my bandolier, and stabbed it into Vesper's left thigh. Her body jerked once, but she didn't stir. I tossed the spent cartridge aside and reached for another one—

Vesper sucked in a breath and sat bolt upright. Her eyes darted wildly from side to side, and she kept blinking and blinking as though she couldn't see very well. No doubt, that was due to the pale blue chemical burn that covered the top half of her face like a space pirate's mask.

She squinted in my direction as though she was trying to see past whatever was wrong with her eyes. "Who's there?"

I opened my mouth, but she cut me off before I could answer.

"Kyrion." She breathed my name like a sigh of relief, and some of that strange, unwanted pressure in my chest eased.

"I'm here. Right in front of you."

I hesitated, then reached out and gently, carefully cupped her cheek. Vesper shuddered, and I dropped my hand, not wanting to cause her any more pain.

"I gave you a skinbond injection. It should close up the worst of your wounds."

"I can feel it. Damn chemicals are like fire running through my veins." Vesper shuddered out another breath, then held her hand out to me. "Help me up."

"I don't think that's a good idea."

"Help me up," she demanded. "Now. Before they get away."

"Who?"

"The Kents and Conrad and whoever else is still helping them."

I grasped her forearm and slowly pulled her upright. Vesper swayed from side to side, but she quickly steadied herself.

"Did you see anyone?" she asked. "Outside the lab?"

"Just your friend Conrad."

I told her which way he had gone, and a grim look filled her face.

"I know where they're going. Come on. Oh, and I need you to get something for me."

Vesper told me what she wanted. I went over to one of the weapons lockers along the wall and used my sword to slice through the metal grate. Then I shoved my sword onto my belt and pulled a large hand cannon out of the locker. I couldn't tell for certain, but it looked like the same sort of weapon Julieta had shot me with on Magma 7.

"What are you going to do with this?" I asked, walking back over to Vesper. "Especially since you can't see right now?"

"I can see just fine," she replied. "If I want to."

Before I could puzzle out what she meant, Vesper jerked her head and held out her hand to me again.

"Come on," she said. "Let's finish this."

TWENTY-SEVEN

KYRION

Vesper clutched my left arm, and I led her out of the lab, still holding the cannon in my right hand. Even though she still didn't seem to be able to see where we were going, she fired off directions, and I took her where she wanted to go. We stepped into an elevator, and she rattled off a code.

"Roof access granted," the elevator chirped, then started to rise.

"How do you know the roof code?" I asked.

"I fixed the elevator a couple of months ago," Vesper replied. "The regular repair guy was having problems. I helped him figure out what was wrong, and he paid me back by giving me the master access code to all the levels, including the roof."

"Nice."

She grinned and looked at the wall where she thought I was.

The elevator zoomed upward, and the floors whooshed by one after another.

"How did you know to come here?" Vesper asked.

I told her about the thumb drive rewriting itself and pinging Daichi's security system. She nodded and told me what had happened here, including Julieta's confession about working with the Kents and the Techwavers.

"I'm sorry," Vesper said. "That Julieta betrayed you."

I started to shrug but then realized she couldn't see the motion. "It's not the first time an Arrow has gone rogue. It won't be the last time."

She frowned and tilted her head to the side as though something about my words bothered her. Even stranger, her eyes flashed that bright silver-blue, as though she was seeing something with her power. Before I could ask her what it was, the elevator floated to a stop, and the door slid back.

"Hold on to my left shoulder and stay behind me," I said. "We don't know how many guards are up here."

Vesper nodded, and her hand landed on my shoulder. Her touch was as light as a butterfly resting on my jacket, but the slight weight of it pleased me in some way I couldn't quite explain, not even to myself. I made sure the cannon was armed, then stepped out of the elevator with Vesper following.

We walked down a short corridor to a locked door. A blast from the cannon fried the keypad on the wall, and the door buzzed open. We went outside.

The roof was typical for a corporate skyscraper, a wide, flat, open space with enough room to land a couple of ships, with a tall, skinny shack that served as a flight control tower and security station.

A couple of guards ran out of the station, probably the same fools who'd fired at me, but a couple of blasts from the cannon sent them scurrying back inside. At the opposite end of the roof, an engine roared to life. I hurried in that direction, with Vesper still clutching my shoulder, but we were too late.

A ship lifted off the platform, rising into the sky. Rowena

Kent was standing on the observation deck, staring down at us, along with Sabine and Conrad.

"They're already taking off," I growled. "We won't be able to stop them."

"Which ship are they in?" Vesper asked. "Is it a small cruiser?"

"Yes." I rattled off the name and identification number, and a beatific smile spread across her face.

"Do you see a round disk?" she asked. "It should be right under the observation deck windows. That's where the navigation sensor is."

"I see it."

"Good. Fire the cannon at it—only that spot, nowhere else."

I frowned. "But won't the ship's shields deflect the blasts?"

"They might, but we'll never know unless you try."

I hefted the cannon up, aimed it at the ship, and fired. Whoever was piloting the ship hadn't engaged its shields yet, and the blast zinged straight into the vessel, right where the sensor was. I pulled the trigger over and over again, sending one blast after another into that part of the hull. The ship veered wildly from side to side, as though it was a living thing trying to shake off the sting of the energy blasts, but it didn't rise any higher into the air.

"Keep going!" Vesper said. "Keep shooting!"

I did as she commanded, sending several more rounds of cannon fire at the ship. Almost all the blasts hit home, and the disk began to glow a telltale yellow, then orange, then red as it heated up.

"One more shot!" Vesper called out.

I pulled the trigger again, sending out yet another blast that hit the disk dead-on. Something exploded, and that part of the hull burst into flames.

The ship veered wildly from side to side again, as though whoever was at the controls was fighting to keep it upright. For a few seconds, I thought they might succeed—until one of the wings clipped the control tower.

The shriek of crumpling metal and breaking glass ripped through the air, even louder than the ship's rumbling engine. Guards poured out of the bottom of the tower, trying to escape the destruction as the ship sheared through the side of the structure. Something else exploded on the cruiser, sending it into a vicious spin.

I started to grab Vesper's arm to pull her back, but she waved her hand.

"We're fine," she said.

Instead of retreating, she strode forward, right toward the still-spinning ship. Vesper reached the edge of the roof. Again, I started to grab her arm, but she stopped herself, almost as if she knew exactly where the edge was, even though I doubted she could see much of anything through the chemical burn on her face.

Above us, the ship stopped spinning in favor of whipping from side to side yet again. Then, with what sounded like an enormous, defeated groan, one of the engines blew, and the cruiser plunged straight down, streaking toward the ground like a meteorite.

WHOOSH!

The ship slammed into the lawn in front of the Kent Corp building, right below the edge of the roof where we were standing. Dirt, grass, and rocks spewed up into the air like an erupting volcano, and the rich, dark scent of churned earth filled my nose.

The cruiser had hit the ground point-first, and with an enormous *creak*, the back end slowly thumped down, as though the ship was an oversize toy some giant child had dropped on the lawn. Fires broke out on the ship's hull, and the stench of charred metal and grass flooded the air.

"Safety hazard!" Vesper crowed in a triumphant voice.

A laugh burst out of my mouth. She joined in with my chuckles, although she clutched her ribs, as though they were still aching despite the skinbond injection I'd given her.

Down below, several guards streamed out of the building and hurried toward the ship. One of the side hatches opened, and Rowena Kent tumbled down to the ground, followed by Sabine and Conrad.

"What are you doing?" Rowena yelled. "Why are you just standing around like brainless idiots? Help me! Now!"

A couple of guards rushed forward, latched on to her arms, and set her on her feet, although Rowena started listing from side to side, as though her equilibrium had been thrown off by the crash. Sabine and Conrad were similarly stumbling around.

More people appeared on the lawn, but these men and women were wearing the dark red uniforms of Imperium soldiers instead of the dull brown of the Kent Corp guards.

The Imperium captain stepped forward, a blaster in her hand. "Lady Rowena Kent. By order of Callus Holloway, you and your associates are to be taken into custody."

"On what charge?" Rowena demanded, still listing from side to side.

"High treason," the captain replied. "For starters."

"Friends of yours?" Vesper asked.

A grin spread across my face. "Something like that. Before I left Corios, I asked Daichi to leak a story to one of the gossipcasts about Rowena's sabotage and how she was trying to flee from Kent Corp headquarters on Temperate 42."

"Nice," Vesper purred.

The Imperium captain waved her hand, and the other soldiers raised their shock batons and surrounded Rowena, Sabine, and Conrad. Rowena kept screeching at the soldiers to let her go. Sabine did the smart thing and held up her hands in surrender, but Conrad started running. He only managed to take about three steps before an Imperium soldier shoved a shock baton into his back. Conrad shrieked and toppled to the ground.

"I wish you could see this," I said.

"Oh, I can see it well enough," Vesper replied in a smug, satisfied voice. "And I'm enjoying every single second."

Side by side, we stood on the roof and watched while Rowena, Sabine, and Conrad were led away from the crashed ship.

Things happened quickly after that.

Another squad of Imperium soldiers arrived, along with Zane, and Rowena, Sabine, and Conrad were placed in holding cells inside the Kent Corp building.

"I want a deal," Conrad said the second I stepped into the cell.

He was sitting down, and his plasticuffed hands were attached to a metal ring embedded in the tabletop. He was sweating heavily, and dark stains had already appeared under his arms.

I leaned my back against the wall and crossed my arms over my chest. "Why should I give you a deal? I already know about you and the Kents sabotaging the navigation sensors on the new Imperium ships. I also know Rowena Kent is working with the Techwave and that this was all part of an elaborate plot to kill Arrows and Imperium soldiers, create instability among the Regals, and wrest the throne away from Callus Holloway. So I see no reason to give you a deal."

Conrad paled at my words, and more sweat popped out on his forehead and trickled down his face. Disgust filled me, and I could barely restrain myself from drawing my sword and removing his head from his shoulders. I had encountered more Conrads in my life than I cared to remember, people who would do anything to get ahead but still wanted a soft landing the instant things turned against them and they started slipping off the treacherous Regal ladder they were trying so very hard to climb.

The door opened, and Vesper stepped inside. She must have found a medkit somewhere, because her face was now free of the worst of the chemical burn, although a bit of blue still ringed her eyes. She had also donned a white lab coat, and the fabric hid some of the rips and blood all over her other clothes.

Vesper pulled out the chair across from Conrad and set a model ship on the table between them.

"What is that?" he asked.

Vesper picked up the plastic ship and pried it open. A microdot drive dropped out of the hollow center of the model and landed on the table. She picked it up and handed it to me.

"This drive contains the original files on the *Velorum* crash, the ones that don't blame me for everything. I took the liberty of uploading them to a gossipcast. Anonymously, of course. I had a contract to fulfill."

"Of course," I murmured, sliding the drive into my pocket. Holloway would want to see it later—and her too.

Vesper sat back in her chair and studied Conrad. Her face was unreadable, but regret flickered off her and twinged my telempathy. I wasn't sure who the emotion was for, though—Conrad for all the trouble he was in now or herself for ever caring about him.

Conrad would be lucky if he was executed quickly, instead of being taken to one of Holloway's labs to be dissected, used for experiments, and then put on display as a visual reminder to all the Regals about what happened when their plots went awry.

Conrad leaned forward and plastered a smile on his face. I had to hand it to the man. He truly was a gifted actor, able to pivot from conniving and terrified to seeming warmth and softness in a matter of seconds. Then again, desperation was a powerful motivator.

"Vesper," he said, wetting his lips. "You have to know that none of this—none of it!—was my idea. The Kents threatened me, and I had no choice but to go along with them."

Vesper tilted her head to the side, studying him the way a hunting falcon would study a rabbit it was about to gobble down. It was a good look on her. "Really? Because you seemed pretty eager for Julieta to murder me in the conference room earlier."

Conrad shook his head. "That was just for show. You know how much I care about you, Vesper. I would never want any harm to come to you."

She laughed, and Conrad flinched at the harsh, caustic sound. "No, I imagine you didn't want any harm to come to me. At least, not at first. You didn't care about me enough for that. You were just using me to advance your own career, and when you got your hooks into Sabine Kent, you finally saw your chance to climb the Regal ladder."

Conrad opened his mouth, probably to keep denying everything, but Vesper waved her hand, cutting off his lies. Too bad. I would have been happy to shut his mouth—and make him eat his own bloody teeth.

Vesper sighed and shook her head. "I can't believe I wasted so much time, energy, and emotion on you. What a fool I was."

She wasn't the only one who had been a fool for what they thought was love. I too had been a fool, years ago with Francesca, and I was starting to think I was being a fool again, right now, with Vesper.

"What else did you do for the Kents besides steal my designs and sabotage the Imperium ships?" Vesper asked.

Conrad wet his lips again. "I don't know what you mean. Like I said before, the Kents forced me to do everything. Rowena said she would have me killed if I didn't go along with her plans for you and the ships and everything else."

Vesper rolled her eyes. "Still going to sing that tired old tune? Fine." She got to her feet, turned her back to Conrad, and gave me a sly wink. "I'm sure Lord Kyrion will be more than happy to ensure your cooperation. Right, my lord?"

I dropped my hand to my sword, pushed away from the wall, and towered over Conrad, my shadow engulfing him.

An ocean of fresh sweat flooded his forehead. "What—what do you want to know?"

"Everything," Vesper replied.

She sat back down and started asking Conrad about the navigation sensors, the ships, and other technical things I couldn't quite follow, but her smart, probing questions—and his replies—revealed even more misdeeds by the Kents. The longer Vesper questioned Conrad, the more her eyes started glowing, and the stronger her seer magic became as it swirled through the air. Her psion power was clueing her in to what Conrad was going to say even before he said it, letting her ask even more pointed questions and steer him exactly where she wanted him to go.

It was . . . *She* was . . . impressive.

Vesper pulled up several files on a tablet, verifying everything Conrad said. I held my position in case he decided to stop cooperating, but he spilled his guts with no further prompting from me.

Conrad was right. He had quite a lot to share.

Not only had the Kents been sabotaging the Imperium ships, but they'd also been secretly developing other tech, although Conrad didn't know whether it was to help the Techwave or for the Kents to use themselves in their attempted coup against Holloway. The more he revealed, the more worried I became. According to Conrad, the Kents weren't the only Regals working with the Techwave, and the group had far more support than I'd suspected.

For the first time, it sounded as though the Techwave might actually be able to overthrow Holloway, and I couldn't stop a bit of dark satisfaction from filling me at the thought. I should have figured out a way to kill Holloway years ago, but I'd been young, stupid, and naïve enough to think I needed his protection.

But the rest of the Regals, as odious as some of them might be, didn't deserve to suffer, and innocent people certainly didn't deserve to die in the crossfire just so the Techwave could assume power. Once again, I was in one of the OBOs that Vesper had described, with only bad options available to me.

Conrad wound down and stared at Vesper with a hopeful expression. "You can get me a deal, right?"

She glanced up at me, and I shrugged, indicating it was her choice.

"Please, Vesper," he pleaded. "Don't you remember all the fun we had together? That should count for something, right? Plus, I told you everything I know. Dig into the Kent Corp mainframe. You'll see I'm telling the truth and that a lot more Regals are involved with the Techwave than anyone realizes."

Vesper stared at Conrad. Once again, I wondered if I'd made a mistake in breaking the bond between us, because I would have very much liked to have known what she was thinking. But even without the bond, I could still sense the tangled mix of emotions washing off her—regret, sorrow, anger, disappointment, bitterness.

Several more seconds ticked by in silence. Then Vesper pushed her chair back and got to her feet. "I can't get you a deal. After all, I'm just a lowly lab rat, right?"

He flinched at her harsh tone.

"But even if I could get you a deal, I wouldn't do it," she continued.

Confusion creased Conrad's forehead. "Why not?"

Vesper's face was as cold as a Frozon moon. "Because I don't *want* to. Good-bye, Conrad. Enjoy the rest of your life. Because if things go the way I think they will, it's going to be very short and extremely painful."

She spun away from him and stalked over to the door.

"Vesper! Vesper!" he yelled. "Help me! Please, please help me!"

Conrad pounded his cuffed fists against the table in time to his desperate pleas. Vesper yanked open the door and strode out into the corridor.

She didn't look back.

TWENTY-EIGHT

VESPER

I walked out of the holding cell. The door banged shut behind me, although Conrad's screams kept echoing in my ears. As soon as he was out of sight, I stopped, braced one hand on the wall, and drew in a deep breath.

Kyrion stopped a few feet away, looming over me, despite the distance between us. But for once, I didn't mind his presence. In an odd way, he comforted me.

"Are you okay?" he asked.

I drew in another breath, then straightened up and pushed away from the wall. "I'll be fine. Eventually."

He tilted his head at the closed door. "What do you want to do about Conrad?"

"Nothing. I can't get him any deal. Even if I could somehow make things easier for him, I still wouldn't do it." I paused. "Does that make me petty and cruel?"

"Perhaps," Kyrion said. "But I'd also say it makes you smart. Never let an enemy get back up off the ground. Kill them as many times and ways as you have to until you know they're dead."

His cold words sent a shiver down my spine, although I couldn't help but agree with his stark sentiment. Despite our previous relationship, Conrad had become my enemy the moment he'd sided with the Kents and tried to hurt me. Maybe he didn't deserve all the horrible things that were coming his way, but I hadn't deserved the ones he'd dished out to me either. Maybe that was just karma for you, the galaxy balancing whatever warped scales of justice it had.

Kyrion and I got into an elevator and rode up to the lobby. Zane Zimmer was there, his hand on his stormsword, grinning at a row of Kent guards like he wanted to kill every single one of them. Several Imperium soldiers were nearby, getting ready to vacuum-seal Julieta into a body bag.

Kyrion went over and stared down at her lifeless form. I stepped up beside him, and Zane prowled in our direction and also peered down at her.

"So Julieta threw her lot in with the Kents," Zane said. "I thought she was smarter than that."

"What do you mean?" I asked.

He gave me a wolfish grin, but his eyes were dim, sad, and tired. "Holloway will never give an inch. He'll hang on to the Imperium throne by his fingernails if he has to, and he'll kill every single Techwaver—and anyone who's working with them—to keep his position and power."

"And he'll use us to do it," Kyrion murmured.

Zane jerked back, as if surprised by Kyrion's candid words. He eyed the other Arrow, then gave a single sharp nod of agreement. Kyrion stared back at him, a bland look on his face, but some emotion passed between the two men. It might have been a flicker of grudging mutual respect, but it was gone as quickly as a comet streaking through the sky.

"Holloway wants Julieta's body brought back to Corios," Zane said. "Along with the Kents."

Kyrion nodded. "You take them. I have a few things to

finish up here. I'll return as soon as I can."

Zane glanced between the two of us, a speculative look on his face, then nodded again and walked away. A couple of Imperium soldiers followed him, carrying Julieta's body in a black bag that swung between them like an old-fashioned clock pendulum.

Kyrion turned toward me. "Where would you like to go?"

I started to say *home*, but I wasn't sure where that was. Temperate 42 didn't feel like home anymore, but I rattled off the address of my apartment building, and Kyrion escorted me there.

To my surprise, Tivona was home, sipping a mug of espresso and watching the holoscreen. The local gossipcast was covering everything that had happened at Kent Corp, and images of Rowena's crashed ship filled the screen.

As soon as I opened the door, Tivona squealed with delight, set down her drink, leaped up off the sofa, and enveloped me in a tight hug.

"I knew you hadn't taken a promotion off-planet without telling me!" she said. "I knew it!"

Between hugs, Tivona revealed how worried she'd been when I hadn't come home that first day and how everyone at Kent Corp had shut her down when she'd started asking questions. Eventually, Conrad had told her that I had been given a promotion on another planet and had to leave immediately.

"I kept digging, but I couldn't find anything about your promotion in the Kent Corp servers. I knew something was wrong, but I couldn't figure out where you were or how to find you. Plus, some of the Kent Corp mercenaries started following me around. They even searched our apartment when I wasn't here." Tivona shivered.

I hugged her again. "It's okay. I appreciate that you tried to find me."

"Well, it looks like you found someone to watch your back."

She jerked her head at Kyrion, who was wandering around the tiny apartment, staring at everything with curious eyes.

A wicked grin spread across Tivona's face. "Maybe he's been watching your front too?"

I rolled my eyes. "It's not like that."

"Why not?" she whispered. "He's even more gorgeous in person than he is on the gossipcasts!"

Tivona shot him an admiring look, which Kyrion pretended not to notice. I rolled my eyes again and introduced the two of them. Tivona blushed and stammered, and she would have even curtsied if I hadn't nudged her with my elbow.

She glanced back and forth between the two of us, and then her face brightened, as though the most marvelous idea had just occurred to her.

"Vesper, we'll catch up later," Tivona chirped. "I should go to the office and start talking to folks. There'll be lots of changes now that the Kents have been arrested."

Before I could protest, she scooped up her bag and left Kyrion and me alone in the apartment. The two of us stood there, facing each other over the low table in front of the sofa. He glanced down at the mess of plastipapers, tools, and wires that were cluttering the surface.

A ghost of a smile flitted across his face, although his features turned serious again. "Tell me about Julieta."

I knew what he was really asking—how I had killed her. So I told him how I had used my seer magic to see what was happening in real time, despite the chemical burn in my eyes. I also told him everything Julieta had said and also that she had figured out we were bonded.

Kyrion grimaced at the revelation, but then he nodded, as if the news didn't really surprise him.

"You were right. The bond *is* dangerous, in more ways than I imagined. When Julieta was talking about turning me over to the Techwave . . ." My voice trailed off, and I couldn't finish my thought about how they would have tortured me—*us*.

"You were right too," Kyrion replied in a soft voice. "It would have been nice to be . . . connected to someone, if only for a little while."

He stared at me, his expression surprisingly open, honest, and hungry. Or perhaps I was just seeing what I wanted to see, a reflection of all the emotions spiraling through me right now.

"This isn't over yet," he warned. "More Imperium soldiers will arrive, and they'll want to speak to you."

I had expected as much. "What should I tell them?"

"The truth—up to a certain point."

I knew he was talking about the bond. "What will you say? How will you explain this to Holloway?" I hesitated. "Will he punish you?"

Kyrion shook his head. "No. I'll tell Holloway that I lied because you were a witness, and I didn't know whom I could trust. That I thought one of the other Arrows was dirty. And I'll tell him that I killed Julieta."

I blinked in surprise. "Why?"

"It will be easier to explain. The quicker Holloway and everyone else accept our story, the safer we will both be."

I thought of everything Julieta had said about Holloway's labs and experiments and his obsession with recreating true-bonds at will. Somehow I held back a shudder.

"Anyway, you've had a long day. I should go and let you get cleaned up and get some rest."

Kyrion headed toward the door, but something propelled me forward, and I stepped in front of him.

"Why did you come here?" I asked.

Instead of responding, he merely loomed over me like usual.

"We got . . . rid of the bond." I stumbled over the words. "You didn't have to come here. My death wouldn't have . . . affected you at all."

He stared down at me, his face impassive. "I wanted to

know who was trying to manipulate us both. I came here for answers, Vesper."

He didn't say anything else, and I knew he wouldn't. Even after everything we had been through together, he had once again reverted to the Arrow I had first met on the Imperium ship—cold, remote, and utterly ruthless.

I stepped aside. "Well, I'd say we both got the answers we wanted."

Kyrion hesitated, then moved past me, opened the door, and walked through to the other side.

The soft *snick* of the door shutting behind him made something crack open inside my chest and flood my heart with feelings that would have been better left locked away.

TWENTY-NINE

VESPER

arly the next morning, several Imperium soldiers came to the apartment and escorted me back to Kent Corp. A couple of them tried to shove me into a holding cell, but I ignored them, entered the R&D lab, and went over to my workstation like usual. Given the growing scandal, no one else was working today, so the lab was empty.

One of the soldiers protested, but I stared him down.

"I know more about this lab than just about anyone else, and I need to access my terminal to answer your questions and type up a proper report. Or shall I call Kyrion Caldaren and tell him the two of you are preventing me from doing my job?"

The mention of Kyrion had the soldiers shifting on their feet, and they relented and let me remain at my workstation. I stayed there for the rest of the day. Between answering questions from one Imperium official after another, I dug into the Kent Corp mainframe, trying to find every scrap of information I could about the Techwave, my designs, and all the other dirty deeds the Kents had been involved in.

I discovered all that and more—so much *more*.

I forwarded most of my findings to the Imperium officials, although I held back the juiciest bits for my own use. I wasn't quite sure what I was going to do with the information, but I'd fought, bled, and almost died for it, and no one was taking it away from me, not even Callus Holloway.

And that was just the beginning of my Regal climb.

Without the Kents around, no one knew who was in charge or what to do about the growing scandal, which was sending shock waves through the galaxy. Kent Corp's stock plummeted, all the board members resigned, and general chaos ensued.

I took advantage of it all.

I cleaned off Conrad's workstation in the back of the lab and commandeered it as my own. I recalled all the workers who wanted their old jobs back, assigned them new projects, tracked the progress of others, and started running the entire R&D division. Tivona returned to her job as a negotiator, and she helped me greatly, giving me access to all the legal documents I needed, as well as financial information on Kent Corp stock prices.

I waited until the stock price had tumbled to practically nothing, then bought every single share I could. With all the chaos and my various anonymous accounts, I became the majority shareholder of Kent Corp within a matter of hours. The money Kyrion had given me helped, as did the second half of my whistleblower payment from the *Celestial Stars* gossipcast, to which I gave an exclusive interview about my many trials and tribulations.

As soon as the gossipcast aired, I became the most talked-about person in the Archipelago Galaxy, at least for a few days.

Not too shabby for a little lab rat.

Two weeks later, I was working on a new, improved brewmaker that featured all my design modifications, when an

Imperium courier approached my workstation, bowed, and handed me an engraved envelope. Curious, I broke the thick wax seal of a bronze hand, Holloway's sigil.

His Majesty, Callus Holloway, has requested your presence at a ball to be held in three days' time on Corios. First-class transportation and housing arrangements will be provided for you and one guest of your choosing . . .

I looked at the courier. "Is this for real? I've been invited to a Regal ball?"

The courier nodded. "It's being held in your honor, miss."

Surprise rippled through me, along with more than a little wariness. From what Kyrion had said, Callus Holloway never did anything without an agenda, and I doubted he had invited me to a ball just to offer his thanks for my exposing the Kents as traitors. So what was he up to?

I didn't know, but I wanted to find out.

I smiled at the courier. "Please tell Lord Holloway that I am delighted to accept his invitation."

The courier nodded. "Very good, miss. I just need to get some information from you."

I put him in touch with Tivona so they could coordinate our travel and accommodations. The courier left to meet with her, but I remained in the lab.

I glanced over at the stormsword that was nestled in a plastic holder at the far end of my workstation. The Imperium soldiers had taken Julieta's sword when they'd removed her body, but they had left the weapon I'd used behind since it was Kent Corp property. I'd commandeered the sword as my own, but it wouldn't help me right now. Not against whatever Holloway was plotting.

My gaze flicked over the rest of my workstation, moving from one half-finished project to the next, before finally landing on the flesh-colored gloves. I still wasn't sure where the idea for them had originally come from, but now I had a glimmer of just how useful they might be.

I pulled the gloves closer and got to work. I had things to do before I left for the ball.

Three days later, I was back on Corios. Tivona had come with me, not wanting to miss the chance to attend a Regal ball. She chattered during the entire pinpoint ride from Temperate 42, and she kept right on talking as the transport took us to our hotel, located in one of the swanky castles along the Boulevard.

"This is . . . this is . . . *gorgeous!*" Tivona sputtered as we walked through the lobby with its blue marble floor, matching columns, and soaring stained-glass ceiling. "It's even more beautiful in person than on the gossipcasts!"

I grinned, glad she was having a good time, but a pang of longing shot through me. I would much rather have been in Kyrion's run-down castle, fixing something, instead of amid all this glossy opulence.

A concierge led Tivona and me to a deluxe suite on the top floor, where a team of designers, stylists, and makeup artists were waiting with gowns, shoes, jewelry, and cosmetics. Being one of Callus Holloway's special guests came with plenty of perks. I just wondered what the real, hidden cost of them would be.

Tivona beamed with delight over everything. Despite my misgivings, I found myself relaxing and enjoying the primping and pampering.

Tivona picked out a long, slinky black dress covered with gold sequins, along with stacks of gold bangles for her wrists, while I opted for a classic princess gown in a gorgeous silver-blue and matching elbow-length gloves. Smoky eyeshadow and red lipstick brought out Tivona's features, while mine were highlighted with silver liner and pale blue gloss. We both left our hair loose and wavy around our shoulders and donned painfully spiky stilettos. I made a mental note to start designing more comfortable high-heel shoes. Undergarments too. I could easily make a fortune combining fashion with functionality.

Once we were ready, the concierge took us back downstairs, where we were put into a fancy open-air carriage and whisked along the Boulevard to Crownpoint. The sun was just setting over the palace's towers, painting the sky a glorious golden pink, and the glow extended down onto the Boulevard, gilding the other carriages and the people inside them in that same soft, shimmering sheen.

The carriage pulled up to the palace, and a valet rushed forward to help us out. Lords and ladies dressed in formal jackets and glittering gowns were climbing out of other carriages, while guards were directing traffic and scanning invitations at a checkpoint. Beyond that area, other Regals were strolling toward the main palace entrance, smiling, waving, and letting the gossipcast reporters pepper them with questions, while the videographers captured images of them all.

Tivona and I moved through the checkpoint and headed toward the entrance.

"Ms. Quill! Ms. Quill!" Several reporters yelled. "Look this way! What do you have to say about your recent heroics? Is this a dream come true for you?"

It was more like a nightmare, but I did my best to answer the questions while walking and smiling into the glaring flashes of light. Beside me, Tivona struck one pose after another, navigating the media gauntlet with ease, as though she was a Regal lady who had been preening for the gossipcasts her entire life.

At the end of the media line, a public relations worker ushered us inside the palace and into a waiting elevator. The ball was being held in the throne room, which was once again filled with fresh flowers, twinkling lights, delicious-looking food, and fizzy drinks. The scene was even more opulent and dazzling than the last ball, and everyone was talking and laughing and seemingly having a fabulous time.

Tivona headed over to the refreshment tables, but I looked around, searching for Kyrion. I hadn't seen him since he'd left my apartment, and I had missed him, as strange as that sounded.

"Back again, I see," someone drawled.

I sighed and turned around. "Hello, Zane."

The Arrow looked as handsome as ever, and his golden hair gleamed under the lights, as did his pale blue eyes. His gaze flicked up and down my body, as if he was searching for injuries. "I see you've fully recovered from that nasty incident at Kent Corp."

"You sound disappointed."

He shrugged. "Just an observation."

"What do you want, Zane?"

"What makes you think I want something?"

I snorted. "The fact that you're speaking to me."

"Fair enough." He peered down his nose at me. "I know you killed Julieta."

I had to work very hard not to show any emotion. "I don't know what you're talking about."

An ugly, mocking laugh tumbled from his lips. "You know *exactly* what I'm talking about. I saw the weapons lab. Kyrion would *never* have made such a mess, much less inflicted all those minor injuries on Julieta. He would have killed her quickly and efficiently. You, on the other hand, strike me as just the sort who *would* make such a mess, both of the lab and especially of Julieta."

A speculative look filled his face. "So I've been wondering exactly how *you*, Vesper Quill, a lab rat with supposedly little magic and no training, managed to kill a much more powerful and highly skilled Arrow."

I didn't respond. Anything I said would only further his interest and curiosity.

Zane arched an eyebrow. "Keeping quiet? Yeah, that's probably for the best." He smiled and leaned down as though he was flirting with me, but his eyes were as hard as permaglass. "I'm going to figure out what you and Kyrion are hiding, and then I'm going to use that information to destroy him—and you too, if you get in my way."

"Why do you hate Kyrion so much?"

He drew back and shrugged again. "It's not hate. Merely the business of being a Regal. Kyrion is keeping me from my rightful position as head of the Arrows, so he must be removed. You wouldn't understand."

Anger flared in my chest at both his threats and his arrogant, dismissive attitude, and I stepped forward, tilted my chin up, and stared right back at him. "You're right about one thing. Kyrion would never take a long time to kill anyone, including you, Zane."

His eyes glittered. "Is that a threat?"

This time, I shrugged. "You're the one doling out petty threats. I'm merely stating facts."

A genuine smile stretched across his face, and he tipped his head to me in a respectful gesture. "Now you're talking like a true Regal. We'll see how you feel about facts when I uncover each and every one of your secrets, Vesper."

Zane bowed to me, then strode away. I watched him navigate through the crowd over to where his father and grandmother were standing. Wendell was chatting with another lord, but Beatrice was staring at me, her eyes narrowed in thought and her index finger tapping against the crystal flute in her hand.

The Zimmers were going to be a problem. I just couldn't see how much of one yet.

Tivona returned with plates full of food for us, and we roamed around the throne room. To my surprise, dozens of people spoke to me. Everyone wanted to congratulate the person who had exposed the horrible corruption that was such a serious threat to the Imperium. At least, that was what everyone said, although the sour notes in many people's voices indicated they wished the Kents had gotten away with their deadly scheme. I wondered just how many folks here were secretly Techwavers—or at least hoped the group succeeded in its mission to dethrone Holloway.

Someone asked Tivona to dance, and I escaped to the fringes of the room, standing in the shadows that pooled around the columns.

"Back again, I see." A voice eerily echoed Zane's earlier words, although this tone was light and friendly.

Asterin Armas glided up beside me, looking as gorgeous as ever in a gauzy purple gown studded with bits of lunarium and other ores.

"Asterin! It's lovely to see you again."

She smiled at me. "You too, Vesper. Your fortunes have greatly improved since the last time we were hiding out here together."

"Just for tonight, I'm afraid."

She laughed. "Sometimes one night is all it takes."

We stood there in companionable silence, watching the Regals eat, drink, talk, and scheme. I spotted Asterin's handler standing with Beatrice, Wendell, and Zane. The man gestured at Asterin, who stiffened beside me.

"Something wrong?" I asked.

She sighed. "Things aren't going to work out with Kyrion, but my family still wishes to secure an alliance with the Imperium."

"With Zane Zimmer? Ugh! He's an arrogant, egotistical jackass."

Asterin let out an amused laugh. "Yes, that's my assessment too, but he comes from a long line of spelltechs and other powerful psions. My family thinks our abilities would mesh well."

I glanced back and forth between the two of them. That telltale silver glow flickered around Asterin and Zane, as though they were already connected. Strange.

A wry smile curved Asterin's lips. "Plus, the Zimmers are insanely wealthy, which is my family's main requirement."

This time, I was the one who laughed. "I think that's a requirement of every Regal."

"As well as the Erzton nobles." She sighed again, then lifted her chin and squared her shoulders. "But I must do my duty to my family, no matter how tedious it is. Wish me luck."

I murmured the sentiment, although Asterin Armas didn't need any luck. She was the type of person who was strong enough to make her own. Asterin winked at me, then glided away, heading over to Zane and his family.

Awareness prickled my skin, and I looked to my right.

Kyrion was finally here.

He was wearing a short formal blue-black jacket, just as he had during the last ball, but somehow he looked much more handsome than I remembered. Over the past few weeks, I'd thought about him far more than I'd wanted to, wondering where he was and what he was doing—and if he was thinking about me like I was thinking about him.

Kyrion turned in my direction, and our gazes met across the throne room. He hesitated, then headed in this direction. His eyes never left mine, and he smoothly skirted around the other Regals as though they were obstacles in his quest to get to me. He reached my side a few moments later.

"Vesper," he said in a low, husky voice. "You look beautiful."

"Thank you. And you look quite dashing."

Kyrion gave me a polite, meaningless smile. I returned the gesture.

"How is your investigation going?" I asked, rushing to break the awkward silence that was creeping up on us. "Have the Kents said anything else about the Techwave?"

He shook his head. "Conrad and Sabine have told us everything they know, which isn't much. Rowena Kent was the mastermind of the whole operation, but so far, she has been surprisingly resistant to all the usual interrogation methods."

I held back a shudder. I could well imagine the physical torture, as well as the truth serums and other chemicals, that Holloway would use to extract answers from her.

"But Rowena's resolve seems to be weakening," Kyrion continued. "I'm set to question her again later tonight."

"After the ball? Why?"

"Holloway wants the Techwavers found and dealt with as soon as possible." A humorless smile curved Kyrion's lips. "It's even more important to him than keeping up appearances with this lavish ball."

A trumpet blared, and I spotted both Tivona and the public relations worker frantically waving at me. My stomach clenched with worry. I'd been nervous about this part of the ball ever since I'd received the schedule for tonight.

"Time for us both to play our parts." Kyrion looked at me, his face tight and serious. "No matter what happens, don't worry. I'll find a way to fix things. I promise you that, Vesper."

Before I could ask what he meant, Kyrion stepped out of the shadows and headed toward the dais where Holloway was sitting on his throne.

Tivona and the public relations worker rushed up to me.

"It's time for the ceremony!" the worker chirped. "This way. Quickly!"

I had no choice but to follow him and head toward the dais as well, my heart quickening with dread with every step I took.

THIRTY

KYRION

I took my position at the bottom of the dais, standing next to Zane. The other Arrows currently on-planet fell in line behind us, while the servants scurried around, getting everything ready for the ceremony.

"Vesper looks lovely tonight," Zane said. "I can see why you're so taken with her."

My gaze strayed back to her. He was right. Vesper did look lovely. Her gown clung to her body like a dreamy cloud, while her eyes seemed even brighter than normal. She looked very much like the space princess she had named herself after when she was a child, but she was much bigger and grander than that, like a blue moon bringing beauty to whoever was lucky enough to be in her shining orbit.

Zane turned toward me, expecting a reply, so I dragged my gaze away from Vesper.

"If you think she looks lovely, then perhaps you're the one who's so taken with her," I said. "Despite your obvious interest in Lady Asterin. I saw the two of you talking earlier."

Zane scoffed. "That's my grandmother's interest, not mine. As for Vesper, well, she's not my type. I didn't think she was your type either—until I realized she'd killed Julieta."

Worry snaked through my gut, but I gave him a cool look. "You read my report. You know that I killed Julieta because she was working with the Kents."

"Oh, I have no doubt Julieta was working with the Kents, just like you claimed. But I also know Vesper killed her, not you." Zane's gaze sharpened. "Curious how a lowly lab rat got the better of a mighty Arrow. I imagine Holloway would be quite interested in learning more about the mysterious Vesper Quill."

Cold fury roared through me. I wanted to tell Zane about all the slow, horrific pain I would inflict on him if he ever hurt Vesper, but I kept my mouth shut. Protesting would only make him even more certain than he already was.

"Nothing to say, Kyrion?" Zane drawled. "Funny. Vesper was also strangely silent."

Before I could respond, another trumpet blared. Everyone fell silent and looked up at Holloway, who was perched on his throne like a viper deciding who it was going to strike out at next.

He glanced around, a benevolent smile on his face. "Lords and ladies, we are gathered here tonight to honor someone who has done a great service to the Imperium . . ."

Holloway droned on for about ten minutes about how Vesper had uncovered the Kents' plot, how evil the Techwavers were, and all the other typical things. Finally, he called on Vesper.

She walked forward and stopped at the bottom of the dais steps, clasping her gloved hands in front of her. A serene smile stretched across her face, but her eyes shimmered, and a telltale swirl of power gusted off her and washed over me. What was Vesper seeing as she peered up at Holloway?

"Vesper Quill, you have done a great service to us all," Holloway said in a loud, booming voice. "To honor your sacrifices and as a reward for your loyal service to the Imperium, I am bestowing the title of Lady Quill upon you. As of this moment, you are a Regal, a House of One, although I'm sure that will grow quickly in the future. Congratulations."

A round of applause rang out, but it couldn't quite drown out the surprised murmurs that rippled through the crowd. In cases like this, Holloway usually just paid people off. I couldn't remember him ever elevating someone to Regal status before, and he would only do it now if he thought *Lady Vesper* could be useful in some way.

Vesper dipped into a deep curtsy, and several photographers stepped forward and snapped her picture. She smiled at them, although her fingers dug into her skirt as though she was trying to keep from flinching at the bright, flashing lights.

The photographers stepped back, and Holloway looked down at me. A small, smug smile curved his face, and he flicked his fingers. One of the servants scuttled toward me, clutching a long bronze dagger studded with red bits of lunarium.

Even though I'd been expecting this, my heart still clenched inside my chest. Beside me, Zane sucked in a surprised breath, although his eyes quickly narrowed in speculation, and he glanced back and forth between Vesper and me.

Everyone stared at me, and several Bronze Hand guards crept into the room, ready to seize me—or worse—if I objected in any way. So I had no choice but to step forward and take the dagger, just as I had done dozens of times before. The weapon was as heavy as an anvil in my hand, but I moved forward so that I was standing off to the side of the dais, between Vesper on the floor and Holloway up on his throne.

"Your Majesty?" Vesper asked. "What's going on?"

Holloway's benevolent smile turned sharp and predatory. "I'm sure you've heard the gossipcast stories about Lord Kyrion's parents and their wonderful truebond. It has long been my wish that Kyrion find his own bond with someone among the Regals. But lately, I've been wondering if destiny has other plans for him."

His smile widened, the hunger on his face clear for everyone to see. "You spent a lot of time with Kyrion, and the two of you survived some very traumatic, high-stress situations. I thought a truebond might have formed between the two of you as a result. Wouldn't that be the perfect romantic ending to this wonderful story? You becoming a Regal lady and Kyrion finding his true partner all in one glorious night?"

Murmurs of agreement rippled through the crowd. Vesper glanced at me, her face calm, but worry flickered in her eyes. The same emotion roiled around in my gut like broken glass. We might have broken the bond in Touma's workshop, but I had no idea if it could come rushing back, especially given how I had . . . softened toward Vesper.

"Lord Kyrion will now proceed with the truebond test," Holloway commanded.

I drew in a breath, then raised the dagger high for everyone to see. Given all the times I'd done this before, I knew exactly how long to draw out the moment. But this was the first—the *only*—time I'd ever been uncertain about the outcome. I waited a heartbeat longer, then brought the dagger down and slashed the blade across my left palm.

Vesper flinched and pressed her lips together. Holloway looked back and forth between the two of us.

"Keep going," he commanded.

I cut myself again—and again and again . . .

Gasps and murmurs rang out, and even Zane frowned in surprise and confusion. Usually, only one cut was required for the test, but Holloway was making me slice my hand to pieces, indicating how eager he was for this to work.

"Enough," Holloway finally called out.

I held my palm out where everyone could see it, although really, there was nothing to see but blood gushing out of the deep, throbbing wounds. Several drops of blood dripped off my fingertips and spattered onto the floor. Perhaps it was my imagination, but the red veins in the white marble seemed to writhe and shimmer, as though they were soaking up every single speck. My gut twisted again, this time in revulsion.

"Now, if you will be so kind as to show us your hand, Lady Quill," Holloway purred in a silky voice.

Vesper shifted on her feet, as if she was uncomfortable, but she tugged on the fingertips of the elbow-length glove that covered her right hand. Then she took hold of the upper part of the glove and peeled the whole thing off her arm.

I held my breath and leaned forward, along with everyone else.

Vesper held her palm out, revealing . . . smooth skin.

The crowd exhaled with a collective sigh of disappointment, but Holloway waved his hand, demanding silence again.

He gave Vesper an indulgent smile, as though she was a child who couldn't follow simple instructions. "I meant your left hand, Lady Quill. Truebond injuries often mimic each other, after all."

"Oh! Of course! Forgive me." Vesper let out a high, nervous laugh. "It's just . . . being here is so . . . overwhelming."

She reached up and tugged on the fingertips of the glove on her left hand, then slowly peeled it off. Vesper cradled her hand up against her chest and peeked down at it, as if she wanted to see the results for herself before she showed them to everyone else.

Once again, I held my breath, although I didn't know exactly what I was hoping for.

Vesper held her left palm out where everyone could see it, revealing . . . smooth skin.

I blinked a few times, but her hand remained the same. Nothing—no cuts, no blood, not even the smallest scratch—marred her palm.

Another collective disappointed sigh rushed out of the crowd, but Vesper ignored everyone else, flexed her fingers, and then held both palms out to Holloway.

"I'm so sorry to disappoint you, Your Majesty," she said in a soft, apologetic voice. "But as you can see, I have no cuts like the ones on Lord Kyrion's hands."

Holloway's smile vanished. "Yes, well, that's very disappointing. I suppose Lord Kyrion will just have to keep searching."

As will I. The thought whispered off him, and the malice packed into those three simple words made my heart clench with dread. He wasn't going to stop. He was *never* going to stop until he had shackled me to him as he had done with my parents.

In an instant, all the worry, fear, and dread in my body solidified into a cold, hard nugget of fury, hatred, and determination. Somehow, I was going to find a way to kill the bastard, even if I killed myself in the process.

"Well, I wish Lord Kyrion good luck," Vesper replied. "A truebond must be such a lovely, wonderful thing to experience."

I almost thought I detected a wistful note in her voice, but that was probably just my own wishful thinking.

Holloway flicked his fingers, growing impatient. He hadn't gotten what he'd wanted, and he was already losing interest in Vesper.

"As a newly appointed Regal, you are free to stay on Corios and set up your House accommodations," he said in a bored voice. "Someone from my office will help you sort out the details."

"Actually, Your Majesty, I was hoping to return to Temperate 42 and resume my work at Kent Corp," Vesper replied.

"Why would you want to do that?" Holloway asked.

"To make sure the Techwavers didn't sabotage anything

else. After all, we wouldn't want everyone's brewmakers to start blowing up, would we?"

Polite chuckles rang out at her joke, and Holloway waved his hand again. "Very well. If that is what you wish."

"Thank you, Your Majesty." She dipped into another curtsy.

I silently applauded her clever strategy. The sooner Vesper left Corios, the safer she would be from everyone, including me.

Especially me.

Holloway waved his hand yet again, dismissing her. Vesper curtsied a final time and melted into the crowd. Several people watched her go—including Nerezza Blackwell.

I eyed the lady, whose lips were puckered in obvious displeasure. I had no idea if she had recognized Vesper as the daughter she'd abandoned, but she definitely wasn't a fan of the newest member of Regal society.

My tablet buzzed in my pocket, and I pulled it out and looked at the alert. I let out a muttered curse. Beside me, Zane was also cursing. A servant climbed the dais and whispered to Holloway. He jerked his head at me.

I handed the bloody dagger off to a servant, then hurried out of the throne room, with Zane hot on my heels. Together we stepped into an elevator and rode it down to the floor where the containment cells were. Several guards were standing in the hallway, worried expressions on their faces.

"I'm so sorry, sir!" one of them said. "We don't know how it happened. One moment they were fine. The next . . ."

His voice trailed off, and I pushed past him and peered into the room, which contained three people in two separate but adjoining cells, Rowena and Sabine Kent on one side and Conrad Fawley on the other.

Rowena and Sabine were sprawled across the floor of their cell, while Conrad was slumped up against the wall of his. Blood had leaked out of the corners of their eyes like crimson tears, and still more blood had dribbled out of their noses and their ears.

They were all dead.

I spent the next two hours trying to figure out exactly how this had happened, when and why, but I didn't come up with any answers.

The water inside the cell was tested and found to contain a fast-acting poison, but the security footage had been erased, supposedly due to a camera malfunction, and there was no way of knowing who had dosed the prisoners or exactly when it had happened. Given Rowena's reluctance to reveal any information about the Techwave, especially the other Regals involved with the group, I was willing to bet another Regal had murdered the lady to keep her quiet, but I didn't have any proof.

Eventually, I returned to the ball, along with Zane. The news hadn't leaked yet, so everyone was still laughing, eating, and gossiping. I glanced around, searching for Vesper, and I found her standing with Daichi and Tivona. The two of them seemed to be hitting it off, although one look at my face had them murmuring excuses and drifting away.

"Conrad and the Kents are dead," Vesper said.

"How did you know?"

"I sensed something strange earlier tonight, almost like a wave of malevolence," she replied. "It's hard to explain. But I knew something bad had happened."

"Your seer magic told you."

"Something like that, I suppose. And that's not all it told me tonight."

She glanced up at the dais, where Holloway was still sitting on his throne. To a casual observer, he probably looked calm and relaxed, but I could see the sour twist to his lips and just how tightly he was clutching his drink, as though he wanted to squeeze the crystal until it shattered.

"What did your power show you?" I asked.

"Your parents standing before Holloway," she said in a soft voice. "I had seen the three of them before, through one of the doors in my mindscape, but tonight I saw even more of the vision. I saw how he manipulated your parents, how he used the truebond to subtly threaten them and keep them both in line. I saw how he took their power a little bit at a time, whenever the mood struck him. And I saw . . . I saw how he finally took too much of your mother's magic at once. How he killed her. I'm so sorry, Kyr."

Kyr. No one had ever called me that before, not even my parents, but the nickname sounded . . . *right* coming from Vesper's lips, even if it didn't drown out the horror and sorrow of what she had seen—and what I had witnessed myself when it came to my parents.

Her left hand flexed, as though she wanted to grab mine, but she didn't. That was probably for the best, given all the people watching us right now, including Lady Nerezza.

Vesper's gaze drifted in that direction. Nerezza smiled and toasted her daughter with her glass, and Vesper nodded back at her mother.

"Nerezza actually came over and congratulated me," Vesper said in a low voice. "She was quite charming. I can see why she's managed to climb so high in Regal society."

"Did she say anything more . . . personal?"

Vesper shook her head. "If she knows who I really am, she hid it well. Even with my magic, she's hard to read. Probably because I'm not objective when it comes to her."

"I'm sorry."

"I'm not. If nothing else, coming to Corios has given me some closure—at least about my mother."

Before I could ask what else she needed closure about, Zane gestured at me.

"I have to go brief Holloway."

"I know," Vesper replied. "I wanted to thank you—for everything."

I shook my head. "I should be thanking you."

She stared at me, and I looked right back at her, trying to memorize the soft curve of her cheeks, the heart shape of her lips, and especially the amazing silver-blue shine of her eyes.

I memorized her in a moment longer, then spun around and walked away before I did something supremely stupid, like ask her to stay on Corios, even though the bond was broken.

THIRTY-ONE

VESPER

E ventually, the ball ended, and Tivona and I were whisked
back to our hotel, where we returned the borrowed
gowns, shoes, jewelry, and other accessories. It was well
after midnight, time for us space princesses to turn back into
regular pumpkins. Or a lab rat, in my case.

Tivona went to bed, but I couldn't sleep, so I stood by the
windows and stared out into the dark.

The ball had gone pretty much the way I'd expected it
to—lots of fake smiles, empty congratulations, and pointless
promises about how everyone wanted to get to know me better.
Please. Lady Quill was a Regal title in name only, and everyone knew it. A House of One, Holloway had called it, and a
mocking moniker had never been so appropriate.

Still, I had been shocked when Nerezza had approached me.
She had smiled and chatted as though we were old friends and I
wasn't the daughter she'd discarded in search of riches, power,
magic, and fame. Speaking with her hadn't hurt nearly as much
as I'd expected it to, mainly because I'd still been reeling from

the horrific vision I'd had of Holloway and Kyrion's parents.

It was a longer, more detailed vision than the one I'd seen through that door in my mindscape. Chauncey and Desdemona had been standing at the bottom of the dais, right in the same spot where Kyrion and I had been, and my magic had made it seem like I was seeing their past and our potential future at the same time.

Holloway had been circling around the Caldarens, talking about some Arrow mission, and he'd kept touching them. A pat on Chauncey's arm, a squeeze of Desdemona's hand. He'd kept touching them over and over again, taking a little bit of their power each and every time, and they'd been forced to let him because he was the ruler of the Imperium, and his Bronze Hand guards were standing by to make sure they cooperated.

And because they were bonded and in love and had a son they desperately wanted to protect, along with each other.

I'd also seen exactly how Kyrion's mother had gotten sick.

After Chauncey had left, she and Holloway had been alone. Holloway had squeezed her hand long and hard—too long and hard—and he'd taken too much of her magic at once. The life, the energy, the power had quickly drained from her body and flowed into Holloway.

People might call him a siphon, but the greedy bastard was nothing but a fucking leech, and he had murdered Kyrion's mother as surely as if he'd shoved a stormsword into her heart. And perhaps even worse, he'd taken advantage of Kyrion killing his father in self-defense. Holloway had forged Kyrion into an Arrow not only because he needed a weapon to help him hang on to the Imperium throne but because he wanted the magic of a truebonded pair more than anything else, and Kyrion was his best chance of getting it.

And tonight, Holloway thought he'd had that power within his grasp again, and he had been eager to doom Kyrion and me to the same awful fate as the Caldarens.

Holloway was going to pay for that, just like the Techwave was going to pay for stealing my designs and using them to murder innocent people. As for the Regals who might be helping the Techwavers, well, I had my suspicions about that, although I didn't have any proof—yet.

But when I found that proof, I was going to destroy the Techwavers and all the Regals working with them, just as I was going to destroy Holloway. I wasn't sure how I would accomplish either goal, not yet, but I was a seer, I was a lab rat, and I was especially good at figuring things out.

All it takes is one person, one tiny mistake, to bring down an entire Regal family. Rowena Kent's voice whispered through my mind. If nothing else, she had been right about that.

Sometimes all it took to change the galaxy was a single person, and I was going to be that House of One.

Even if I wasn't exactly *one* anymore.

I looked down at my left hand. My palm was a bit puffy and pinker than normal, but that was the only indication that something was wrong. My invention had worked even better than I'd anticipated.

I grimaced, knowing this was going to hurt, then pressed in on what looked like a button-size freckle on the inside of my wrist. A soft *hiss* sounded, and I hooked my right index finger under the bottom of the thin layer of flexible polyplastic and peeled the flesh-colored glove off my hand to reveal . . . a cut, bloody palm.

My bond with Kyrion wasn't broken.

It had *never* been broken.

Touma might have given us a chemical cocktail, but it hadn't disrupted the bond. Maybe the spelltech had thought the chemicals would really work, and maybe they had worked on other people, but not on Kyrion and me.

The cold might have numbed the bond, but it hadn't broken it, at least not for me. That was why I'd been able to hear Julieta's thoughts and call the stormsword and other objects into my hands in the R&D lab. I had been tapping into Kyrion's psionic abilities, his telepathy and telekinesis, and not just my own seer power.

And I didn't think the bond was broken on Kyrion's end either, considering what he had carved into his own hand and into mine too.

An eye.

I held my palm up to the blue moonlight streaming in through the windows. Kyrion had cut a crude eye into his own palm, and it had appeared in the center of mine as well.

Did he even realize what image he'd carved into his own flesh? Did he actively know that the truebond was still intact? Or was it just a whisper from his subconscious? Perhaps I would ask him when I saw him again.

And I *would* see Kyrion again. I could *feel* it, although I couldn't quite see when or how our paths would cross again.

As I stared down at the bloody eye in my palm, I reached out with my magic and went to my mindscape. All the eyes were wide open and staring at me, but now I found their watchful gazes comforting.

Even more doors were crowded in here than ever before, and I could open and shut them at will, just by thinking about what I wanted to do. I peered in through some of the doors, but my gaze kept straying to the Door, the one in the back of the room that contained nothing but darkness. I walked over and stood in front of it. I still couldn't see into the black depths, but I'd finally figured out what lay inside.

I'd had so many theories over the past few weeks about what the Door was—a future that hadn't yet come to pass, my death, my bond with Kyrion, even his darkness creeping into me through the bond. But it wasn't any of those things.

It was *my* darkness, *my* magic, *my* power.

It was the strength that had been lurking inside me all

along. Julieta had said that trauma could sometimes trigger a truebond. For a while, I'd thought that was what had happened between Kyrion and me, but now I had a different theory.

I thought the darkness, anger, pain, and loneliness in him had recognized the same sort of darkness, anger, pain, and loneliness in me. Perhaps that was what had drawn us together and formed the bond. As for when the bond had formed, well, since I had been wandering around Castle Caldaren in my dreams ever since I was a child, I thought it had been percolating far longer than either Kyrion or I had ever imagined.

I kept staring at the blackness beyond the Door, and a few wisps of smoke curled out, almost like fingers beckoning me to come closer.

Kyrion had long ago embraced his inner darkness. He'd had to in order to survive.

Me? I could still walk away. I could return to Temperate 42, run Kent Corp, and live a good, safe, long, happy life. I might even meet someone in the future, someone kind and generous who would love me for who I was and not what I could do for them. Oh, yes, I could finally have the kind of life I had always dreamed about. But that wasn't the life I desired. Not anymore. Because those weren't the things I desired anymore.

Oh, I still wanted to live a long, happy, fulfilling life. I still wanted to connect with someone, love someone, and not just because of a truebond. I wanted to love someone for just being themselves, and I wanted that same love in return.

But right now, I mostly wanted revenge—on the Techwave, on Callus Holloway, on everyone else who had ever used, abused, or wronged me.

But perhaps most of all, I wanted to keep myself—and Kyrion—safe from Holloway's and everyone else's greed. Holloway had been right about one thing. A truebond should be celebrated, not twisted into shackles to control other people.

And the only way to protect Kyrion, to protect myself, was

to make sure Holloway never used anyone else like he had used Kyrion's parents or the way he wanted to use us.

So, with all those sapphsidian eyes still watching my every move, I drew in a deep breath and slowly let it out. Then I strode through the Door and embraced the darkness within myself.

ABOUT THE AUTHOR

Jennifer Estep is a *New York Times*, *USA Today*, and internationally bestselling author who prowls the streets of her imagination in search of her next fantasy idea.

Jennifer is the author of the **Galactic Bonds, Section 47, Elemental Assassin, Crown of Shards, Gargoyle Queen**, and other fantasy series. She has written more than forty books, along with numerous novellas and stories.

In her spare time, Jennifer enjoys hanging out with friends and family, doing yoga, and reading fantasy and romance books. She also watches way too much TV and loves all things related to superheroes.

For more information on Jennifer and her books, visit her website at **www.jenniferestep.com** or follow her online on Facebook, Twitter, Instagram, Amazon, BookBub, and Goodreads.

You can also sign up for her newsletter: **https://www.-jenniferestep.com/contact-jennifer/newsletter/**

Happy reading, everyone!

OTHER BOOKS
BY JENNIFER ESTEP

THE GALACTIC BONDS SERIES
Only Bad Options

THE SECTION 47 SERIES
A Sense of Danger
Sugar Plum Spies (holiday book)

THE ELEMENTAL ASSASSIN SERIES
FEATURING GIN BLANCO

BOOKS
Spider's Bite
Web of Lies
Venom
Tangled Threads
Spider's Revenge
By a Thread
Widow's Web
Deadly Sting
Heart of Venom
The Spider
Poison Promise
Black Widow
Spider's Trap
Bitter Bite
Unraveled
Snared
Venom in the Veins

Sharpest Sting
Last Strand

E-NOVELLAS
Haints and Hobwebs
Thread of Death
Parlor Tricks
Kiss of Venom
Unwanted
Nice Guys Bite
Winter's Web
Heart Stings

THE CROWN OF SHARDS SERIES
Kill the Queen
Protect the Prince
Crush the King

THE GARGOYLE QUEEN SERIES
Capture the Crown
Tear Down the Throne
Conquer the Kingdom

THE BLACK BLADE SERIES
Cold Burn of Magic
Dark Heart of Magic
Bright Blaze of Magic

THE BIGTIME SERIES
Karma Girl
Hot Mama
Jinx
A Karma Girl Christmas (holiday story)
Nightingale
Fandemic

THE MYTHOS ACADEMY SPINOFF SERIES
FEATURING RORY FORSETI

Spartan Heart
Spartan Promise
Spartan Destiny

THE MYTHOS ACADEMY SERIES
FEATURING GWEN FROST

BOOKS
Touch of Frost
Kiss of Frost
Dark Frost
Crimson Frost
Midnight Frost
Killer Frost

E-NOVELLAS AND SHORT STORIES
First Frost
Halloween Frost
Spartan Frost

OTHER WORKS
The Beauty of Being a Beast (fairy tale)
Write Your Own Cake (worldbuilding essay)